Amazon reviewers' praise for the story formerly published as *High Treason*.

"I love how the author twisted in some of today's political arguments, vaccines, government cover-ups, finances, etc. This book dives into so much of what is going on in the US today and what could possibly come later."

"This is a story of love and of bitterness, rising up in the heart of a man and in the highest corridors of government."

"I will say it is not your typical feel good Amish fiction book! I read this book cover to cover non-stop. It shows the Amish struggle with the same feelings, doubts and fears that we in the English world struggle with."

"If you have been into Amish fiction, but are tired with the same old love stories and happy endings, then please grab this book — it will have you seeing Amish fiction in a brand new and much needed light."

"How should we then live? This is a question (with apologies to Francis Schaeffer) that has been burning in my mind since I started reading. Regina Owens is a young, liberal, black, female minister who is not content with leaving well-enough alone. But this book is not about a young, liberal, black, female minister. Enos Yoder is a young Amish man whose world has been completely obliterated by death, mayhem and destruction. Yet this book is not about a young Amish man. Instead, this book is about how every person who claims the name of Christ is to live in a society where corruption, violence and anarchy are the order of the day. It strikes at the very foundation of one's faith, and challenges you to ask the really hard questions, such as, Does God still care? And if God does still care, where is He now? This book will either strengthen your faith, or cause you to question it. And if you are questioning your faith, this book will not leave you alone until you've settled the questions, once and for all."

Worlds Apart

Jerry Eicher

WORLDS APART

Futuristic political thriller

Published by Horizon Books
Contact: www.eicherjerry.com

ISBN 978-0-9787987-8-9

Chapter One

Enos Yoder stood by the barn and looked out across his father's newly sprouted corn fields. The tender stalks reached skyward as if they yearned for life from the skies above them. The sun set behind him. The dying rays cast long shadows across the lawn. He thought they looked like outstretched fingers of some deformed giant that reached for what he could never find. His single buggy sat half in and half out of the sun's rays, its spindly shafts pointed toward the paved road.

Inside the house there would be little supper on the table tonight — no mashed potatoes and gravy, no roast slathered with savory mushrooms. Enos's stomach growled at the thought. There had been no such foods in the house all week, the place gripped in sorrow. They ought to be thankful, his father said, even for bread. What his sisters managed to cook on most evenings was much better than that. Bread and water, his father claimed, was what the Amish martyrs ate in their cells more than five hundred years ago. Their children should be content with the same.

But he should not think such things tonight. Mom lay dying from the horrible thing that had the whole country in an uproar. And if he did not get out of the house tonight, words would be spoken between him and his father, words that should not be spoken, words that a righteous man did not allow to pass his lips. Why then did they well up inside him and push to break out, like cows who strained at the fence for a bit of grass on the other side?

The front door of the house opened behind him, and the

screen door snapped shut. Enos listened, the sound muffled in the heavy evening air. That would be his father coming out to see where he was; he would question why he wasn't in the house already. His father would see the buggy shafts pointed away from the barn, and he would know.

"Enos," the low voice of his father reached him across the lawn. "Are the chores done?"

Enos nodded but didn't turn around.

"Then come in with us. You know that Mom's time is approaching."

"That would be why I'm not coming in." Enos stayed turned away from his father's face. "I've had enough of this."

He was nearly as tall as his father now, and his chest had broadened in the past few years. His arms were still not as thick or his hands as hardened from years of work in the fields, but he had become a man almost without realizing it.

Not that many years ago those words of rebellion he had just spoken would have brought an immediate response. Hands would have clasped like steel on his arms, his boyish legs propelled to the barnyard for a leather strap applied vigorously to his backside. Enos breathed deeply, the memory still fresh, but his father no longer used such methods; he was too big for strapping, or perhaps his father feared something that neither of them had yet placed into words — a son who resisted his father. Such a son would not be allowed to stay home, and Norman Yoder needed his son at home.

"You would blame me for your mother's dying? As if it were not *The Lord* who gives and takes life."

"You know what I mean." Enos turned to face his father. "There is help right down the road, as you have known for weeks. Mom would not be dying if you had taken the medicine the *English* people are offering."

"And sell my soul to the government? Give up our highest beliefs? Who do you think we are, Enos? Has it really come to this?"

"But you know Bishop Mast has approved the vaccine. The *English* people are not requiring what the government people were. It's not evil. You just go down and ask for help."

"Bishop Mast is not God, and you know that man can be wrong. There are others of our people, Enos, who also have doubts about accepting help from the *English* people."

"I don't care," Enos said. "Let them say what they want to, they are going down to the *English* for help. I know, because I have asked around."

"I will not allow it," his father said, his lips tight above his lengthy beard. "It does not matter if the whole world approves of a thing. I will have no part of the world, and I will not have my children going to war."

"I don't have to go to war, Father," Enos said. "That was the government's requirement for giving us the medicine. It's not the *English* people's requirement."

"It is a trick, Enos. They are taking our people's names when they give out the medicine. It will all be the same thing in the end. Instead, we will live and die by the will of God, as did our forefathers before us. They died at the stake for their faith. The flames scorched their flesh. Can we not die in our beds?"

"Die like Mom is dying? That is worse than flames," Enos screamed, as he stepped closer to his father. He knew his face was contorted.

"If you do not come in soon, you will miss your mother's passing." His father turned his back and walked towards the house.

Enos waited as he watched his father's stooped back enter the front door. His father never paused or looked over his shoulder. The man was impossible, like a mule who got its feet stuck in the mud and refused to budge. His father spoke lofty words, lived his life with high convictions, but it all ended in tragedy — in his mother's pain and agony while she writhed on a bed in the back bedroom.

Soon the blackness would come for them all, and there would be no escape. Well, for his father and his younger siblings there might be none, but he would not stand for it on his own account. There was no sense in dying without a reason. And if his father was wrong on this, he might be wrong on many other things.

Enos sighed as he turned to walk to the house. He would go inside and see, but that was all. Mother would be out of her head with fever anyway, even if she was close to crossing over to the other side. He opened the front door and held the screen so it didn't slam behind him. The bare white walls of the living room greeted him, the simple couch and rocking chairs empty.

Here his mother had sat all those evenings of his childhood. Here she had rocked and knitted while his father read the Amish *Budget,* searching for news of family and acquaintances in far flung Amish communities. It had all come to an end, so abruptly, so suddenly, when the outside world they had separated themselves from all their lives had crossed the threshold of their door. The world now breathed the sickness of the *English* people upon the most beloved member of the family.

Already two of his sisters showed signs of the infection, and there was no escape apparently — not if Father didn't change his mind.

"She's speaking!" His father appeared in the hall to the first floor bedroom. "Come, she's calling for you."

Enos shook his head, but his feet already obeyed. He followed his father's broad back. Inside the room some of his siblings knelt around her bed and some stood, leaning over to touch her. She lay in her plain dark blue dress, washed and pressed only yesterday.

"Enos," she whispered. Her eyes glistened without tears. Red sores on her arms oozed white pus. On the dresser the flickering kerosene lamp cast light on all of them. "My son, my oldest son. I must speak to you before I go."

"Mom." He fell to his knees and clutched her fingers. They weakly wrapped around his, the bones hard against his strong flesh. "I'm so sorry, Mom."

Her face brightened as her eyes searched the distance. They didn't seem to see him now. "You must not say such things, Enos. We all must cross the river one day. It is only a moment, and then everyone must follow."

"No, Mom," he said. "It does not need to be so."

"Your father knows what is best, Enos. You must not question his word. Only in obedience can any escape the evils of this world. I have heard the angels sing tonight. You must not doubt what the *Will of God* is."

"Mom." He touched her face, but her head lay back, her breathing shallow.

"Come away." His father's hand pulled on his shoulder. "Do not disturb her last moments; they should be spent in peace."

There is no peace in this place, he wanted to scream. There is no peace in dying like animals from a plague in the barnyard. But he kept silent, his eyes fixed on her face. She opened her eyes again. They searched the room and settled on him. A soft smile crossed her face.

"Take courage," she mouthed the words. "*Dawdy* and *Mommy* are here, and the angels. Do not fail to follow when your time comes — especially you, Enos. Your heart must not forsake the narrow path."

"Come back," his father's voice spoke in his ear, but he lunged forward to lay his head beside hers on the pillow. He wept, great sobs in his agony, but she had her eyes on the ceiling, smiling with joy on her face. Her hands feebly lifted off the bed quilt for a brief moment, only to fall limply back again.

"She's gone," his father declared. "Come now, we must prepare her body for the ground. Her soul has gone to her eternal reward."

Enos stood. He still wept, his own sobs joined by those

around him. They gathered at the foot of the bed, their arms around each other. His father touched her eyes, which still stared blankly at the ceiling. He closed them with soft pressure and drew the quilt over her head.

His father turned to face them. "Enos, Paul, James, Andy, take the shovels to the back field and begin the grave. We will have the funeral tonight, once you are done."

"But is the Bishop not to be here?" Enos asked, not moving.

His father's tone was harsh. "I want no man who has defiled himself with the world to be at my wife's funeral. *The Lord* will forgive him, as I will forgive him, but tonight will be a time when only the pure will bury the pure."

I am not pure, Enos wanted to scream. *I have thought the thoughts of the English. I was going to leave tonight, to visit my beloved Rosemary. I want to visit the English house and bring medicine for the whole family. I want to forget the horror that life has become. Are those not the thoughts of the world? Thoughts which defile the soul?*

But he said nothing and turned to lead the way out of the house, past his buggy with the shafts turned towards the road, out to the little tumbled-down storage shed with the shovels.

"Here," he mumbled, and gave the three shovels he could find to his brothers and took the pick in his own hands. Silently they walked across the fields, the sun now set. The full moon rose above the tree lines. The soft globe in the sky threw their moving shadows across the tender corn stalks.

"Mom's in glory now," one of them said. His voice was scratchy and rumbled.

Enos said nothing, his head held straight forward, his black wool hat pulled low over his face. They reached the end of the fence row, where he pointed and struck his pick hard into the ground.

They dug as one man, their muscles honed from their years of labor in the fields, their movements perfectly timed like a finely tuned Swiss watch. The hole deepened. The bank of dirt rose to cast its own shadow as the moon rose higher.

"It's deep enough now." Enos pulled himself out of the depths.

"Why do we put Mother down in the ground when she has gone with the angels?" the youngest, Andy, asked.

"I don't know," Enos told him. "You'll have to ask Father that."

"It's so that God can find us when He comes back with Mom's soul," James the third son suggested.

"Is that true?" Andy wanted to know.

"I don't know." Enos struggled to control his voice. "But what I do know is that we will all be digging holes for each other soon if Father doesn't accept medicine from the *English* people down the road."

"But they are not like us, even if they look like us." James's voice trembled. "Father said they are up to a great evil. That the Lord hates those who pretend to be what they are not."

Then why doesn't He hate me? Enos wanted to shout into the night air. *Why does He allow me to stay alive?* He wanted to howl at the moon like a dog who has lost its bearing in the night and sings his agony to the heavens. But his brothers were here and he must not damn their souls.

"Let's go get Mother," he said. "Father can't bring her here by himself."

They walked back up the fields, past the house. Enos paused to push the open spring wagon up against the house steps.

"Shall I harness the horse?" James asked.

"No," Enos said. "We can all push ourselves. It will be better that way."

Why was it better? It was hard to tell, he thought, but it just was. They should take her to the last resting place by themselves, with their own hands, with the pull of their own muscles and hearts.

His mother's body lay on the floor, dressed in her black dress. His sisters now wrapped her in the best quilt from the upstairs cedar chest, used only for special visitors.

"We have washed her," his father said. "And we are ready."

"You should not have dressed her in black," Enos said. "Mom has a nice dark gray dress that she loved."

"Black is the color of the ground our souls came from," his father said. "We must not think ourselves above the earth the Lord has taken us from."

"But she is with the angels," Andy joined the protest.

"Yes, she is, but not yet all of her. You will understand someday. But now, come, let us go."

They carried her, two on each side, as the three sisters held open the door. Enos felt the softness of her flesh under his fingers, the body from which he had come, soon to harden and turn finally into the soil of the fields.

"You should have brought out the horse," his father said as they lowered the body down on the back of the spring wagon.

"It is well that we should push it ourselves," Enos replied, and for once the father obeyed the son. He took up the shafts as if he were the horse himself. They moved across the fields, slowing for the ruts in the ditch. When they arrived at the grave, two went to the back to lower her body into the hole, and two waited at the bottom with hands outstretched.

His father removed his hat, and they did likewise, while the girls wept softly.

His father began to pray, "And now unto the Most High God we give thanks and praise for the life He has given, and for the life He has taken. Blessings and praise be to his name. Be now with us, oh God, as we continue on with this life. Let us come to the same blessed end as this soul you have received into Your gracious hand. In the name of the Father, the Son, and the Holy Spirit. Amen."

Enos waited until his father had thrown the first shovel full of dirt, and then he bent his back and joined his brothers in smooth swings. The moonlight glistened on the metal surface of their shovels.

Chapter Two

Colin Anderson paced the corridor outside the Oval Office. The stoic-faced Secret Service men who stood motionless at their stations seemed to pay him no mind, but he could imagine their smiles when he turned away. Let them laugh, he thought; he didn't care. They could think what they wanted about aides who were summoned abruptly by the most powerful man in the world. It was the President's opinion that mattered in the end, and his alone. And he was not being summoned to be chastised. Of this he was certain.

"The President will see you now," one of the agents by the double doors said, his voice clipped.

Colin entered.

"Mr. President," he said as he smiled broadly.

"Colin ... it's good you had time to come."

President Michael Doyle motioned towards the pair of couches. "Make yourself comfortable. It's nice weather tonight, isn't it?"

"Yes it is, Mr. President. The moon should be up before long."

President Doyle laughed. "Washington gets very confusing sometimes, but I'm glad to see that you still keep track of such little things."

"Well..." Colin shrugged. "I do walk outside once in a while."

"As I try to." President Doyle stood to pace the floor.

"You really shouldn't work this late," Colin ventured.

"It's a twenty-four hour job," the President said. "It makes little difference whether it's here or over there at the residence. They always find you. It's Mr. President this and Mr. President that."

Colin nodded as the President continued.

"'What shall we do?' they ask. 'Mr. President, the nation is almost at war. Mr. President, the epidemic still hasn't abated?' Tell me, Colin, what would you do if you were Mr. President?"

Colin smiled. "That's why I'm not president, sir. And let's keep it that way."

"True ..." the President allowed. "So why don't you at least tell me where we are going with the country."

"But ... Mr. President." Colin motioned toward the unseen distant Cabinet room. "We had the Health Care meeting this morning. Nothing has changed since then, sir."

The President looked long out of the tall windows before speaking. "The epidemic is out of control, isn't it Colin?"

There was a long moment of silence. "Yes it is, Mr. President. And we have begun to implement the emergency procedures we spoke about. The plan to use the prisons to house the sick has begun this morning; as well we have brought in fresh supplies of vaccine from another plant in China. And we plan to use a counter insurgency program to blame local militia groups should unrest...."

The President raised his hand to stop Colin. "I don't have time for every detail. That's why I give you guys the power I do. But I want you to make decisions as I would make them. We have to save this country from itself, and that will take big, bold decisions that some may not understand. But you understand me, don't you?"

"Yes I do, Mr. President." Colin kept his gaze level.

President Doyle stood and walked over to the window behind his massive desk. "But tell me again, Colin. Why aren't there enough vaccines to go around? You guys saw this coming years ago, or you should have. Why was nothing done?"

"Mr. President, please," Colin protested. "I thought you said you trusted me. That you left decisions up to us."

President Doyle came back to the couch and sat down. "But why is it that the people are refusing them — large portions of the population from what it sounds like? Why is it that the vaccines are inferior? Why is it that in some cases — perhaps in many — they spread the disease?"

"Mr. President, really, I must protest, sir." Colin cleared his throat. "You shouldn't concern yourself with these matters. We are doing the best we can. If it helps anything" — Colin cleared his throat again — "The Northern States and California are doing fine. It's elsewhere there are problems. The South — Virginia primarily — Utah, Montana, and most of the western States."

"And what exactly is the problem?" The President stared out of the window.

"Well ... sir," Colin began. "We are short on almost everything medically related. But I'm sure you're aware of that."

President Doyle nodded.

Colin continued, "The supply of vaccine is no different. We are short everywhere and corruption is widespread. It seems to spread almost as fast as the epidemic itself. And we have sent directives repeatedly, with all the appropriate instructions, to our operatives in charge, along with strict orders to pass it down the chain of command. Appropriate penalties have been spelled out — with your approval of course."

The President nodded and stood to pace again.

Colin continued. "I suppose people figure things out ... that we can't enforce the rules. Then it just goes wild it seems. Deliveries are not made on time, deadlines for research are missed. Even Mayo let us down on the vaccine. We sent a billion or so their way to find the latest match on this fever, and their vaccine is what gets most people infected. Not always, but most of the time."

"And?" The President turned to face Colin.

"A little lab in North Carolina has the perfect match, but you know the problems associated with that. The Northwest director, Mr. Howard, had a perfect fit when that news hit the fan. And I couldn't ignore him. So we produce what vaccine we can from North Carolina. We send it to the best places — where it is most needed — but they can't be given priority or sent more monies than they already receive. That could be a scandal all of itself. And then the problem of a clinic in the South *finding* a solution when Mayo couldn't. Imagine that. It's the principle of the thing, sir."

"Can't Treasury give you more funds? You don't have to use the Mayo stuff. Set it aside, and increase the supply out of North Carolina."

"I would, Mr. President, but I have no control over Treasury. They tell me if they print any more money the whole economy will go over the edge. The dollar ... but it's not my department, sir. And Congress has its own priorities right now. You think one of those fat cats would lessen his chances of reelection to take any risks? It takes plenty of money sent home for that. Which is monies we don't have."

"You know that none of this looks good, Colin. And it will make things worse if a few martyrs kill themselves on top of everything else. Thank heavens that hasn't started yet."

"You would know more about that than I do, Mr. President."

"And the news media has been cooperative." The President paced again, as if he hadn't heard Colin's last remark. "They at least understand the panic that could result."

"That is correct, sir. And I hope this holds." Colin wiped his brow with the back of his hand.

"These detention centers ... why not build more, instead of using the prisons? You know how explosive an issue that could be?"

"I thought the press was under control, sir!"

President Doyle shrugged. "We work hard on that angle.

And I don't need you to remind me of our greatest vulnerability. But I imagine the answers will all be the same. There are no funds for building detention centers. And tent cities would be too obvious, attract too much attention. So you turn out the prisons and make use of what you have. Practicality, you say, and all that, and of course making the best use of the limited available funds."

"Yes sir. And I thought perhaps this would help on another front, sir. With our plan this will increase the crime rate, shall we say, with the prisoners out in the appropriate areas, and allow us greater control later … when measures might then be taken that otherwise couldn't …."

President Doyle held up his hand. "You are a visionary, Colin … but spare me the details."

"I'm sorry if I have disappointed you, Mr. President."

"Not in the least." The President's smile was cold. "Perhaps we could call it the law of the unintended consequences. And it's perfectly explainable in case our friends in the press find out. But I hope you have taken the appropriate precautions?"

"Yes, Mr. President. The governors oversee the parole boards, or will be involved if they aren't already. The most violent offenders … the ones not even our friends could explain away … are consolidated. That still leaves plenty left for our purposes."

"And no governors have objected?"

"A few, sir, but they have been persuaded, shall we say."

"By normal means … I hope?"

Colin laughed. "Medical control makes for great persuasion, sir, especially in times of crisis. Most of them have family members … if nothing else. So I wouldn't worry, Mr. President. We are using Directive 901 extensively … in the converted prisons. I wished only to inform you of how beneficial the directive has been for us. And that it took a lot of courage to sign it, sir. That even if this should leak, I think the public would understand."

The President shook his head. "I don't know about that. But I do know that I visited Washington Adventist Hospital yesterday. I saw firsthand again how these fever victims suffer. And I believe no human being should have to die powerless under those circumstances. I saw the suffering in the children's eyes. I saw the sores on their skin, the agony of the death that lay ahead of them. I saw his parents, solid religious people, standing there, watching their child die, and I could hardly stand it. Yet what can I, even as President, do? You can't tell people to let go. You can't order them to accept the inevitable. Because God's hand causes it all, they think. Yet how can we escape responsibility if we stand by and don't do what lies in our power to do?"

"It was a good directive, sir." Colin dropped his eyes. "Most of the sick make the correct choice. If they don't, we leave them to experience the full version of their illness in the prison yard. It doesn't take long for them to decide. And if that wasn't enough reason, sir, remember the limited recourses we have on hand."

President Michael Doyle held out his hand. "Get some sleep, Colin. You need it."

"Not more than you do." Colin turned to walk out the double doors, his steps brisk. The agents in the hall never turned their eyes. Let them think what they wished, he thought. He was under the President's orders, doing what was best for the country.

Chapter Three

The young reverend of the black AME church in Farmstead, Virginia, Regina Owens, stepped outside the front door of her church parsonage. She glanced up Main Street as an old gray pickup pulled off from the intersection. Its bumper nearly dragged the pavement as it clattered along.

Across the street sat the historic Baptist church visited by Martin Luther King, Jr., before he was assassinated. Farmstead was that way, Regina thought — steeped in history, proud of itself one moment with what remained of the old Southern bravado, and ashamed of itself the next.

Here the public schools had been shut down rather than integrate during the heated confrontation in the sixties. Apologies were made by the present day public officials from time to time, but the fact remained like an old scar long after the wound has healed.

But thoughts of the distant past were not what troubled her tonight, Regina told herself. It was the present — the turmoil in the world and the upheaval in her own life. She had turned Travis Jones — the energetic chairman of the church board, her boss, and the best attorney in town — away from her house last night. He usually stayed over a few times a week. This was a well known practice of theirs for over a year now. Not that anyone from the town or the church cared. She planned to marry Travis, and he her—at least she had thought so--until the past few weeks. Travis was up to something. She was sure of it. What, she didn't know. Another woman, no doubt. Wasn't that what it always came down to?

Well ... she didn't like it any more — sleeping with a man while she wondered. A right old fashioned thought, of course, and not like her at all. But perhaps life eventually took her where she hadn't expected — back to the old ways her parents had brought her up with. Regina shook her head. She had no plans to go there. She just wanted Travis gone last night to help clear her head. Travis, of course, had not taken kindly to the rejection. He had looked positively upset, so perhaps there wasn't another woman.

Regina pushed the dark thoughts out of her mind. She had her duty tonight. She cared for the welfare of her parishioners, and if they were in the hospital they would be visited regardless of the circumstances. Had that not been the guiding philosophy of her call to the ministry? One was bold, and one did what the job required.

And much was still right with the world. The soothing voice of her father on the parsonage phone today had assured her that all was well with her family. They had taken the vaccine offered by the government, and the sickness had not darkened their door.

She began her walk to the hospital. The news said everything was under control, but Regina still hesitated at the corner of High and Main with the late evening sunshine in her eyes. Two ladies approached her, middle-aged, white, and well-dressed. This was a college town, and they looked like professors with their brisk walk and briefcases.

"Good evening, ladies." Regina smiled.

They walked by as if they hadn't heard, their eyes focused straight ahead. Regina resisted the urge to glare after them and continued to move up the slope of the street.

Why didn't people care enough about each other to at least say hello? Apparently the friendly college town had become withdrawn in the midst of the present difficulty. And she probably was out tonight only because she was a reverend—or to get away from Travis. He'd be back tonight at the parsonage door, his hang dog expression firmly in place, and she likely would let him in. She'd give in to the plea in his eyes. And that would get neither of them anywhere. Travis was a good lover, and she did miss him — a lot, in fact. But a night spent with him would only complicate things further. She didn't really need that right now.

Regina set a brisk pace up the slight incline. Ahead of her lay the expanse of red brick college buildings laid out in a sweep of grandeur along grassy lawns. The campus conveyed a sense of age, wisdom, and connection with the learned peoples of the past. The Civil War monument on the other side of the street blazed with glory as the setting sun broke through clouds. The rays flooded the hero on horseback with deep shades of red and orange.

The police cruisers didn't have their lights on, the two vehicles parked on each side of the street. The roadblock of yellow sawhorses with reflector tape spanned from the college lawn to the nearby sidewalk café. Regina kept going, looking straight ahead. There was little question what the officers were doing; they had their duties.

"Good evening, Reverend," the nearest officer nodded. He apparently recognized her.

"Good evening." Regina didn't slow her pace. They would expect her to continue and not to interfere. There were new laws these days about such things, even for Reverends.

The officers stood on either side of a blue suburban. The windows were down, the words easily heard.

"Let me see your vaccination card, ma'am," one of the officers said.

Regina stopped and turned around. Surely she was far enough away that neither officer would object. This might not be one of her own parishioners, but weren't all God's people part of her flock?

"I've already gotten my shot," the woman said, her sleeve pulled up high on her arm.

"Is anyone else in the car with you?" demanded one of the officers. "I still need to see your card, ma'am."

Regina saw the look on the woman's face change to fear.

"Mommy," a small voice said. A head popped up from behind the seat. "I'm scared. I can't stay down here anymore."

"Will you please step out of the car, ma'am," the officer said.

Regina saw the woman hesitate as the officer reached for the door handle, his face resigned to another unpleasant confrontation.

"I'm okay, officer." The woman attempted to smile, but the effort contorted her face. She pushed his fingers away. "All of us are fine."

"Just step out of the car. We need to check your son, ma'am." The other officer repeated the command.

"I know what you will do to him." The woman's voice had become a harsh whisper. "It's worse than the real thing."

"We are here to help your child, ma'am ... and you." The officer reached for the door latch again. "It will do no one any good if your son comes down with the fever."

The woman grimaced. Regina heard the click of the latch and the door swung open hard, right into the officer's knees. The backwards leap came too late as the officer landed on his backside in the grass. He sprawled across the lawn.

"Rotten," the uninjured officer muttered. "What is this world coming to?"

"I'm sorry, Reverend." The woman looked beseechingly at Regina before she pulled the car door shut. "Pray for our souls."

The officer was back on his feet and moving quickly. Regina paused, frozen in place. Should she interfere? Officers all over the country forcibly vaccinated people on the spot on a daily basis. She knew that. Wouldn't her interference only make matters worse?

The woman decided the matter for her as she jerked the

car into gear, her knuckles white on the steering wheel. She squinted into the full glare of the setting sun. The roar of the engine filled the air as the car accelerated and swerved wildly.

"Don't shoot," the officer on the street side shouted.

"I'll only get her tires," the other shouted back.

"No. I've got her license number. The health department can take care of this one."

Regina heard their voices as if they were far in the distance, her eyes still fastened upon the careening car.

"No, dear Lord. Please don't let this be happening," she prayed out loud as the car caught its wheel on the curb and bounced high into the air. It missed another vehicle by inches, then righted itself. Still it accelerated, until the car blew a front tire and swung to the right.

"No," Regina screamed, watching in horror as the car catapulted over the curb and clipped the fire hydrant on the corner. The vehicle missed the Episcopal Church sign in the lawn but crashed into the heavy wooden doors.

"I don't believe this," the officer in the street said. "What did she do that for?"

Regina stood still, her body cold from head to toe. Water roared from the broken hydrant. The arch of spray nearly reached the tree tops, now dappled red from the setting sun.

"Lord, no," Regina screamed again, forcing her legs to move. She ran into the street, her heart pounding. She heard the quick slap of shoes on pavement from the officers just behind her.

The explosion caught them all by surprise. Flames erupted into a great ball of fire and filled the entire front of the church. Smoke billowed upward, a mass of roiling blackness that darkened the sky. The percussion of the blast momentarily deafened Regina's ears. Wood and concrete pieces flew as high as the old oaks in the lawn.

The voice of the officer squawked into his microphone behind her, the words unintelligible. Regina forced her feet forward again. The heat was heavy on her arms, but something had to be done. She had to reach the woman and child, but how?

"You have to stay back," the officer shouted. He grabbed her arm and pulled her back to the sidewalk. "This is for others to take care of."

"What others?" Regina hollered. "There is no one here who can take care of this."

"It was nobody's fault," the officer shouted back. He still held her. "I didn't shoot."

Perhaps you should have," Regina yelled louder. The words made little sense, she knew, but did anything make sense at the moment?

"It's too dangerous." The officer still didn't loosen the grip on her arm. "Help will be here in a moment."

Regina sank to the ground and felt the grass come up to meet her. The softness was a reproach, she thought, the relief to the ache in her legs an insult. There should be no pleasure at the moment of such tragedy. The pain of the officer's fingers dug into her arm and cut into her thoughts. She turned her face up to his. Regina beseeched him, "I won't go near there. I'll stay here. Just let go of me."

He studied her for a moment before he nodded. Moments later he ran down the street towards the cars that had stopped haphazardly as they came up over the grade towards the college.

In the distance came the sound of sirens, and emergency vehicles rolled into sight from the north. Regina watched. What else was there to do but watch? The woman and her child's lives had been snuffed out, just like that, with no recourse, no undoing of the terrible accident.

What had just happened? Regina wondered. Why did the car blow up? Cars didn't blow up because they ran into church doors. It was incomprehensible.

"Would you please move back?" A burly fireman jumped

down from his truck to approach her. "We need this area clear."

Regina turned to go, but the fireman motioned for her to stop. "Aren't you the Reverend down at AME?"

"I am."

Were you here when this happened?"

"Yes, and it shouldn't have," Regina retorted.

"Well, Reverend," he shrugged. "I doubt the officers are to blame."

"Then who is?" Regina's voice rose again. "What just happened here?"

The fireman looked away. "Sorry, I don't know. And I have to go before the church burns down."

"What about the woman and the child? Don't you care about them?"

"Look, ma'am, no one could have survived that inferno." He pointed at the roiling flames. "Please move back. We have more trucks coming in."

Regina didn't answer as she walked across the college lawn. There she could watch from a safe distance. She glanced back at the flames that now licked the roof of the church. The water arched from the fire hoses to douse them and fought to gain the upper hand.

She wanted to sink down onto the grass again and watch the struggle play out against the darkened sky. Her charges at the hospital would understand when she explained why she had been delayed. But she would do no good here; she had to keep active. Stillness would only leave time for more questions she didn't want to face right now. Questions whose dark faces stared at her from the billowing, writhing flames on the church roof.

Regina forced herself to walk up High Street, past the wail of another fire truck that rushed down from the north. Two more sirens shrieked from downtown as the drivers lay heavy on the horn.

People gathered on their front porches to watch the old church burn. Surprisingly, no one bothered to holler and ask her what had happened. Regina forced her feet to move again. She turned up Oak Street and climbed the hill to where another police blockade stood. The post had been momentarily abandoned, the yellow sawhorses pushed to the side of the road.

Empty syringes lay nearby, and Regina stopped to pick them up. After the twelfth one she gave up the count. She cast them into the ditch where they could cause less harm. They landed with a soft rustle in the tall grass. The city wasn't mowing here, she thought — only three blocks from the college. How strange was that?

Regina shook her head and glanced back over the treetops. She had to stop worrying about things. She had enough problems in her life with Travis. This was not her area of responsibility. She was a minister of the gospel. She dealt with the souls of men, and she must trust those who were in charge of the rest of the world.

Below her stood the hospital, a sprawl of low red brick buildings, expanded a few years ago and now under new management — the pride of her small town. The parking lot in front of the hospital was almost empty. Regina stopped herself from a glance toward the south lot. It would do no good anyway. She knew what was there, and she could do nothing about it.

A child's cry of agony, audible even above the noise of the passing cars, broke her resolution. She ran forward to look. Vehicles were parked askew, as they had been all week, as if someone had tried on purpose to find a random pattern. In the falling darkness only the faintest of details were visible, but it was a world set apart. Between the two lots sat three police cars. The officers stood outside their cruisers, batons at the ready. Cold circles ran around Regina's heart. Tonight looked like it might be even worse than anything she had seen before.

The child had ceased his cries, and silence hung heavy in the air. The dark clouds that rolled in from the west seemed to reach down to join the earth below. A car turned into the lot behind her. Its headlights cut the evening air like a stab of a sword and lit the emergency room doors for a moment before jerking skyward. Regina held her breath as the car hit the little knoll and the lights dropped to sweep the south lot with light.

Indeed, it was worse tonight. Many vehicle doors stood ajar, with patients' legs extended out from the seats. Backs were bent over the forms and moved slowly as if they struggled with burdens too heavy to bear.

The light faded as the car stopped by the emergency room doors. The driver's door swung open. A man leaped out and glanced around. He pushed open the hospital door and ran inside. Regina stood still as she watched the gentle swing of the double doors. A moment later the man was forcibly thrust back outside, with two burly white-clad figures on either side of him, their hands on his arms. Regina could hear their voices loud and shrill.

"No vaccination card … no treatment … no exceptions. You should have thought of that before you took the chance."

"But I have one." The man's voice rose in desperation. "Here it is … if you'd just let me show you."

"Is your girl really sick?" The question was asked with a raucous laugh.

"That's what I told you! She's in the back seat. My wife has it too, but not as bad. That's why she's not with me."

One of the white-clad men looked into the back seat. "She does look sick to me, but why didn't you get your girl vaccinated?"

"We did," the man screamed, his hand raised, his finger pointed in their faces.

"He said he got her vaccinated." The while-clad man by the door laughed. "Let's see that card again."

The man fumbled in his haste and seemed unable to find

what he looked for. He dug deeper. With a shout he produced the card. "There … now please help my daughter. If my wife gets any worse … I'll bring her in later."

The white clad man held the card high, as if he needed light from the emergency room lights to read by. "They get better all the time," he laughed. "Don't you think so Fred?" He handed the card over to his companion.

The other gave it a cursory glance. "Sure do. Now why do you think you could fool us like this? People have been trying this all day."

"What's wrong?" The man's voice trembled as he held himself in check.

"This is a fake … that's what. You people are so stupid. Telling us the government vaccine doesn't work. Who does your dirty work on these cards anyway?"

"It's not a fake. It's the real thing." The man was in their faces again.

Both of them laughed. "Soon you'll tell us the real fever is not as bad as what your girl has now."

"How would I know that?" the man screamed.

"Just don't try anything. Now get out of here."

"Or over there." The other pointed. "And something must be done about those people before long."

They disappeared through the double doors, their movements abrupt. The man didn't move for long moments before he turned his head skyward and wailed his agony. The sound reverberated into the corners of the street and hung in the shadows before it seemed to burst into the heavens themselves.

Chapter Four

For long moments Regina didn't move. What choice was there to make? Tonight the pull on her heart for action was even stronger. There was but one answer, even if the road stretched out into the distance before her, filled with unnamed danger and fear. Perhaps her rejection of Travis last night had given her courage. Regina took a deep breath and walked toward the south parking lot. The cops looked her way but offered no resistance. Their job apparently stopped only movement in the other direction.

"Careful there Reverend," the one who appeared in charge said.

"I've had the vaccination," Regina told them. The words felt as if they needed to be spoken — not for information value, but as contact between two entities who were still human.

The man laughed, "That's what we keep telling ourselves. Good luck now, but we're staying here. We don't carry divine protection."

The others joined in the laughter, and Regina smiled. It felt better than the icy stone that sat in the pit of her stomach.

"You wouldn't have seen what's happening with the commotion down the street?" one of them asked. He pointed towards the red blaze in the sky over downtown. "We can't make sense out of the radio chatter."

"I was past it," Regina told him. The officer didn't need any further explanation. He could find out the details on his own.

"There are crazy people out there tonight," the officer said.

Regina didn't respond but moved toward the erratically parked cars. Blank stares met her eyes, yet she didn't stop. The first few people she passed had the fever only in their eyes, their skin still fair. She paused by a red car where a boy was laid out alone on a blanket, his body covered with a thin sheet.

"How are you son?" Regina asked.

He didn't say anything.

"Are you alone?"

The boy nodded. "Dad left me some water, and he told me he'd be back soon."

Regina laid her hand on his forehead. She felt the hot, fiery, flushed skin.

"Will it be easy?" The boy's voice was a whisper.

"I don't know," Regina told him. Because she didn't know.

"Are you a minister?" His gaze searched her face.

Regina nodded.

"I thought they said so. I don't think anyone else dares come here. Except Dad ...."

"Do you want me to pray for you?" The need for words rose up inside her. There were no other answers anyway, but they both already knew that.

The boy attempted a laugh. The effort caught him in his chest, and made him gasp for breath. Coughs racked his body. Regina held his head off the blanket until calm returned, the prayer frozen on her lips.

"Do you think there's a God?" The boy searched her face again.

"Of course." The answer came without thought.

"It seems like He could do something to help us." The boy's breath caught again, the look of pain on his face intense.

Regina turned her head before she answered. "He is, son. We just can't see it right now."

The boy grimaced. "That's what Dad said ... before he left."

"Do you want me to stay with you?" Regina lowered the boy back onto the blanket.

He shook his head. "There's worse here than me. So you'd best pray for them."

Regina got to her feet. She waited, uncertain. Her charges were still inside, but it was too late for that now. She would hardly be allowed entrance from the south parking lot.

"May the Lord bless you," Regina whispered.

The boy smiled, his white teeth showing. "Dad's coming back soon."

Regina pushed herself to move on. Several people looked up at her but said nothing. Everywhere empty water bottles were strewn around. Stacks of them sat in the shadows near the parked cruisers. In the distance a woman motioned for her with her hand. Regina approached the car slowly and saw a young girl in the back seat. The woman who had beckoned her was red-faced, her eyes puffy. Sores oozed on her arms. Regina got on her knees as small stones on the pavement cut into her flesh. She ignored the pain.

"We both have it," the mother said. "Darla doesn't have much time though. It seems like the children get it the worst."

"Shouldn't you take her home?" Regina asked.

"My husband still hasn't got it, and we can't infect him," the woman said. "Can you pray with us?"

Regina nodded. She let her gaze move over the form of the young girl. She had never seen the full extent of the disease before, and this was worse than any of her fears. There was blood on the girl's mouth. Streams of red came out of her ears. Puffy lesions laced her skin. The fingernails were purple, blackened and broken as if from a brutal force within.

Regina overrode her fear with great effort. She called on reservoirs of strength laid up by her faith, by her firm belief that one honored God by service to one's fellow man. Regina reached out and touched the girl's hand.

"Does it hurt much?" Regina asked, as the sound of the words mocked her.

The girl nodded.

Regina struggled for words to comfort her, but her attention was jerked away by a loud shout behind them. Startled she stood, and her head hit hard on the car roof.

"I'll be right back," Regina whispered. She turned towards the hospital and saw the man from the emergency room altercation confronting the row of officers.

"So why can't I get inside? I need my child treated," his voice shouted.

"We don't make those decisions." The officers stood firm.

"Then what good are you?"

"You had best go home, sir." The officer pointed down the road. "There's nothing we can do here."

"But I paid my dues! We got the vaccination. You know why I can't take her home."

The cop said nothing and held the line.

The man came closer. He leaned forward as the shadows from the street lamps played on his face. "I'm not going home, because at the first roadblock I come to you know where they'll take us. They only let me through because I was coming to the hospital and that's worse than this." The man's hand swept across the south parking lot.

"I don't know what you mean." The officer placed a finger on the man's chest. "On the road with you ... or stay here. I really don't care, but you can't go inside."

Regina saw the man lean backwards and almost fall over.

"Wait a minute," Regina shouted. The words were drowned out by a mighty bellow from the man as he leaped forward and grabbed the cop by the throat with one hand while with the other he wrestled for the officer's weapon.

Regina watched with horror on her face. The officers on each side sprinted towards their comrade, their hands on their drawn weapons.

Their commands rang into the night air, "Drop to the ground ... now. You're under arrest."

The man's hand came up with the weapon. With a fling of

the other, he shoved the cop backwards and turned towards his own car. Guns trained on him as the man ran the few steps back to his vehicle. He dove into the open back door of his car.

"Get him out ... now." The order came from the fallen officer on the ground, his voice hoarse.

"I'll cover for you," the closest officer said, and the other holstered his weapon. The man's unmoving legs were visible, sticking out of the open back door, as the officer approached.

"Get him out," the order was repeated.

When the officer grabbed the man's legs, the shot came, the sound muffled from inside the enclosed car. The officer recoiled and fell backwards while he tried to draw his own weapon. Another muffled gunshot came from the car. The man's legs thrashed before they lay still.

"Why did you shoot him?" The question was angry. "Now we really have trouble on our hands."

"I didn't, sir," the officer said.

"Then who fired the weapon if it wasn't you?"

"He shot himself." The officer stood to his feet.

Regina watched with her hands on her cheeks. It was clear what they would find long before the officer reached the car. Obviously the demons of hell were out tonight, ravaging the land. She fell to her knees in the darkness, wordless groans on her lips.

"We'd better call for a stretcher," the officer in charge said.

"They won't give us one."

"Then let's at least get him out on the grass. Perhaps the girl can be saved."

"She's already dead, sir."

They fell silent and moved as if by instinct. They pulled the man out first and dragged his limp body to the curb. They slid a blanket under the girl before pulling her out. Blood oozed from the wound in her head.

"She's gone," the mother's voice whispered from behind Regina. "Could you say a prayer for my little girl's soul, please?"

"Of course," Regina mumbled.

"Thank you," the woman whispered. "The whole world has gone mad. Do you still believe in God?"

The question made Regina flinch. But there was only one answer.

"Yes I do; and I'll pray for your child now."

"Pray that God would forgive our sins," the woman said.

Regina's fingers brushed the girl's cheeks. They turned red by the faint light from the street lamp. The girl opened her eyes and sought Regina's.

"Are you an angel?" the mother asked.

Regina shook his head.

"It hurts," the girl said. In seconds her eyes lost their focus before they glazed over; then she was gone.

"You haven't prayed yet." The mother's voice was urgent.

"Our Father which art in heaven," Regina began. The words caught in her throat for a moment. "Thy kingdom come, thy will be done, on the earth as it is in heaven …."

She couldn't go on, and the woman seemed to understand. Her own voice finished the prayer. The woman said the words as they should be spoken, with passion, with love, and with hope.

"She is at peace," Regina said when the prayer was done. She wiped her bloody fingers on her handkerchief before she closed the girl's eyelids.

"Thank you. I'll wait now." The woman smiled. "Perhaps I'll make it, because I don't look too sick do I?"

"I hope you'll be okay," Regina said. What else could she say?

"You're a minister, aren't you?" The woman's eyes had an eager light in them.

Regina nodded.

"I thought so. No one else would have dared to come here. Will you bury us tomorrow morning?"

Regina met her gaze. "I'm sure there is someone who will take care of you."

The woman looked towards her daughter's still face. "It doesn't matter now, does it?"

Chapter Five

Enos pushed his horse hard through the gathering darkness, pulling up only slightly for the roadblock on the main road. Two police cars sat in the ditch, their lights off. The officers stood in the middle of the road. They stepped aside as he approached and waved him through. Their faces looked grim in the dim buggy lights.

A faint glow of red fire hung on the horizon towards the town of Farmstead. Shouldn't the local Palmer fire department have joined their brethren in fighting the fire? Enos wondered. Yet he had heard no sirens heading up Hwy. 460. Perhaps the locals in Farmstead could handle the fire themselves.

What did it matter what burned in town anyway? All of his sisters were in bed with the disease that buried his mother. His father would kill all of them by the time this was over … unless he could do something quickly. He was the oldest of the family and responsible, he told himself.

So what should he do? He could drive past the *English* place tonight after he saw Rosemary. Perhaps he should ask if Rosemary's folks had any medicine left? They had followed Bishop Mast's counsel, and the government had not come to knock on their door. But had that been what Mom meant by her last words? *Keep to the narrow path, Enos. Do not stray from what is right.*

But he didn't want to stray. He wanted to stay alive. Enos urged his horse on. He turned west towards Rosemary's place and pulled into the driveway to tie up at the ring by the barn. He had come here for three years now. Happy times they had been as he drove Rosemary home on Sunday nights after the *hymn singing*. He had laughed with her in the buggy and eaten the food she had prepared and served in the living room. Those had been times of love. They looked forward to the day when he could buy his own farm and say the sacred marriage vows with Rosemary's hands in his.

At least Rosemary and her family were still alive, which was something to be thankful for. But there would be no wedding this fall. It would have to be enough to simply give thanks for what they had and not cry over what they didn't have. He would hold her hand tonight, speak soft words to her, and that would have to be sufficient.

The barn door opened as Enos climbed out of the buggy. Rosemary's father, old John Dan Troyer, looked out, his white beard in the shadows, his head framed by the light of the lantern behind him.

"Good evening," John said. "I wondered who it was. We don't get many people visiting anymore."

"I had to come over," Enos told him. "I haven't seen Rosemary in a while."

"I know." John stroked his long beard. "Someday we can have church again, but *The Lord* knows even his chosen people cannot gather when the disease is running rampant among us."

"Father says the martyrs would have gathered anyway," Enos said.

He shouldn't have said the words, Enos told himself at once, but they came out of him like water forced from a spring.

John stepped outside the barn door. "Your father is a hard man, Enos, and yet who is to say what is right in this time of trouble? Your father may yet be proven correct. I know my heart is troubled sometimes when I think of the times we are living in, but Bishop Mast has spoken. I cannot but follow his leading."

"I wish father would listen to him." Enos's voice ended in

a sigh. They both knew how he felt, Enos thought, and they both knew little could be done about it.

"We must not give up our faith," John said. "Come on in the barn, if you wish. Rosemary is helping me with the late chores."

Enos said nothing more as he followed the old man inside. Of course John knew what he wanted and only made an attempt to tease. Even that, a faint sweet taste from days gone by, brought a pang of sadness to his heart.

"Hi," Rosemary greeted him. Her eyes were hollow but a smile brightened her face. "It's good to see you tonight, Enos."

"Good evening." Enos returned her smile.

"We're so sorry to hear about your mother," Rosemary said. "And not even time for a funeral. That was horrible. I don't know what the world is coming to."

"I know." Enos moved closer to stand beside her. She stood and looked up at him before her fingers reached out to grasp his.

"I'm ready to return to the house," Rosemary told him. "Do you want to come with me?"

"I'll come in a little while," Enos said. "I need to speak with your father, first."

"Okay, I'll be waiting for you." She slipped out the barn door and closed it behind herself with only a faint snap of the latch.

John looked at Enos after Rosemary left. The old man seemed to understand the thoughts that rushed through John's mind. "This is not a good time for love, or for speaking of love," he said. "I am sorry that things have come to this. I know you wished to wed her by now, but it seems *The Lord* has chosen another path. I hope your heart has not spoken harsh things against the will of the Almighty."

"I have tried to walk on holy ground," Enos said as he met John's gaze. "If I have failed, I will seek repentance, but father does not make things easy."

"I know." The light of the lantern reflected on John's face. "Is there something you wish to speak to me of?"

Enos didn't hesitate. "The medicine the English give ... do you have any left ... that we could take in case the others are willing to disobey my father?"

John's countenance saddened. "So things have come to this?"

Enos rushed on. "Perhaps, but I don't know what else to do. We will all soon be dead if we don't."

John stroked his long beard. "Yes, and we may all die, medicine or no medicine. My heart is much troubled about these matters."

Hope flitted on Enos's face. "So do you have some that you could give me?"

John shook his head. "The *English* only give medicine to people who visit their houses. They do not give any to take home. I wish it were not so, but it is. Perhaps you had better obey your father and put these thoughts far from your mind?"

"I cannot." Enos's voice was clipped. "Or do you wish me to die?"

John sighed. "No, Enos. I wish a good husband for my daughter, one who will raise godly children with her — children who will live on after we have gone to our reward. This is what I desire, but it may not be what *The Lord* desires."

Enos groaned. "Then there is no hope for us?"

"Hope." John's laugh was bitter. "Not in this world there isn't. The president talks of hope in the papers, but there is none with the plans he has for the country. They are enacting new laws against us every day in Congress. No, Enos, we have only our God to hope in."

"Do you believe God will help us?" Enos regarded the old man for a long moment.

John took his time. "He does all things after the counsel of his own will, Enos. He does not always tell us what that is."

Enos looked away. "I read the paper the other week — one

that I picked up in town. It spoke of a new vaccine, a better one that would solve this problem completely. Do you think our people will take it when it comes?"

John's eyes shone with zeal. "We will take nothing from the government, Enos, as long as they make us go to war in exchange for it. Even Bishop Mast would never agree to such a thing."

Enos paced in front of the old man. He still wasn't done with this conversation even with such a powerful argument brought out as proof. "Then why did the Bishop agree to take the *English* medicine? Father says it's the same thing."

John hesitated. "Your father may be right, but I honestly do not know, Enos. These are hard questions. But most of the others agree on one thing: the *English* people in that house are not the government. They are our neighbors, and Bishop Mast believes we can take help from neighbors. I happen to agree with him."

Enos continued, "Father says there is something going on at that house which isn't right. That there is no reason for *English* people to pretend they are like us. Father says they have purchased another property besides the two they already have and that in the end the government will come after us."

"I don't know, Enos. We have enough troubles of our own without having to think about these *English* people."

Enos paced a few steps before he stopped. "I'm going in to speak with Rosemary now if that's okay with you?"

John nodded. "Her mother is in the house, but you may go upstairs if you wish to speak in peace."

"I will do that." Enos left and walked across the lawn in the darkness. The moon hadn't risen yet, but he found his way, his feet familiar with the path.

Rosemary opened the front door for him, as if she knew he was coming. Her white *kapp* glowed in the flickering light of the kerosene lamp.

"Is Dad coming in?" She glanced toward the barn.

"Before too long." He entered and waited.

"Mom's in the kitchen." Her gaze sought his. "So we can go upstairs."

"I'd like that." He reached out to touch her face in the shadows. "Your father said we could."

"I thought he wouldn't mind." She smiled and took the kerosene lamp with her as she led him up the steps.

They went through the door into her small bedroom. The ceiling sloped in the back where the bed sat snug against the wall. The familiar quilt was draped over the top, its outlines of carefully hand-stitched patterns visible in the light of her lamp.

"You can sit on the bed." She motioned with her hand.

He sat down and she left the lamp on the dresser. She came over to sit beside him. He found her hand while he looked at her face. Rosemary smiled, her face weary in the flickering light.

Here he would bring her on their wedding night, Enos thought, and take off her *kapp.* He'd let down her hair and kiss her white neck. He had never seen her breasts, but they would appear like two roes on the hillside, the Song of Solomon said. This must be a sight too great for the eyes of a man, Enos told himself, yet *The Lord* had given man such beauty to behold. A thousand times he had thought of this, and a thousand times he had told himself it could never happen to him. This was too wonderful, too sacred a thing — and apparently he had been right. *The Lord* would take Rosemary away before He had ever given her to him.

The day would never come when he could feel her face, or touch her, or pull her body tight against his. He turned away as he felt his body tremble at such thoughts. They were forbidden by the command of the *Most High God* Himself — the one who chose whether to give or whether to take away — and yet he thought them.

"You can kiss me tonight," she whispered. "Our wedding night should have been many months ago."

He pulled away from her. "Your father has trusted me. I cannot violate your father's trust."

"Father understands." Her voice was soft. "You can kiss me, Enos, and perhaps even more. Father allowed you to come up to my room, so it's okay. I am to be your wife some day."

"But we have not said the vows." His voice was a groan. He sprang to his feet as the blood pounded in his head.

"I know how you feel." She reached for his hand. "But you know how it is. Our wedding may never happen, Enos. You could die; I could die. Your father does not believe in taking the medicine."

"But...." He tried to breathe at the sight of her upturned face. "We are not wed, Rosemary. Have you gone mad?"

Her gaze was steady. "I do not know about such things, or what tomorrow may bring. Isn't it enough, Enos, that you love me tonight?"

"I cannot!" He tore his gaze away.

She stood to wrap her arms around him and her softness pressed against his chest.

"I can't do such a thing." He spoke into her hair.

She whispered the words. "When you are ready, I am Enos."

He groaned again and pushed away from her. "I will stop tonight at the *English* people's house. After I've taken the medicine we can be wed. Then we will not be tempted like this anymore."

She clutched his hand. "You would disobey your father because of me?"

His voice was hoarse. "I would, Rosemary. You know I would. Perhaps we can live beyond this time of trouble to have children together, to raise a family in the holy ways of God. That is when I can love you, not before."

She pulled him tight against her again. He tried to breathe

as he kept his hands on her shoulders. He felt the tenderness of her skin through her dress, like the softness of the morning breezes that moved over the corn fields. Then moving through his fingers he felt a fire that burned more than the hoar frost on the metal barn gate.

"We must not sin, Rosemary." He tore his hands away.

"You're not angry with me, are you Enos?" Her question followed him.

He shook his head and tried to smile. "I must go now. I am but a weak man, Rosemary. You must not do this again."

She appeared pleased. "Then kiss me, Enos. Just once. You can surely do that."

He hesitated.

Her voice pleaded. "Please Enos. I love you."

He bent towards her and sought her lips in the light of the kerosene lamp. Her face came up to meet his, and he closed his eyes. He could feel her mouth form to his, her lips move.

She was like a well for which he thirsted, and the first taste of its waters flooded his senses. She was all wildness, and he stepped away from her.

"Thank you, Enos." She came close to whisper in his ear. "I will always remember this kiss. Our very first one. But go now."

He fumbled for the doorknob and closed the door behind him without a backwards glance.

Chapter Six

Enos drove his horse through the night, urging him on. His father would soon ask why he was out so late and state that he couldn't possibly rise promptly for the chores tomorrow morning at four o'clock. Enos snorted to himself — as if chores mattered when the world had gone mad. But perhaps they did matter? Perhaps that was how men kept their sanity, finding solace in their daily routines when the world fell apart around them.

Rosemary would have done more than kiss him tonight. He was certain of it. And he wanted to with all his heart. He had almost given in tonight, and this must not happen again. So next week, or the week after that, they must visit Bishop Mast's place. Even if it was in the night, and even if only her parents would come, the vows must be said.

After the wedding he would live in her house for the first weeks of their marriage. And he would taste her kisses all night long. The thought ran though him like a flame, broken only by a yet more startling one. His father would soon be dead, as would the rest of his family, and that included himself — if something wasn't done. Enos pushed open the buggy door and pulled to a stop beside the road.

"It is madness," he shouted to the heavens.

When after long moments there was no answer, he slapped the reins and hollered to his horse, "Let's go."

The horse jerked forward, and he soon turned up the road toward the *English* people's homes.

He would do this, Enos told himself. He would have to do

it, for Rosemary's sake, for his own sake, and for their future children's sake. He pulled into the lane and stopped by the barn. Everything looked like these people really were Amish. They had gone so far as to put a ring on the barn for buggy arrivals. He climbed out and tied his horse before he walked toward the house.

Everything there was also as it should be. The sidewalk with little bits of grass had been left uncut on the edges. The front door was darkened. The light of the moon played on the solid wood. A woman answered his knock, her white *kapp* crooked on her head — the first sign that they were not what they said they were. But no one but another Amish person would have noticed the difference.

"Can I help you?" The woman regarded him with suspicion.

"I would like some of the medicine you give our people." Enos took off his black hat.

"Do you live around here?" The woman still hadn't moved.

Enos cleared his dry throat. "Yes, on the farm not far from here. My father is Norman Yoder."

"Has he been here, your father?" Her face hadn't lost its suspicion.

"Please," Enos begged. "I'm asking for myself and for my family. They all need help, and also I wish to marry soon."

"Ah, a wedding." A small smile played on her face. "At least some of normal life continues on. Do step in. What was your name?"

"Enos," he said. "Enos Yoder."

She hesitated. "Just a minute, Enos. I'll be right back."

He waited and studied the room while she was gone. These people were good, he thought. There were no signs of electric power or appliances anywhere. A gas lantern hung in the living room, visible through the open doorway. No television cast its blue light; an almost total silence hung over the house. As it should be in any good Amish home, he thought.

The silence afforded them all time for reflection and repentance from fleshly desires.

"Take this." She reappeared to hold out a small capsule. He took it in his fingers and felt its plastic roundness.

"Thanks." He tried to smile.

"You have to take it here." Her face was stern.

"I need water?" His voice caught.

"Just a minute and I will get you a glass." She disappeared again.

When she came back he tipped his head and swallowed. He always obeyed a voice of authority, even if it was a woman. Had not his mother commanded many of his days, and did not the Holy Book say that God gathered his children as a hen did her chicks? This woman felt like a mother hen. She soothed raw spots his father had left wounded and bleeding.

"Thank you." He stepped back. "Is that all there is to it?"

"That's it." She smiled.

"Does it work for people who are already ill?" He didn't hide the hope in his voice.

She nodded. "Yes it does. Is your family ill?"

"My sisters are. Can I take some for them?"

She shook her head. "They must come here. We will take care of them. Shouldn't neighbors take care of each other?"

"But you are not Amish." He blurted out the words, then wondered what she would think of his boldness.

Her smile only deepened. "We need peace, my family and I. Sure, we haven't fully joined as perhaps we should have, but doesn't that take a long time?"

"*Yes*." He shrugged. "It does."

"Isn't it almost impossible, becoming Amish?" She gave him a knowing look.

Again he nodded.

"That's what we thought, and it's also what our friends thought. We have several of them who have joined us. These are troubled times, and your people are such a shining example of what a Christian life should be. Does it bother you that we wish to live like you do, without really joining?"

Enos winced. "I'm not the bishop and don't know about such matters."

She smiled at him as if to say she understood.

Enos took a deep breath. "Did you get this medicine from the government? I ask because how else could you give it out for free?"

Her smile froze in place. "You are a curious fellow, aren't you? Well, we are definitely not with the government. In fact, we are opposed to the government in the same way your people are. That's what we explained to your bishop — what was his name?"

"Bishop Mast."

"Yes, Bishop Mast. My husband told him we are people of some means, and we'd like to help out in return for being allowed to live among your people without disturbance. Your bishop said you don't have any dealings with the government anyway, so there would be no problems."

"That is true," Enos said. "We believe in the will of God, but we do obey lawful authority where we can."

"Of course," she said. "You are a wonderful people. I wouldn't wish to change a thing about you. We have access to this medicine through a private company, so no one has to worry about it being from the government."

"I will tell my father," he said. "Perhaps he can be persuaded to come. Thank you again."

"Have a good night, Enos." She smiled and closed the door behind him.

Enos lingered for long moments in the darkness. He looked around as his horse neighed once in the background. Enos ignored the sound to walk around the edge of the house. He tried to find a basement window. He had no business here, but he had to know. Something more went on here than what the woman had said. Perhaps it was his sense of how an

Amish farm should feel. He could feel something hum under the surface that should not be here. What these people did was really none of his business, yet.... He crept along.

There was no window, only a basement door. The steps went down with dirt embankments on either side. He took them in the darkness, and his fingers found the doorknob. He felt the lock hold. Then he heard someone come behind him. He leaped upward, found a ledge with his hands, and swung over the edge of the bank. He landed softly and lay flat on the ground. The person came down the steps, rattled keys in his pocket, and opened the door to the basement.

The man turned on the light — an *English* electric light — and looked over his shoulder before he closed the door. In the darkness, Enos caught his breath. Could he believe what he had just seen? Rows and rows of *English* equipment sat in the basement — radios, computer screens, and wires that ran everywhere.

He had seen no one move around inside, but this house was not what the woman had claimed. Still, this was none of his business. If he spoke up, his father would never change his mind and would never come here. But his father would never come anyway. They would all die, as his mother had died.

Enos walked across the lawn and climbed into the buggy. He glanced once over his shoulder. From up here everything looked as it was supposed to. The low light of the lanterns burned in the window. The basement level was in total darkness. Whoever really lived here was good at disguises, no question about that.

Enos drove home but took his time now. His father would already be upset about his late arrival. It was likely close to midnight by now from the looks of the moon. But the medicine was safely down his throat. How had he dared take it? His father must never know, but even if he found out there was nothing his father could do about it.

His thoughts strayed back to Rosemary. Surely Bishop

Mast would agree when they arrived to say the vows. And they would live together upstairs, not only one night but for the rest of their nights on this earth. Perhaps *The Lord* who sometimes gave and sometimes took away would allow such a thing after all.

Enos pulled into the driveway of his home. There was still a light on in the barn. His brothers would have completed their chores hours ago, so it must be his father who waited up for him. Enos stopped and unhitched the horse, then opened the barn door. There was nothing to be ashamed of, he told himself, even if he had *English* medicine inside of him.

His father sat in the horse stall, his head in his hands. "You are late." He raised his head to look at him. "Were you doing inappropriate things at Rosemary's place?"

Enos led his horse to the stall. He gave the horse a slap on the rump before he closed the door and turned to face his father. "I stopped by the *English* house. They said there is no connection between the government and their medicine. They are private people with extra money. They wish to help us, but we will have to take the rest of the family as well as yourself there to get it. They said the medicine works even for sick people."

His father rose to his feet. "And so you make your mother's death to be of no value? Would you do that, Enos? Is that the respect a son owes his mother?"

Enos's gaze fell to the straw-strewn concrete floor. "Mom is with the angels. I do not think she wishes for us to suffer on her behalf."

"I will not go to these people!" his father roared. "Nor will any of my children go. If you were not full grown I would strap you like the *Good Book* teaches. You are a disrespectful son, Enos. How I wish it were not so. You had no right to stop in that place. There is evil there, a great evil which has no name. If you were the man you think you are, you too would know this."

"Then you will all die, because there is no other cure," Enos told him.

"There is the *Will of God,*" his father shouted. "And I will trust in His care, not in the arms of the world."

"Then it will be as you wish." Enos turned to go. "I will bury you when your time comes."

"And you expect *The Lord* to have special favor on your body?" his father asked. "Already one of your brothers shows signs of the sickness."

"I will also bury him," Enos said, not answering the question. There was no use anyway, he figured. It would be like water that ran off a steel roof. None of the moisture would ever go inside. He would bury his father when the time came and the rest of the family if necessary, but at least he would live. He would live to see the day when he could exchange his vows with Rosemary.

"Your time will also come." His father followed him out of the barn.

Enos looked up at the moon to contemplate its golden glory. "Mother is with the angels tonight, and that is good enough for me."

"She wishes for you to join her, along with us."

"I know," Enos said. "And someday I will, but not like this."

Chapter Seven

The old parsonage walls were lit by the rays of the early sun, the warm off-white colors reflecting the light. Regina sat at the kitchen table, her breakfast in front of her — still untouched. It all seemed a dream this morning and very far away, as if it had never happened.

And yet it had, Regina thought. She searched the front page of the local paper again but found no reference to the events of the previous night. The cable news had nothing important to say either. Perhaps there hadn't been time in the rush of the news cycle. No doubt there were camera crews at the old church site right now. She could walk up or drive around and check to make sure the people in the hospital parking lot were at least given basic care. But that wouldn't happen either. She also must have dreamed that idea.

The door bell rang and the door opened before Regina could even rise from her chair.

"Good morning, Reverend." The grim face of Travis Jones appeared. "I see you're having breakfast. Have some for me—after a night like I've just had."

Regina flinched. "For you? If you stay on the chair over there." She had hoped he wouldn't show up, but at least Travis seemed occupied with something at the moment that didn't include her.

Travis laughed. "Is that all the welcome I get?" He didn't wait for an answer. "At least I see these awful times haven't affected your sense of humor. Though I must say these deaths cut into my business. And we're going to have to adjust your salary if we can't get the offerings back up to where they belong."

He came closer and Regina stiffened. Surprisingly he sank into the offered chair, his face sober again. "I suppose you know about last night, the church and the hospital incidents. Something tells me you were in the middle of it all — like you always are."

"In that you would be correct." Regina ran her hand over her eyes. "So I guess I didn't dream it."

"No. I wish you had. I just came from the local editor's office — he arrived early this morning. There were a lot of us up late last night. Thankfully he's of the same mind as the rest of the town council. This thing has to be kept under wraps — lest it spread. You know how people like to copycat."

Regina hesitated. "I was there for both of these incidents, if you want to call them that. And I think they should be news. People should be made aware of what is going on if for no other reason than the danger to their souls if they take this kind of action. I do pastor a church, you know."

"That's another thing." Travis gave her a brief glare. "We really have to talk about this ... as friends of course. You shouldn't have gotten involved like you did."

Regina allowed the question to show on her face. "You don't like what I did last night? I was comforting the hurting and dying."

Of course Travis didn't like it, she told herself. She knew him well enough to know that.

"It's not like that." Travis appeared pensive. "It's that our own people need your spiritual guidance. Why weren't you inside the hospital instead of outside ... with those others ... with the ones who disobey the law? It's not our fault, you know — if people are stubborn and won't take the vaccine."

Regina let her gaze move over Travis's shoulder and out the window. The sun rays hit the floor and reflected light onto the kitchen table. She remembered last night, the shouted words, the insinuations.

She met his gaze. "You don't think I should have been there?"

His eyes gleamed for a moment. "It's dangerous; I wish you wouldn't get involved. There are people who can take care of these things."

Regina took a deep breath and plunged forward. "I saw some very strange things last night for which I have a lot of questions. Why did that church blow up? Sure the woman's car crashed into the doors, but that wasn't enough to make the entire place go up in flames."

Travis shrugged. "How should I know? Things happen."

"You should at least care," she said. "We should all care, even when it's easier not to."

Travis laughed. "Don't go preacher on me now. I'm not a theological major like you are. I'm out here in the real world, where things are not always black and white. Take for example the situation we're in now. People have to take the vaccination, whatever their religious or political beliefs, or it will cause the disease to spread even faster."

"You're not answering my question about the woman's car."

"Hey, Regina," Travis said and held up his hand. "I don't know anything about what makes vehicles explode. But anything is possible, I guess. What are you getting at?"

Regina frowned at him. "She was just trying to get away, Travis. The car should not have exploded simply by crashing into the doors; they should not have had to die like that."

"I understand, and I'm sorry it happened," Travis said, obviously trying to placate her. "But back to you and your hospital rounds. Please leave those people outside alone from now on."

Regina looked away. "Look Travis, I can't leave them alone, not when they need help. I held a little girl's hand last night while she died. That seemed more important to me than talking platitudes to those who are being well taken care of inside the hospital. I didn't hear of anyone dying in there, did you?"

"Look." Travis held up his hand again. "I know you and I know how you think, so I'm not surprised you did what you did. That's one reason everyone in church likes you. But you'll have to remember that your responsibility lies with pastoring your flock first. We can't have you interfering with the police by ministering to people who have broken the law. That isn't good, and it doesn't look good."

Regina stared at him and knew her eyes blazed with anger. "Were you there last night, Travis? Of course you weren't. You didn't see what I saw. I can't make you any promises if I see someone in need and you know that."

"I suppose so." Travis sighed. "I thought you'd say so. Why do you have these strange ideas lately?" He mumbled to himself. "Throwing me out of the house, but I still had to try. Let's just say you've been warned when the members start to complain. I'll speak up for you if I need to, but it sure would help if you tried to watch yourself. Things aren't going to get much better."

"You're involved, aren't you?" Regina tried to control her anger. "With this … with what's going on."

"I don't know anything." Travis shook his head. "It's a sign of the times, I suppose. The world is going crazy."

"I think you're going crazy."

A smile crept across his face. "I like that about you. The temper. Your drive."

Regina struggled to think of something else. His words affected her more than she wished they would. She rushed out the words. "There was a lot of hope that accompanied the reelection of the president to his second term. The president overcame tough odds, and he's a good man. But tell me, where are the people being taken … the sick ones?"

"To the hospitals ... of course." His gaze moved over her. "Where else would sick people be taken?"

She forced her thoughts to stay on track. "I've never seen any there — at least the advanced cases like they had outside. I noticed it last night for the first time; but perhaps it just didn't register before. The hospitals ought to be full of people, as widespread as the disease is."

Travis laughed. "That's the hospital's affair. I don't know how they do things. They probably have them quarantined somewhere where you wouldn't have access to them."

"Maybe, but I have been all over the hospital and haven't seen any. You'd think I would."

"Look," Travis said as he stood to his feet. "Please stay out of trouble. For my sake if not your own. Like you said yourself, you're a minister of souls, so you'd best stick with that and leave the rest of this for those whose responsibility it is. I don't know how all these things are handled, and frankly, I don't want to know."

"Well, someone has to care."

Travis continued as if he hadn't heard her comment. "There are wiser and better people in charge — officials who care and who make the best use of the monies we have to work with. With the economy the way it is, and tax revenues falling through the floor, we can thank God we are where we are. Think of the shape we'd be in if some people were in charge. They'd have sick people lining the streets, throwing them out of their homes. At least we are trying to help those we can."

Regina studied his face. "So you don't know where the sick are being taken? Because I heard things last night. Strange things, Travis, that sound like more than rumors. Why would a woman flee from officers and intentionally wreck her car over a mere rumor? She didn't seem to care about much except getting away. I was there and saw it. Why would a man kill his child? There is something going on that we aren't supposed to know about."

His laugh seemed forced. "You really have a good heart, but enough of this subject. I think we have unfinished business, don't we?" His gaze burned into her, its reach deep and hungry. He couldn't have been with another woman, Regina thought. But that was exactly what she shouldn't think right now. Moments later she knew her resolutions were too late.

"Come," she told him. "You might as well get it over with."

His face was grim. "Is that all you feel for me."

"Is that not enough?" She led the way to the bedroom.

He followed her, and when they finished he pulled on his clothing while he sat on the edge of the bed. His voice was weary. "I need to get going, as I'm already late for the town council appointment." He gave her a quick glance. "Just keep your mind focused on your flock and we'll be fine. You're a really good pastor, and we all appreciate that. And you're also a great lover, Regina."

She tried to smile. Travis reached the front door, where he lifted his hand in a quick wave, and was gone. The house settled into silence around her. Regina dressed, but her mind refused to focus. She returned to the kitchen to sink in her chair, the paper still open on the table. She picked it up and paged through it with quick movements. Now she'd never get rid of Travis. But what did it matter? It all seemed so trivial right now.

She finished the now cold breakfast, got her coat, pulled it on, and stepped out into the street. Where she was headed, she had no idea. Last night, and now Travis, had unsettled her. Anywhere seemed good enough. The few people on the sidewalk passed her. They didn't meet her eyes, and a few glanced away. Apparently no one wished to be engaged in conversation. Halfway up the hill, Regina tried anyway.

"Good morning," she said to a middle-aged man, but he passed her by without answering. A young college girl, her hair all in a mess, dodged sideways. Her face appeared tear-stained.

"Excuse me," Regina offered.

"That's okay." The girl didn't slow down.

Regina paused to catch her breath. Was Travis on target with his admonitions? This might be none of her business, yet how could she not want to know or care about what was going on?

The questions and possible answers all seemed to run together, as if one were the same as the other. Had her professors in seminary somewhere touched on this point — where caring was to stop? Could they even have imagined what she saw last night?

Regina continued up the slope on High Street. There ought to be news cameras and people here. They ought to be milling about, standing by the rubble in shock or at least in curiosity. But by the time she reached the little café on the corner, she saw that wasn't the case. Only a simple tarp hung over the front of the church, soot marks from the fire flared upward on the brick wall, and the grass lay trampled in the front yard. Yellow tape went down the street as far as she could see.

A few young people hesitated on the sidewalk before they moved on. But no media vans or camera crews trained their lenses on the rubble. Life carried on as though nothing had happened.

Her eyes searched the parking lot again. Surely at least a police cruiser would be parked somewhere, but there was nothing.

"Good morning." Regina approached a young college boy who came towards her on the sidewalk. "What happened here?"

The boy grunted and half turned. He shook his head. "The police say there was a fire last night. At least that's the word going around the campus."

"Thank you," Regina told him, but the boy didn't respond as he walked on. His backpack bounced with each step.

Regina remained for a moment as thoughts raced through

her mind. Why was she the only one concerned about what had happened here? Had fear gripped the town, or was there some other obvious reason she couldn't see? Had she perhaps imagined this nightmare? Regina shook her head when no answers presented themselves. Moments later she walked past the burned church and up Oak Street toward the hospital. Obviously there had been a fire at the church, but what about the hospital? Had that nightmare been real? Regina reached the place where the roadblock had been. She stopped to kneel and ran her hand over the grass in the ditch. It was freshly mowed, with no signs of debris or syringes lying around. There was not even a trace of plastic chewed by the lawn mower blades.

Regina rose to her feet and crested the hill. Below her the hospital came into view. She froze with her hand on her mouth. There were no police cars visible anywhere, no yellow sawhorses to keep the two parking lots separated. All was clean and orderly with parked cars here and there as they should be. It resembled none of the craziness from last night. A car turned into the driveway and pulled up to the emergency room doors where the two attendants had confronted the man the night before. Had this all been a nightmare? Regina wondered. But what about the screams, gunshots, and pleas for help when the woman and her child were dying? She couldn't have imagined that. Someone had covered up this mess — someone with the power to get the work done fast.

Regina turned to go back. Travis might be right? Whatever had happened here was way beyond the reach of her calling, but there was no way she could not get involved. This entire situation defied reality, and she was right in the middle of it.

Chapter Eight

THE TWO MEN CREPT OUT OF THE BUSHES after they'd watched the road and neighboring farmhouses all afternoon. Now they crossed a little stream. The darkness shrouded their movements. Their shoes flooded in the stream.

"We shouldn't have come this way, you idiot," the smallest one snarled. "You know those cops are around somewhere. We've got money in our pockets and civilian clothing on our backs. Let's stick to the main roads and get our sorry behinds out of this county."

"That's what got us in trouble in the first place, remember Bill?" The tallest one bent forward, his face close to the water which muffled his soft laughter.

"Don't be bringing up those old stories, Donny," the other protested. "We're out now, and we can do things right this time."

Donny turned, a smirk outlined on his face. "I can just see you hanging on to that marijuana bag, driving like the devil down those back roads with the cops on your heels. Why didn't you throw it out the window?"

"That was just a story. You can't believe half that stuff."

"Well, do you believe this?" Donny pulled a bundle of cash out of his pants pocket and ran his thumb over the edge of the bills, making them rustle in the night air.

"It's money, but the cops gave it to us," Bill protested. "That's reason enough for me not to trust them. So let's get out of here."

"And have them stop us at one of those road stops? You

know we already had to dodge one blockade. Those cops didn't look too happy from where I sat, and if those rumors in prison were correct there's a few more of them around. To say nothing of the officers who let us go. I want more food, money and guns before we move across the country."

They reached the far bank, clambered out, and slapped water from their pants.

"I didn't see any cops from the prison van," Bill said. "Did you?"

Donny laughed. "Who can see out of prison van windows? They twist your eyeballs, and they wouldn't stop prison vans at blockades, now would they? They're just waiting to shoot us the first chance they get. That's what I say this whole thing's about — getting rid of us the legal way."

Bill only grunted as Donny continued. "What other reason could there be for this sudden release? Just *poof* and we're outside. For good behavior? Like I believe that. As if the whole prison has good behavior all at once. I expect we weren't supposed to notice that, blinded by the green in front of our eyes. 'Here's the money,' they said, 'just take it and keep your mouths shut ... if you know what's good for you.' Well, I know what's good for me. I'm going to get something done for once ... really get something done before I have to walk miles on these feet, or get blown away."

"We have enough, Donny," Bill protested. "Plenty and enough to get somewhere like Richmond, Lynchburg or even South Boston. From there I heard there were good jobs to be had most anywhere. We can get a fresh start: brand new driver's licenses and everything."

"Just shut up," Donny said. "We're staying away from the main roads. And I'm getting myself a woman ... tonight. I haven't had one in years, and I know you haven't either. Let them shoot me after that — at least I'll die happy."

Bill grunted, "There's a light ahead."

"I already saw that." Donny marched across the field and

didn't look back. "It's the place where that buggy was at earlier. You would have seen him too if you'd had any eyes in your head instead of worrying about things all the time. Come on, and keep quiet."

"I don't want to go back to jail so let's be careful; and what does a buggy have to do with things?"

"Easy pickings, my man. They should at least have a hunting gun or two to blow the cops to kingdom come if it comes to that." Donny laughed as his figure faded into the dark. Bill forced himself to run. The form of a white farmhouse and barn soon appeared. Donny stopped and held up his hand.

"Stay with me, and don't make a sound," he whispered. "We have to find the phone lines first."

They circled the house as they ran their hands along the foundation, but found nothing. They ended up where they'd started, back at the front porch.

"So what's going on?" Donny whispered. "There are no phone lines."

"Then let's get out of here," Bill said. "They must have cell phones."

"I'm not going anywhere." Donald thought for a moment, until a smile crossed his face. "Of course — they're Amish. They don't have phones in the house. And no cell phones either."

He grabbed Bill's arm and hauled him towards the front door in a wild run. They burst through the front door, taking the latch off in the onslaught, and both came to a halt in the living room. They stared at an elderly Amish man seated on a rocker. Beside him sat his wife, and on the couch his young daughter.

"Don't move!" Donald ordered them. "Is there anyone else in the house?"

"There is only us," the old man said. "Me, my wife, and my daughter. Are you in need of help?"

The young girl on the couch shifted her eyes wide with fright.

"Keep an eye on her, Bill." Donald approached the rocker. "So where are the guns, old man?"

They were all silent. Bill watched the girl, but she didn't move.

"Guns?" Donny leaned closer to the old man. "Where are your guns?"

"We don't have any," the woman spoke up. "We are a peaceful people."

Donald laughed, "Okay, I buy that. But you've got a shotgun or two around, right? What about money? Don't lie to us now — it gets people hurt when they lie. Just tell us where the guns and money are and we will be on our way."

The woman shook her head. "We're poor folks. We don't have any money other than the few dollars in John's billfold."

Donny laughed and moved towards the girl. "So let's talk with this person then — if Mom and Pops don't want to talk, maybe the young one does. Where is the money, sweetheart?"

The noise of the wind stirred in the trees outside. The sound rose above the nervous breathing of the Amish family. Their frightened eyes fixed on Donny as he glared at them.

Bill looked out the window and listened. He reached over to slap Donny on the arm. "Let's get out of here." He motioned with his hand towards the door. "Now! This is not what I thought it was."

"And leave this?" Donny laughed. "Not in a million. Remember, you're in it now too, Bill. It's not just Donny who's doing this."

"You are a rotten, low down, good for nothing poor excuse for a human being," Bill snarled.

Donny threw his head back and laughed. "So little Bill has gone moral on me. He sees some religious people, and bam, he's gone. My, my, what shall we do now?"

Donny waited, as if for an answer. He tilted his head at the girl. "What do you say, sweetie?"

"No," Bill said. "You leave her alone. They look like good people."

"If I wasn't concerned about leaving a trail, I'd kill you now, you little twerp. Come on, shape up, or I will anyway."

"The Lord wishes all men to live in peace with each other," the old man spoke up.

Donny whirled towards him. "Shut up!" Then he turned to the girl. "I just want to know where the money and the guns are. Tell us, and I mean now, or do I need to use the chair?"

The girl gasped, and her gaze flew to her mother.

"We have no guns in the house, or money," the woman repeated.

"Surely the girl can talk for herself." Donny grinned.

"There is no money other than what's in Dad's billfold, like Mom said," the girl whispered. "And some small bills in the jar above the cabinet where I keep change. There's an old shotgun in the barn, near the hay loft."

Donny laughed and moved towards the couch. He grabbed the chair and swung it in the air, bringing it down hard over the mother's head. The girl gasped, her eyes wild and pleading. Strangled noises came from her mouth, but she didn't scream.

"You didn't have to kill the woman," Bill yelled. "There's better ways to get information."

Donny shrugged. He turned to walk down the hall towards the bedroom. Bill stayed with the girl. He held her arm. She seemed in a daze as she stared at her mother. "Is she dead?"

"I don't think so." His voice was touched with sympathy. "But Donny laid into her pretty good."

"Are you going to kill me and my father?"

"Not if I have anything to say about it, but you have to be quiet."

Donny's growl came from the bedroom, and he appeared in the hallway with empty hands. He held them up.

"They said there was no money," Bill told him.

"Silence, Bill. I know the man's lying," Donny roared. "Who doesn't at least have hunting guns around, other than an old shotgun in the barn?" He grabbed the chair and brought it down over the old man's head. The body fell sideways and lay still.

"You killed him." Bill stared. The girl's lips were white.

Bill lunged forward, but Donny sidestepped and placed a kick in his behind. Bill sprawled across the floor, sliding into the homemade rug on the hardwood floor with his hands extended.

"What a clumsy thing you've always been, Bill. Now lay there until I'm done or go look for the guns. We'll need them."

Bill rose to his knees as Donny jerked the girl off her feet, forcing her towards the bedroom. Donny paused in the hallway to tear off her white *kapp*. He threw it on the floor, a look of disgust on his face, before they disappeared.

What was he to do now? Bill wondered. There was nothing he could do. Donny was a mad man and had been ever since they met in jail. Why had God chosen to pair him up with a mad man? God … as if He were really in charge…. No matter who was responsible, Donny was a mad man and had to be stopped. Donny wouldn't leave the girl alive in the bedroom, not once he was done with her. He would leave no witnesses. The old man groaned on the rocker, and Bill walked over to feel for a pulse. It still beat. But the old woman looked dead with her mouth open.

He must find the guns somewhere and stop Donny. The cops would understand. Someone would understand. He could prove things. He would show them what he had done and why. He would live to see another day, and he would know he had done what was right. That was the best thing, that feeling in his heart, amongst this trouble, amongst this bloodshed, something would be right.

Bill raced upstairs where he groped for the wall switch

and realized there was none; the house had been lit downstairs by some other means. He retraced his steps and took the kerosene lamp from the kitchen, then searched through all the drawers and closets upstairs. He found nothing but simple dresses and shirts, all solid colors.

Back in the kitchen he still found no guns but stopped at the knives. He might as well have a pea shooter as go up against the cops with kitchen knives. But he didn't need to go up against the cops; he only needed to stop Donny.

He paused to think. The noises had now moved from the bedroom to the living room. The girl had never cried out, never uttered a sound — it had been all Donny, crazy Donny. Bill walked to the kitchen opening and looked into the living room, his knife clutched behind him. Donny had tied white strips of bed sheets around the couple's necks and pulled tight the last knots. The girl was nowhere in sight. Donny turned to look towards him. His eyes gleamed. "They're dead now. The little thing said her name was Rosemary. That's all she would say, 'Rosemary is going to heaven.' Think about that. How delusional these stupid religious folks are."

Bill moved fast as he stepped up behind Donny and plunged the knife down from above. He drove the blade into the broad flesh between his shoulder blades. Donny tried to reach around, his eyes terrified as he turned his head. Bill held him for long minutes until he was sure he was dead, then lowered his body to the ground.

Bill left the gas lantern lit and stepped outside to look around for a vehicle. Escape was still possible, he hoped. Should he take a chance and try to explain all this, or run the roadblocks by force? But there was no car. There was no garage. There was only a buggy behind the large door in the barn. What good was a buggy?

Bill laughed at his own question. The whole world had gone crazy, and that included his own thoughts. He ran across the open fields. He could yet reach the creek, he figured. Halfway across the beam of a police torch bounced across the field, overshot him, then came back.

"Halt! Now!" came the voice on the bull horn, but Bill didn't stop. He didn't throw up his hands. Somehow it would all be useless anyway, he told himself.

The bullets reached him before the sound of the gunshot blast. His body leaped forward, his arms akimbo before he struck the ground. His body twitched, but not for long.

Chapter Nine

Enos drove his horse at full gallop through the morning light, thrashing the reins. Mist rose from the creek as he rattled across the bridge and never slowed for the bump where concrete met pavement. His buggy wheels left the ground for a moment, and he heard only the heavy pound of the horse's hooves in his ears.

This could not be, he repeated to himself over and over. Someone had received wrong information. Rosemary and her parents dead? Yet Bishop Mast had been sure of himself. He had even stayed to speak with his father. The two had stood beside the barn in earnest conversation. The tragedy last night had apparently brought them together where the death of his mother had failed.

Enos pulled back on the reins as he approached the farmstead. The house, barn, and everything else still looked the same; all was normal except for the English police cars in the yard. Enos took the turn into the driveway and nearly slid the buggy into the ditch. The horse stumbled and fell to his knees. Enos left him there as he leaped from the seat and ran towards the house.

"Who are you?" the officer demanded as he blocked the door.

"I'm the future son-in-law," Enos gasped.

"Then you don't want to go in there," the officer told him.

"So it is true then, they are all dead?"

The officer's face darkened. "I'm afraid so, son. You had

better wait until we're done. Then you can see your girlfriend at the funeral home."

"I'm coming inside." Enos pushed forward. "I want to see her. And there will be no funeral home; we bury our own people."

The officer shrugged. "I can't blame you. They've got more to do at the funeral home than they can handle. I guess it's nice that some people still take care of each other, and since we're letting your people get away with most everything else these days — why not getting close to a crime scene? The photos are already taken and this won't be going to trial anyway. Both of the bad guys are dead."

Enos didn't listen. He slipped past the officer and entered the living room, where he took in the two broken bodies in a quick glance.

"Where is she?" Enos asked. "Up in her room?"

"In the downstairs bedroom, son," the officer said from behind him. "But I warn you, it's not nice."

Enos moved forward, his hands at his side, his thoughts flying. Rosemary was in her parents' bedroom. She would never have gone in there except by force. And what force could have caused such a thing? What could have moved her to obey? It would not have been her father or her mother. Neither had reason to. And they would not have hid there from danger. So this must have been the work of one of the *English* men.

He glanced back at the fallen body behind the couch. There was blood on the English man's mouth, and a puddle of blood in a great circle on the floor around him. He must have been Rosemary's assailant, Enos thought. He forced himself to move on. Blind hate filled his heart as well as the desire to use his hands to tear pieces of flesh from the man's body.

He knew the feelings rising within him came from the enemy of his soul. They sprang from his fallen nature and were forbidden by God. He would be damned if he yielded; he would never cross the river to see his mother if he did not cast them from his heart. The man was already dead, and there was nothing left to be done anyway. Enos moved down the hallway with his eyes blinded. He groped with his hand to feel his way forward.

In the bedroom a still form lay on the bed, covered in a white sheet. From the center the blood showed red and oozed onto the bedroom floor. He stood there and stared. This was not Rosemary. Rosemary had been alive. She had kissed him. She had waited for him. This had to be someone else, someone he didn't know.

Enos reached out to pull the sheet back to her hairline. Joy leaped to his throat — she had no white *kapp* on. Rosemary would never be without her *kapp.*

His hand paused, as uncertainty burned in his mind. But he had to look. He had to be certain.

Enos pulled the sheet down further. Her closed eyes appeared first, then her nose and mouth with their white lips. There was a piece of bedsheet wrapped around her neck where his hands had once caressed. It really was Rosemary. A sob caught in his throat. Someone must have torn her *kapp* from her head. It could have been no other way. She had died after her honor had been taken by force.

He moaned and touched her face. He felt the coolness of her cheeks under his fingers. The softness was gone. He moved the sheet further down. The bruises on her chest were pronounced and bloody. He dropped the sheet and cried out in anguish as he lifted his head towards the ceiling.

"Come." The officer appeared at his side. "I tried to warn you."

Enos allowed himself to be led away. He was now unseeing, past the bodies in the living room. Once outside, he struggled to draw a breath. He sprawled on the lawn and sank his hands into the mown grass. He wept and fought down his nausea. Oh, why had he not taken the chance to love Rosemary when she had asked him? Now her virtue had been so cruelly stolen by wicked hands. She had never known a righteous man. Enos roared his agony towards the heavens.

Two buggies rattled into the driveway behind him, but he didn't care. Let come who wished, he told himself, but he would stay here. Close to the ground Rosemary had walked on. In sight of the house she had lived in. Here she had crossed in her bare feet only a day ago on her way to the barn. Here she had worked and hung wash out on the line. And here she had died.

He remained on the ground as his father and Bishop Mast came across the lawn.

Bishop Mast laid a hand on his shoulder. "I'm so sorry for what has happened, Enos. But you must not allow bitterness to enter and grow in your heart. These were evil men. *The Lord* will judge them according to His own will."

"He has judged them already," Enos choked. "Rosemary was taken. But the *English* man is dead and I'm glad."

"You must not say such things." The bishop knelt beside him on the grass. "Rosemary is with the angels now. And the unjust suffering we experience in our bodies will be turned by *The Lord* into jewels for her crown."

"I would have killed the *English* man myself if he had not already been dead," Enos whispered. "My hands would have taken the life from his throat, just like he did theirs. Yes, I would have killed him."

Bishop Mast stared at Enos and moved closer to his face.

"Enos, my son," he said. "What you are feeling is the wrath of man, which works no good in this world. You must let it go and allow forgiveness to flood your being."

"Forgiveness I can give since the man is dead," Enos told the bishop. "But I wish it had been I who had killed him."

"You will speak no more on this matter." His father pulled on the bishop's arm. "Leave him alone until his senses have returned. This is too much for any of us to bear. Enos will forgive and he will repent later for the words he has spoken."

"I want them buried today," Enos said.

His father and the bishop looked at each other and nodded.

"There is no reason why it cannot be," the bishop agreed. "I will summon our people and send some young men over. They can begin digging the graves at the graveyard. The women will prepare the bodies."

"I will return home then," his father said. "My youngest girl did not rise from her bed this morning, and her sister is not far from following her over the river."

"I will not dig more graves for our family," Enos told his father. "I have Rosemary's family to dig for now. I will bury her with my own hands."

Bishop Mast ignored Enos and grasped his father's shoulder.

"There is no reason we cannot help you, Norman," the bishop said. "Shall I send the young men over? I can come myself later to say the words over the grave."

Enos's father paused, a faraway look on his face. "It is good of you to offer, but nothing has changed at our house. I still believe in being undefiled by the world."

"But we have spoken this morning, Norman, about the things of the Lord," Bishop Mast protested. "Surely there has been peace restored between us?"

"Perhaps peace," his father said. "But my wife died without you there and so will the rest of my family if it is the Lord's will. Enos will come home to bury the last of us. If not, then we will join you again when this is all over."

"As you wish, Norman." Bishop Mast shrugged. "You know I hold nothing against you. We live and die by the Lord's will. But I will always consider you my brother."

"I go then in peace." His father left with his buggy, without a glance back over his shoulder.

"I'm sorry about this," Bishop Mast muttered, when Enos's father was out of sight. "It breaks my heart what you have been asked to suffer. But draw comfort, Enos, from the fact that *The Lord* has all things under his care. This sorrow will be over when He wills. In that day we will be able to say that truly *The Lord* has given and *The Lord* has taken, and His name is greatly to be blessed."

"But I was never given," Enos whispered, but the bishop didn't hear him; he had already turned to walk back to his buggy.

With bowed head, Enos walked to the tool shed and found the shovels. He placed them over his shoulder and headed out to the road where his horse and buggy still stood. Enos climbed in and drove past the wide open fields to where the corn came together near the fence row. There the community's graveyard lay. He picked his own spot and began to dig.

In the hours that followed, footsteps came from behind him, but he didn't raise his head. Men's hands joined the dig, and women's hands came to offer them glasses of water, but he looked at no face but Rosemary's. Not as she had been in the bedroom, sightless, white, and cold, but warm and alive, her eyes full of love for him.

He saw her head raised in joy while she rode beside him in the buggy. He saw her take deep breaths on warm summer evenings. He saw her beaming smile as she brought him food on Sunday evenings and sat on the couch beside him. He heard her rippling laughter when she unwrapped the lamp he had purchased for her first Christmas present. He saw the concern written on every crease of her face when he told her of his father and the things he endured at home.

"We will soon have our own place," she had whispered. "And our own children, and you will be a wonderful father."

"Perhaps." But he had allowed her confidence to wash over him. "At least I hope so."

"It is more than I hope so," she had said. "It is for sure, because I love you, Enos. Love is all anyone needs besides *The Lord,* and we already have Him."

He paused to lean on his shovel. Love wasn't everything.

One needed soil to work, fenced fields, cattle to graze the grass, plows and disks to work the land. He had all of those now, but he had lost love. Perhaps it was everything after all because without it, all the other things didn't seem to matter.

He might as well bury it all in the ground, but that could not be; life must go on. Bishop Mast would soon come to say so. Yes, his life must go on without Rosemary, because he had no choice. He had to choose to forgive or to hate, but over life and death he had no choice.

Bishop Mast soon came to lead the funeral. He walked in ahead of the bodies being borne on the spring wagon. Enos climbed out of the hole and reached to help lower the box. He laid it tenderly in the ground. The life was gone from her body, and the ache in his heart was like a heavy rock that wouldn't move. Tomorrow he would decide whether to hate or to forgive, he told himself, but today he would bury Rosemary.

When they were done, they stood back, and Bishop Mast opened the prayer book to read the words, "Oh Great and Heavenly Father, most Gracious God. We beseech you now, casting our voices up to the *One* who gives and the *One* who takes away. Have mercy upon these souls we have given back to You. Remember the day You formed their bodies with the fingers of your own hand, and hold not their iniquities against them, or shut the doors of your dwelling place from their eyes. Receive them unto yourself, humble our broken souls who trust only in your Will and in the pleasure of your heart."

Enos listened as Bishop Mast read. There had been no such prayers said over his mother's grave, but surely she had gone into the angels' arms. And without question Rosemary and her parents had been carried on angel wings from their earthly pains into heavenly glory. It could not have been any other way. Rosemary was too beautiful, too wonderful, too sacred, to have the last memory on this earth be the hands of an evil man who tore at her body. The angels must have touched her even before she was gone.

They threw the dirt in and he helped. Afterwards, Enos threw his body upon the mound that now covered his beloved. He wept and didn't care that the dirt covered his face. What did it matter when he would never touch her again? Bishop Mast and the others pulled him to his feet and brushed the soil from his clothing, but he couldn't move from the grave. And he didn't need to wait until tomorrow to decide; he already knew his choice: he would hate. He would be damned for it, but he would hate with all of his heart.

Chapter Ten

Regina glanced at the Richmond newspaper the following morning on her way to the refrigerator for milk. The paper slipped from her fingers to the floor. Regina grimaced as she set the milk down and gathered up the pages.

She sat down to scan the headlines: *Governor Has Concerns On Available Funds for Highway Construction; General Assembly May Pass Bill For Additional Tax Revenues; Fed Aids States with Vaccine Monies; Health Secretary Believes Virus Epidemic Almost Contained.*

There wasn't much in it that interested her. She dropped the paper onto the table and stared at the milk sitting beside her cereal. What was the world coming to anyway? Travis hadn't been by last night, and he should have been here by now if he planned a stop this morning. His absence disturbed her more than she imagined it would. And not because she needed anything from him, she told herself. She could live without a man. And hadn't she wanted to get rid of him? Only this wasn't about another woman any longer. She was sure of that. Something more sinister was abroad, and Travis was involved. But how? That was the troubling thing. And should she care? All night long she had turned the question over and over in her head.

The classes in seminary on societal justice weren't much help, she thought. They were about preparing to meet the needs of the poor, readying one's spirit for battle against the evil capitalist, or helping the needy with government aid. They taught her how to help the lower classes in society obtain a fair chance at life or reach their potential with a college education. There was no preparation on what to do when a mother and child died tragically because she feared the hand of government.

She wanted to know why. Regina poured the milk into her cereal and listened to the soft crackling sound. She almost wished Travis would come. The distraction from her thoughts would be nice, and if she was honest, enjoyable. She did love the man. Yesterday morning had proven that, if she needed any proof. Regina made a face at the milk carton. In Travis's absence the questions buzzed around her mind and wouldn't stop. Shouldn't the events of the past few days bother people? Yet they didn't seem bothered. Or perhaps they didn't know? Did the reporters at the Richmond paper know? And if they didn't, why weren't they asking the proper questions to find out?

Regina finished her bowl of cereal and went out the front door. The morning was too nice to use her car parked behind the parsonage, and the café on Fifth and Main was not that far. She would walk and treat herself to an espresso and pick up some information while she was there.

"Good morning." She nodded to the few people she saw on the street. Most of them went by without a greeting in return.

Mrs. Grunter, though, from the Pastries & Deli, stood on her threshold and returned her "Good Morning." At least there were still people in the world who acknowledged each other, she thought. Should she stop in? But Mrs. Grunter sold coffee and donuts on the go, and a different atmosphere would be right for this morning — a place where people sat around, where they lingered and talked. If such a place still existed!

A half a block further down, Regina pushed open the door of Gilbert's Corner Café. She held it open for two young college girls coming out. They nodded and smiled, their coffee cups in hand. Regina smiled back. Perhaps there was hope in the world after all. These young people still appeared cheerful. A quick look inside showed no one at the tables, but perhaps if she waited there would be.

"A large," Regina told the girl at the counter.

"Decaf or regular?" The girl smiled, her head mid-level to the steel coffee machines, her pressed uniform spotless.

"Regular." Regina returned her smile.

"I should have known," the girl laughed. "What else would one drink this early in the morning?"

"I suppose so." Regina's mind was elsewhere. Two people now stood in line behind her. Perhaps she might overhear something of use.

The girl set the coffee cup on the counter. "My girlfriend goes to your church. She always has such good things to say about her pastor. So I came with her the other Sunday. But I'm sure you didn't notice with the crowd you have each Sunday."

"I'm glad to hear that." Regina handed the girl a five. "I hope you decide to come again."

"Oh, I will." The girl handed back the change. "You know how it goes ... with church and all."

"I hope to see you then." Regina picked up the paper cup and noted the heat under her fingers. She grabbed a cardboard sleeve and slipped it on the cup. The girl had already turned to the person behind her, so Regina selected a table in the middle of the café. This seemed like a good spot to pick up on others' conversations.

Out of the corner of her eye Regina saw a man pay for his coffee, turn around and sit two tables down from her. So far, so good, she thought. Now if someone would talk with him. Maybe she should move down, say *good morning,* and ask a few questions.

The chair scraped at her table and surprised her. She looked up.

"Care if I sit with you, Reverend?" The man's voice was soft.

"Sure," Regina shrugged. She didn't know the man, but neither did he appear dangerous. His suit was nice. And he was white. Not that it made any difference, but....

"Couldn't help overhearing your exchange with the cashier." He pulled the chair in and rested his arms upon the table. "So you're a Reverend?"

"Yes ... at AME. And you?"

"From the college." He grinned. "But there's nothing like the holy calling of the church, eh?"

"Perhaps." Regina met his gaze. His eyes were warm. "I'm sure there are other worthy causes in the world."

"Ah ... but the church." He held her gaze. "Does she not minister to men's souls?"

Regina didn't hesitate. "Yes, that she does. Or at least I do."

"But these are times that call for more ... don't you think?" He searched her face, as if he wanted an answer he knew she wouldn't give.

"I'm not sure what you mean."

He kept her gaze. "You were at the college the other night ... weren't you?"

Regina winced. "I was, but I didn't see you on the street."

He shrugged. "Actually I wasn't. But I can see things without being on the street."

"I see ... you were looking out of your window, I suppose. Why didn't you come out?"

He hesitated. "Sometimes it's best to stay in one's own world. Don't you think so?"

Regina gave him a sharp look. "Did you think I was out of mine?"

He smiled. "It all depends ... doesn't it?"

Regina took a deep breath and gathered herself together. She had wanted information and conversation, but this was a little too much with a man who was a stranger.

"I wouldn't know," she finally said. "You're not making a whole lot of sense."

He stood to leave. "Professor of Social Works, actually the head of the department. I hope you make good choices in the days ahead. It's not going to be easy for anyone, and we can use all the help we can get."

Regina didn't look away. "I have no idea what you are talking about, professor, and what was your name?"

"Lester Blanton, the fourth." He offered his hand.

Regina hesitated before she shook it. "How do you know me?"

"All in its own good time, huh." He grinned. "Hope things go well with that boyfriend of yours. Wouldn't want love destroyed along with everything else these days. You take care now and have a wonderful day."

Regina watched the professor get up and walk out without so much as a backwards glance. For a moment he paused to hold the café door open for an elderly man, then he was gone. She shook her head and took a sip of her coffee. Now how strange was that? Some professor from the local college sat at her table for no apparent reason and talked like he knew her. Why? That was the question. Perhaps she had gotten more than she bargained for this morning, but that's how things had gone the last few days. Trouble showed up, and she didn't have to look for it. She had a feeling, though, she had made it easy for the professor to contact her by her venture into such a public place. But then she had no plans to avoid public places either. Regina glanced around. An old man at the counter paid for his coffee and tottered across the café to a nearby table. All the other tables were now empty. She might as well leave, Regina figured, and rose to her feet.

"You have a good day, Reverend." The girl behind the counter waved as she went past.

Regina waved back as she pulled open the door and stepped outside. On the street she walked with quick steps past the courthouse. A lawyer or two scurried across the street, and a few scattered shoppers lingered near the window fronts.

All seemed intent on their own business, or was it stress she saw in their faces?

Ahead of her Professor Blanton's figure appeared out of the donut shop. Regina slowed down. She had no desire to see him again so soon. Moments later she saw him turn the corner up High Street with his head down. He moved at a brisk clip.

Who was he really? she wondered. A professor? Really? But he wouldn't lie would he? What benefit lay in that? The light turned green, and Regina crossed the street. She entered the parsonage to grab her keys off the hook by the refrigerator and walk out the back door. Her car started on the first try, and she headed out of town going north on State Route 45. Where exactly she planned to go she wasn't certain, just somewhere. She needed to think. Too much was happening right now to process in familiar surroundings.

State troopers had set up the first roadblock at the town limits.

"Pull over please," the officer told her. "Routine check." He smiled, but Regina felt a chill creep down her neck. There was nothing routine about this request to pull over. Normally they just glanced at her card and waved her on through. She stopped the car and showed him her inoculation card.

"I'm the pastor at AME," she told him.

"Ah, one of the good guys." The officer smiled. "But pull up to the curb, and please pop your trunk. I'm sorry, but we have to check everyone."

She pulled forward and reached down to spring the release as a second officer joined the first. He opened the trunk lid, and his head disappeared inside.

"All clear here," he said. "Are you checking the back seat?"

"She's the pastor at AME," the officer by Regina's window replied.

"You'd still better look." The order was curt.

"Sorry about that," the officer apologized. He motioned for her to unlock the back door, opened it, and made a quick sweep with his gaze before he waved Regina on. She accelerated out of town. Now why had they done such an extensive search? There seemed no obvious answer unless some unknown danger lay about. Which wasn't difficult to imagine. Danger seemed to lie everywhere.

A mile out, Regina drove past the last of the subdivisions. Her eye caught sight of a tractor at work in the fields, the farmer's hat pulled tight over his eyes. The young corn bent over as if driven by the wind. A few cars passed her, all of them on their way towards town, but no one glanced in her direction.

Regina made a split-second decision and turned off onto a side road. Her tires kicked up a cloud of dust from the unpaved shoulders. The road narrowed, and she slowed, as her wheels hummed on the rough pavement. A ramshackle of a house came into view, its foundation rotted. An old man sat on the front porch. He leaned forward as she approached, obviously curious. Regina waved, but the man only stared back. His gaze followed her around the bend.

In front of her the morning mist had drifted in from the river and obstructed her vision. Regina slowed down even more. What was she doing out here? She should really turn around, she thought. The road showed no sign that it went anywhere. Perhaps she should have stopped and talked to the old man on the porch. But what would he know?

From out of the mist behind her the form of another car, a gray Porsche, appeared. The vehicle pulled up close to her bumper and flashed its headlights. Her heart pounded. Should she flee? Make a run for it? But where to?

When the flashing lights didn't stop, she slowed to a crawl and then to a stop in a farmer's lane that led into his fields. There was no escape anyway, since she didn't know where this road went. Clearly whoever this was wanted her to stop.

The gray Porsche stopped behind her, and a man got out to walk towards her door. She rolled the windows all the way up and clicked the lock. With the mist around him he approached her side of the car. It was only when the grinning face of Professor Lester Blanton appeared in her car window that her fear changed to anger, and she cracked the window. The nerve of the man to follow her like this.

"Hello, again." The professor was all cheerful.

"Why are you following me around?" Regina demanded.

"Because you seem a curious sort of Reverend. That's what I like about you. Why else would you wander the back roads of the county?"

"That happens to be none of your business." She rolled the rest of the window down.

"Perhaps," he agreed. "But you're only going to get in trouble if you don't stop this. You can't stick your nose in where it doesn't belong."

"So you don't care either — with what's going on in the world?"

He raised his eyebrows. "The question is whether you wish to know, not whether I care."

"No! It's always about caring," she retorted. "I figured a professor of social work should know that, or are you of the uncaring kind?"

He smiled. "Perhaps we should keep the subject on yourself. If you really want to know, drive down the next road about a mile and turn left at the stop sign, five miles or so. There's an open field on the left and then woods. See if a man's still there. That is if you really care. I don't blame you if you don't. And it might be wiser if you didn't, you know."

She caught her breath. "So what are you saying? And what do you want from me?"

"Let's see if you care first. Go see, and maybe you'll find him and maybe you won't." He walked back to his car. Once there he turned around in the road and drove back the way he had come. His gray Porsche was soon swallowed up in the mist.

So now what should she do? The man talked nonsense.

What could possibly lie down that road? A secret project of some kind? A hidden danger? Why would he have suggested she go? He didn't look like a man who would send a woman to her death.

Regina restarted her car. She might as well go see, she figured. So she made the turn at the next road and drove several miles to the stop sign. Her gaze searched both sides of the road. Across a field, her eye caught sight of a man in the wood line. He disappeared into the trees the moment she slowed down. Before he vanished she saw his arms hang limp at his side. He had a shuffle to his gait as if he were completely exhausted. Regina bounced over into the side of the ditch and brought the car to a stop.

So was this who the professor spoke about? Someone who ran off into the woods? A man in trouble, no doubt! Someone she could help. Regina glanced back over her shoulder but saw nothing, the road empty behind her. Professor Blanton must have left the decision on whether to pursue this matter up to her, she decided.

Regina hesitated as she reached for the doorknob. Did she dare? Did she really want to know this badly? What if the man was a fugitive from justice? But hadn't the people at the hospital parking lot been considered fugitives from justice? Yes, they had, she told herself, and she would also take this chance. The man might have the information she looked for or really need her help.

But Travis was right. After this she did need to change. Let those who knew best take care of the important matters. Not that long ago she would not have pursued anyone, dangerous or otherwise, into the woods.

Yet the lecture didn't help, really. Neither her own nor Travis's. She wanted to know, in a perverse sort of way. She, the pastor of AME, was tired of secrets, of headlines in papers that never mentioned what really happened, of veiled references from church officials, of people who took matters into their own hands as if driven by a force over which they had no control. And she wanted to know why the man she loved was involved in this.

Before her was another man — in flesh and blood — who might not be afraid to speak his mind. That could well be what Professor Blanton tried to say. She could turn him over to the officers at the roadblock later if he was in need of help she couldn't supply. Regina climbed out of the car and locked the door.

Chapter Eleven

Regina entered the woods, her steps cautious. Branches scratched her face, and she sidestepped. How did anyone walk through such heavy foliage? Especially with nerves on edge and this stifling stillness. Each footstep crunched the leaves and seemed to echo through the woods. Wild images flashed through Regina's mind — the flame from the explosion of the car the other night, the smoke as it curled around the red tiled roof, the howl of despair outside the hospital, the sound of muffled gunshots. But she continued forward, even as she fought down her fear. She would not be turned back, not after all she had seen already.

The man she followed had entered the woods a little further to the south, she figured, which would place him deeper in the woods by now. A car rattled by on the road behind her and Regina froze in place until the sound faded away. It wasn't the gray Porsche, so apparently Professor Blanton didn't plan to come. Hopefully no one would think to stop and investigate a parked car along such a remote road.

If the man hadn't lifted his arm when he did, Regina would have stepped on him. Leaves covered most of his body, apparently pulled over himself in the shallow depression. She saw clear signs of the fever in the man's eyes.

"Water," the man moaned. "Or kill me now."

Regina approached to squat on her heels. "Why are you here? Are you running away?"

The man grimaced. "I was, but now I wish I hadn't. Death

will find me anyway, and death by thirst is worse than I imagined."

"I have water in the car," Regina told him. "I can take you into town, or drop you off at the checkpoint up at the roadblock."

"Not to the police!" The man's eyes widened. "Don't you know about them?"

"No, I don't know," Regina said. "So why don't you tell me."

The man looked at her with wild eyes. "You may not want to know. Most people are like that, and it could get you in a lot of trouble."

"Please let me help you." Regina offered her hand. "I'm a pastor, and I can't just walk away and leave you here."

The man groaned, "Then it's worse than I thought. Just leave me, please."

"Perhaps if you told me what the problem is …."

"For your own safety, you must leave." He tried to lift his head.

Regina shook her head and pressed her lips together. "What if I can get you past the roadblocks to the parsonage? I just came through them; they shouldn't check me twice. They know who I am."

"I'm already as good as dead, Reverend. Why place your life in danger? You know there is no cure for this fever."

"Perhaps." Regina shrugged. "But I won't leave you to die out here like a dog. At least I can offer you a cot in the back room and make you comfortable."

The man attempted a laugh, the sound a raspy cough. "I guess life is hard to let go of even for a condemned man. So your offer tempts me. And I think I am in no condition to resist, but you are taking a great risk in helping me. Is there something in your Christian creed which compels you to this foolishness?"

"Something like that." Regina grasped his hand. "I am

compelled to help you because of my beliefs but also for my own reasons. I think you have information I need. So why are you out in the middle of the forest? Are you avoiding the law?"

"Because they have killed us all," he said, "and that's no lie. But I dare not tell you any more until we get through the checkpoints. That way if you are caught you can honestly say that you knew nothing."

"I plan to always tell the truth." Regina studied the man. How much had the fever affected his mind? Would this explain the radical actions she had witnessed the other night, and the man's own present condition?

"I'm not crazy." The man seemed to read her thoughts. "These things are the truth." He struggled to get to his feet.

"What's your name?" Regina held out her hand to steady him, but he drew back.

"It is best if you don't touch me … even if you have been vaccinated. And the name's Frank."

"I have been vaccinated, Frank," Regina assured him. "I should be safe."

Frank attempted a smile. "So was I, but I got the fever from the vaccine itself. I suppose a lot of people have figured that out by now. The government's out of money, I think, and who knows what's in the stuff."

"The government does the best it can," Regina told him.

"As you wish." Frank stumbled to his feet.

"Come." Regina offered to touch him again. "I have a water bottle in the car."

They took their time with Frank's slow walk. When they reached the car, Regina gave him her half empty water bottle. Frank drank in gulps while he clutched the side of the car with one hand to steady himself. Regina popped the trunk and motioned with her hand for him to climb in.

"Oh, no, Reverend." Frank shook his head. "I'll ride in the front. I have my vaccination card on me, and since I'll be inside the car now it might work."

"But you look sick."

"It's my chance to take. If they raise questions, you can say you picked me up along the road. Don't Reverends do such things?"

"I think you'd better get in the trunk. I already said they won't check me again."

Frank brushed himself off with his hands. "And if I'm found in there, then what? It will look like you're hiding me. You don't put people you've picked up in the trunk."

He climbed in the front seat and pulled the door shut after him. Once he was settled in the seat, he ran his fingers through his hair.

Regina sighed and climbed in. With difficulty she turned around on the narrow road and drove back the way she had come. She took deep breaths as she watched the river fog fade away in her rearview mirror. When she reached Route 45, no cars were coming from either direction. She pulled out and accelerated back towards town.

"Perhaps the checkpoint is gone," Regina offered.

"I wouldn't hold your breath." Frank glanced over at her. "You need to relax; you look too tense and worried."

"Who wouldn't be under these circumstances?"

"I would," Frank said, then added, "I'm very grateful for what you're doing."

"I hope you have things to say when we get through this," Regina told him.

"If we get safely through I will tell you everything I know."

The fear was evident in his eyes now. Ahead of them the familiar police cruisers and yellow sawhorses came into sight. Regina slowed the car and waited behind another vehicle while the police searched the trunk and the back seat before they gave the signal to proceed.

"Howdy, Reverend," the officer from earlier greeted her.

Regina tried to smile. She kept her gaze on the steering wheel and flipped open her wallet.

"You're clear on that. I saw it earlier." The officer dropped his head to look into the car. "Did you pick up a friend?"

"Yes. And I'm giving him a ride back into town."

"Let me see his card."

Frank lifted his card and attempted a grin.

"I've got to see that closer, and pop your trunk, Reverend."

Regina reached for Frank's card and passed it across. The officer glanced at it. "That's fine, but we still have to see the trunk."

Regina kept her eyes away from his face as she bent down to pull the trunk lock. It popped, and the lid rose moments later. The back car door on Frank's side was jerked open and a flashlight beam searched under his seat.

"Ready to go." The officer on Regina's side signaled her on. The one at the trunk nodded and waved. She took off.

"I told you so," Frank said when they were out of earshot.

"I guess you were right," Regina agreed. "So will you get going with your story now?"

"If you would be so kind … I'd like more water first."

"And a bed to rest in later perhaps?"

Frank shook his head. "A barn floor is good enough for a dead man like me."

"All of God's creatures are worth proper care."

Frank laughed. "God's creatures? How can you be one of God's creatures when they treat you worse than animals?"

Regina ignored his comment. She watched her speed as she drove through town and arrived at the parsonage without further mishap. After she parked behind the house, Regina let Frank open his own car door. He struggled to stand but refused help when Regina offered her hand. Inside the house, Regina seated him at the kitchen table and brought him a large glass of water.

"Ice?" Regina asked, the water-filled glass still in her hand.

"No thank you. Just water is good enough for me." He drank in great gulps.

"More?" Regina offered when the glass was empty.

Frank nodded.

Regina returned to the kitchen and refilled the glass. Frank set it on the table in front of him before he hung his head, his eyes weary.

"Your story," Regina told him. "Are you strong enough to start?"

Frank sighed. "I don't know if you'll believe me, but please for your own safety don't repeat this to any of the authorities. You will find out then that it is true ...."

"Just cut the drama, okay. I'll decide what to believe."

Frank shrugged. "What's going on is the government has emptied the prisons. Where the prisoners are I don't know, but they aren't in prison anymore. How many other prisons are doing the same thing, I don't know. But the grounds are now being used to house the sick who have the virus."

"That makes some sense," Regina agreed. "The government must be driven to extremes with the epidemic because the hospitals are all full also. So this is where the rumors are coming from, no doubt magnified in people's minds."

Frank leaned forward. "These converted prisons aren't hospitals, they are killing centers. There's no way they can take care of all the people who are sick. No one knows of a cure, and no one is expecting to find one. They offered us a drink ... voluntary of course, but it wasn't. Our choice was lying in the open prison yard under the elements, or going out easily. No one said anything, but no one lasted for more than a few hours. They made their choices soon enough."

"And so how did you get out, if this is true?"

"I pretended everything — taking the drink, dying, being loaded onto the truck with the real dead bodies. Didn't I look like a good pretender at the checkpoint?"

"I don't know; you might also be a good liar."

"I've come from hell, Reverend, from hell on earth. I wouldn't lie about that. And I'm still dying anyway. But isn't it better out here under the silent heavens than with the whimpers of torment in my ears?"

Regina stood to pace the floor. "There's no way such a thing could be happening."

"Perhaps not, but it's still true." A little blood oozed from his eye and Frank rubbed it. He looked at his finger. "I'm sorry. I'd best leave soon, especially now since I told you."

Regina pushed the Kleenex box on the counter towards him. "Throw the used ones in the waste basket."

Frank complied, as Regina studied him. "So are you sure your mind isn't affected? A few nights ago I saw a woman drive her car into the church up on High Street. She ended up killing herself and her child. The same evening I saw a man purposefully kill himself and his girl at the hospital."

"I am not here to convince you," Frank said. "You are the one who asked and now I have told you."

"But such things just don't happen in this country," Regina protested.

"I know," Frank said. "Look, I'll leave for your own sake. If you could give me a sandwich or two, I'll take them with me."

"But ...." Regina stopped as her phone began to ring on the desk.

"Get it," Frank said. "I'll wait that long."

"Hello," Regina said into the mouthpiece.

"Reverend." The voice sounded familiar. "Professor Blanton here. I hope I didn't alarm you today, but listen carefully."

Regina hesitated. "I'm listening."

"I suggest you get that man out of your house quickly. Force him to go, and if he doesn't, tell the police he entered by force."

"They've already seen me at the roadblock with him," she replied, "and I couldn't do it anyway; he needs help."

"Suit yourself, but I've warned you. I didn't intend for you to bring him home. You know they knew he was sick at the roadblocks. Right now they don't care, but tomorrow they might."

"So then what was today all about?" she asked, but the line had already disconnected.

What was Professor Blanton up to, she asked herself again. She now had more questions and fewer answers.

"I'll go now," Frank told her. "It sounds as if someone has seen me already. And I've gotten you in way too deep, Reverend."

Regina threw her hands in the air. "But why? I don't understand any of this, but you're not going. If you must die, then at least die in some sort of comfort upstairs on the floor. It's the least I can do for another human being."

"You're serious, aren't you?" Frank stared at her.

"Of course. This is what God commands us to do — to help those in need."

"God bless you!" He attempted a laugh.

"God commands us to be his hands and feet," she told him. "So upstairs with you, and let me deal with the consequences." If Travis came tonight this might help him explain what all went on in the world around them. Travis knew. That much she was certain of.

His gaze wavered between her and the door; he looked ready to bolt. Instead he shook his head and followed her hand motion up the stairs. She stayed behind him and laid out an old sleeping bag on the bedroom floor. He settled in with a sigh and dozed off even while she stood there.

Regina went back downstairs and looked out the window at the traffic in the street. Who was Professor Blanton — if that was his real name? What were the answers to her questions? And what did Professor Blanton wish her to discover? That might be the question she should ask.

Chapter Twelve

Enos stood on the front step of Rosemary's house as the darkness fell around him. Inside, the gas lantern hung in the living room window. It cast its soft glow out across the lawn. Rosemary was now buried in the graveyard along with her parents. Today two of his sisters had been added to the ground at the farm. Father still wouldn't budge from his ways, even when Enos had begged for understanding. His brothers had looked at him with hope in their eyes, but he had let them down, just as he had let Rosemary and her parents down.

"Bishop Mast has nothing against taking the medicine," he had repeated as they walked back towards the house with his father by his side. Already the man showed signs of the fever, his eyes glazed.

"I will join my wife on the other side with my soul pure from the world," his father had replied.

To beg was useless, Enos knew, but still he had begged. He had pushed back the black mass of hatred in his soul long enough to get the words out. He had kept them free of bitterness. His father hadn't seemed to notice, but now the hatred ran over him again. The blackness squashed any other emotion he had and left him cold and dry on the inside.

Tonight, he was here on her farm, even though Rosemary and her parents were gone. None of Rosemary's family had been by to tell him he couldn't be here. Likely they had enough things to worry about without the care of another farm on their minds. When life resumed again he would be gone from this place, probably eaten up by this hatred or dead from it, he figured. But he didn't care anymore — either way, Rosemary would never come back.

He ought to harness the horse to the buggy, but instead he headed across the fields at a fast walk. It felt good to walk; he felt the strength of his legs as they navigated the rough ground of the corn field.

Here the two *English* men must have crossed the night they came to Rosemary's house. Here the one must have crossed again, after he had left behind the three lives torn and soaked in blood. When Enos asked, the officers had taken him to see the man with his head half blown off. He had needed to see it, but it hadn't helped. The sight hadn't taken away the hatred.

The officers said one of the *English* neighbors had driven past and thought he saw strange shadows in the house. This was who had notified the police. Enos walked faster as the evening breeze blew across his face. Soon fall would arrive and he would need a warm coat, he thought. But that wouldn't matter either with Rosemary gone. He usually enjoyed winter and the work in the cold. Now the cold was inside his soul. He again quickened his pace.

He climbed the fences to walk across a hay field and pulled the barbed wire apart to slip through to the next field. The wire twanged in the darkness behind him. He should have brought his flashlight, but what did it matter? His eyes would adjust in time to the night sky, and soon the moon would be up.

Enos crossed the last field to approach the *English* people's place, the ones who lived like Amish but weren't Amish. Tonight he would learn their secrets and understand what they were really about. Perhaps they held the answer to how he could purge his hatred. Perhaps they could point the way to revenge, because he must avenge Rosemary's death.

There had to be more than the two men he had seen dead who had killed Rosemary. Many more. The officers who took him to see the dead man had lied about something. Rosemary could not have died because of only two men. She was too sweet, too close to the angels. It would have taken hundreds, thousands, to reach her, to break through the defenses *The Lord* put up around holy people. Rosemary had never spoken an unkind word in her life, never breathed an evil prayer against anyone. It would have taken Satan himself to kill her through many, many evil men.

A low light flickered in the window as he approached the house. Enos stepped up on the porch and knocked. The front door burst open and he was pulled roughly inside by strong arms. Steel barrels were stuck into his side and took away his breath, but Enos smiled. "I knew I had come to the right place. I need your help, please."

"It's an Amish boy," a man's voice said.

A flashlight shone in Enos's face.

"I want to avenge the death of my Rosemary," he said.

"Who is Rosemary?" the voice of one man asked.

"The Amish girl whose parents were killed along with her the other day," another man's voice answered from beside him.

There was silence for long moments while the flashlights still beamed into his face.

"Can I sit down?" he finally asked. "My name is Enos."

"Okay," one of the men said. "But don't try anything funny. And where is your buggy? We didn't hear anyone driving in."

"I walked in." He lifted his chin. "Is that a sin? Walking?"

They chuckled.

"Go get Clare," one of them finally said. "See if she has seen him before."

Before any of them could leave there were footsteps on the stairs and a door opened behind him. Enos didn't move, and the woman came in. The flashlight shone in his face again, but he refused to blink. Enos stared into the whiteness.

"It's the boy who came with the buggy the other day," she said. "I think he lives down the road a ways. He took the medicine I gave him."

"If it was the police they wouldn't be walking in or driving in with buggies," one of the men said, laughing. "They'd blow us out with tanks, Clare, if they knew we were here…."

"Right now it wouldn't take tanks," the other said. "So what does this young fellow want from us?"

"I want revenge," Enos said, before anyone else answered. "I want to kill them all."

"Kill them — who do you want to kill?"

"The ones who killed Rosemary." Enos's fingers tightened on the rim of his hat.

"But they are already dead," Clare replied with surprise in her voice.

"It took more than two to kill Rosemary," Enos answered her. "Rosemary would not have died because of only two men."

"But you are Amish." The question was still in her voice. "Amish don't kill."

"I know, but I want to — it's necessary," Enos said.

The two men laughed. "That sounds like a good enough reason for killing to me," one said.

"But your faith?" Clare obviously was not convinced. "I know how strong it is. You can't be sure of yourself. Tomorrow you may repent and change your mind. Why should we help you?"

"I know my own mind," Enos said. "I know this is a great sin, but I cannot help it, and I will not change my mind."

"Sounds serious to me," one of the men said. "And we could use him, you know. It might help to have a real Amish person on our side. Now wouldn't that be something?"

"I don't know." Clare fell silent.

The flashlight had been out of his eyes for some time. Their faces formed in the low light of the kerosene lamp. Clare had on her white *kapp*, he saw, and they had beards on their faces, but their fingers were wrapped around guns. Real guns, he thought, not like the rusting shotgun his father kept in the basement to hunt with. Enos searched for an *English* way to tell them what lay on his heart. How would they describe what he felt, what he wished to do?

Phrases and sounds from his school days rolled around in his head, things he had learned under the tutelage of the *Old Maid,* Susie. They had used *English* textbooks in school and read *English* ways to say things. Slowly he remembered a picture, a firm look on a man's face as he stood in his small ship pushed across an ice-filled river with oars that stuck out the side. Beyond lay the snowy bank of the river, where men gestured and waved the man on. What had Susie said? How had she explained this thing the *English* were doing?

"Yes." Enos stood to his feet. "I know what it is now. I plan to commit *treason — the* great sin."

Enos held his breath as he looked at their shocked faces. What had he said wrong? Because it explained exactly what he felt inside about his faith. If he killed, things would never be the same again.

"You are accusing us of *treason*?" Clare asked.

"No," he shook his head. "It is I who am committing *treason*. There is no higher sin in our faith than killing."

"I see." Clare stood still for a moment. "But are you sure you can do this?"

"Yes." Enos sat down again. "It must be done."

The two men raised their eyebrows to Clare, and she nodded. "I think we may have a true convert here."

They smiled at him then as one by one they extended their hands. Enos smiled and shook them in return.

"Well, I guess he's joining the rebellion." One of them laughed again. "Welcome to the revolution, son."

"Don't tell him more than he wants to know." Clare patted his arm. "This is hard enough for him."

"So when can I kill those who are responsible?" Enos asked. "I want to start tonight."

They smiled again and motioned him to a seat at the

kitchen table. They brought over the kerosene lamp, and Clare sat down beside him. "So tell me your situation. You live with your parents, correct?"

"Not anymore." Enos clasped his hands. "Not since Rosemary was killed. I'm keeping up her parents' place. Until life starts again and her extended family wants the farm."

"Normal life isn't starting anytime soon," one of the men said.

"So you have the place all to yourself?" Clare asked.

"Yes," he nodded.

"And the rest of your family?" Her gaze was intense.

"Father has the virus and we buried two of my sisters today. The others won't last long."

"Have they come here to receive the medicine?" she asked in surprise.

"No. Father won't allow it and I can't bring my brothers here while he's living."

"What if we gave you enough for your family — to take home with you? Would you agree to do something for us?"

"Like what? I don't need a reward to kill. I only need a gun and to know where the people live who are responsible for my Rosemary. I think you know that — if you will tell me."

One of the men laughed behind him. "I wish we had such faith in ourselves."

Clare silenced him with a look. "See, Enos, this is not only about killing. It's also about keeping innocent people alive. That is what we are most concerned about. Do you think you could do that? Allow us to use your place to give out the medicine? Later, perhaps, we will have to fight, but not now."

"You want me to wait?" he asked.

"It's really the only way, Enos," she told him. "But we can teach you how to handle a weapon. Is that good enough for now? We really need your help."

"How would I do that? I already know about the things in your basement. But you are welcome to use Rosemary's place.

However, there will be trouble if my people find out, but it will not be worse than hating and killing."

"A real *Hardy Boy,*" one of the men said. "He knows about the things in the basement."

"Just ignore Moe and Joe here." Clare smiled. "Do you think you can do that?"

"What about fighting?" Enos asked. Their amusement made no sense at all, but at least they had not turned him away.

"Joe will teach you how to use a gun, and if you're any good at it, you might get your chance before long. There are many, many of them, remember."

"That's what I thought." Enos got to his feet. "I need to get back, and it's a long walk across the fields."

"Not so fast there, *Rambo,*" Clare said. "Give me a minute so I can pack my bags. Joe can drop us off at the end of your driveway, and then I'll be in business."

"You're coming tonight?" Enos looked at her face.

She looked serious enough, but this all happened so fast. He had never lived in a house with girls other than his sisters. Not even with Rosemary.

"A deal's a deal," Clare said. "Come on now, I don't bite. And I'll have the medicine for your siblings tomorrow."

"Are you sure about this?" one of the men asked.

She looked at his face for a moment, then disappeared up the stairs when the man finally nodded his agreement. Moments later Enos sat in the car's back seat as he waited for Clare to come out. She reappeared and threw her suitcase in the trunk, then climbed in beside the driver.

Joe started the car, pulled out the driveway, and headed down the road. He dropped them off at the house and waited long enough for Clare to retrieve her suitcase from the trunk. Enos stood beside her in the light of the red taillights and reached for the handle of the suitcase. He applied steady pressure when Clare resisted until she released her hold.

"Come," Enos beckoned. He led the way towards Rosemary's house. Clare followed behind him and her feet whispered in the grass.

Inside the gas lantern still burned. He showed her the upstairs bedrooms. "You can have whichever one you want."

She didn't choose Rosemary's, because she was a *good* woman, he thought. Somehow she must have known.

"Good night," Clare called after him. She smiled in the dim light of the kerosene lamp.

"Good night," he said. "I'll be downstairs if you need anything."

He settled himself on the couch in his usual place and faced the bedroom door where Rosemary had died and gone home with the angels. Eventually he fell asleep.

Chapter Thirteen

Regina tiptoed up the stairs of the parsonage in the glow of the early morning light. Travis hadn't shown up last night or this morning, and in a way she was glad. It might be best if they approached these questions between them without another man in the house. And a sick man at that. Outside the sky over the town was streaked in deep reds and oranges. The weather man had predicted more than three inches of rain by late evening. There was a chance the storm might track to the north over the mountains of West Virginia, but it would hold off its heaviest rains until the following day, they said.

Regina pushed open the bedroom door and studied the gasping form who lay on the sleeping bag. The now familiar sores had broken out on Frank's arms and face. Clearly he would not last long. She wondered what she could do with the body. To carry a dead weight downstairs by herself was out of the question, and neither could she call Travis. That would only precipitate what she had been thankful to avoid earlier.

"Water," Frank whispered, as he rolled over on the sleeping bag. She retreated to the bathroom and returned with the glass filled to the brim. He drank greedily.

"Is there anything else I can get for you?" She touched his arm. He flinched and drew back to shake his head. She went downstairs and stared out towards the street to watch the morning traffic move past. Everything looked normal, but she knew life was not back to normal. She had the evidence upstairs if she needed any.

The ring of the parsonage phone made her jump, and she

raced to answer. Someday she would give in and buy a cell phone, but that day hadn't arrived yet. Call it her old fashioned quirk, a rejection of modern life, or just plain stubbornness, but cell phones were not a part of her life.

"Good morning, Reverend," Professor's Blanton's voice said. "Do you still have that man in your house?"

"It's really none of your business," she snapped, but didn't hang up on him — though she should have, she thought. She had expected Travis to call, not this pesky stranger from the college.

"I'm going to share a secret with you," the Professor continued. "Not that I should, but you're a nice person."

"I don't want to hear more secrets," Regina protested.

"Really?" he countered. "Even if it can save the life of your friend upstairs? Would that not be in the will of God?"

"Are you also the religious professor now, Mr. Blanton?"

He laughed. "Let's say I grew up in church. Is that good enough?"

"No, it's not."

"I guess I could attend one of your sermons," he said. "Would that be helpful?"

Regina sighed into the phone. "So what do you want, Mr. Blanton? I'm getting tired of games. There are people dying, and no one is doing much about it."

"That's exactly the point I was coming to." He cleared his throat. "I'm giving you the chance to do something about that problem."

Regina sighed again. "Mr. Blanton, just how do you know so much about these things? How did you know Frank was in the woods yesterday?"

"Well...." He paused. "I didn't know you'd bring him home, so obviously I don't know everything. You are full of surprises — good ones I must say. But we will leave that for now. Would you like to know where to take your friend so he can get the help he needs?"

She laughed now. "You're not God."

"No, I'm not," he allowed. "But I do know where this can happen. I trust you know enough not to share the information, since I see you haven't called any of your church people yet."

"How would you know that?" Regina demanded. "And that could be for different reasons than you think."

"I think I've judged you correctly." He obviously avoided her question. "So here it is. Take your man — if he's still alive — out to Puckett. Have you got a pen? I'll give you directions. They'll know what you need when you arrive. Take him with you and leave him there. You don't want him dying at your place."

"I don't know if I trust you." She held the phone tight against her ear. How did the professor seem to know so many things?

"You may not trust me, but I know you want to help poor Frank. Trust me on that."

"Just a minute." She made up her mind and scrounged around for a pencil and paper. She copied the address as he dictated it and hung up when he was done.

She had meant to ask him about the roadblocks, but it was too late now. Maybe he was a miracle worker, an angel in disguise who could blind the eyes of prison guards. Regina laughed at her thoughts. The craziness of the world must have driven her crazy. Still, to drive a man to Puckett for medicine that might not exist, all on the word of a college professor she hardly knew, was a big risk. But why not? The world was crazy already. She might as well join. And perhaps Travis would give her answers if she did enough crazy things. Regina climbed the stairs two at a time. Breakfast would have to wait. She went into the bedroom and knelt by Frank's side.

"Frank, we have to go," she told him.

"I'm staying here," he said. "I'm dying anyway. Can't I die here like you said?"

"There's a place I can take you for help," she told him. She hoped her voice sounded convinced.

He rolled over and looked up at her. "I'll die here, okay."

She jerked on his arm again. "Frank, you must come with me." He cried out in pain, but she pulled again.

"Okay, okay," he muttered. Slowly he rose to his feet.

She helped him down the stairs. Once in the car, he stared after her when she ran back inside but didn't move. She retrieved two water bottles from the refrigerator and a small bag of bagels before she rejoined him to drive west out of town.

At the roadblocks the immunization cards were enough to satisfy the officers, even with their curious glances at Frank's obviously diseased face. Apparently the professor was correct and the officers now left you alone if you met their basic requirements of a vaccination shot.

"Why are they allowing me through?" Frank asked, as she accelerated towards Puckett.

"I don't know," she told him. "Maybe they don't have orders to arrest sick people."

"They don't know where I've been," he said.

"Are you sure you were telling me the whole truth yesterday?" she asked him.

He sighed and leaned his head back against the seat. He closed his eyes and didn't answer.

Regina found the correct exit off the four-lane, where she passed Amish farms as she drove south. So the professor had sent her into Amish country. It would be interesting to know how these people had survived the meltdown of the nation. Had their religious separation benefited them?

She slowed down to pass a buggy. The horse's head hung low. His ribs showed. He was either a naturally skinny horse, she thought, or the Amish also suffered from the hard times.

The next road west was the one she wanted. She made the turn and pulled into the driveway a few minutes later. Not only had the professor sent her to Amish country, he had sent her to an Amish home. Well, perhaps they were the only people left who engaged in good works. But how had they managed to find a miracle cure?

"I'll be right back," she told Frank. She walked up to the front door and knocked. The Amish woman who answered had a smile on her face. "Hi. Can I help you?"

"Professor Blanton from the college told me to come here," Regina told her. "I have a sick man with me."

"Sure." The woman never batted an eye. "Bring him in and we'll take care of him."

Just like that? Regina wanted to say, but kept her mouth shut. Help was help and not to be looked down on. Frank didn't protest when she opened the car door, but he brought one of the water bottles with him. The Amish lady helped him into the house, and she made no effort to keep Regina out. Once he was settled on the couch, Regina looked around. She had never been inside an Amish home before. There were no electrical plugs on the walls, no lights hung from the ceiling, and there were no sounds of a TV — the Amish indeed were different.

"Okay, we'll take care of him from here." The lady still smiled. "When he's better we'll drop him off in town, or wherever he wishes to go."

Regina retreated while Frank gave her a weak smile. Well, if he was comfortable with these people then she should be. There was little hope for recovery on his own. A quiet Amish home was as good a place to die as her parsonage. Regina closed the door behind her and walked across the lawn to find an Amish man by her car. He looked about her age, she figured. No doubt he was the husband of the woman inside. But why was he in front of her car?

The man's eyes looked troubled and had black circles underneath them as if he had witnessed horrors too awful to imagine. But then so had she, Regina told herself.

"I'm sorry if I frightened you," he said when she

approached. "My name is Enos. I see you have a Bible on the seat."

"Yes. I am a minister in Farmstead, at the AME church."

He studied her for a moment, as if processing this information. She wondered if the Amish had ever seen a woman pastor before, not to mention a black one at that.

Finally the Amish man pushed his hat back on his head and rubbed his cheek. "Are you a Christian?"

Regina laughed. "Of course I am. Perhaps I'm too liberal for you, and do things you wouldn't, but nevertheless Christian." He said nothing, and she rushed on. "Does that bother you? Will it affect the care your wife gives Frank? Because if it does, I'll go back inside and get him." The nerve of the man, she thought. He had more gall than she would have imagined possible. Or was he so backwards, stuck in some kind of time warp.

He glanced down and moved out of the way of her car door. "I'm sorry for the question, ma'am. I did not mean to anger you. I do not know what such things mean, but the woman inside is not my wife. Still, she will take care of the man you brought, as she also gives our people the help they need."

Surprise registered on Regina's face. "Who is she then? She looks like you."

"She is my sister." His face was pained. He stroked his face for a long moment before adding, "That's not really true, but we will call her my sister for now."

His words made no sense at all. Either the man was touched in the head or sick with the fever, though he didn't appear sick.

"I'm sorry to have bothered you," he continued. "I should speak to you about my soul. It is very dark inside of me and I cannot speak to my own people."

Regina studied his face. Should she speak with him? The question troubled her. Yet a talk with the man could do no harm, though he looked as if he needed more help than she could give him. What terrible things had he seen to cause such pain on his face? But he appeared harmless enough. There was no wild gleam in his eyes.

He turned to go toward the barn when she lifted her hand. "I have a few minutes. What is it you want to talk about?"

He faced her. "Your church believes in killing, doesn't it?"

She stared at him. Was the man mad after all? Somehow she found the strength to answer. "We do not."

His face fell. "You do not go to war?"

"Oh, that. Of course. My father was a veteran, but that is not wrong."

His face was puzzled. "But the men are dead, aren't they? The ones they shoot at?"

Regina managed a smile. "I'm sure Dad hoped they were, but killing in defense of your country is not murder."

"Oh," he said. "Is your father with the angels?"

Now she looked puzzled. "My father is still alive in Georgia. That is, he was last month — if this craziness hasn't wiped out the whole family since I spoke with him last."

He nodded. "Then he will be with the angels when his time comes to cross over."

"Of course!" She sounded indignant. "My father is a good Christian."

"Then there will be souls in heaven who have killed men? My people say we cannot go there if we kill."

"I wouldn't wish to argue with your ministers," she said. "But I would disagree."

His face darkened even more. "But you are not one of our people. *The Lord* may judge you differently."

Regina shrugged. "I doubt that. God seems to be of the same mind with all His people."

The words didn't appear to soak in.

"My soul will be damned," he muttered, "and yet I must do this."

"Are you planning to kill someone?" She stared at him. How in the world was an Amish man going to kill anyone? With his bare hands? He looked strong enough, she thought.

"I will when I find them and those people will help me." He pointed towards the house. "But I should not bother you anymore. You have given me some comfort, but I still am who I am."

"You really shouldn't kill anyone," she told him. "That's what the law is for. You could turn this person in and they would take care of him."

"I don't know," he shrugged. "I only know what my heart tells me. So you really are a minister? You look young for a minister." He contemplated her, as if he'd forgotten his own agony.

"Yes, I am." She pulled herself up straight. There was no reason to be self conscious, even in the face of disapproval from these strange people.

"Do you talk with God?" He squinted at her.

"I'm afraid I do. Do you have objections?"

"No." He shook his head.

"I'd better go." She crept closer to her car.

He watched her as she climbed into the car and put it in gear. He still watched when she pulled out of the drive. She waved, and he waved back. A smile seemed to form on his face, she thought. At least she had enlivened his apparently dark day, even if she had given no other help. That was worth something, wasn't it?

Chapter Fourteen

Enos sat at the supper table and watched Clare where she sat across from him. She certainly knew how to cook, but the food wasn't quite Amish. Something was different, he thought.

"You don't have to stare at me," she smiled. "I'm just like any of your women, especially in this dress."

"I know." Enos felt the red creep up his neck. This was a very strange situation to be in even though Frank lived with them in the house. That did help some — a lot in fact. In the old days, the bishop would have been over to speak about this. But those were the days before Rosemary died.

"What are you thinking?" She looked at him. "The least you can do is tell me since we do have to live in the same house."

"I was thinking about Rosemary." He ducked his head. "And about how different things are now."

"You can say that again." Her voice was sympathetic. "I expect I'd miss my boyfriend if he were taken suddenly from me—that is, if I had one."

Enos didn't answer as the silence settled over them. She ate with her gaze on the kitchen wall.

"Do I get to take the medicine over to my family tonight?" he finally asked. "As I was promised?"

"Sure." She got up from the table. "How much do you think you'll need?"

He ran the question in his mind and came up with a guess. "Five. Three brothers, my father, and one sister. That is if they are still all alive."

"I thought you said your father wouldn't take the stuff."

"I did, but I still have to try."

"Will you bring it back if your father turns you down?"

He nodded.

"It's good of Joe to trust you like this, you know that?"

He nodded again.

"We don't have a lot of the medicine, okay? We have to use it sparingly. Things are getting worse each day."

"Where is the medicine from?" He looked up to meet her gaze.

"You're curious, aren't you?"

He shrugged.

"I guess it doesn't matter if I tell you. Well, sort of tell you. If we get in trouble, you know that includes you now, don't you?"

He looked away.

"It's like this, Enos," she told him. "Some of the government's vaccine is good, but much of it is not. You wouldn't know that since your people haven't been taking the government vaccine. Anyway, we have our own lab in the south, a private firm that manufactures the vaccine for our organization."

"Are there more of you?" he asked.

She laughed. "Of course, many more."

"Are they all in Amish communities like ours? Because that is what you're doing, hiding among us."

"You shouldn't become too curious," she told him. "It's not good for people, but we are not that stupid. This is just one way of hiding, and a good one at that, you have to admit. We almost fooled you."

He managed a smile. "Perhaps, but not quite. You can't speak the language."

"That is true, but we don't have to since we're not trying to convince the Amish. And we've purchased the community's goodwill with the medicine, so your people won't be telling anyone."

"Then Father was partly correct." He stood to his feet. "Thank you for supper, but I must be on my way."

"Here you are." She gave him the medicine in a brown paper bag. "And remember to bring back what you don't use."

"Yes," he said, then walked out in the gathering darkness. In the barn he harnessed the horse and hitched him to the buggy. He drove toward his old home place and wept as he held on to the lines with one hand. His soul was damned, he figured; there was no way around that fact. The English people were up to something evil. So how could he take home medicine from their hand now that he knew? Would it bring darkness into the souls of his brothers and sisters?

Enos looked up at the starry skies and imagined he saw the picture of Bishop Mast's face form in the clouds. He even saw the bishop's eyes and heard his firm voice. "I've taken the medicine and encouraged my people to do the same."

Were all their souls filled with darkness? Enos asked himself. No, this was not possible at all.

The darkness must not be in their souls, because they did not know what was in the English house — what now was in Rosemary's house. So his family must not know, and the blame would fall upon himself. The vision of Bishop Mast's face faded from the skies, and Enos dried his tears. If he must suffer, then he must suffer. The life of his family was worth the cost.

The woman pastor from this morning would likely say this was all foolishness, but how would she know? She came from another world, from the *English* world where many wrong things were considered right. She had soft eyes and long arms that came out of her short dress sleeves. How could she be a minister? Enos looked up at the stars and shook his head. The *English* world was very strange.

What would it be like for a man to love such a woman? Love her as he had loved Rosemary? Of course such a person would be a man of her own race, born among her own people, raised to be like her. It could not be any other way. They would be like he and Rosemary had been, in love. It was strange, but it had to be true.

Enos slapped the reins and urged his horse on. He wanted to get this over with, to face his father and win this time. How he would do this was still to be seen, but somehow he would win. Some argument would have to be found, some reason to overcome the man's stubborn mind. His father was like a high boarded fence in the barnyard, over which the strongest Belgian could not climb. But there were cracks between the boards, places a mouse might slip through.

He would be a mouse tonight, he decided. There would be no hard words spoken. He would not bang against the fence, for that would never work. His soul was black now, dipped in hatred. He no longer needed to fear the lowly crawl of the mouse. The crack would appear tonight, and he would crawl through. There was no other way the deed could be done.

"Whoa." He pulled back on the lines. The driveway into his father's place was lit only with starlight, the barn dark already. His brothers must have completed the chores early, or they were already dead.

His heart hurt in his chest. Was he too late? He climbed down from the buggy and tied the horse. He took the bag with him on a fast run toward the house.

A single kerosene lamp burned on the kitchen table when Enos burst into the house without a knock. His sister Edith sat at the table and wept, with no one else in sight.

"Are they dead?" he whispered.

Edith looked at him with hollow eyes. "Father is very bad tonight. And Paul died this morning. James and Andy couldn't dig the grave. They couldn't do the chores. They are both upstairs sleeping. I'm the only one able to take care of them."

He stroked her hand and took her in his arms as she wept. Her thin shoulders shook. Then he pushed her away from him to break open one of the bottles of medicine. "Here, take this."

Her eyes became large and her face flashed fear. "But Father said we were not to."

"Father isn't in his right mind at the moment," he said. "And I am the oldest."

Edith nodded. She stared at the capsules but swallowed obediently when he brought a glass of water.

"Where is Father?" he asked.

"In the bedroom. He's out of his head. All he wants is water."

He smiled, and she looked at him as if he were mad. "Where have you been, Enos? You don't smile while your father is dying."

"I was only smiling at the thought of being a mouse," he said. "A lowly little mouse. Is there anything wrong with that?"

Her eyes were wild as she watched his face. She thought he surely had gone mad.

"Come." He motioned with his hand. "Give your father a drink again."

Edith followed him into the bedroom, where she stood beside him as he studied his father's face. He held out the glass of water for his father to drink. Before the first swallow went down Enos slipped the capsule into his father's mouth, and it disappeared without complaint.

His father's eyes searched the room but saw nothing as he moaned under his breath. It may be too late, Enos thought, but he had tried. His soul was black, and this deed would not be held to his father's account even if he saw the angels tonight.

"I'm going upstairs," he whispered, and his father's eyes jerked open.

"Enos?" his father called out.

Quickly Enos ducked out of sight in the hall, and Edith stroked her father's fevered forehead.

"It's okay," Edith told him. "You'll be better soon."

The girl was smart for her age, he thought. She caught on

quickly. If his father lived she would never tell him, as they all would never tell. They trusted him even if his soul was dark.

He went up the stairway to his brothers' room. They made no complaints and asked no questions when he brought them water and the medicine.

"Sleep well," he told them. "I will bury Paul for you. You don't have to worry about him."

Relief flooded their faces, and he wept on the way down the stairs. Edith waited for him at the kitchen table. He took her in his arms again and pulled her tight against him. His tears joined hers.

"Everything should be okay by morning," he whispered in her ear. "I will bury Paul tonight. If father dies, send James or Andy down to tell me, and I will come help. I'm staying at Rosemary's place."

"Is it true then?" she asked. "That the English men killed all three of them? That they ripped out her insides and spread them around the bedroom floor? Father wouldn't let me come to the funeral. He said he wanted us all to stay home."

"They are dead." He pulled her tight against him again. "But the rest is not true. I think the angels came before Rosemary died, and they took her home."

She need not know what else had happened; her heart was too young for such horrors, her mind too pure to know what evil could do. But then Rosemary had been the same. He wept great sobs. His chest shook against his sister's white *kapp.*

"Will the angels come for me when my time arrives?" Edith looked up into his face.

"*Yes,*" he said. "They will come, because you are one of those God loves. But be quiet now, because I must go."

She followed him to the door and closed it behind him as he went down the porch. Why were some spared and others not? He wondered as he ran across the lawn. It was very strange how *The Lord* worked.

He found the shovels and the body on the spring wagon

beside the barn. They had not come any further than this — his two brothers who had struggled with their duty. Their bodies had refused to obey what the mind commanded.

Enos pulled the spring wagon towards the back field and dug until the hole was deep enough. The hours passed. His back ached. His lungs burned. After he lowered the body, he paused to look up at the stars again. Should he say the words of prayer? Was he worthy of such a thing? Bishop Mast could not come even if he wished to. There were too many other things that needed his attention. Yet was his brother not worthy of this respect?

Haltingly he began, "Our Father which art in the heavens, Holy be your name, your kingdom come, your will be done on this earth, even as it is done in the heavens ...."

He continued on, uncertain, but filled in the best he could. It was good enough, he told himself at the end. His brother had been honored. He bent over and filled in the grave with dirt.

Afterwards, Enos studied the stars again in the blackness of the heavens. There was a beauty there, a glory he had never noticed before. He had always seen the stars before. Now the darkness stood out and called his name. But this was as it should be, he thought. He had blackness in his soul, and he loved the darkness. Enos shook himself loose from his thoughts and threw on the last shovel of dirt.

Chapter Fifteen

Regina stood in the old church sanctuary. The sweep of the elevated speaker's platform rose above her. These hushed early morning hours, alone with her thoughts, were treasured moments when she could catch them. For a moment she hesitated, then entered her office to slip on her preaching robe and step back into the sanctuary. Travis still had not come around, and she needed to calm her soul this morning.

Regina allowed the awe to sweep over her. She tried to become lost in the moment, to forget the outside world, the sickness, the death, and Travis. Her heart ached even as the last few days seemed far away, almost as if they had never happened. Here, hidden away, the heavens seemed closer. God seemed more real, and the world and its troubles faded away.

She walked to the center of the platform and raised her hands into the air. Worship in the presence of God was a cure for whatever ills crept into one's soul. It did not need to wait until the pews were full. It was a matter of the heart. Slowly she moved her arms and swayed to the unheard music. She sang the made-up words of the moment.

Praise be to God, Immortal Praise. How great His love, from heaven came. How can mere mortals speak His name? Jesus, Jesus, who died, and lives the same. We praise and praise and praise the sweetness of your name.

As the last sound died away into the high ceiling, she sang the words again. She changed them as she went along. This lifted her spirit and refreshed her soul. Even if someone walked in, she would continue. Let that person join in or think what they wished.

Her hands were still lifted in the air when the dull percussions reached her through the thick church walls. Regina paused. She listened and lowered her hands. Had something exploded? And what were the sounds that continued in the street? They sounded like human cries, like a woman's voice, shrill and terror-filled. She rushed towards the front door. Was even this, the sacred sanctuary, to be invaded by blood and bullets? Was there not enough agony in the world already?

Regina pushed open the wooden front doors and glanced up and down the street. How appropriate it would be, she thought, in this moment when God felt so close, to leave the world in one's clergy robes and go straight into glory itself. She waited in the silence. She imagined awful things that tore into her body, but nothing happened. The percussions started again, rapid and steady, with no corresponding human sounds this time. Regina heard the distant roar of vehicles downtown and the long squeal of tires. She wanted to remain hidden behind the church doors because her heart pounded in her throat, but she had to see what had happened and if something could be done about it.

Across the street in the Bethesda Plaza under the tall apartments a man stepped outside. He looked at the church, then raised his hand to point towards the corner on High and Main.

"Terrorists," he shouted. The man clutched his throat as the words left his mouth. The glass doors behind him splintered into a thousand pieces, and blood gushed down the front of his shirt. Regina screamed as her courage disappeared into the blue sky. She ducked back inside the church doors as the man collapsed to the ground.

Regina stood behind the solid wooden doors and kept her breath steady. She prayed, "Please God, what is happening? Whatever it is, stop it." The spattering of gunshots continued outside. They seemed to come from the local government building on the corner of Main and High. Was it under attack, or was the Bethesda Plaza under attack? That was where the man had stood.

Regina ran across the floor of the sanctuary to the phone in the church office and dialed 911 but received only a busy signal. Others must have called in already. She left her robe on the floor and returned to the front door. There she pondered what to do next. With her heartbeat in her throat, she pushed the doors open again. A glance up and down the streets showed no approach of emergency vehicles. There was no sound of sirens either.

Energy and anger seemed to come out of nowhere and fill her. The wise action would be to wait here until the proper authorities arrived to deal with this, but she had waited long enough. The man across the street lay motionless, the puddle of blood around his head bright red even from this distance. Was she supposed to hide and wait inside her church doors while others died outside?

Regina ducked low and ran down the church steps and up the street. She saw the bodies on the front concrete steps of the federal building long before she arrived and threw herself down beside them. Two women lay face down, raw wounds ripped into their backs, arms sprawled towards the street. Long streams of splattered red ran down the steps.

Regina felt for a pulse and found none. She crawled upwards to the second and got the same result. Even without medical training, she knew they were dead. Towards the top of the steps a uniformed guard groaned, and Regina crawled towards him.

"Hold still," she told the man. A pool of blood lay below the man's punctured leg, the side of his face was torn away, and his breath bubbled out between white shattered teeth.

What was left of his mouth opened. The words came out in a shrill rasp of unintelligible sound.

"There's help on the way," Regina assured him. She finally heard the shrill scream of sirens from the south. The town police were on Main Street, and the sheriff's office two blocks away.

The wounded guard's hand tapped hers, and Regina met his gaze. Again the mouth opened and gurgled. A weak hand motioned towards his weapon. There was no mistaking the message. The silence of the street was heavy, almost as if the whole world had gone to sleep or waited for the next horrible thing to happen.

Weapons kill people, Regina thought as she lay on the concrete steps, and there had already been too many killed. Still, she took the revolver and felt the heavy weight of the steel as she put it in the guard's hand. Before her eyes Regina saw the front double glass doors of the government building move and swing open.

A man stepped out with a heavy black weapon clutched in his hand, the long bullet clip arched out underneath. He wore a black scarf wrapped over his hair, his face twisted with hate and rage. Regina held still where she lay. Neither did the guard move beside her. The man's gaze swept towards them. He searched the street, and Regina closed her eyes. She knew her body would be dead by the time the percussion of the shots reached her ears, and suddenly it mattered a whole lot whether she lived or died.

Regina opened her eyes. The man's head had turned to look down the street towards the scream of the sirens. Then the side of his face exploded. As the man fell his weapon fired into the street in a great blast of noise. The bullets traced a smattering path of stone and dust across the concrete steps. Beside her the guard fired again as the man crumpled to the ground.

Behind her a siren screamed to a halt and Regina saw officers in black scramble out, hiding behind their vehicles. The guard still held the revolver in his hand, his eyes glazed. She rolled over once to move herself farther away. Surely the officers wouldn't shoot a woman who lay in the street, even if she had just moved.

A bull horn blared from the police vehicles behind her, "Police officers. Freeze."

Regina raised her hands and wondered if she should crawl down the steps. Emergency vehicles poured in from the center of town to scream into Bethesda's parking lot. A large square police van, steel webs in its windows, skidded around the corner from Third Street. It stopped directly across the street from the government building.

The back doors swung open and black helmeted officers leaped out as Regina held up her hands. They took their time, their bodies strapped with multiple layers of clothing and equipment. They formed a line and carried transparent shields in front of them. Slowly they moved up the stairs. Most of them entered the building.

"All clear," the shout came minutes later. The ones on the steps moved into action. They ran back to the police van and returned with collapsible stretchers. These they lay on the ground beside the bodies.

"I'm not injured," Regina protested, but they only lifted their fingers to their lips. Quick hands transferred her on to the stretcher and straps came up over her body. They were tightened with a jerk, and she was airborne.

They shoved the stretcher into the back of an emergency vehicle and Regina could see the street begin to move, the back doors still open. Across the street, a hollered command came from the building, followed by a solid percussion greater than she had heard all morning.

The government building exploded before her eyes. Whole chunks of concrete lifted high into the air as giant clouds of billowing dust rose heavenward.

"Step on the gas," the attendant beside her shouted. "They just blew the federal building."

"Hang on," the driver shouted back. "I'm getting us out of here."

He accelerated, taking the corner at Main and Third with tires squealing.

"You'd better go back and see if you can help," Regina said. "I'm not hurt that badly."

"I'm afraid there's not much anyone can do to help with that explosion," the attendant said.

The emergency vehicle raced forward, and Regina watched the street signs whiz by through the side windows. It couldn't be that far to the next light and the driver didn't slow down. Perhaps the road had been cleared by the flashing lights and the scream of the siren.

"Slow down," the attendant hollered. He stared out the side window, his face frozen in fear. Moments later the squeal of tires again filled the air. Wrenched sideways, the emergency vehicle slid to a halt with a loud thump.

"What's going on?" the attendant asked. He pushed away the object that had fallen on Regina's head. She struggled under the straps and used her body weight to help him.

"Someone pulled in front of us," the driver yelled back. "But we've got everything under control now."

"Sorry about that," the attendant said. "Did you get hurt?"

"I wasn't," Regina said as they topped the hill above the hospital. "I don't know about now."

He looked at her with concern, then turned to open the back door as the driver pulled to a stop in front of the emergency doors. They wheeled her inside. She watched the doors recede behind her. These were the same doors the man with his child had tried to enter that horrible night not so long ago. Now she was being taken inside where he had been shut out.

"She suffered a slight blow to the head," the attendant's voice said to the doctor. He didn't say where, but it didn't really matter. She was alive, and many people back there at the attack site were not. Good people were dead.

She struggled to focus on the doctor's face but her head throbbed. Around her the room was filled with white curtains and cloth-draped carts. Regina struggled to rise, but a hand pushed her back down again.

"You'd better lay back and rest awhile. We don't want you to injure yourself any further."

"I want out of here," Regina told him. "I have things to do."

"Stubborn, aren't we?" the doctor said. "Well, there is someone here to see you, if you are up to it. What do you say?"

"I want to discharge myself," Regina told him.

"Later." The doctor disappeared through the drawn curtains.

Another face came into focus, his features unfamiliar. But then everything was unfamiliar of late.

"Looks like you had a rough time of it." The voice wasn't unpleasant. "I'm Agent Beatty with the FBI. Are you up for some questions? If not, I can come back later."

"I can talk," Regina said. "But then I want out of here."

"Sorry about the head," Agent Beatty said. "You can be thankful you weren't injured worse."

"Thanks for the concern. Were many people killed in the attack?"

He ignored her question.

"You're the pastor at AME?" he asked.

Regina nodded.

"So you went out to help the injured on the steps. That was a mighty courageous thing to do. I'm sure your members will be proud of your actions. I might even put you in for a medal or something."

"Don't bother." Regina shook her head, as stabs of pain ran down her neck. "I just want to get checked out of here."

"Were you with the guard when he shot the hostage taker?" Agent Beatty didn't smile any longer.

"I was there when the shots were fired," Regina said. "Why do you ask?"

"Was he still alive when you got to him?"

"Yes, he was." Regina tried hard to focus, but the man's face drifted away.

"You wouldn't have fired his revolver by any chance?"

"Me?" Regina forced her aching face into a smile. "No — I take care of men's souls."

"You wouldn't have to be embarrassed if you did," Agent Beatty said. "It might even bring an extra medal. The story of a local hero who saves the day. I can see it now all over the front page."

"That would be nice," Regina said. "But it looks like I wouldn't have saved much anyway. Wasn't the building blown up?"

"Yes, it was, and a sad ending to the story," Mr. Beatty smiled. "Well … you have a good day. And I hope you get better soon. Good to see a Reverend on the job in the face of danger. Thank you — from all of us."

"You're welcome." Regina winced.

The doctor's face appeared a moment later. "You're not leaving just yet, young lady. That's for sure. Not with your head banged up like that."

"That's not fair," Regina protested. "You tricked me into talking."

The doctor smiled. "No," he said. "I just need to take some x-rays and keep you overnight for observation."

Chapter Sixteen

As the evening light streamed in through the window, the form of Travis Jones appeared in the hospital room doorway. Regina squinted her eyes.

Why had Travis shown up? Just when she was dressed and ready to leave. He'd ignored her for how many days now? And it had been at least a whole day since the explosion downtown, if not longer. And things were still dizzy in her head.

"I see the Reverend's got herself quite a thing going on here." Travis waved a copy of a newspaper under Regina's nose.

"Just leave me alone." Regina swung her legs out over the edge of the bed. "I was just at the point of getting out of this place."

Travis grabbed her hand, a fake smile on his face. "Let me be the first to congratulate you — our local town hero. You do the church proud, if I must say so myself."

"Why are you here?" Regina asked him. "Where have you been?"

Travis grinned and ignored her question. "The doctor said you were discharged this afternoon. So let me join you on your ecclesiastical rounds this evening, and we can get in double duty. I want to see the smiles on our members' faces."

"I don't want any attention at the moment," she told him.

"Hah," Travis snorted, unfolding the paper with a flourish. "I'd call aiding the injured under hostile fire worthy of praise. I think that should do just fine for a story. The local paper has a feature and it's on the front page of the Richmond Daily. Right here before my very eyes. Listen to this."

He read in a loud voice: "The pastor of the AME Church in Farmstead found herself in an unusual situation yesterday. A vicious attack was made against the local government building next door to the AME church. The Reverend Regina Owens was in the church at the time and did not hesitate to offer aid. She exposed herself to considerable danger while the attack was in progress — all in the hopes that help could be offered to the wounded outside. An officer who did not survive because of his extensive wounds shot one of the attackers on the front steps of the building after being aided by the Reverend.

"We spoke with ATF spokesperson Arthur Mullins on site in Farmstead. It is the initial belief of investigators that a white supremacy group was involved in the attack. The alleged group shot up the place and then blew up the building with a bomb. None of the attackers survived. Authorities believe the bomb to have been a homemade IED of yet unknown composition. Mr. Mullins said that initial investigation points to possible similarities between these attacks and others in the past from other militia groups. Further testing is ongoing in the matter. No arrests have been made, but are expected soon."

"There you go." Travis tossed Regina the paper. "I see you're dressed so let's get going."

"How do they know it was a white supremacy group?" Regina groaned as she stood to her feet. Travis was already at the doorway.

"How would I know?" Travis glanced over his shoulder. "I'm not with the FBI, but it's in the paper. Do you need more reason than that?"

Regina walked faster to keep up, "Slow down, man. I got my head whacked yesterday. How come the newspaper missed that?"

"Just be thankful for what you got," Travis grinned. "We can make quite an honor out of this."

"They should have talked with me," Regina protested. "I would have told them some things."

"That's why they didn't talk with you," Travis said. "That's why they talked with me. And I know what to do when someone wants to thank me."

Regina clutched the newspaper and kept up with Travis's long stride.

"We only have one person from the church in today." Travis pointed down the hall. "Probably the fever. Old Ronnie Lewis, stuck back in his cabin in the woods. I guess he doesn't understand what taking the vaccination means."

"Is Mrs. Hendricks out already?" Regina tried to think but her head hurt too much.

"They released her this morning," Travis said. "Her hip's still a little sore, but they needed the room. People have to make the sacrifices they can."

"So I'll check on her at home."

"The elevator." Travis pointed. "They've got the entire two floors above us for the fever patients, and they might have to expand again if this thing doesn't slow up. Perhaps you'd better spend your time in prayer instead of trying heroics." He laughed.

Regina bit her tongue and held back her questions. The elevator doors opened and they stepped inside. On the ride up, Travis kept his eyes on the indicator light and offered no comments. Regina followed him as he stepped out, her nostrils instantly assailed by the rank smell. Medical personnel walked by, all with white masks over their faces. Travis made a beeline for the girl behind the desk, and she handed him two masks without a word.

"You can't be too careful." Travis pulled on his mask.

Regina followed his example.

"What room is Mr. Lewis in?" Travis asked the girl.

She typed rapidly on her computer and said, "402." Her eyes were cold, and Regina shivered as she followed Travis down the aisle. She had lots of questions for Travis, but clearly here was no place to ask them. Her eyes glanced into the rooms as they passed. She stood back so Travis could go into 402 first.

"Well how are you?" Travis boomed. "Brother Ronnie Lewis done himself in, I see."

Regina smiled at the little man in the bed. He looked sick, his eyes watery with fever, his breath heavy, but he did nod his head. Tubes hung all over him. A nurse rushed in and punched keys on the control board. Moments later she was gone again.

"They've got me *souped* up good." Ronnie tried to chuckle.

"Feeling any better?" Regina touched his hand.

"Not much." Ronnie met her eyes. "I wish I'd taken the vaccine now. Just stayed home, even from church. Didn't want to run those roadblocks. I figured the bug couldn't find me there, I guess."

"Weren't you in church lately?" Regina asked, her mind foggy.

"Not really," Ronnie shook his head. "It might have been my brother. People say we look a lot alike."

"That you do." Regina forced a smile. She cringed even as she asked the question. "How did you get in the hospital if you didn't have the vaccination?"

Ronnie looked surprised as he waved his hand at the other two beds in the room. "Just like those folks did, I guess. I called the ambulance when things got bad, and they came to get me. I was mighty glad for the service once I got here. It looks like we're all being taken good care of."

"Just be thankful," Travis snorted. "At least they're taking care of you."

"That's a good attitude to have," Regina said. *"The Lord* always has a blessing hidden away somewhere."

"Well, we've got to get going," Travis boomed. He pumped Ronnie's weak hand. "You get well now."

"Hard not to, with all that stuff hanging on me." Ronnie tried to laugh as he pointed at the tubes.

Regina smiled and followed Travis into the hall.

At the elevator they waited as Regina gathered her courage. With the doors shut behind them she launched, "So what is going on, Travis? I'm tired of being in the dark here. You don't come around, and we've got all kinds of trouble afoot ... accidents, people killing themselves, bombings, and no one seems to know or care enough to find out why. The papers are silent. The cable news says nothing. Where are those sick people from the parking lot the other week? Why did I see people with the fever turned away from the hospital doors — and now the hospital is full of people who didn't have the vaccination? And they weren't here that long ago. I know, because I visit here regular. And I think you know what's going on, if not involved yourself."

Travis shook his head. "Just mind your own business, Regina ... and your church's business, I might add. You are the hero, remember? Just leave well enough alone, okay? There are people in charge who know what they're doing. Smarter people than us, people who know how these things have to be done. What do you and I know about a fever epidemic? Do we know how to control it? How about stopping it? How about getting everyone vaccinated? How about where to put all the sick people? It's all too big for one man or for one mind, Regina. It takes all of us ... together ... working for one common good."

"And what would that be?" Regina felt the anger rise in her voice. "Killing people, or driving them to it? That's what it looks like to me. And what about that new prison the next county over? You know anything strange going on out there?"

"Now ... now," Travis tapped Regina on the arm. "I know nothing about any of that. What I see is all I know, and I don't see much."

"I want to know, Travis, and now. You do know something, don't you?"

He laughed, but sobered moments later. "I must say you have me worried, Regina. That's the real reason I came up to see you. But I suppose you already know that?"

The elevator doors opened and they stepped out. Regina glanced down the halls and waited until they were outdoors near Travis's car before she spoke again.

"Maybe I do, and maybe I don't, but what about you answering my questions?"

"I will answer one thing for you." Travis's finger pointed in Regina's face. "I know what you saw at the government building. But you have to trust the authorities, okay? If you go blabbing about this, only my personal intervention can keep you from being hauled up to Washington or some such place. And I'm not sure if that will be good enough. Remember, it doesn't matter if what you saw and what the papers say aren't the same thing. You've got to learn to mind your own business, Regina. You're a pastor ... not some vigilante loose on her own. The world has no use for vigilantes. It only has a place for those who work together."

"You call this working together?" Regina waved the newspaper around as she got in the car. "A white supremacy group? Really. You and I both know that was no white terrorist I saw shot. Now why would someone want to hide that fact?"

"I don't know." Travis accelerated the car. "How would I know? That's what I'm trying to tell you. Others have this thing under control. Maybe they have a reason for spreading the disinformation. Have you thought of that yet?"

"Then why don't you find out for sure?" she retorted.

Travis didn't look happy. "Because I am smarter than you are, Regina. This is not how the world works now. No one can go around on his own, barging into things he doesn't need to know about. Take my advice and stop this behavior of yours. There are tough times ahead for this country. And as God knows — they are already here. Don't make it worse for yourself. You have a good position at the church. You have respect from the community. You're a hero in the paper." Travis smiled. "Sure ... you're still single, but you know I've got that covered."

"I know you know, Travis. Tell me!"

His smile only grew as he pulled up to the parsonage. "Come on now, Regina. I'm here, and the world is right again."

"This is not the time." Regina met his gaze. "And I still want answers."

"Afraid, are we?" he teased.

Regina sighed. "I'm afraid love will have to wait until these troubled times are over, Travis. Sorry. It would be for the best."

Travis got out of the car. "Put that mind to rest, Regina, okay? And we'll all be better off. Take that from a very dear friend who wants the best for you. And now we have the night in front of us."

"Thank you for the ride, and good night, Travis." Regina entered the doorway.

She heard his footsteps behind her but didn't turn around. His hands came around her waist, and she resisted him. But tonight strong fingers sought her face and tightened their grip. There was no pain yet, but it would come soon if she continued her rejection of him. It wasn't worth it, she decided, and she wouldn't win anyway. His temper had been aroused. And what good did a scream do her, or even many screams. She didn't want her reputation shattered. Strangely it wouldn't be if she slept with him, but it would if she caused a scene. She went limp and he carried her to the bed. He must have wanted to make up for his harshness, but the niceness soon ceased. A sob escaped her lips by the time he finished.

"Let that be a lesson, and don't forget it," he said as he dressed and left the house.

This was not good, she told herself when Travis was gone. Her body ached and her heart was bruised even worse. The violence in the world seemed closer tonight, and there was little she could do about it. She buried her head in her hands and wept.

Chapter Seventeen

Enos followed the man they called Moe through the woods. Only he wasn't Moe — his real name was Milroy. Behind him came Joe who carried the guns. The black bag in Joe's hand darted in and out of the shadows as they moved among the darkened tree trunks. Dusk had settled over the fields hours ago.

Tonight was the night he would learn how to use the things that kill people. Father's rusty shotgun used to hunt deer was nothing compared to these guns. From the looks of them no squirrel could outrun a discharge from their barrels.

No news had come from home today, so his father must still breathe. Someday his father would find out about this, as all Amish found out things about each other, and there would be a price to pay. If he killed, there would be an even larger price to pay, a price too large to imagine — but that was how it had to be.

The men paused, and Enos waited, unable to see their faces in the darkness.

"It's right around here somewhere." Moe pointed. "The valley will keep the gunshots down — what there will be of them."

"There won't be much," Joe grunted, and undid one of the bags. "This is good enough."

They stepped out into a clearing and motioned for Enos to follow. He could see more by the starlight now as the guns came out of the bag, the long muzzles wrapped in something.

The men's hats shadowed their faces until they tossed them aside into the grass. He followed their example.

Moe showed Enos where the shells went into the clip and where the clip went into the gun. Enos waited while Joe walked across the field and set up a candle at the other edge of the meadow. Its small flickering flame looked like a firefly in the distance.

"This is how you load." Moe pulled back the clip. A soft rattle sounded, followed by a click. Enos did the same to his gun. "Now you raise your weapon to your shoulder, look through the scope, place the crosshairs on the candle flame, and fire."

A soft poof sounded from Moe's gun.

"Missed on purpose," Moe muttered when Joe laughed. "I don't want to walk all the way across the field again."

"Really." Joe laughed again.

"This shoot is not for my benefit," Moe said. "So shut up. Now you try it young man."

Enos raised the gun to his shoulder and looked through the scope. He gave a cry of alarm before he cast the weapon aside.

"Now what?" Moe said. "Are you afraid of the gun?"

"It's daylight," Enos said.

"Stupid you, Moe," Joe said. "You should have explained. He's never used a real gun before, let alone a night scope. Look, son, there's technology in there that turns starlight into daylight. So don't be afraid. It allows you to see at night. Just remember during the daytime to take off the converter on the front of the scope."

"Try again," Moe said. "You'll see the candle plainly."

Enos raised the gun, focused on the candle flickering in the scope, and fired this time. Nothing happened.

"Why isn't there a loud noise when we shoot?" Enos asked.

"Silencer equipment," Moe told him. "You don't think we're stupid enough to advertise our presence for all the world to hear?"

"What is that?" Enos asked.

"Just fire," Joe groaned, "we haven't got all night."

Enos tried again, and again nothing happened to the candle.

"Keep going," Moe muttered, and Enos did, but the flickering candle still gave off the steady flame.

"Here," Joe said. "Let me try that gun. Maybe Moe messed up the scope when he carried it over here."

After he handed the gun over, Enos watched as Joe lifted it to his shoulder and fired smoothly. The candle went out.

"See there," Joe chuckled. "That's how you shoot."

"There's someone coming," Moe hissed, fear in his voice. "Who could be following us back here?"

"Who's down there?" a voice called out moments later, as a searchlight streamed across the field.

Both men threw themselves down on the ground and began to crawl back towards the woods. Enos also lowered himself, after he picked up one of the guns. He waited until the beam from the man's searchlight had gone in the other direction before raising his gun and aiming it. He found the man in the darkness. He saw the face look after the light, and then he placed the crosshairs on the man's chest. He tightened his finger on the trigger and took a deep breath — but he couldn't do it. As Enos waited the light went out.

"Good Lord, Almighty," Moe whispered. "That was close enough; probably some game warden roaming around out here."

"I almost fired at him," Enos said. "But I couldn't."

"Thank God you didn't." Joe snatched away Enos's gun. "You would have given away our position or worse. He would have called in on his radio for sure."

Enos followed the two men at a run over the top of the next hill. There they slowed down and walked back to the barn. Once inside, Joe lit a gas lantern and the guns disappeared.

"From now on young man," Moe said as he sat on a straw

bale, "remember this ... no shooting at people until we tell you to, okay? When that time comes we'll need you, but it's not here yet."

"Aw," Joe interrupted the lecture, "don't be too hard on the boy. We have deep cover, remember?"

"Sure we do," Moe said. "But there's no need to use it before it's time."

Enos nodded, "I can do what you tell me to do. I know how that works."

Joe laughed. "At least we know the boy is with us. Surprised the heck out of me, I must say. Amish boy, bang. Ready to fire away, *hah*. Of course you couldn't hit much, now could you?"

They laughed, but Enos didn't laugh.

None of this felt good, he thought, and the darkness lay heavy on his heart.

The two men left and closed the barn door behind them. Their buggy soon rattled out of the driveway. This was so wrong, all of it, Enos thought. *English* people shouldn't drive around in buggies. They were not holy. And his father should never have been driven to such extremes, having to make choices between life and death. He should be home tonight, laughing with his brothers and sisters, looking forward to seeing Rosemary on Sunday night after the *hymn singing*.

Now there was no *hymn singing* to attend, no church services at all, not with things the way they were. His father hadn't been to one for months. Enos groaned and buried his head in his hands. An hour passed before he walked back to the house. How he longed to see Rosemary's face again. But she was gone now, and nothing remained from the past to bring peace back in his heart.

Clare was sitting in the living room on the couch when he entered, where she read by the light of the kerosene lamp. She had fed him supper at dusk, before Moe and Joe had arrived for the shooting lesson.

"Sit." She motioned with her hand at the empty space beside her. "How did the shooting go?"

"Okay," he said, but he didn't move. What right did he have to sit beside a woman who was not his sister or his wife?

"Tell me about it." She repeated the gesture. "I won't bite."

He sat down beside her and held his breath for a long moment.

Clare smiled. She wore the same night dress his sisters always wore. It was long and flowed down to cover her body. He wondered how she knew what Amish women wore when they went to bed. She had never worn it downstairs before, and he had never gone upstairs after she went to bed.

"So did you learn how to shoot tonight?" she asked.

"I almost shot at a man," he said.

She laughed, and her cheeks dimpled. Obviously she didn't believe him.

"I did," he insisted. "I was afraid, so I couldn't. Joe chewed me out good for even thinking it."

She raised her eyebrows and pulled a cell phone out of her pocket to punch in numbers.

"You have a cell phone?" He stared. "You know that the Amish don't have cell phones."

"I know." She winked. "We are careful with them."

The phone rang as he listened. "Hello Moe, it's Clare. Young Rambo says he almost shot someone tonight. Is he serious?" An astonished look spread over her face as she listened. "He did? ... And he didn't die of fright? ... Well, bravo for him.... Yes, I would say so ...." She closed the phone and hid it again. "Well, look at you."

"So do you believe me?" he asked. Somehow the darkness inside dimmed as she sat beside him.

She touched his arm. "I think I do. Now isn't that something? You have more in you than I supposed you did."

"They killed Rosemary," he said, and the darkness returned.

She took his hand this time and placed her other arm around his shoulder. "I know how that feels. Most of us have lost people in life — people we loved."

"Have you lost your promised one?" He searched her eyes.

"No, not quite in the way you mean." She reached up to stroke his face, and he didn't pull away. "Mine sort of ran away, which isn't the same."

She nestled against him. Rosemary had also nestled against him in the buggy. He held his breath for a moment.

"You're a strong man." She looked up at his face again, touching his smooth cheek. "You almost killed a man tonight."

He looked away as the darkness rushed in.

"Come upstairs with me. I would love that."

He looked at her. At the smile on her face. At the warmth in her eyes.

When he said nothing, she teased, "What happened, little Rosemary think herself too good for you?"

He leaped to his feet and threw off her arm.

"Rosemary did nothing of the sort!" he shouted.

"I'm sorry." She reached for him. "I didn't mean to offend you."

"You know nothing about the souls of my people." He stepped away. "*Yes*, we are ignorant. And *yes*, you have learned many of our ways, but I will not sleep in your bed."

"I said I was sorry. Okay? What's wrong? Am I not good looking enough?"

His face softened. "You are good looking, Clare. But there is a darkness in my soul, and I will not add more than is necessary."

"Your people take killing pretty hard, don't they?" She studied his face.

"*Yes*." He winced. "They do."

"It's okay." She touched his arm again. "I said I'm sorry."

He nodded and tried to smile.

She had meant no harm, he thought. That much was clear.

Perhaps the darkness would have left if he had gone upstairs with her, but he could not. He had said *no* to Rosemary, and he would not say *yes* to this.

"Sleep tight," she said moments later and closed the stair door behind her.

Chapter Eighteen

Regina stood inside the front door of the parsonage as the sun came up over the horizon. She watched the empty South Main street. The few cars that tried to come through had to circle around in Bethesda Plaza and cross behind the Baptist Church. A stillness hung in the air, as if the world waited in expectation of something momentous. Her heart still bled this morning from its own explosion last night. Never had Travis used her like that before. The revelation seared and tore through her senses. But if Travis thought such actions would cause her to back off from her search for answers, he was sorely mistaken. And surely there would be no repeat performance in the future. But the fact was she could do little if they did occur again. From what she had discovered so far, a report to the police would go nowhere. And someone would be sure to bring up the point that an unmarried Reverend shouldn't have slept with her boyfriend in the first place. A chill ran through her at the thought. It was amazing indeed how some people could bring up old fashioned morality when it suited their purposes.

She stepped out on the front porch. Double yellow tape was strung up a few feet beyond the church. The line went across the street from there, held up by a long line of yellow sawhorses that wrapped back around on Third Street. About her pieces of concrete still lay in the street, the roof of the government building almost gone. Several town officers stood guard below the steps, their cruisers parked on the North side. ATF and the occasional FBI jacket were visible, spread out over the rubble. They still probed and scribbled in their notebooks. Several held an occasional conversation among themselves.

Regina stepped off the porch for a closer look.

"You there, please move back." One of the officers came closer.

"I'm with the church." Regina motioned towards the church with her hand. "I live in the parsonage."

"Well, please stay on the other side of the tape then, ma'am."

Regina nodded, and the officer moved away. But they seemed uncomfortable and took glances in her direction as she studied the rubble. She took her time. It was after all her territory, and it felt good to exert some kind of control after what Travis did last night.

Regina forced her mind to focus. Now was not the time to get bogged down in personal problems. And they were minor anyway compared to what else went on in her world. She glanced around. What kind of bomb had it taken to blow this solid concrete building to smithereens? How had the attackers brought it in without being observed? The nearest officer's radio squawked, but Regina couldn't understand the words. He turned away for a moment and raised his microphone to answer.

Moments later he approached at a fast walk. "For your own safety, ma'am, you had best get back inside. Things are very unsettled out here."

Regina smiled and turned to go. Things were unsettled in more ways than loose concrete and unstable structures, she thought. Inside the parsonage, she lowered herself on the couch to think. She deserved the day off with this throb in her head, but the questions wouldn't stop. What did Travis know? An awful lot if half of what Frank claimed was true. And how did Travis know what she had seen in the attack? Someone must have seen her, a nearby witness perhaps, but there hadn't seemed to be anyone around.

She turned on the television and checked the news channels. It was the same story as before. They said things, but nothing useful. She picked up the phone and called the number in Georgia. Her mother's voice answered.

"Hi, Mom, it's Regina.... Is everything okay? ...Yes, I'm fine. We had some trouble in town the other day, but don't worry. I'm okay.... What kind of trouble?...Government things.... Someone blew up a building.... Yes, I know it's probably not on the national news with everything else that's going on, but it was a big thing around here...."

She hung up thirty minutes later and her gaze caught sight of Travis's rumpled newspaper from last night. The front page was half exposed. The top headline glared at her, *Virginia Governor Seeks Emergency Powers*. Travis had not mentioned this.

Regina retrieved the paper and spread the front page out on the kitchen table. She read silently. "Citing the extraordinary nature of what faces the Commonwealth and the nation at large, Governor Pat Westing has requested emergency powers from the Federal government. It is uncertain at this time whether such powers can be granted, or if a possible presidential order may be necessary. Governor Westing stated that while such a consideration should be viewed only as a short term solution, no option should be off the table.

"As justification for his request, the governor gave multiple examples of what the Commonwealth is dealing with. The fever epidemic shows few signs of abating, and local authorities are overrun with cases of ill people who have somehow avoided the mandatory vaccination procedures.

"There is also the urgent need for more hospital beds and treatment supplies. This need has baffled local officials across the Commonwealth. A repeated plea from the governor to the legislature to act and appropriate the needed monies has apparently fallen on deaf ears. Excuses and fears, the governor says, can no longer be used to block changes that must be made. Human lives are at stake.

"The governor said further that violence has erupted across the Commonwealth. He has assigned a task force to look into the causes, but no conclusions have been reached at this time. Robberies and break-ins have become widespread and in some cases have turned into homicides. Local law enforcement has become overwhelmed. These incidents are too numerous and distressing to detail, according to the governor.

"Added to all this are the egregious twin attacks yesterday on the Federal buildings in Farmstead and in Roanoke, of which a full account is given elsewhere. Initial investigations point to a growing swell of homegrown terrorism. Calm is urged until the authorities can gain a full understanding of both the design and scope of the terrorist groups. The governor expressed hope that his request could be acted upon quickly."

So Roanoke also had an attack, Regina thought. She laid the paper on the floor and walked out on the front porch again. The Bethesda Plaza still looked quiet, a few cars parked here and there, the street on South Main empty. Apparently the traffic had finally been diverted up at McDonalds. Only the bombed-out federal building emitted any sound, as officers moved about in the roped-off area. Was there some way to obtain information other than the official sources?

Memories of her father flashed through her mind — his form at work in his garage when he fiddled around on hot Saturday afternoons with a cheap shortwave radio he found in the attic. He finally persuaded the thing to work and listened all summer long to voices from half a world away, until the novelty faded away. But he taught her how to listen to what the world had to say. Regina got her keys and started her car behind the parsonage. She headed south on Main Street.

She expected a roadblock somewhere around the Countryside Restaurant, which would have provoked the customary flash of the vaccination card, but there was none. On the edge of town nestled a Radio Shack in the Wal-Mart shopping mall. Regina chose a spot as close to the front door as possible. They ought to sell shortwave radios here, with a quality good enough for what she wanted.

The short blast of a car horn sounded behind her, and Regina jumped. She craned her neck to follow the sound but could see nothing. Likely the car was owned by some excited teenager who wished to show off to his friends. She opened the car door, clicked the lock, and prepared to cross the parking lot.

"Well, if it isn't the Reverend," called out a familiar voice from a distance. Regina whirled around to see Lester Blanton come towards her at a brisk stride. He wore a dark navy blue suit.

"Good morning," Regina greeted him. "Why are you following me around?"

The world might be going to pot, she thought, but somehow Lester Blanton always showed up.

Lester laughed. "Now what makes you think I'd do such a thing, Reverend? But of course I was following you around. Who wouldn't follow a beautiful woman around the streets of Farmstead? And what are you doing here? Looking for a diamond ring across the street?"

"Not yet." She met his gaze. "But I don't like to be followed around."

"Actually," Lester smiled, "I was going to Wal-Mart and saw your car ahead of me. I couldn't resist coming over to say hi. I hope everything is going well."

"I dropped off my visitor like you told me. I hope he is doing well."

Lester nodded, "Of course, and congratulations on the feature in the paper. It's a nice write-up for your church."

"Yes, it is, and thanks."

"Town's having a lot of trouble, isn't it?"

Regina glanced away. "I think the whole country is, from the looks of it."

"I suppose so," Lester allowed. "But there's not much simple college folk like me can do about it."

Regina grimaced. "And you expect me to believe that? You know more than you are letting on."

He appeared weary.

"Are we at war with ourselves, Professor?" Regina asked him.

He thought for a moment before he answered. "Not yet, I don't think."

"I wonder sometimes," she replied.

He cleared his throat. "What I'm really trying to say, Regina, is that perhaps we could have supper at Charley's? If you're not busy, of course. I know we just met not that long ago, but I would enjoy an outing with you."

"You want to take me out for dinner?" She stared at him.

"Why not?" He looked around the parking lot. "Am I not from the male species, and are you not a beautiful woman?"

"I suppose so." She smiled at his humor. "That would be nice, but you're up to something, aren't you?"

"I guess you'll have to find out." He made a face.

"And when shall the magic hour be?"

"Would seven tonight be okay?"

"Splendid," she said. "I'll be looking forward to it."

"Till then." He nodded and retreated to his car to drive off with a wave.

"You have gone crazy," Regina told herself as she marched across the parking lot.

Yet how could she resist? The desire to know was too strong. And Lester knew a lot, she told herself. Regina forced her thoughts back to the task at hand. She checked for traffic before she crossed the last lane in the parking lot. Radio Shack was almost empty when she stepped inside, which was fine.

"Can I help you?" a young sales girl offered.

"Sure ... I'm looking for a shortwave radio of fairly good quality."

The girl led Regina towards the back of the store. When she found what she looked for, the girl pointed. "This is a real nice model."

Regina ran her fingers over the front of the radio and glanced down at the price. "It's exactly what I want."

The girl smiled and moved back down the aisle with the radio in hand. Regina followed her. She pulled out her credit card, and the girl took it. The pause came a moment later. "I forgot to tell you, the State people have to approve this first."

"For radios?" Regina made no effort to hide her surprise. "Since when?"

"Oh, it's just for short-waves. We got the order from the governor's office last month."

"What if I pay cash?" Regina asked.

"It makes no difference. I have to call in your Social or driver's license. We've not had anyone turned down yet, so there shouldn't be a problem."

Regina hesitated, as wild scenarios ran through her head. This was crazy, but she would not be intimidated.

"Here's my license," Regina said, and the girl dialed the number to give the info in clipped tones.

The girl turned from the phone moments later with a big smile. "That's all it took. Now we can do the credit card."

Regina nodded, her face grim.

"It's not our choice, of course." The girl appeared concerned. "I'm sorry if that bothered you, but I could have my job taken away if I don't comply. We even had an official visit from Richmond last week. The guy from the state went through all our records and matched everything up. So I guess it's a big deal to someone."

"Well, thanks anyway." Regina allowed her face to relax. It wasn't the girl's fault, whatever the government ordered.

The girl gave her the box, and Regina walked out the door. She glanced up and down the street, uncertain. The shadows under the storefronts seemed to carry sinister meanings now, but she shouldn't give in to this jumpiness. Let them come and ask her why she purchased a shortwave. The reason was no secret. She wanted to listen to the news. Since when was that a crime in this country?

There was still no roadblock when Regina drove back up South Main. The checkpoints could change at a moment's notice, she knew, apparently part of the strategy to find what the police looked for at the moment. Would a shortwave radio pass inspection? Now that was a troubling question to ask — really, too troubling to ask. Regina unlocked the door of the parsonage, which opened with a squeak. She removed the radio from the box and set it on the table in plain sight. Let someone see her if they wanted to — she didn't care. Regina flipped the dial and found static, then voices, then stranger voices in many languages. The English voices spoke only of personal concerns and local issues. An agitated voice finally caught her attention, and she stopped, adjusting the dial. Agitation was good to a point — she felt agitated and perhaps the man had something worthwhile to say.

"My family lives in America," the man said. "Right now they're cowering in fear at home, captives in their own country. I can't believe what's happening. There is no news in the papers; nothing is being said about what's going on.

"I'm in New Zealand, and we have a strict quarantine placed on us right now, or I'd be flying home tomorrow to see what's going on. I'm afraid the whole world is going mad."

Regina continued to flip through the dial. She already knew the world had gone mad, so that was not news. She found a broadcaster in Germany who gave grim statistics in English on the deaths in his country from the epidemic. He didn't sound hysterical and ran through the numbers as if reading the latest stock report. Apparently no one knew much more than she did.

She turned off the dial. It was time she thought about dinner. The world might have gone mad, but she needed food.

That seemed strange somehow, but perhaps even everyday things became strange in a mad world.

Chapter Nineteen

Regina sat at the table in Charley's and fidgeted. The officer who stood outside the front door had let her pass through without incident when she showed her vaccination card. Her thoughts were dark at the moment. Would Travis be by tonight? And if he was, how would she handle him? But really, there was little use in thoughts expended on that matter. She could do nothing about Travis at the moment. Other than try to ease him out of her life. Her heart ached at the thought, but there seemed no other option.

"Just one for tonight?" the smiling waitress asked as she cleared her throat.

Regina jumped, then held up two fingers and forced a smile.

"A drink for you then?"

"Water." Regina nodded, and the waitress left two white cloth-wrapped utensils and menus on the table before she retreated.

Below her the river ran past the huge glass windows. The sound was a soft gurgle along the tree-lined banks. It was almost crystal clear this time of year, no longer sullied with mud from the heavy spring rains. Only a few people sat at the tables nearby, as Regina glanced around. But it was still early, and these were not normal times.

Regina opened the menu and studied it but saw nothing of interest. If Lester didn't show in a few minutes, she would wave the waitress back and order before people began to stare. Who was the professor anyway? That was a recurring question, and still she could find no answer.

Regina took a deep breath and held it until her chest hurt.

"Waiting long?" Lester's voice caught her by surprise and Regina jumped.

"Just thinking." She tried to recover her senses.

"Well, there's plenty to think about." Lester slid into the seat and pulled his long legs under the table.

"Work at the college getting a little overwhelming?" Regina wished the nervousness wasn't in her voice.

"I got a little detained." Lester tilted his head sideways but still smiled. "I hope you can forgive me."

"Sure, and what's so funny?"

He shook his head. "I just saw a picture of you in my mind, working in the kitchen, your white apron on, and deep into … well, let's see, perhaps a ham casserole, or an upside-down pineapple cake. I think you could still do that, right?"

Regina laughed, "I bet you know nothing about either of those. You just pulled that off the top of your head to impress me."

He nodded. "Well, I take it that my guess wasn't that wild, and that you actually have made those foods. But seriously — I've made both. When I couldn't stand take-out food anymore."

"Surely we aren't that bad?" The waitress had come up to stand beside them.

"No, dear, my goodness, no." Lester laughed. "Your food is wonderful. That was only a figure of speech. Though you know I can't afford your prices all the time — at least not on my salary."

The waitress cleared her throat. "Would you be ready to order? If not, I can come back later."

"We are," Regina said. The words had leaped to her lips. "Well … I guess we are."

Lester didn't answer but motioned with his hand. "You go first. I'll be ready when you're done."

"Ah, then…." Regina tried to collect her thoughts. Nothing had attracted her attention earlier, so what did it matter. "Let's make it the Chesapeake Bay Crab Cakes."

"Would you like the Napa Cabbage Cole Slaw or corn relish?" The waitress waited for her answer.

"Cole slaw," Regina replied.

"And you?" The waitress turned towards Lester.

"Oh … I'll take the Filet Mignon."

"Baked potato or rice pilaf? The salad comes with it."

Lester nodded, "Baked potato with butter and sour cream … even if it's an extra."

The waitress scribbled. "We have our own bread. Would you like that?"

"That would be excellent," Lester smiled. "And bring some extra for the lady. Her ribs look like they need fattening."

"Looks like he's starting on you already." The waitress laughed. "I'll be right back."

"You have a reputation here … perhaps with the girls?" Regina asked, when the waitress had left.

Lester smiled. "Surely you're not jealous."

"No. Just checking your reputation."

"Oh, I have a sterling reputation," he said. "As clean as the wind-driven snow. Isn't that how the *Good Book* says it?"

"Something like that," Regina agreed, and met his gaze.

"So tell me about yourself." Lester leaned forward. "I know you are the Reverend Regina Owens. But is that all? Never married I assume?"

"No, and yourself?"

His eyes flickered for just a moment, but he shook his head.

"It seems like half the world is divorced."

"I know." He didn't meet her gaze. "I was almost married once, but not all the way."

"Sorry," she muttered.

"Thanks." His eyes didn't smile. "So tell me more about yourself. Worthwhile things, good things, like your family, your dreams, your memories, youth, childhood, that sort of thing. And of course love, if you wish."

"Funny how it all seems to lead back to love — or begin there."

"Sort of," he agreed, "but why talk about that now? The world is falling apart you know, and you still haven't told me about yourself. You're liberal, I assume. Tell me how a liberal gets to be a liberal. What's she like when she's a little girl?"

"Does that mean you're not?" Regina looked at him over her glass.

"Liberal?" he asked.

She laughed. "Yes ... you know what I mean. I thought all social work professors were liberal."

"Head of the *Social Works Department*." His eyes gleamed. "I worked too hard not to rub it in at every chance."

"So how does a little boy get to be a conservative?"

Lester pondered the question as he stared out the window.

"Come on," she teased. "Answer me."

He finally laughed. "Well ... I don't know, I guess I was born that way."

"That doesn't cut it," she retorted.

He leaned back in his seat and waited as the waitress came towards them with their plates of food. She beamed. "Piping hot out of the kitchen. The filet mignon for you" — she passed Lester the steaming steak — "and crab cakes for you, ma'am. Is there anything else I can get for you?"

"I'm fine," Regina nodded.

"I'll take steak sauce," Lester told her.

"Certainly." The waitress scurried off.

"She should have brought that with her," Regina said. "I guess service is bad tonight."

"Life's a little troublesome right now." Lester put on a sympathetic look. "So it's understandable."

Regina saw the waitress return at a rapid stride, and Lester smiled. "Thank you so much."

"You're welcome." The waitress left again.

"So now back to your story." Lester turned towards her.

She held his gaze for a moment before she gave up. What was the use? He probably couldn't explain how he got to be a conservative. Regina took a deep breath. "Well, I was once a little girl. I played with my doll and ran around the house. One day I said to myself, why should I not be a liberal? Isn't the whole world a liberal place? The sun rises and gives its light freely. The moon has no shame at night. The stars twinkle for everyone. Why should we be so tightfisted and deny others what should be freely shared?"

"I didn't know you were a comedian," he said. "Did you learn that in a seminar?"

Regina laughed. "Not really, but the world isn't coming to an end; all that apocalyptic stuff is little more than fairy tales. Humankind has been here for thousands of years, and no one is going anywhere that I know of."

"You call what's happening out there normal?" he asked with a strange look on his face.

She shrugged. "No. It's terrible, and it's deep, and people I love are involved. Isn't that bad enough?"

He leaned forward. "Frank told you plenty, I think. What are you going to do about it? That's the question."

"How did you know Frank was out there? Let's start with that."

He looked away. "I can't tell you that."

"You don't have to be so mysterious."

"Perhaps not, but I have my reasons."

"I'll remember that in the future," she said.

He pulled on his napkin. "Okay, let's be serious Regina. Why were you interested in Frank?"

"I like humanitarian causes." She shrugged. "They bring out the liberal side of me."

He smiled. "You're a hopeless case, Regina, you know that."

"So why are we having dinner?" she asked.

His smile didn't fade. "Perhaps because I like the company of a beautiful woman and because I'm lonely."

"Oh, you break my heart, Lester. Is that the best come-on line you have?"

"I thought Reverends had divine protection against such things," he said laughing.

"Okay." Regina joined in. "Enough with the teasing. What is there to know? Because I don't know what's going on. I don't know what would drive a man to kill himself and his child."

"And now you think you should find out?"

"Perhaps, but I don't know. Sometimes I think I've gone far enough. But then I keep being driven on by events out of my control."

"Really?" He studied her.

"I'll find out in my own way," she said with a shake of her head. "When the time comes, that is."

"What if I told you? Would you believe me?"

"So why don't you tell me?" she retorted.

"You know we're just going around in circles."

She sighed. "So let's not go around in circles anymore. You seem to know a lot more about what's going on than I do. So tell me."

He looked out of the window for a long moment to watch the river float past before he answered. "Number one, the government is corrupt and rotten to the core. The president is ordering all sorts of illegal things — well I suppose he figures they aren't illegal if they come from him. But that aside — the bombing at the federal building here in town and in Roanoke were federally ordered. The church that blew up the night that woman drove through the doors must have been set to go off overnight by the same people. She just got there at the wrong time. All for what reasons? I have no idea. I'm sure it fits in someone's sick scheme of things."

"You sure about this?" Regina shifted in her seat.

He continued without an answer. "On top of all that the epidemic is being totally mismanaged by the health care officials. Vaccines are corrupted. In some cases they are killing people outright, in others it's leaving them open to the virus or something worse. Exacerbating everything is the corruption of the health care officials themselves. The prisons are being emptied out, releasing them on the general population, apparently to wreak havoc on purpose. It serves the added goal of making the local police appear virtuous when they solve these mad crimes easily. In some cases, they are simply shooting the released prisoners on sight. Before or after the crimes, it makes no difference. In this uncertain climate, the population loves the government. Well, some of them do."

"You're positive?" She studied his face.

"I'm afraid so." He met her gaze. "They are allowing the sick to die in these transformed prisons. What else can they do? There are too many of them, and there is no money. The world is out of money, Regina. The government, the state, the economy, the colleges — I mean, we've had our pay cut twice already. Do you think you'll be exempt?"

She shrugged. "That would be a small worry if what you say is true."

"There's more to come." He played with the last of his steak. "And that's really what I want to talk about. Can we count on you to help?"

"I'll help however I can. I'm a pastor," Regina replied.

"I meant something else," he said.

"I thought you did."

"I think you're one of us. We aren't that many, but we have to protect ourselves."

"Are you trying to overthrow the government?" She held up her hand. "Because I want nothing to do with that."

"We're trying to survive, that's all," he said. "And we care about people. Let's see ... I almost forgot that."

She managed a laugh. "Perhaps we'd better finish our food before it's cold."

Lester nodded, and silence draped over them.

"I had a good father," Regina broke the silence. "He worked hard for his family ... so we could go to college and have what he didn't. There were seven of us, three boys and four girls. All of them married except me."

"Is your dad still alive?" His voice was gentle.

"Yes, but he's old now. He loves his grandchildren. So does Mom, as far as that goes, but not like he does. I don't get home much anymore, other than holidays and that sort of thing. School took so much of my time, and now the years with the church. You sort of get away from things."

Lester had finished his steak while she spoke. His potato was scraped down to the skin.

"So, what are some of your memories?" She glanced towards the river.

"They don't sound as good as yours." He made a face.

"But we still share them; they are a part of living."

Lester smiled. "Am I now a counselee, needing to look into his troubled past?"

"Well it might do you good — might bring you peace," she told him.

"Peace." Lester leaned forward with his elbows on the table. "That was promised with the coming of the Christ child, and that's been over two thousand years ago and we're still fighting each other."

"Perhaps God meant peace in the heart," she told him.

"Then He should have mentioned that, instead of getting our hopes up. Isn't there something about full disclosure in human relationships, let alone the divine?"

Regina didn't answer, averting her gaze from his.

The waitress appeared in her line of vision. "Can I get you something else?"

Regina shook her head.

"We're ready for the check." Lester handed over his credit card.

The waitress nodded and walked back to the front counter.

"So when will you do the first job for us? This caring thing of course." The waitress returned and gave Lester the credit card receipt. He filled in the gratuity amount and signed it. Regina kept her gaze focused on the table.

When the waitress left, Lester stood, waiting.

"We will have to see, I guess." Regina got to her feet.

"Here's the address." Lester paid no attention to her obvious uncertainty. "Pick the lady up tomorrow and take her out to the Amish farm where you took Frank. You can use my car. Pick it up at the other address – the one in Farmstead. The lady has her vaccination card, so there shouldn't be any problems with the roadblocks. You can do that, can't you?"

"What kind of trouble are you getting me into?"

He smiled. "None at all! And you might thank me someday...." Lester offered his arm, and Regina took it.

"Are all girls this mysterious?" he asked on the walk out to her car.

"Just me." She leaned on his shoulder. "And thanks for dinner. That was nice of you."

"Don't forget now." He opened her car door and waited until she climbed in. Moments later he was lost in the shadows beyond the streetlights, walking away with quick steps.

Chapter Twenty

Enos drove towards home, allowing his horse to take its time, the lines limp in his hands. Faint shadows bounced along the ditch, thrown there by his low buggy lights. He watched them, glancing back towards the road every few moments. His horse knew the way, and he would arrive without incident, he figured. What awaited his arrival was the question. Was his father still alive? He assumed so since no word had been sent by his sister. But perhaps they were all dead. Who said the medicine always worked? Few things in life ever did.

Beneath his seat was one of the long guns from the other night. Enos remembered the conversation. "Take it along," Clare said. "You never know who you will meet along the way. It's not safe for anyone to be out on the roads after dark anymore."

"What if I have to use it?" he asked. But how could he use such a terrible thing? Still he asked, because someday he would have to use it.

"No one will suspect it's under the buggy seat." Clare flashed him an understanding smile. "Don't use it unless you shoot to kill. If you meet any police, they'll let you through without any problems. You are still Amish after all, and the real thing at that. Just be careful; we don't want any dead officers."

Enos nodded as he studied her features. Clare had been nice to him this morning. She fixed him breakfast and said nothing about his refusal to sleep upstairs. He studied her

Amish dress while she wasn't looking. He thought of Rosemary and what had been done to her, and raw emotions nearly choked him.

"Is there anything wrong with the food?" Clare asked.

"No, it's good food. As good as my mother used to make."

"Well, that's a compliment." She smiled.

Clare was that way, Enos thought, his eyes once again following the shadows in the ditch. A nice woman, but she was not one he could ever marry.

But then, why did he worry about the sacred vows said to an *English* woman who pretended to be Amish? His heart wasn't Amish any longer. He had a gun under his buggy seat, and he would use it when the time came. How easy it would be to slip up to Clare's room tonight, he thought. She would welcome him. Her eyes said so. She would show him things more wonderful than the food she prepared for him. But he could not. That darkness was too deadly, perhaps even deadlier than the gun under his seat.

No, that was not true, Enos told himself. There was no greater sin than to kill a man. To kill was the sin that sent another man's soul to the judgment seat without benefit of repentance.

He shuddered and felt the darkness approaching again. This darkness was darker than the shadows along the roadside, darker than any light could ever change. It had invaded his soul, and it would never leave. Enos reached outside the buggy to run his hand over the low light, noticing the lines in his hand and fingers. He drew in long breaths. The darkness had still not reached everywhere, he told himself. Not as long as he could see his own hands.

His horse shook its head, and Enos tightened the reins. He turned his head as he passed an Amish farm. It was Mose Mullet's place, and something wasn't right. The wash room door was open, swinging in the night air. The low light of the interior spilled out onto the side porch. Also a light in the barn shone through the windows, but that wasn't so strange since Mose and his boys could still be at work on the late chores.

Enos pulled back the reins and turned into the lane. He tied up his horse to enter the barn door but found no signs of anyone. He hollered, softly at first, then louder, but still got no response. He left the gas lantern on the ceiling and walked towards the house. He entered through the wash room door and didn't knock. This was not his home, but the door was open.

He stopped to stare at the sight in front of him. Mose and his wife Ruth sat on kitchen chairs with ropes tied around their bodies. The soft light of the kerosene lamp played on their bruised faces. They were gagged with washcloths; the length of Mose's gag had fallen over his long beard. His eyes were weary, stricken, sorrowful, as if he had beheld evil itself and lived.

"What is going on?" Enos whispered, but Mose could say nothing. Neither of them moved on their chairs. Faint noises came from the living room. Enos reached to pull the cloth out of Mose's mouth, but the man shook his head. He motioned with his eyes towards the living room.

Enos stepped through the kitchen opening and paused to look around. The gas lantern hung from the ceiling hook. Before his eyes a man rose from the couch, his face shining with sweat, his chest bare.

The man grinned and muttered to himself. "Another stupid Amish boy I missed. Where did you come from, *bozo?* I thought I sent all you *idiots* upstairs."

The man stood to his feet. His bottom was bare. Enos glanced down at the couch as Mose's oldest daughter, Marilyn, pushed herself upwards with a cry. She pulled her torn dress together to cover herself. But not before Enos saw the marks of her injuries.

"He's got Mom and Dad tied up in the kitchen," Marilyn

gasped. "I couldn't keep him off me, Enos. You know I couldn't. I'm not strong enough."

Blind rage swept through Enos — the black hatred that no righteous man should ever hold against another human being, but he was no longer righteous or in control of his emotions. This was what they had done to Rosemary, and this man was one of them. Enos moved towards him as the man bent over, his bare back white in the gas lantern light. The man fumbled with his trousers. When Enos stepped closer, the man's hand flew upwards and he flourished a sharp knife blade.

"Back off you Amish *idiot*." A wild laugh came from the man's lips." I know you people don't harm a flea anyway."

Enos's hand moved through the air and caught the man's arm at the wrist. He wrenched it backwards to grab the knife with the other. He lifted his arm and plunged the weapon up to the hilt into the white chest. He pulled it out and drove it into the throat this time. He tore upwards in his rage. The body stiffened in mid-air and seemed to hang for a long moment before the man slide to the floor.

Enos bent over to gather up the man's shirt thrown on the hardwood floor. He threw it onto the bleeding, twitching body. He slid his hands underneath it and hoisted the man aloft.

"Open the front door," he croaked to Marilyn.

She moved as if she were dreaming, her hands still on the torn edges of her dress. Enos went through the door sideways and threw the body out into the dark yard. It landed with a soft thump. The shirt floated through the air after it.

"You killed a man," Marilyn whispered. She stood frozen at the front door.

"*Yes*, I did." Enos felt nothing. The darkness ought to rush in about now, he thought. It ought to overwhelm his soul, but there was only the pound of his own blood in his ears.

"What are we going to do?" Marilyn asked, as she closed the door behind him.

"Get a wash bucket in the kitchen and clean this up." Enos stared at the living room floor.

Marilyn moved fast and disappeared into the kitchen. Enos looked at the knife in his hand. The sharp blade reflected light from the lantern. He had committed a grievous sin, he told himself. This knife had committed the greatest sin known to his faith. Yet it was not the knife, it was his own hand that had done this. He had betrayed the Most High God.

"Here is the water," Marilyn said, one hand still holding her dress, "and a rag. Mom and Dad are tied up, but they are alive."

"I know." He pointed with one hand. "Go upstairs and put another dress on. I'll cut your parents loose. Tell your brothers to stay up there. Make them listen. I'll clean up down here."

She didn't move while he wet the rag.

"Are your brothers still alive?" He glanced at her.

"*Yes.*" She still didn't move. "Am I with child, Enos?"

He studied her bare feet. He didn't know much about men and women, but he knew about cattle and horses. She could well be, but it was best if he didn't tell her. Perhaps his promise would tear the evil from her body.

"No." He shook his head. "You will not be with child."

"Oh, Enos," she sobbed. "You know I couldn't keep him off me."

He stood, wrapped his arm around her shoulder, and pulled her tight against him. She sobbed, great gasps that gave off little sounds, as if her chest would tear apart.

"You didn't have to kill him because of me," she finally wailed. "I would have lived. But you have now sent his soul to judgment without it being right with God."

"I know." He touched her lips. "And you must never tell anyone what you have seen."

She sniffled hard. "Will Henry still marry me, Enos?"

"He will, Marilyn — it will be okay." He pulled her close. "You tell him what happened to you the next time you see him, and he will understand. He's a *good* man."

"Thank you, Enos," she whispered, and left to run upstairs.

He washed the floor until there were only a few streaks. He wiped the knife and dried it on his pant leg. He walked out to the kitchen where Mose and his wife still sat and pulled the gags out of their mouths.

"What is going on?" Mose asked, his voice hoarse.

Enos cut the ropes and helped Mose stand. "The man was attacking Marilyn. But he is outside now, and I am cleaning up the blood."

"The poor girl!" Mose exclaimed. "But we must all bear our trials during this time of trouble. And I believe *The Lord* will give her grace."

"I hope so." Enos laid a piece of rope on the kitchen table. "Are you well?"

"By the Will of God, I am." Mose flexed the muscles in his arms. "*The Lord* must have decided the rest of us are to be spared. I had begun to think He wanted us all to cross over, but we have not."

"I am glad to hear that," Enos said, as Marilyn reappeared in a fresh dress. She still looked tear-stained, her face puckered as if she was ready to burst into sobs again.

"My poor, poor daughter." Her father brushed her arm with his finger tips.

Her mother took Marilyn in her arms as the two rocked against each other beside the table.

Enos pushed past them to enter the living room with Mose behind him. He bent down to wipe the hardwood floors again.

"How did you get the man to leave?" Mose surveyed the damage to his home. "Was he done with Edith?"

"I made him leave." Enos didn't look up.

"Surely you did not use your hands on him?" Mose said with horror on his face.

Enos said nothing for a long moment as he wrung out the washcloth. "I killed him, Mose. He's lying outside in the yard."

Mose gasped. "May *The Lord* forgive you—if He can? But your father will be ashamed that his son would choose to forsake the ways of *The Lord* in his time of trouble."

"I'm sorry," Enos told him. "But it had to be done."

"What will happen to him now?" Mose glanced towards the heavens. "I will pray that he found repentance from his wicked deeds before he passed."

"Do you want me to call the police?" Enos looked up at the man. Mose should be the one to decide, he figured. It didn't matter either way to him.

Mose said nothing for the longest time. "I do not wish to call them — they will only ask questions." He paused and added, "But perhaps you should. *The Lord* does not look kindly on those who seek to hide their sins."

"Okay." Enos rose to his feet. "I will go to the neighbors and call then. It might be best that way."

Enos left the bucket of water on the hardwood floor. He walked past his buggy and down the road for a quarter of a mile. He knocked on the door and told the basics of his tale to the man who answered. Before he was back to the house, flashing lights approached in the distance. He went inside and waited.

The officer who arrived began to ask questions. Enos answered them the best he could, then listened as Marilyn told her story and went upstairs to bring down the torn dress. Mose and Ruth gave what they had to say in the kitchen. And there were the cut ropes that still lay in the kitchen, and the body outside.

When he was allowed to go, Enos felt the darkness cling to his heart as he walked back to the barn. He climbed into the buggy and left his dim lights turned off. The full moon had risen and flooded the land with light. As he went out of the driveway, he looked back only once before he turned towards

Rosemary's place. It was too late now to visit his father's place. Besides, the moonlight soothed his soul, as if it washed away some of the blackness inside of him. He stuck his hand outside the buggy. He could still see it as before, but on the inside things were not the same. They would never be the same. He had committed the greatest sin of all against God.

Enos arrived and left his horse in the barn to chew on a bucket of oats. Inside the house he found the kerosene lamp still lit on the kitchen table. Clare had left it there for him so he would not come home to a dark house. But there was no way she could know of the darkness inside him, he figured. Could what lay above him in the bedroom with Clare be a greater sin than what he had already done? He didn't know, but he was drawn as with an invisible force.

With bated breath, Enos tiptoed upstairs and pushed open the door to her bedroom. He whispered towards the moonlight form on the bed, "I killed someone."

There was only silence. Enos moved closer to push aside the drapes over the window. The moonlight poured in and she stirred on the bed but said nothing. This was forbidden to him, Enos told himself, as he lifted the covers. He waited and couldn't move. He had sinned greatly tonight, but there was no reason to add further to his transgression. This was not necessary.

His hands grew cold as he draped the covers over her again. He had reached the door of the bedroom when her voice stopped him. "You're welcome to stay, Enos. You don't have to be afraid."

He didn't answer, but slipped out into the hallway and down the stairs to settle on the couch. It was a long time before he dropped off to sleep.

Chapter Twenty-One

Regina slowed for the speed limit as she approached the little burg of Puckett, then turned north on the side road. The thick trees that lined the road rushed past as she accelerated. Sharp curves brought her foot only slightly off the gas pedal.

At the Holiday Lake sign she turned again and let the professor's gray Porsche have a little of its head. The car sprang forward for all of three minutes before the next sharp curve came up. Regina braked, and the car hugged the blacktop like a leopard on the last dash before the kill. She laughed aloud, then slowed and turned into a driveway without the use of the signal. Not that anyone was around, but why advertise one's intentions?

The Porsche bounced over the ruts in the grassy driveway. Its bottom scraped at regular intervals until the lane began to climb. Close to the house door, Regina stopped and climbed out. She knocked twice, then stepped back.

"I've come for Mrs. Nellie Brown," Regina told the man who opened the door.

"She's ready." The man motioned for her to enter.

Regina followed, and he soon arrived at the back bedroom. The windows were draped in dark cloth, and the ceiling fan ran at a slow cycle. Its blades creaked in low groans.

"Hi." Regina smiled at the older woman.

"I'm so thankful you could come." Nellie tried to climb out of bed. Regina got on one side, the man on the other. They lifted the woman gently to her feet.

"It was the least they could do." The man's voice was sharp.

"Really." Regina paused. "I don't know exactly what's going on. I'm just the taxi on this job."

"Sorry." The man's face softened. "I didn't mean to sound ungrateful, but Mom's been through a lot."

"You should have taken the vaccination," Regina said, and watched his face.

"Right . . . . " The man attempted a smile. "I guess it's no good to say she did."

"The hospital takes special cases," Regina told him. "Don't you want to try their good graces?"

"I'm afraid Mom didn't vote correctly in the last election." The man shook his head. "Neither did I. We tried the hospital but they turned us away. But I suppose you knew all of that?"

"I didn't." Regina forced a laugh. "Sorry."

The man joined in, the sound hollow. "I'd go down and change the situation, but I don't think it would do any good. My friend from work tried it, but they said late converts weren't welcome, that the slots were already full. They told him to try and straighten things up at the next election. But you know that doesn't work. We'll all be dead by then."

Regina supported Nellie while her son opened the door. Together they helped her into the front seat of the car.

"Thanks a lot." The man shifted on his feet beside the car. "We appreciate it."

Regina nodded. She turned the car around to drive back down the lane. The Porsche took the bumps and cradled them as if they rode on pillows.

Regina still asked. "Are you doing okay? I'm not jostling you too much?"

"I'm fine." Nellie appeared in a stupor. "Are you really taking me where I can get better?"

"Of course." Regina tried a smile.

Nellie didn't look convinced. "For some reason I'm worried. I did try hard to get better on my own, but nothing worked. Brandon has connections at the college with some secret group he says. I thought it was a joke at first, but now you're here."

"No, it's the real thing." Regina nodded. "I took a man there the other day and dropped him off. I think he's doing better."

"Okay." Nellie seemed to settle down. "So where do we go from here?"

"If I told you, it wouldn't be secret anymore, would it?" Regina smiled.

Nellie stared at her for a moment before she seemed to space out. Apparently the woman had lost interest in the question. Regina glanced at her watch and a look of concern crossed her face. She needed to get back before too late. She accelerated and headed back towards the four-lane.

What were the professor and his people up to? It was too late to ask now that she drove his car. Thankfully Travis hadn't shown up last night to complicate things further, but when he did find out about this little jaunt of hers, he wouldn't he happy. Regina sighed. She already knew that, and she still continued with her own plans. Hopefully Travis had done his worst. She would resist him from now on, and eventually he would get the message. That was the best way out of their relationship, she figured. A public ruckus with Travis would help no one.

"Where are we going?" Nellie interrupted her thoughts.

Regina glanced over towards the woman. "Could you please stop asking, because I can't tell you."

"You can't tell me?" Nellie sat up straight.

"Don't worry." Regina smiled over at her. "It's a place close to Puckett, that's all."

Nellie's eyes got big. "There is no help for me in Puckett. You're going to kill me, aren't you? You're one of them."

Regina forced a laugh. "Now why would I do such a thing to a lovely lady like you? I could have left you alone in that house if I wanted you to die."

Nellie's eyes bulged. "How do I know how people's twisted minds work?"

"Just try to calm down," Regina told her. "We'll be there soon. Would you like me to put down the windows for you?" Perhaps the smell of fresh air would soothe the woman's nerves.

"I'm not doing it." Nellie's voice was tense.

Regina shrugged. "That's fine, Nellie. Whatever makes you comfortable."

"I mean, stop right now!" Nellie hollered. "I'm getting out of this car."

"What!" Regina lifted her gaze from the road to find the short stubby nose of some sort of pocket pistol close to her ribs. Where had the woman gotten hold of such a thing?

"Put it down. I'm your friend." Regina allowed her frustration to come through.

"I'll use it." Nellie shook the gun. "I swear I'll use it, if you don't take me back home."

Regina met Nellie's eyes. "I'm not going to hurt you."

"Take me home then. Like right now."

"Okay." Regina threw up her hands. "I'll take you back home."

Regina slowed down and pulled into what looked like a hunter's lane. The trees rose high above their heads. Where had this crazy woman gotten her gun? Or for that matter, why was she even out here driving her around? She stopped and put the Porsche in reverse. Her foot slipped and the engine roared. The tires spun on the loose leaves.

"That's better," Nellie said, but she didn't lower the gun.

Regina swung the car out on the blacktop and shifted into first. As the car accelerated back towards Nellie's place, her eye caught the fast approach of a vehicle in the rearview mirror. She slowed down, and Nellie stuck the pistol into the base of her neck.

"Keep going," Nellie hissed.

"Just put the gun down," Regina told her. "There's a car coming up behind us, and I don't like the looks of him."

Nellie laughed. "You won't trick me so easily. That's really, really lame. A car behind us — is that what you're afraid of? Well, I can tell you what I'm afraid of — that's you."

"I hope you're right," Regina muttered, her eyes on the rearview mirror. The dark blue sports car behind them made no effort to pass, and moments later its blue and red lights blossomed on the car's dash.

Nellie only grunted.

"Put the gun down," Regina yelled. She made no attempt to hide her anger.

"You're taking me home," Nellie said from between clenched teeth.

What was the use, Regina thought. The woman was frightened out of her senses. Talk would do no good, but she had to try.

"There's someone behind us." Regina tried a calmer voice. "Just look for yourself."

"I'm not falling for such a simple trick," Nellie snapped. "If I look back, the next thing I know my brains will be going out the back window."

"Then look in the rearview mirror!" Regina shouted.

"I will do no such thing." Nellie menaced with her weapon. "Now take me home."

"Have it your way." Regina sighed. "If we get out of this, you certainly won't have yourself to thank. Some people couldn't help themselves if they tried, but never mind. Just don't pull the trigger on that stupid gun of yours. Where did you get it anyway?"

"That's none of your business," Nellie spat out. "If we don't protect ourselves … who will?"

"I will," Regina muttered. "If it's not already too late."

"What are you muttering about?" Nellie demanded. "Just get me home."

"Sorry, my little dear." Regina stomped hard on the gas, and the Porsche took off like a rocket.

"Stop," Nellie screamed, her eyes wild, but the gun shifted off Regina's neck.

With one hand on the wheel, Regina slapped the gun further backwards. The report of the shot was solid inside the car, and the bullet left through the open back window with a blast of air.

"You stupid woman ... you!" Regina jerked the gun out of Nellie's hands and shoved it under her seat. A glance in the mirror showed the blue sports car tight on her tail. She took the next sharp curve with both hands and felt her way through it.

"You're going to kill me!" Nellie wailed.

"I'm trying to save you, now shut your mouth," Regina hollered.

"Slow down!" Nellie screamed. "Take me back home!"

Regina ignored her and accelerated again. A yellow sign flashed by. It proclaimed the curve must be taken at thirty-five miles an hour. She made the turn doing well over sixty, but the Porsche never faltered.

Regina took the next side road, uncertain where it led but liking the open stretch that cut through the trees. Minutes later the curves were back with quick turns leading to a little bridge in the hollow whose metal railing rattled as she crossed. The trees thickened and the curves got worse. Behind her the blue car still followed.

"We might as well have this out," Regina muttered. "I hope the professor still likes me when he picks the pieces of his car out of the woods."

"Stop!" Nellie screamed.

At the next curve, the Porsche slid sideways. Regina shook her head and took the next curve at even greater speed.

"If we get stopped, just tell him the truth," Regina told Nellie. "Remember that. I'm taking you to get medicine for your illness. Show him your vaccination card, and we'll be okay."

Nellie said nothing, but her lips trembled.

Regina watched her rearview mirror as the distance increased between the two cars. The officer had just made the last curve as she took the next one. The Porsche slide sideways again. She turned at the next side road and again increased her speed. For the next few minutes she slowed only for the curves, first left, then right, until she was sure she had lost him.

Lester would be proud of her if he ever learned how she drove — though she hoped he never would. She didn't dare turn south, so Regina headed straight north towards the next distant state road. It would take more time, but even if she had to go as far around as Lynchburg she couldn't risk being seen by more police. A reckless driving ticket would be one thing, flight from an arresting officer quite another.

"I want to go home," Nellie moaned.

"I'm certainly not doing that," Regina snapped. She tossed the pistol out of her open side widow and watched the weapon bounce among the trees. "That was a very stupid thing for you to do." But so was what she was did. It was all stupid and dangerous.

"God help us, please," Regina whispered. "Because I don't know what in the world I have gotten myself into."

Chapter Twenty-Two

Regina drove east on 460 and kept her eyes on the rearview mirror. Nellie's head lay over the back of the seat with her eyelids closed. Regina had looped around before she reached the north state road 60, and had found 460 again by a southern route on the back roads. If Nellie made any more problems, she would stop the car, roll the woman out into the ditch, and drive off. Let Nellie handle that situation. The insanity of it all, she thought. To shoot off a pistol inside the car. Nellie could have killed someone.

She ought to pull over right now, call the police herself and tell them the whole story. So why didn't she? But that answer was easy enough. Because of what had happened already, she figured. The stories she had heard sobered her — Frank's tales of average citizens driven to choose their own deaths in converted prison yards, the professor's claim the government was behind the bombings in Farmstead, and multiple claims that government vaccines caused the illness they were supposed to prevent. The trouble was, the wild stories sounded more and more believable.

She had seen fear that drove a man to choose death along with his child rather than continue with life. And if that wasn't enough, she'd seen a dark-skinned man brought down with the officer's pistol only to be told by both Travis and the papers that it was a white militia conspiracy. From the looks of things, Travis must be in on the evil at least in their town.

She could take Nellie back home, but that wouldn't be nice or very Christian. Like being nice was of much value any more, but it felt good at least, a strand of the old life to hang on to. Before long there would be no room in this torn and broken world for people who cared.

"We're coming up on the place." Regina reached over to prod the woman.

Nellie's eyes snapped open to look around. "We are stopping at an Amish farm," she croaked.

"Don't go bonkers on me again, please." Regina pulled into the driveway. A buggy sat out by the barn, its shafts pointed towards the barn.

"I guess you weren't trying to kill me," Nellie muttered. "I know the Amish would never hurt anyone."

"I hope someone can help your sick mind." Regina got out to open the car door.

"Did I really shoot in your car?" Nellie asked as she climbed out and stood with her hand on the car hood.

Regina offered her no further help. "Yes, you did, and the sin is on your hands, not mine."

"I'm sorry." Nellie looked mournful. "I shouldn't have done it."

"Just come." Regina motioned towards the front door. Nellie followed her on the walk across the yard. The same Amish woman answered the door and welcomed them with a smile.

"Hi," Regina said. "The professor sent me again."

"I know." The woman held out her hand. "I'll take her from here."

"Ah," Regina cleared her throat. "What happened with Frank? Did he get well?"

"Sure, he's already gone." The woman still smiled. Nellie hobbled inside, and Regina stepped back. The woman closed the door, her hand on Nellie's arm.

Regina took a deep breath and walked back towards the car. The woman was cool under her smile. And where was the Amish man? The one who claimed the woman wasn't his wife? Perhaps she should check up on him.

Regina pushed open the barn door and looked around the dim interior. There seemed to be no one around, but the man had to be somewhere. Amish men didn't leave with their buggies parked in front of the barn. As if in answer to her questions a bale of hay slide down a wooden chute to land on the barn floor. Men's work shoes soon followed, and the Amish man appeared. He dusted off his clothing, but bits of hay still stuck in his hat.

"Hello." He appeared surprised.

"Good morning." She smiled. His eyes seemed clear today.

"Aren't you the pastor woman from the other week?" He regarded her with a steady gaze.

"Yes, I am. How are you doing?"

"Okay, I guess." He didn't sound too convincing.

Regina smiled again. "Doing as well as one can with the whole world gone mad, I suppose. I have to say I'm sick and tired of all this killing."

A look of fear rose in his eyes.

"Have you killed anyone yet?" she teased, and wished at once she hadn't.

The fear flamed on his face. "I'm afraid I have, and that my soul will be forever damned."

"So what happened?" Regina stepped closer.

He gazed at the shadows on the barn ceiling. "A man was with Marilyn, one of our young girls. He had broken into their home, and he pulled a knife when I approached, so I killed him."

"You did what?" Her voice sounded more startled then she intended.

"He was on her," he intoned. "Like it must have been for Rosemary. And I couldn't stop myself."

She reached out to touch his arm. "That sounds like self defense to me."

"Sit." He motioned with his hand.

She lowered herself on the fallen hay bale and he walked around the corner of the manger to come back with another one. He bounced it on the floor and sat down. "I have sinned greatly."

Regina ignored the remark. "You said your name was Enos?"

"It is." His mouth worked silently for a moment. "But what does that matter?"

She shrugged. "I just wanted to make sure. Who we are is important. I'm Regina."

He looked away. "I only know you as *the preacher*."

"That's not funny." She made a face. "Why does that bother you so much?"

His face was expressionless. "You do not understand the faith I come from. Women do not preach, and men do not kill."

Regina chuckled. "That's quite a list."

He nodded. "It's longer than that, but those are two of the big ones."

She raised her hands. "Then we are different. Is there anything wrong with that?"

He gave her a quick glance. "I see that you understand, and *yah*, that's okay."

"Thanks." Regina forced a smile. "Should we talk about something else?"

He thought for a moment. "Perhaps. But the killing seems to be all I think about. I am glad I could say this much about the matter. I cannot speak with her about the condition of my soul." His gaze drifted towards the house.

What was she to say? Regina wondered.

Enos stared towards the barn ceiling. His voice was cold. "The world has become a crazy place. There is so much changing, and there seems no place to escape. Perhaps to the grave, but who wishes to go there?"

Regina leaned forward. "What do you think is happening with the world?" But how would he have an opinion on that subject? The Amish were pretty much locked away from it all, confined to buggies and barns.

He didn't hesitate. "I think it will end very badly. Many more of my people will die."

Surprise showed on her face. "Has someone told you this?"

"No one tells me much of anything." He winced. "But it may be because nobody knows. They are all afraid in their hearts."

"Are you afraid?" She regarded him with a steady gaze.

"Only for my soul." He set his face. "But I will do what needs to be done. That has been decided for me."

She pulled back. "Have you been talking with God?" Was Enos some crazy self-professed prophet perhaps? Was that how she found herself on a hay bale beside an unknown Amish man?

He dropped his head. "I do not even pray anymore. My heart is too dark. But I cannot but know and follow what seems best."

Regina took a deep breath. "And this is all because you killed the man in self defense?"

He nodded. "And because I hate."

He definitely was no self-professed prophet, Regina decided. Traumatized perhaps by what had happened. In spite of his strange words, there was a clear-eyed honesty and strength about him.

"Let's not talk about killing anymore." She shifted on the hay bale.

He cleared his throat. "The darkness in my heart is driven away by your goodness."

She ignored the comment. "Who was Rosemary?"

His eyes became troubled. "She was the one promised to me. The one with whom I was to say the sacred vows. But she is dead now. I buried her in the graveyard."

"And you did it all by yourself?"

"The bishop and some of the others came," he said. "The

women washed her body, and that of her parents. Some of the men helped me dig the grave, and I helped place Rosemary in the grave myself." The tears now ran down his cheeks, and he made no attempt to wipe them away.

"I am sorry for your loss." She reached over to touch his arm. "I really am."

"There is worse coming." He was distant again. "And we must be ready. We must even be ready to kill, if necessary."

"I don't know about that." She rose to her feet. "I was hoping things would get better."

"Only God knows for sure." He still sat on the bale of hay. "Are you leaving now?"

"I really have to get back. I'm already late."

"Are you an angel?" He looked like he wanted an angel. "Have you come to cleanse my heart of sin?"

She laughed, "I'm afraid not. I might be a pastor, but no angel."

"It feels like an angel has been here." He touched his chest. "Because I have sinned greatly."

She bent over to stroke his arm. "You should stop feeling guilty about defending the girl. Didn't the police let you off? They must have or you wouldn't be here."

His eyes were on the barn floor again.

She took his silence for the affirmative. "I've got to be going. By the way, did Frank actually get well? The woman in the house said so, but I wanted to ask you."

"He did. Frank left a week after you brought him here."

"That's good to hear." She moved towards the barn door. "Take care."

"Only God can really help us." His voice followed her.

"That's always true." She paused at the door. "It's just that we don't know it, or forget it. Perhaps that's the lesson we are supposed to learn during these hard times."

"It may be." He shrugged. "God has His own ways of doing things."

She left him on the bale, and his gaze followed her as she went out the barn door.

The man surely didn't think she was an angel. It must have been a figure of speech he used. And yet it felt good, being thought of as an angel. Her presence had obviously affected him for the better. He was troubled but still a marvel. Honesty was a beautiful thing, Regina thought, and confession. She climbed into the Porsche and pulled out of the driveway. There ought to be more men in the world like the Amish man Enos. He comforted her heart with his wholesomeness.

Chapter Twenty-Three

Clare had supper ready — a meat casserole of some sort — and Enos sat to eat with her. The new woman, Nellie, was in the living room. She sipped on a glass of orange juice.

"So how did your day go working in the barn?" Clare glanced in his direction.

"Okay." Enos didn't meet her gaze.

He had seen her last night under the covers, and the thought was almost more than he could bear. He wished she wouldn't sit so near to him, but Clare was not to blame. Was this how it would be when one was married? Enos wondered. Did the hands and the eyes know things that you could not speak of around the supper table?

"There's a buggy pulling in the driveway." Clare broke his thoughts as she got up. "Someone must need the medicine."

Enos followed her gaze out the kitchen window but said nothing. He didn't trust his voice.

Clare rambled on. "I wonder why they would come here to this house? I told Joe to tell your bishop about the change. I thought with the extra traffic, it would be better this way. But Joe doesn't do anything fast."

"I will speak with them." Enos stood to his feet. "If they want the medicine, I will send them in." He rushed out.

"But your supper will get cold," Clare hollered after him.

"I don't mind eating cold casserole," Enos hollered over his shoulder as he went out by the washroom door.

The low lights were still on as Enos approached the buggy. Whoever this was did not plan to stay long, or they would have climbed down and tied their horse. Enos ran his hand through his hair. His hat was still inside. He had forgotten it in his rush to leave his memories of Clare behind.

Enos stopped short. A man did not go outside without his hat even in the dark. Had he already lost all of the old ways? Had he allowed everything to slip through his fingers when he killed? Enos sighed. At least he had not slept with Clare. Was there not some comfort in that fact? Enos shook his head and continued on.

"Good evening," Enos spoke to the darkened buggy door.

"Good evening," Bishop Mast's voice replied. One of the bishop's black rubber boots reached down for the step. The man lowered himself to the ground and leaned against the buggy wheel.

"I did not know who you were." Enos ran his hand through his hair again. "Or I wouldn't have come out without my hat on."

"Were you eating supper?" Bishop Mast looked at him sharply.

"Yes." Did the Bishop know that Clare lived in the house? Enos glanced behind him and saw the shadow of Clare's form pass in front of the living room window. Now the bishop would certainly know someone was in the house.

"You have someone living with you?" The bishop had followed his gaze. "Is this one of your family helping with the farm?"

"No." Enos added nothing else. Hopefully the bishop would leave the subject alone.

"Your father has been over to speak with me." The bishop looked away.

"I suppose he has?" Enos jerked his head up.

"Yes. And your father is greatly troubled over the matter the other evening — as we all are, when you forced a man out of Mose's house using your own strength."

"But he was trying to molest Marilyn," Enos protested,

"like they did Rosemary. I cannot but hate, even if it condemns my soul."

"That is what your father said was happening, but there are worse things than suffering for your faith, Enos. We must all learn to lay aside our natural desires and seek the will of God. There is never a right time to kill a man."

Enos took a deep breath. "I will not hide this from you. Darkness has entered my soul since Rosemary died. I will kill those who took her away. It is something I cannot help."

"But those men are dead." The bishop grabbed his arm. "Why do you need to hate them, Enos? This only harms you."

Enos lifted his head so that the dim light of the buggy shone on his face. "I suppose you are right, but there are others who are just as bad. One of them was with Marilyn the other night, and I cannot but use my hand against them."

"But you are killing." The bishop clutched Enos's arm. "You—a man who was born among us."

"Yes," Enos agreed. "I know, and you must do with me what you wish."

"I have never heard of such a thing." The bishop stared off into the darkness. "Not since the days when our forefathers took up the sacred vows of the faith has one of our own killed."

"I do not explain myself well," Enos said. "Nor do I know why my heart has grown dark, but it has. I am at war with evil men."

Bishop Mast focused on Enos. "Did not your mother wish you to keep the narrow path?"

Enos remained silent.

The bishop continued. "I know this is true. Your father told me so. He used it as a reason for his own stubbornness in not taking the medicine from the *English*. Listen Enos, you will never see your mother again if you do not repent at once and make your confession in church."

"I cannot!" Enos's voice was clipped.

"That is no way for you to speak, Enos." The bishop stepped closer.

Enos looked at the ground. "I do not say you are wrong. I only know that the sickness may be over for us— now that everyone has taken the medicine — but there are greater dangers coming. The roads will soon be too dangerous for our people to travel on. I cannot turn back now."

Bishop Mast's face was grim in the low lights of the buggy. "Have you lost your head, Enos? Are you a prophet now, that you know the future? How can that be with darkness in your heart?"

"I do not know." Enos hung his head. "I do not try to explain these things."

"Your father and I have made our peace, and so I will have to deal with you." The bishop stepped back. "I believe you understand that. It is the least I can do to respect your father's wishes."

"I am sorry it has come to this." Enos met the bishop's gaze.

The bishop hadn't given up yet. "Then you will not return home at once and make confessions for this?"

Enos kept his voice to a whisper. "When this is over, my heart may be too black to ever return."

The bishop climbed back into his buggy. "Then you are no longer one of us, Enos. I will tell your father at once, and we will cleave the darkness from the light as the Holy Scriptures instruct. In the days past more time would have been taken with you, Enos. But now we cannot."

"I am sorry," Enos muttered. "I know I have fallen low."

"Then repent." The bishop waited.

Enos shook his head and the bishop continued. "Then I must say what I have to say. Enos, you have been a much trusted brother in the community, but no longer is it so. Even the greatest trees can fall in the forest and yours has been a mighty fall. Until you repent to me, or to one of the other ministers, and give proof of a complete change in your life, you are out. Out, Enos. Outside of God and outside of the Church. I give you over to the devil for the destruction of the flesh, until you repent. Do you think your mother desired such a thing on her death bed?"

"I buried her," Enos groaned. "I know she desired no such thing."

"And yet you go on in your darkness?"

"Until the light finds me again, I do," Enos said. "I cannot help myself."

"Every man can help himself — if he takes hold of the tree of life," the bishop said. "Take a hold, Enos; pull yourself back from where you have gone. It is a terrible thing you have done, this taking the life of a man. But remember that my door is always open to you."

"It is best that you go now." Enos pushed the buggy door shut on the bishop. He took the halter of the horse and turned him around. He slapped the horse on the rump with his hand. The animal jumped and ran at a trot out the driveway and onto the road. Enos stood aside to watch. He waited to walk back towards the house until the lights of the buggy had grown dim.

They would all know now what he had done, he thought. They would always know. Even if he came back when this was over, they would still know. They would look at him and know he had killed with his hands. He was a traitor to his people. He was a man who had broken the holiest commandment of all.

A horrible darkness rushed over him so that he choked for breath. Would *The Lord* smite him now, right where he stood? There would be no hope for him if he died here, shorn of the blessing of *The Lord* and of *The Church*. He had been cast out by the bishop himself, condemned to walk alone among the wolves of the world, until such a time he was cleansed.

Enos stumbled toward the house.

Clare met him at the door in her nightgown and peered into his shadowed face. "Who was that?"

"Our bishop." His gaze swept over her.

"You still have the bishop visiting you in these times?"

"They will visit us until time ends." Enos stepped inside. "They watch for our souls."

Clare laughed. "That doesn't sound very comforting. What did the dear bishop wish to speak to you about? You sure were out there a long time. Your supper is more than cold by now. I was ready to ride out to the rescue, thinking he had kidnapped you."

"He wished to speak to me of private matters." Enos pushed on into the living room. "And I have no hunger for supper anymore."

"He must have really spoiled your appetite." Clare followed him. "You were eating well enough before he came."

Enos didn't look at her. "That cannot be helped now."

"The old woman is sleeping in the other bedroom." Clare touched his face. "I'm heading upstairs now. Did the bishop talk you out of coming up with me?"

He lifted his face. "You are beautiful and lovely, but I cannot."

A smile flitted on Clare's face. "I've never seen anything like you. But I will say no more about it."

She took the kerosene lamp and slipped up the stairs. What a fool he was, Enos told himself. This couldn't be a worse sin than what he had already done. And the bishop had thrown him out into the darkness. But he had said *no* to Rosemary's beauty. So how could he say *yes* to this? He would not dishonor her memory.

Chapter Twenty-Four

Regina tried to even her breathing as she stared at the front door of Professor Blanton's apartment. His instructions had been to keep the car until today and return it to his driveway. But he had been arrested earlier that afternoon, the girl said. On what grounds, she wondered. There obviously was no ready answer. Like there was none for so many other questions.

She left the professor's porch and drove her own car back towards town. Carefully she kept under the speed limit. As she approached downtown, the peaceful streets were bathed in soft lamp light, giving no indication of what lay ahead at the corner of Main and High. A few officers were still in front of the bombed-out Federal Building. They stood behind the yellow sawhorses, with a single searchlight spread out over the rubble. Her eye caught sight of a knot of people on the other side of the roped-off area. They must be curious onlookers, but it was a little late in the evening for that.

Regina turned right to circle around. As she turned back on to South Main, she surveyed the crowd of people. They carried signs, vaguely visible in the light of the street lamps. She hadn't seen the extent of the crowd before; it stretched halfway up the hill. Relief rushed through her. She hadn't known how much she dreaded the next face off with Travis until now. With the crowd here, he wouldn't dare pursue his violent course.

Where had they all come from? She read a sign immediately in front of her that proclaimed, *Where is the Government?*

A tall fellow, dressed in leather and black boots, carried a placard reading *Down with White Terrorism.*

The group moved out into the street and milled around. They seemed peaceful enough. Regina turned on her left turning signal, and they parted. She waved even though she did not recognize anyone, but no one waved back. Regina parked in her usual spot behind the parsonage and went in the back door. She walked to the front window for a look outside. Thankfully there were no shouts yet, so she wouldn't be disturbed even if this went on into the night.

Maybe the radio would work tonight? Little more than static and useless programs had come through last night again. The radio in hand, Regina went up the stairs and glanced out the window at the crowd below her. It was unlikely anyone could hear whatever she found on the dial, but why should it matter anyway? This was a free country, wasn't it?

She fiddled with the dial and came across static voices here and there who droned on and on in monotones. Surely someone had to be discussing real news. Maybe the agitated New Zealand man would be on a rant with news from his family in America.

Frustrated, she set the radio on the dresser and went for another look at the crowd below. The Bethesda Plaza parking lot was now half full and cars lined South Main. Vehicles were parked wherever drivers could find a spot. A man came from his pickup truck with a makeshift podium, followed by others who carried a piece of plywood. Another man pulled apart a stack of five-gallon buckets. Apparently a speech was in store for the streets, but that was understandable. The destruction of a small-town Federal Building was not a common occurrence. It was a wonder there hadn't been protests before this.

Regina returned to the soft buzz of the radio. She flipped the dial around the spot where the agitated New Zealander had been. She flinched as his wild voice in mid-paragraph broke through the static. "… New Zealand stands in calm today while much of the world lays in turmoil."

The man's voice faded out again, and she adjusted the dial. The shriek returned. "Reports of the fever plague decimating much of Europe and reaching into Russia and the Far East are all over the place here. How much of it is true, I don't know, but one is driven to believe that many of the reports are in fact true. The United States has only recently become acquainted with the savagery of the epidemic after their heroic attempts to keep the virus off shore. My family in America is surviving, staying mostly indoors. Thank God we are safe here on the islands — at least for now. Are we afraid, as they are afraid? Well, of course we are, but we must remain courageous in good and bad times. So we hope and pray for the best, and offer our prayers and concern for those who are suffering.

"The government here is enforcing strict quarantine measures as the only answer. Any and all who leave the islands are not being allowed to return. For once the oceans that separate us from the rest of the world are truly our friends. In the meantime, my contacts through email and phone calls to my family in America tell me that the government of President Doyle has moved in, placing strict controls on all radio, television, and print media. At least that is what they say. One has no absolute proof, since the news is not in the paper. But they claim things are happening that are not appearing in the papers. How much of this is their paranoia I don't know. They are citing experience with this president as their main evidence. They claim he is capable of almost anything, and that the current Congress is going along.

"Where this will lead to no one knows, or as they say, only God does. Many prayers are being offered both for ourselves and for what is happening. The news here claims the world markets are reflecting this instability and could possibly fall to their lowest levels since the crash of the great depression.

The worst is still to come, it is feared, as even our own government struggles to deal with this tragedy with very limited funds."

The man's voice continued, but Regina was distracted with shouts from outside. The parsonage had been well insulated in the remodel a few years ago, so the noise that penetrated must be much louder on the street. Apparently the demonstrators had begun to broadcast speeches, from the sound of it. Regina walked over to the window and glanced out.

The police were at the government building, now in a solid line, and the chanting crowd spread across the Bethesda parking lot. Regina returned to the radio to catch the tail end of the sentence.

"... being used for this nasty work. I have my own feelings on this matter. I believe this is all with full government approval at the highest levels. Mr. Doyle's administration is using the emergency provisions in many of the health care bills passed by Congress a few years ago to deal with this epidemic. And worse news lies ahead, I'm afraid. Rumbles have been heard here for weeks already about the world financial situation. Governments in both Europe and America are struggling to deal with the monstrosity of their public debt.

"The American deficit is now unimaginable with no end in sight. China has abandoned its slow approach to divesting from the dollar and is dumping green backs by the billions. If that is not panic, then it will come soon."

Regina flipped off the dial. The man was clearly on a rant again tonight. Some of it made sense — way too much sense – but nothing could be done about it anyway. Lester's news at the restaurant the other night had been just as serious an accusation. Regina took the stairs of the old parsonage two steps at a time, the sounds from outside even louder now. In the living room she kept the light turned off and hesitated for a moment. A quick glance out the front window showed a speaker on an elevated platform in the middle of a fiery speech. His listeners shouted back and pumped the air with their fists.

Regina opened the front door to step out on the porch where she paused to listen.

"I tell you," the speaker roared, "how are we to put up with this any longer? Have not our children suffered enough? Have not our people been oppressed long enough? Have we not been afraid of the night long enough? And now they would bomb us in our heart and in our soul, setting off their terror right next to our churches. Haven't we the Baptist Church directly across the street, a black church, the very church where the Reverend Martin Luther King spoke?

"And haven't we here behind us the AME church? Do any of you actually believe this is all an accident? I tell you, it is no accident. And I say this is enough. We have seen enough blood, enough terror, enough fear in the night. It is time our government did what it claims to do. Protect us from destruction. It is time to take back our country from those who sow only discord and fear."

"The Reverend is out on the porch," someone in the crowd shouted. "Let us hear from her."

The speaker paused to look towards the parsonage and wave his hand. "Why yes, come on down here Reverend Owens. Let us hear from you about the events of the last few days."

Should she disappear back inside? No, it was too late now, and someone would only follow to urge her back out again. There was nothing to do but move towards the podium. As Regina walked off the steps the crowd parted. They were men and women with fright in their eyes and alarm written on their faces. Regina nodded to those she knew and tried to still the rapid beat of her heart. What in the world was she supposed to say?

Chapter Twenty-Five

The round street lamps cast a hazy light as Regina mounted the steps of the flimsy platform. She felt the plywood give way under the pressure of her feet. The squeak of wood on plastic was audible over the cries behind her.

"Speak up there, Reverend," a man yelled.

A woman's voice added, "No more white power … no more ever again …."

The roar of the crowd drowned out any other noise.

"The Revered Owens from the AME church will now address us." The moderator turned over the microphone.

Thankfully it was dark and the fear on her face didn't show as much.

"Let's hear it," the distinct voice of Travis thundered from the edges of the crowd. So this was what Travis had occupied his time with lately. No wonder she had seen so little of him. Regina took a deep breath. She might as well plunge in. "There was a grave injustice done to this town," Regina began.

"Louder," the moderator whispered from beside her. "They can't hear you."

"Someone is failing us," Regina hollered. Wasn't that true? The crowd roared its approval.

"What is happening to our country?" Regina kept her voice at full volume. "How can there be justice in the land when the sick and dying are no longer treated? How can there be freedom when the buildings of our towns are bombed out in front of our eyes? Where was justice when men died here in the explosion? Where is the protection of the police force when there is danger?"

The moderator motioned for her to move aside and screamed into the microphone: "I say it was because the white man got his way again. That's what I say, and it's enough. It's enough, I say."

"Enough," the crowd yelled back.

Regina saw the officers across the street speak into their microphones. They shuffled on their feet, but they stayed on the sidewalk.

"I say we take the fight back to them," the moderator yelled. "I say we take it back to their places of business, back to their schools, back to the streets of our town, back into the homes of those responsible for this."

"Fight back! Fight back! Fight back!" The chant grew louder and soon changed to the rhythmic flow of "Fight back now … fight back now … fight back now."

Regina saw two police cruisers pull up from South Main and another from the street behind the college. They pulled to a stop, but no one got out.

"I say we take the fight right back to them white folks," the moderator continued while Regina flinched. Things didn't look good.

"Now!" The crowd roared. "Now! Take the fight back now!"

"Let's go," the moderator said and waved with his arms towards downtown. "Let's make our voices heard tonight. We are tired of discrimination, tired of oppression, tired of second place, tired of being told we can't be protected."

She had to move or the opportunity would be gone. Regina grabbed the microphone back. "Hello, hello," she yelled. The silence started at the front of the crowd and moved to the back. She had one chance and one chance only.

"I have a better plan," Regina said. "It's late and we have seen enough upheaval in this town today. Let's not risk our passions and be led into temptation. As the Lord told the devil, man must not tempt *The Lord God*. He is on our side, but let us return tomorrow, gather in front of the police station, and there, in the light of day, express our grievances. Isn't that a much better plan?"

"What about justice?" a voice called out.

"We shall have justice. I will come myself tomorrow to be with you. I promise ... but tonight let's go back home and allow our emotions to cool."

"Cool down," the moderator yelled beside her. "Give me that mic back."

Regina held the microphone away from him and blocked his forward movement with her body.

"They'll blow us all up by the morning," someone yelled, and the words were echoed in the crowd. "We want justice tonight."

"We are not the aggressors," Regina shouted into the microphone. She noticed the size of the crowd had grown considerably in the back. "Remember Dr. King. Dr. King did not choose the path of violence, and neither should we. There is justice to be had without destruction. We can all go home tonight and return tomorrow. We can then go down to the proper authorities, and our concerns will be heard."

The moderator grabbed her arm, and Regina lost control of the mic.

"I say we go downtown tonight," the moderator hollered. Here and there Regina saw heads that shook no.

"You turned them against me," the moderator whispered, his microphone held at arm's length. "I expected better things from you."

"I expected better things from *you*," Regina retorted.

"Tonight ... we march for justice," the moderator tried again, but the damage had been done.

"You had to bring in Dr. King's name," the moderator said as he glared at her.

"I guess I know what works." Regina cut off her smile as Travis approached the platform. He had to force his way through the crowd. He would not be a pleasant man to face at the moment, but Regina stepped forward to meet him. The dressing down or worse would be easier to take where the others couldn't hear as well.

The concussion behind her thrust her forward. She stumbled and felt the plywood slip under her feet. Travis, at the edge of the platform, turned his face with a look of complete horror.

Regina regained her balance and looked up to see a ball of fire burst out of the back of the Baptist church. It hurtled skywards to hang for a long moment above the tree line before it fell back to earth.

The crowd stood transfixed with eyes turned upward. The very sky seemed to burn. Then fiery cinders rained down and lit many of those who stood nearest the building. Men and women slapped wildly at their clothes. Regina rubbed the loud ring in her ears.

"So you want to back down now?" The moderator bellowed above the din. "They are bombing us openly!"

"Wait for the police," Regina cried, but she had no microphone and the sound was drowned out by the angry cry of the crowd.

Driven as if by the wind the crowd surged forward. Two police cruisers came down from High Street and officers were deployed on the other side of the yellow sawhorses. Regina stayed on the platform as the people ran past. The fire at the end of the church exploded again, the flames not quite as high this time. In the distance she heard sirens and the blast horns of fire trucks.

"We'll take them out before our incompetent government can arrive," a man shouted.

The yellow sawhorses in front of the bombed-out federal building tumbled sideways, the tape torn to bits by the rush of the crowd. Bravely the officers on top of the hill stood their ground. They swung their short night sticks and shouted in fear more than fury.

"Out of our way. Out of our way. It's not your war," someone in the front line hollered, and the officers scattered to the sidewalk at the last minute as the mass of people swept by.

"Is this what you wanted?" Regina asked the moderator. She turned towards him, but he was gone.

"He's not here," Travis said, seated on the edge of the platform. "I think he joined the stampede."

"Is this what you wanted?" Regina asked him. "Is that why you were going to chew me out?"

"You don't see me running after them ... do you?"

"Then you should have done something to stop it. You knew what was going to happen."

"Don't worry," Travis said. "It doesn't matter. There are plenty of white folks mixed in there. This is not just a black problem. Let them vent their anger ... it will do them good."

"I didn't say anything about white or black," Regina told him. "Why didn't you stop them? You could have spoken up ...."

"I couldn't have even if I had tried," Travis said, sober faced. "You know that ... don't you? Not after that church blew up. Only God can stop them now."

From the street above them came the sound of breaking glass, followed by angry cries of "No more oppression ... no more ... no more ever again ...."

The fire trucks screamed around the corner of High and Main, their horns blaring, and took up positions on either side of the church. Men ran from the trucks like shadows in the glare of the fire to attach hoses to fire hydrants.

With a roar a ladder truck on the Bethesda Plaza side began to extend itself. More cruisers came from south of town. Their lights added weird blasts of color to the night sky. They turned right and gathered below the church. Officers jumped out to bark into their microphones, then milled around as if uncertain of themselves.

"I'm getting myself over to the parsonage," Regina said. "They might get it into their heads to sweep every black man off the streets."

"Not likely," Travis muttered.

His voice sounded tender, she thought, as he walked with her to the porch. But he surely didn't plan to come inside while this ruckus went on in the streets. Still he might, and she had best forestall him. "You know something I don't." Regina studied Travis's face in the street lamp light, as the fire from the church cast crazy shadows on the parsonage wall.

"Nothing more than you do." Regina saw the glint in his eyes as he looked towards downtown. The man lied.

"I'm not going to stay here." Regina moved forward even though Travis stood right in front of her.

"I wouldn't go." Travis blocked her on the parsonage steps. "Just let this thing run its own course. It's best that way."

Regina slipped past him, and he made no effort to grab her. She was already in a fast run past the bombed-out federal building. She avoided a block of concrete on the sidewalk and moved out into the street. A quick glance backwards showed no headlights, so she ran in the middle of the road.

The first office building she came to had the glass front broken out and faint forms dashed about inside. Regina stepped closer and waited for her eyes to adjust. "Don't do this," she hollered into the shadowy darkness at the vandals.

"Just shut up," a man's voice answered, followed by a loud crash. "Leave the brothers in peace. Tonight is our night to show them what justice is. At least we won't burn the place."

An object flew through the air and landed with a crash as sparks flew off the walls.

"Watch it there," a voice laughed. "Wait to burn this place until I'm out of here."

"This is not the way to settle scores," Regina hollered again. "You've got to stop it."

"Maybe I will burn down the place ... if the sister won't shut up," the voice taunted her.

"This is not Dr. King's way," Regina said. Surely there had to be some way to reason with them.

A form came towards her, its face mere inches from her own.

"Do I look like I need lectures from you?" The man's eyes glimmered in the street light. "I say we do this the white man's way ... fire with fire. Isn't that better?"

Regina heard laughter from the others as they moved around her.

"Spoken like a true brother," someone said.

"This is a time for principles that transcend race," Regina responded.

They laughed again.

"Spoken like a Reverend," the first man said. "Well, practice your preaching down the street. That's what I say. Tonight is a night for action."

They jumped out through the broken glass and were gone. Their wild cries drifted down the street. When Regina stepped outside herself, flames already wrapped themselves around the wooden doors of the Farmstead Baptist Church beside the courthouse. Glass and objects from storefronts flew into the streets. Nowhere was there any sign of law enforcement. She turned with a sigh to walk wearily back towards the parsonage. The officers near the burning church turned to watch her go past but offered no resistance. The world truly had gone mad. But thankfully Travis was gone when she walked inside the parsonage. She couldn't deal with him tonight on top of everything. Tomorrow maybe, but not now.

Chapter Twenty-Six

Enos slipped off the couch in the middle of the night and found his clothing in the darkness. Restlessness stirred deep inside of him. He lit the kerosene lamp and dressed. Afterwards he walked over to the window to look out across the darkened lawn. Last evening had certainly been a low point in his life, he told himself. Maybe he should still go up to Clare's room, but he couldn't with the strong memory of Rosemary on his mind. She was like a rose that had bloomed in the spring only to be blown to pieces by a hail storm. The bishop would likely say he should resist Clare out of principle. But he had transgressed the law of God greatly when he killed a man. If Rosemary kept him from a further slide into the darkness, then he was thankful. And Clare was darkness, he was sure of that. The beauty of her body would lead nowhere else.

The tears ran down his face and he let them flow. Was this how Judas felt when he betrayed his master and sold him for thirty pieces of silver? His reward had not come close to the price of that silver. In fact, there had been no reward for the man he had killed. Rosemary could not be brought back again, and that was the only reward he wanted. Indeed, he had lost much and gained little.

He wiped the tears from his eyes and peered into the darkness. He would not think of Clare now but focus on the very real danger facing his people. Would the time to kill come again? Outside nothing moved, but he would feel better with a gun in his hand. Enos retrieved one from the closet by the front door. He clutched the cold steel as he stood by the window. Long moments later he blew out the lamp and returned to the couch, leaving the gun propped against the window frame. He undressed again, lay down, and pulled the quilt over his head. The world would never be the same, he thought as he fell asleep.

Enos slept with troubled dreams and rose while it was still dark. He stood on the front porch to look out across the fields. A glow of fire shone against the sky. It looked as if all of Farmstead was in flames. But that wasn't possible. No sirens had traveled towards Farmstead all night; he had been up and would have heard them. Did the world burn like his heart burned inside of him?

Footsteps behind him interrupted his thoughts, and Clare's voice, still heavy with sleep, whispered, "What's going on?"

"I don't know." He turned around. She was still in her night clothing, and he looked away.

She surveyed the scene outside. "I'm going over to the other house to find out. This looks serious."

"How would they know?" he asked.

"They have their ways," she told him.

Images of TVs, radios, and wires in the basement flashed though his mind. "I guess so. Shall I get the horse ready for you?"

She chuckled. "Prince Charming this morning, *hey*. Why didn't you come up last night?"

"I couldn't," he muttered. "I still remember Rosemary."

Her face said she understood, and he left her to walk across the yard. In the barn he lit the gas lantern. He whistled for his horse and patted him on the nose when he came on the run. How simple and trusting the animal's eyes were in the glow of the lantern. Not like the world he had chosen to join. Clare was not simple nor did she trust. She would be warm in bed, but his heart would still be cold. That much he knew. Perhaps he had learned this when he ran a knife into a man's body, or perhaps he had always known it?

Enos stroked the animal's neck and threw on the harness to lead him outside. There he hitched him to the buggy and held the bridle until Clare came out and climbed in.

"I'll be back to fix you breakfast," she told him. "Is that okay?"

"I can handle the food," he told her.

"Like an Amish man can find his way around the kitchen." Clare didn't wait for an answer as she slapped the reins.

He let go of the halter and watched the buggy leave. "I'm not Amish anymore," he hollered after her. There was no one around to hear, but he needed to say it. The words placed distance between him and the huge hole Bishop Mast's words had torn in his heart.

"You are no longer one of ours," the bishop had said. The words still cut like a knife. He had to get away from the pain. But how?

Enos turned to look towards Farmstead again. The flames still reached towards the sky, even higher than before. Was the whole world to burn now? Was his own soul to be consumed by literal flames before the eternal ones came? Enos shuddered and turned away.

Even now he could bring out the other horse, Enos told himself. He could ride bareback across the fields and beg Bishop Mast for forgiveness. The bishop might not give it quickly or easily, but the matter would be changed in the end. But was he sorry? That was the question. Would he not kill again? When another man stood over an Amish girl or over another man's Rosemary, would he hold back his hand and refuse to plunge in the knife or fire the gun?

Enos stared as the flames rose into the sky and wondered. This whole thing was far from over. The world had apparently only begun to burn. This was not the time to be sorry or to question the path chosen. Such moments would come later, when peace had returned to the land.

"I will not turn back," he shouted to the heavens. "What *The Lord* says about the matter is up to Him."

But what good did that do? Enos wondered. He should move on now. He was not one of them anymore. Had not the bishop said so? And it was best that way. So he must get rid of these clothes. He must find *English* ones to wear. There was much trouble ahead, and if he killed again they must not lay the blame on his people. The Amish would never lift their hands against another human being, because they were righteous, and he was not.

Enos ran back towards the house and rushed into the bathroom. He pulled off his hat and tossed it against the dresser. No more would he wear such a thing. Enos took the scissors and chopped at his hair. He cut the best he could. Afterwards he took a good look in the cracked mirror. He looked different, changed, transformed, but wasn't that the point? He stared at his reflection in the mirror. Did this man carry a dark heart inside him? Was this still Enos? It didn't look like Enos. Not since his early youth, all those many years ago, had his head been without his long hair.

Outside he heard Clare return and went out to meet her, leaving his hat behind. She gasped when she opened the buggy door and whirled about, then emerged with a gun pointed in his face.

"It's me, Enos," he shouted.

She lowered the weapon. "*My,* you know how to scare a woman. What have you been doing? You look like you went through a threshing machine."

"I am no longer Amish," he told her. "That is what the bishop said."

"They sure mess with your people's minds." Clare climbed down from the buggy. "So what am I supposed to do now? I can't live in a house with an *English* person. And you were the only real Amish person we had. If I could get my hands on that bishop, I would let him have it."

"I don't know." Enos hung his head. "I hadn't thought of that."

"Never mind, we'll think of something." Clare rushed about in circles.

"What is happening in town?" he asked as he tied the horse to the barn ring.

"They had riots in Farmstead last night. It looks like the whole downtown might be in flames."

"Are people hurt?"

"I suppose so, although I wasn't worrying about that. Joe said the stock market's crashing all over the world. That might not mean much to you, but it does to us. China and Russia have pulled out of the dollar, so our money might be worthless this morning, for all I know."

"I don't know what that means."

She turned to face him. "It means we are all in a bunch of trouble, Enos. That's what it means. It's time to tighten the hatches, so to speak. So no more giving out medicines; no more playing good guys. This is what we were getting ready for."

"I will not help you any longer as an Amish person."

"I think you've already made that clear." She waved her head at his shorn head. "That was really stupid you know. Now the authorities know exactly who to look for. No more hiding behind the Amish face."

"I will not hide anymore."

Fear flashed in her eyes. "They arrested one of our contacts at the college. You're going to wish you had that Amish hair back."

He stroked his bare face but shook his head.

"Come inside." She motioned with her hand. "God knows we're all in plenty of trouble. I'll fix you breakfast and get that awful haircut of yours straightened out, but after that I'm gone. And sorry, you can't come along. I'm going back to Joe's place, and no *English* people allowed."

"That's okay," he muttered. "I have made my choice. But you will leave me with the guns?"

"You can have all of them," she snorted. "And the ammunition. But it will take more than that — for what's coming. There will be mobs roaming the countryside before long."

"I will do for my people what I can," he said.

He would pay for his sins in some manner. He would stand guard where he could and keep away the evil men who had killed Rosemary. Bishop Mast and his father could not stop him; they would not even know who he was. He would look like the *English*, and they would not feel shame. He would not show his face but hide in the shadows.

"Whatever good deeds you have in mind, keep me out of them," she told him. "I'm making breakfast, and then you're driving both of us over to Joe's place."

He nodded and entered the barn while she walked towards the house. Inside, he sat on the hay bale again. Here the preacher woman had sat with him. She was a good person, of that he was sure. She was good like his people were good, and yet her father had gone to war. How was that possible? But it was good to think about. If she could have such a father, one who had killed, then perhaps he could also someday be good again.

Even if he never saw her again, he would always know there were *English* people who were good. She was also troubled by the condition of the world. She felt what he felt, and yet she lived in a world where they killed. Enos knelt down beside the hay bale. He lifted his head towards the barn ceiling and allowed the tears to flow. *The Lord* must have mercy upon him already, he thought, to send an angel from heaven so he would know that all was not lost.

Could there be forgiveness for his sins? For the first time in a long time his lips moved in prayer. Slowly the words formed into sound. "I have sinned greatly, Father in heaven. I don't know how to make anything right or how to stop doing what needs to be done. Rosemary is dead, and men like her killers are still out there. I cannot promise you that I will not kill again, and yet you have sent an angel to me, to show me that even though my heart is black right now, I can be good like she is good. Thank you for that. I know that Bishop Mast has thrown me out of the church, and so I am walking in a great darkness. Yet you have sent help, and I am thankful."

He got up from his knees and walked towards the house. Clare had breakfast ready for him when he entered by the washroom door.

"The guns are all in the upstairs closet," she told him. "Nellie is not eating this morning. Hurry and eat yours before we have to leave."

He said nothing but pulled up his chair.

"So have we been crying?" She stared at him.

He nodded and began to eat.

"Well, you little sweetheart." She stroked his face with her hand. "I'm sorry, but I can't stay around anymore. Poor boy, you'll find love someday, I think, even in this crazy world."

He ate and avoided her gaze.

"You're a nice man, Enos." She touched his arm. "And I'm sure your faith had better things in mind for you than me."

He shook his head and finished his food while she ate across from him. "My hair," he said when she finished.

Clare jumped up from the table and came back with the scissors. "I'm not much of a barber. But a squirrel could do better than that."

He held still while she snipped away. The hair fell all around the chair. If she didn't quit soon, there would be nothing left, he thought. His head already felt light.

"There." She stepped back. "That's done. Do you want to see yourself in the mirror?'

He shook his head. "Do you want me to carry anything out to the buggy?"

"Only my suitcase in the hallway. Nellie didn't bring anything."

He took the suitcase outside and waited until the two women came. Nellie grumbled, still a little unsteady on her feet. He offered his hand to help Nellie into the buggy. Clare climbed in after him. Enos pulled out of the driveway and allowed the horse to take its time. The skyline over Farmstead was no longer as bright, since the sun had taken away much of the glow. But great billows of smoke poured skyward.

"It'll burn for days," Clare said. "I don't think anybody's doing much about it."

"Maybe they can't do anything." He hung on to the buggy reins.

She laughed. "That wouldn't surprise me. Nobody has any money left."

He slowed down to pull into the driveway and bounced to a stop beside the barn. He jumped out to help Nellie climb down. Afterwards he carried the suitcase up to the house. Clare motioned for him to wait while she dashed into the house. She came out minutes later with a paper bag and handed it to him.

"*English* clothing," she said. "It will go with your new haircut."

"Thanks." He walked numbly back to the buggy. He really was an *English* man now, he told himself, as the blackness rolled over his soul.

Chapter Twenty-Seven

Regina walked outside again and shielded her face from the heat that came from across the street. A gust of wind stirred the smoking debris. It lifted dusty ash and smoke into the air. The ladder truck, extended out over the bombed back section of the Baptist church, disappeared in the dark billowing clouds.

Another army truck, draped in camouflage green, roared up from South Main to join the others scattered around Bethesda Plaza. The firefighters had fought until early this morning to keep the flames away from the Plaza building. The AME church had also been saved. That had been easier work, though, since the bombed-out federal building provided a greater distance for the fire to cross.

Sleep in the parsonage had been almost impossible with the racket outside and the fear that gripped the town. Regina rubbed her weary eyelids. Clearly the National Guard had been called out overnight. That must be the governor's action, but these were not local units from the marks on their vehicles. Someone must have shuffled territories, she figured, so local sympathies didn't interfere with official duties.

What had possessed the mob last night to wreak such chaos? From the looks of things, the entire length of Main Street past Third had been given up for lost. Only blackened ruins of burned-out brick buildings remained, where yesterday there had been a clean, friendly hometown street. The new courthouse stood almost alone, its sides smoke-marked but still intact.

Regina felt the tears spring to her eyes and allowed them to run freely. Where had all this hatred come from? Hatred never solved anything, and it certainly didn't help matters in this town.

Hopeful thoughts seemed like a faint dream this morning, something that would have to wait for church on Sunday. That is, if any parishioners showed up. Hatred was that way. It stole more than you bargained for.

Hearing footsteps, Regina turned to see a grim-faced Travis striding up the street. She caught her breath and took a step backwards.

"Regina." His voice was stern. "We have to talk."

He only wanted to move inside the house, she thought, the fear tight in her chest. "About what, Travis? I know it's awful what happened last night."

He sat on the parsonage steps and she let out a long breath of relief. "I'm sorry, Regina, but I was very disappointed in you. I had hoped things would never come to this, yet in a way I'm not surprised. The signs have been there for some time."

She took another deep breath. "The signs for what, Travis? Please don't talk in circles. My head hurts too much."

He glanced up at her. "Okay, then here it is, Regina. You can't go on serving at AME. Not after last night, not after the way you handled yourself, not after the things you said. I was there. I heard them myself. Otherwise I would stick up for you, but it happened, Regina."

"What happened, Travis?" She waved her hand towards downtown. "This is what happened, and I certainly had nothing to do with it. You were there, and I heard little protest out of you. What have you to say for that?"

He sighed. "Regina, you know how it is. We're all sorry for things getting a little out of hand. Perhaps I should have spoken up, but that's not the point. Some things can't be helped. Things like this. What's more important was your attitude beforehand, trying to speak over Rodney James and insulting him in front of the crowd."

"Who is Rodney? The moderator?"

"He was more than the moderator, Regina. You should know that, even if you don't know him personally."

"I thought I recognized him, but he was out of line. Encouraging the crowd in what it planned to do. And I was right, Travis. Look what happened."

"Mr. James is a Reverend, Regina. He's a high official in the Black Baptist churches. You should have known about him, Regina, and you should have known why he was here. That's the problem with you. You seem to be with us, but you're not. This can't go on any longer. Not after last night, and the Baptist church being blown up right before our eyes. Whatever Reverend James had to say last night was the right thing to say."

"You're right, Travis, this can't go on any longer. I didn't know who he was, but he was still wrong. He encouraged this." Regina pointed at the burned-out blackened section of Main Street.

"And this was not wrong?" Travis waved his arm towards the Baptist church. "I didn't bring along the morning paper, but it claims the same white militia group that bombed the government building is responsible. The destruction of downtown is a tragedy, Regina, but our anger was justified. And you were wrong disagreeing with it. You will have to leave your position, Regina. There is no choice about the matter."

"So I am not to have any chance of reconciliation, Travis? Isn't that what we are all about?"

"Don't preach to me, Regina. Are you willing to give your apologies to the people, to Reverend James? He will be speaking this Sunday. Right here at AME. Are you ready for a true reconciliation gesture, Regina? Are you ready to give up these subversive activities of yours? Associating with Professor

Blanton, who is in prison, I might mention. Can you do that, Regina?"

"Just like that, you would throw me out?"

He attempted a smile. "I have not forgotten about us Regina. If that's what you mean. And I know I was a little rough the last time I was with you, and I'm sorry. That is why this is so hard on me, and why I am offering you a way out — one without public disgrace and without having to face Reverend James again. Resign, Regina. Since you haven't answered my questions, I have assumed your answer."

"I suppose Reverend James has quite a fiery sermon prepared for Sunday. All about justice, reconciliation, and responsibility?"

"You need to be thinking about yourself, Regina." Travis leaned closer. "And about us. Think about your future, and swallow your words. You'll be much better off, even though it might hurt now."

"I'm not going to do it, and you know that."

He grimaced. "I know, Regina, but please realize that it's over for you. No black church will ever touch you again, and I'm certain the white ones won't either. Think of what your father will say when he hears. All that potential lost, gone down the river."

Regina forced back the tears. Travis's words were hurting much more than he even knew. "Just leave my father to me," she snapped. "So when do I have to be out of the parsonage?"

"I'm sorry." He touched her hand. "I really am. I wish it could be otherwise, but that choice isn't yours."

It's yours, she almost said. And all the rest of you. But she held back the words. It would do no good anyway, and would only leave them worse off than they already were. Time could heal, her father had often said, and it could heal better if one didn't cut the wound deeper than necessary.

"So what papers do I sign? Or do I walk out on the street tonight?"

"Regina, please, don't make this harder on me than it already is." He pulled a piece of paper out of his suit coat. He unfolded it and handed her a pen.

"You brought this along? You were prepared?"

"I know you better than you think, Regina. But I'm still sorry."

She scribbled her name on the bottom line and didn't meet his gaze. "So when do I have to leave?"

"You can stay until we find another pastor, but I'll have to charge you for the lights. The rent we can forgo. I think the board will go along with that."

"Thank you," she said. "That is nice of you."

A ghost of a smile played on his face. "I'll be stopping by, and you know how to get a hold of me."

She nodded, and he turned to go. She watched him walk up South Main. Thoughts raced through her mind. She should have seen this. She should have known she had gone too far. All the risks she had taken, all the things she had said. Travis and their love. She would miss him, and it was all her own fault. Or was it?

Regina placed her head in her hands and let the tears come. An engine roared somewhere across the lot, and she looked up. Not that it mattered, but any sound right now was a welcome distraction. Another army truck pulled into the plaza. She stood and turned to walk up the steps into the parsonage.

Perhaps a call to her father in Georgia would be the thing to do. Confess everything to him. Tell him what she had done. He would understand, and there might be someone he could call. Someone connected to Reverend James, who could talk him down from his high horse, because Reverend James was clearly the person behind all this. But was that the way to handle the situation? Run back to Daddy when real trouble showed up?

Regina shook her head. Somehow she needed to solve her own problems, and right now that involved her departure from the parsonage. She had to find somewhere else to live. It would be nice to find at least one person who was not involved in this trouble, someone who didn't need a lot of explanations, someone who wouldn't try to talk her out of her stand. But who in the world would that be? Lester was in jail, and Travis was no help. The church parishioners were about the limit of her personal acquaintances in town, and they had best not be compromised even if they might be sympathetic.

At home there would be Aunt Courtney and Uncle Ben, but even that would filter back around to a conversation about what her father thought. Regina sighed. Perhaps all things came back to your father, and maybe she should face him, drive down to Georgia for a good cry. But at the end of the day she still had to live her own life. Her father would see to that. He would not tolerate a girl at home who crawled under the covers and cried for months over her failures, however unjustly she had been treated.

A vision of the Amish man's face, his hat full of straw pieces, came to her mind, and Regina laughed out loud. She turned the doorknob to enter the parsonage. Now that would be a change of worlds. What a time warp.

Regina wiped away the tears and thought of Enos's honesty, his open face. Could she gain shelter with the troubled man? It was a hard question, but who would have thought the question would ever come? She? Thrown out of her job? The town burned down? Who could have told her yesterday that she would speak out at the mass gathering last night? It was a mad world, and was it any madder to desire comfort from a source where it could be found? Maybe the Amish man was mad too. Maybe he had prisoners hidden in the basement of his house, where he fattened them for slaughter in these hard times.

She laughed out loud again. Amish people were about as innocent as they came, if she remembered correctly. How else did you explain the man's guilt over his use of force to protect his sister in the faith? The poor man. He genuinely did seem tormented, and yet he could reach out and touch her heart. That was more than could be said for Travis. He was neither tormented nor able to comfort her.

She would do it. Why not? There was no one to stop her. Travis certainly wouldn't care, and if he did, that was his problem. He sure hadn't made much effort to persuade the board on her behalf.

But she couldn't simply arrive at the man's place with nothing to offer. "Could you put me up until I can find another place to stay?"

That would really fly well. It might even make an Amish man laugh. No, she would go past the grocery store, gather up some of the basic items people need to live, and after that pay a visit to the Amish man. If things didn't go well, the parsonage was always available. But what a relief it would be to get away from it all and leave the town until things settled down.

"Thank you, Lord, for that inspiration," she whispered, and rushed upstairs to pack.

Chapter Twenty-Eight

Regina drove down South Main towards Wal-Mart. She kept her eyes open for any roadblocks, but none appeared. There were only soldiers in their green camouflage uniforms who stood in the major intersections and in front of the businesses. Those she passed looked young, with weariness written on their faces as they scanned the passing cars. They must have been ordered out of bed last night and pulled away from family and spouses to patrol their own country. Yet they protected it from its own citizens. Did the world seem as crazy to them as it did to her? It didn't look like they thought so, but perhaps they were trained to hide the fact.

In the trunk one of her suitcases banged against the other as she braked for the light. She would have to situate them better at the shopping plaza. She didn't want noises in her trunk, even for the short trip to Puckett. Which raised a point — she needed gas, and Sheetz was the cheapest place for that.

Regina gasped as she drove past Wal-Mart. Soldiers lined the whole front of the huge superstore, and the parking lot was full clear out to the street. Lines of cars crept along, or attempted to get in. Well, she wasn't the only one who needed groceries. Fortunately she had all day with little to do. The Amish man didn't know she would arrive, and Travis sure didn't care where she was.

How wonderful it would be to head straight south on route fifteen, her suitcases packed in the car, and never stop until she reached the Georgia state line. Daddy would be waiting there — but life also would be waiting afterwards.

Her eye caught not only the number of soldiers at Sheetz, and the lines of cars again, but the gas prices listed on the billboard. Regular at $6.69 per gallon. Super at $7.29. Was this a local shortage? Had the gas merchants exploited their chance to line their pockets with a little extra? But how did they do this under the watchful eyes of the National Guard? Wasn't that what the government was for — the protection of its citizens from greedy gougers when crises like this came up?

Regina rolled down her window. "Excuse me. Are these prices a local problem?"

The solider shrugged. "I wouldn't know, ma'am. They were all right last night, that's all I can tell you. I guess if people try to burn down their town, things like this happen."

"I guess," Regina told him.

She had to stay in line. The car wouldn't run without gas. Before she reached the pumps an hour later, the price on the billboard was up another quarter. She filled her tank and paid with her credit card.

Cash might be a problem, she figured. So she pulled back out on South Main. She needed to stop and make a withdrawal. This could be done at Benchmark after she got groceries, but another glance at Wal-Mart convinced her it wasn't worth the hassle now. Kroger downtown was more expensive, but there had been no visible lines when she drove past. Regina took another look at the packed parking lot and drove on to the South Benchmark Bank.

"Can I help you?" the lady at the open teller's cubicle asked. She didn't look friendly today, her face strained.

"I'd like to make a $600.00 withdrawal, please." Regina began to write a check.

"I'm sorry, ma'am," the teller said, "but we are limited to $200.00 withdrawals today."

"Two hundred?" Regina stared at her. "I have a much larger balance than that."

"I know, ma'am, but we are restricted in our cash flow."

"What about tomorrow?"

"I don't know," the teller said. When Regina still stared at her, she leaned closer. "To tell the truth, tomorrow might be worse, but that's just what I've heard whispered. Don't quote me, okay?"

"Is it just Farmstead?" Regina made no attempt to hide her unease.

"It's statewide," the teller told her. "Beyond that, I don't know."

"Well then." Regina adjusted and finished the check. "I'll take the two hundred."

"I'm sorry." The teller counted out the money. "Your funds are fully insured by the government, so don't worry. This is only a temporary cash flow problem, I'm sure."

Regina said nothing as she placed the money in her purse. In her car again, she drove to the Kroger's plaza and found a parking spot after two circles. Thankfully there were no lines outside the store. She left her car locked and entered the store to take one of only two carts left. One small blue hamper sat on the floor, askew, the bottom lined with stringy dirt. Each aisle had several customers who pulled items from the shelves in large quantities. No one seemed to push half empty carts.

"My sister told me things are cheaper down at Wal-Mart," a well-dressed lady whispered to her. "But I wasn't going to fight the lines."

Regina nodded. "Same here. So what are the prices?"

"Going through the roof. That's why everyone's hoarding. I'd advise you to do the same."

Regina smiled at the woman and pushed her cart towards the milk aisle. She gasped at the marked price, $10.24 a gallon. A pound of butter was $7.59. She wouldn't shop for much today, even if she wanted to. One gallon of milk would have to do. Hopefully the Amish man would take this as a token of her good intentions and have cows in his barn. Life on an Amish farm looked better all the time.

This was an angle she hadn't thought of before. But she still must pay the man. Amish people were honest folks, and she couldn't take advantage of Enos. He wouldn't know that milk now sold for over ten dollars a gallon. She would have to tell him and pay accordingly.

Bread was just under five dollars a loaf, and Regina took three. Breakfast cereal was $8.49, and she selected a box of Wheaties and Corn Flakes. As she went through the checkout counter, the girl looked at her and then at the carts behind Regina piled to the brim. "Expecting better times?"

"I don't know." Regina smiled. She wrote out a check for the amount the girl rung up. "One can only hope."

The girl nodded, but glanced sideways at her as if Regina were some weird creature inflicted with a malady. She took her three bags of groceries and exited the store. At the car she placed the items in the back seat. Now, what else to take? Maybe she could come back for other things later once she saw what was needed at the farm. But she really should just go out first before she made more plans. The Amish man might not even want her to stay. Somehow that didn't seem possible, but she had no rational reason for her optimism. It was just there, like a hope that rose up inside of her.

But one thing else she needed to take along yet, and that was the shortwave radio. It might keep an important link with the outside world. Given her strange penchant for life without a cell phone, a little news would be welcome. Regina returned to the parsonage to find Travis on the front porch. She parked in the back, then took a bag of groceries inside with her. He followed her.

"I figured you were out shopping." The old hunger was in his eyes, and she hesitated.

"I was," she said, but added nothing else.

"Really, Regina." He reached for her hand. "I think you ought to rethink your position. I got to thinking about how much I'll miss you — both now and, you know, in the future.

Please consider an apology to Reverend James. It shouldn't be that hard a thing to do."

"I'm not going to, Travis," she said. She moved away from him. "But thanks for trying. I just wish you cared enough to stick up for me. You know I'm not a bad person."

"I know that, Regina. I would never say you were." His gaze begged.

"Then why are you treating me like one, Travis?"

He threw his hands in the air. "You know I'm caught between a rock and a hard place, Regina. You know it's my love for you that is giving you the break I'm giving you. I could demand that you leave the parsonage tonight. That's how strong the feelings are against you."

"Then why don't you tell the dear people I have served faithfully for the last few years that I am leaving the parsonage tonight?"

He seemed startled. "But where are you going, Regina? The whole town is in an uproar. The governor has the National Guard out everywhere. You're not going to find a cheap place to stay with prices going through the roof like they are."

"I suppose the Lord will provide." Regina left him to go upstairs for the radio. His footsteps followed and her heart beat faster. She knew what would happen, and she knew she must resist this time regardless of the cost. Hadn't she lost everything already that pertained to Travis's world?

The hunger burned in his eyes. His hands were on her, but she pushed away. "No, Travis. That's over."

Anger flashed in his eyes. "It's not like you're the only woman in the world."

Strangely the words now caused hope to rise in her heart, and she forced the advantage. "Then you'd better find her, since I'm leaving."

"Don't say it was my fault," he muttered.

"I don't, Travis." She tried to hide the relief in her voice. He already had found another woman. He wouldn't have given in otherwise. This news ought to cause the pain to throb in her heart, but right now it didn't. Maybe later. She had won. In ways she didn't fully comprehend.

"It doesn't have to be like this," he said.

"But it does." She retrieved the radio from the other room, and he followed her down the stairs.

He still hadn't given up. His voice was insistent. "Please, Regina, I must insist that you stay at least for the night. Let me talk to Reverend James, and perhaps something can be done."

"Like changing my mind, because he's not changing his?"

"Why do you have to be so stubborn, Regina? I love you, I really do."

Now she wiped away a tear but said nothing.

He continued. "I've always known I love you. You've known that I do. Hasn't that been clear enough? You wouldn't have this job if I hadn't spoken up for you to the pulpit committee. I wanted to marry you from the first time I laid eyes on you."

"Five years, Travis," she managed. "It's been five years. Why aren't we married?"

"Now Regina, that's not fair." He rung his hands in frustration. "I had other things on my mind, and it just didn't seem the right time. We're both still young. How did I know this would come up and separate us like this. I'm sorry, Regina. I really am."

"Sorry Travis, but the answer is no."

He got to his feet and sighed. "And where are you going?"

"Maybe I'll drive home to Daddy," she said.

"I can't imagine you doing that."

"Thanks. That's the nicest thing you've said all day."

"Well, the parsonage is still here if you should need it. Take the key with you, and I'll watch things until you come back."

"Thanks Travis. That's nice of you."

"Why do you own a shortwave radio, Regina?" He stared at it as if he had just noticed.

"Because I like to know what's going on."

He sighed again. "You could have gone a long way, Regina. All the way to the top, you and me. It's too bad. That's all I can say."

"If the top is where you are, then I'll pass," she said, her voice bitter now. "Would you please leave? I need to go."

"Goodbye." He closed the door behind him and didn't look back. She watched him walk down the street, just as he had done so often before. How had such a good thing gone so wrong? It was a good thing, wasn't it? Their love? Their passion? Maybe she had been all wrong about it. Wrong about even this morning. She certainly felt nothing but an emptiness inside of her now.

Regina wiped away the tears. "It's the world gone mad," she said out loud. "And I'm going mad along with it."

Chapter Twenty-Nine

Regina pulled into the driveway of the Amish homestead and stopped her car near the barn. Everything looked much the same as last time, yet something was different. The buggy was no longer in the barnyard, for one thing. But this had to be the same place.

At this place she had spoken with the Amish man and sat with him on the hay bales, and he had comforted her with his honesty as much as she comforted him with her encouragement. Was that what she was after now — comfort from him? It hardly seemed possible. She might find some relief that way, but it wouldn't solve the problems she faced.

She got out and closed the car door. Well, first things first. Imaginations of the future were futile until she actually met the man again. He might send her out on the road again, and that would mean one long trip to Georgia, which would end at best in tears shed on Daddy's shoulder. Maybe that's what she needed — to hit bottom, to be fully humiliated and disgraced. Didn't such experiences cause growth, unpleasant though they are?

As she pushed open the barn door, the hinges squeaked in the still evening air. The Amish man came out from the back at a brisk walk. Only he wasn't Amish anymore. His black hat was gone and his hair was cut in rough edges around his head.

"Hello," he said as she stared.

The voice was the same, so why was everything else different? While the question raced through her mind she noticed the buggy parked between the wooden stalls, its shafts raised to the ceiling, stuck in between the floor beams.

"Hi," she managed. "What happened to you?"

He ran his hand through his hair. "I guess I've joined the *English* world. Do you object?"

The words rushed out. "Oh, no, of course not. It's just that you look … different. I was expecting you to be like you were the other day."

His face fell. "So are many others. My father has not seen me like this yet, nor has Bishop Mast. But it is too late to go back. They have thrown me out of the church."

She wrinkled her brow. "Out of the church, like … you mean, the temple or something? I didn't know you people had temples."

The sorrow was heavy on his face. "We have no temple but the one in our hearts. That is why the pain is almost greater than I can bear. To be cast out is to be cast out of hearts you love."

She stepped closer. "I'm sorry, I had no idea. Is this a bad time? I mean, I can leave, if you don't have time to talk. But…."

"I would love nothing better than to talk with you." His glance was genuine. "But perhaps you are also in trouble. Farmstead is…."

"In flames," she finished for him. "And I lost my job. Which is—I admit—really why I'm stopping by … not just to talk." She gave him a pleading look. "Would there be any way I could stay with you for a few days? Upstairs in the spare bedroom perhaps? I know there is your — what did you say — almost sister staying with you, and maybe Nellie is still here? Would one more person be too much of a bother? I would be glad to pay something. I brought some money along, and some groceries. The bank wouldn't let me withdraw a lot of money, but I can go back into town tomorrow."

She paused to catch her breath. Was he going to ask her to

leave? She studied his face. He looked out the barn window and seemed lost in thought.

She cleared her throat, but he spoke first. "I have prayed again. I cannot believe *The Lord* would hear me, and yet you are here. Is that possible? Did you come because I prayed?"

"I don't know." She met his gaze. His eyes looked troubled, but not wild. He thought deeply, more deeply than she had imagined possible for a man.

He pointed towards the barn door. "Did you come in your car?"

"Yes. I couldn't have walked, and there was no one to bring me."

"Then this is what I need — a car parked outside. This must be an *English* place now — for what I have to do — protecting my people from what is coming."

"Protecting your people? You need a car?"

He nodded. "I need to make it look like an *English* place. That is why my buggy is inside the barn, but I did not know how to make the outside look right. A car will be exactly what I need."

"So I get to stay here? If I leave my car outside?" She tilted her head.

A ghost of a smile played on his face. "Of course you don't have to. But you are a good person. And I would be honored to have a good person in the house for the troubled times that have come."

She still asked. "And your *sort of sister,* and Nellie?"

He shook his head. "They are not good like you. But they are not here anymore. Perhaps that is what you mean. They have gone back to the *English* house. So it's just me now."

She searched for words. "So … I would be staying alone with you?"

A look of distress crossed his face. "I'm sorry if you don't trust me. I know that I have sinned, and that you are a good person."

Regina laughed. "I'm afraid you overrate me, but I can take care of myself, I think. And you don't look like you would assault women."

He stared at the barn floor. She stepped closer to touch his arm. "I'm sorry. I didn't mean to add to your discomfort by implying anything. I'm sure that whatever you've done, *The Lord* will have mercy. He always does. I know *The Lord* will; he has forgiven me often."

A full smile crept across his face. "You speak the words of *The Lord,* even if you are a woman. It is all so strange. You bring hope and light into my dark life. Who would have thought such a thing was possible?"

Regina took a deep breath. Her lungs filled with the sweet fragrance of cut hay, the faint smell of his sweat, and the lingering hint of harness leather. Enos was a man. A strong man of faith. There was no question about that. He made Travis seem like a distant memory, too faint to recall. She focused again. "You're going to have to grow your hair back," she told him.

His eyes opened wide in surprise. "But I have to look *English.*"

"You'll look *English* enough." She noticed his clothing for the first time. "You're already wearing our clothing. That's what really makes you look different."

"What really makes the difference is the heart." His face had fallen again. "I will never be *English* in my heart. No matter what I do to the outside."

She smiled. "I don't know that I would want you to. I like you the way you are."

A shadow crossed his face. "I have killed, and I am afraid there will be more killing ahead because I wish to protect my people. I do not ask you to share in that sin, but I must do it."

Regina didn't hesitate. "It is not a sin — to protect yourself against attack. I'm assuming that's what you have in mind. And by the way, how do you know there will be one?"

His looked pensive. "That's not so difficult. My people

have food stored in their basements, canned goods laid up for many months. We have grain in the barns. How long will it be until the *English* people who are hungry figure that out? I don't think it will be very long."

"Have you been in town this morning?"

He shook his head.

"Then how do you know about food shortages, or rather the soon-to-be food shortages? Which is true, now that I think of it. Milk just jumped to ten dollars a gallon, a price not sustainable for long."

"I only know it's coming" he said. "How I know, I don't know. Perhaps I'm getting old before my time. Not that many months ago I was an Amish boy looking forward to his own farm and family. Now my hands have killed and this has filled my heart with sickness like an old man's body. You bring light into my soul, for which I am very thankful. Are you sure you're not an angel?"

"I am not an angel." She laughed.

"Angels would not lie," he agreed. "So I must believe you, but it's difficult. But come, let me show you what I have in the house, and then you can decide what you wish to do."

"Then you are allowing me to stay?" She heard the hope in her own voice.

"I think so." His smile was soft.

What had she taken hold of? Regina wondered. Some wild dream inspired by the current frenzy in the world. After all, Enos was from another faith far removed from hers, not to mention their difference in race. Even in the modern twenty-first century that was a stretch. What in her childhood could have pushed her towards this moment? This moment when she walked towards an Amish man's house with plans to stay for the near future at least. Travis would say she had lost it, and perhaps she had.

Regina followed him as he closed the barn door. She muttered, "What a strange sight we make together?"

He chuckled, "It is strange. But no stranger than everything else I have seen. I know I've stopped thinking about strange things. I accept them now. The world grows stranger and stranger as everything changes."

"That's a good idea, acceptance." She fell in step beside him.

He opened the front door and motioned inside. "I hope you like the place. It's not much but Rosemary used to live here."

Her voice caught. "Then I'll love it, I'm sure." She touched his hand. "I'm so sorry, Enos. It must still be hard."

He nodded. "I'm glad you think the house is good. There is the door to the upstairs. You will be staying in one of those bedrooms. I sleep on the couch downstairs, near where Rosemary was killed."

She stared at him. "You shouldn't do that. It's not good for you. That does strange things to people."

"Perhaps." He looked away. "But that is where I sleep. And downstairs in the basement are more guns. I can show them to you later."

Chapter Thirty

Enos waited at the kitchen table, staring into the flickering flame of the kerosene lamp. Regina's radio sat on the floor near the front door. The soft light played off its silver sides. She was upstairs now. He had gone up with her to see if she had found the room satisfactory. Her *thank you* and smile had drawn him in all evening. It soothed his soul.

Regina was different from Clare in so many ways. Regina was good like Rosemary. When Regina smiled, she brought back those feelings of everything being right that Rosemary always gave him. But how could an *English* woman, a minister, ever give him what Rosemary had given him? It wasn't possible — at least in every way. But for the health of his soul she had been sent by God. He was sure of that. Enos shook his head and got up to stand by the front window.

He thought back over the evening. Regina had insisted on making supper. It was good food — not quite as good as Clare's, but still good. She warmed a can of corn from the basement, sliced potatoes, fried them on the stove, and made gravy — from memory, she said. Something about her childhood in the south. Peaches also came from the basement. Simple, but good, as she was good.

She told him the prices of milk and bread in town, which troubled him. How could something like that change so fast, almost overnight? Her face grew pinched with fear when she listened to the radio. It gave out little snatches of news. But what she seemed to look for wasn't there — a man from New Zealand, she said, from way across the ocean on the other side of the world. She brought strange things into the house.

"Do you know what the *National Guard* is?" she asked him, and he shook his head.

She explained. It was like an army each state kept available, and the governor of Virginia had called out his guard to help keep the peace.

"Do you know what the stock market is?" she asked.

He nodded. "That's where greedy men sell their things on Wall Street."

She laughed, the worry momentarily gone from her face. "Not quite, but it doesn't look good for our money. Both China and Russia have started selling off their US debt holdings. The value of our dollar has fallen like a rock."

"Why do China and Russia owe us debt?" he asked.

She appeared puzzled but still answered him. "They buy bonds from us, which are promises from the government to pay it back at a later date."

"Why would they do that?"

She shrugged. "I guess for our interest rates, who knows? They have their reasons. Anyway, they have gotten rid of them, and the value of our dollar is done for. I don't know that the two are exactly connected, but maybe they are. Like a dog chasing a rat, or the other way around."

He laughed, one of his few laughs of the evening. "Did you grow up on a farm?"

"Not like yours." She made a face. "Ours was only a few acres, but we had a cow, a few goats, a pig for meat, and chickens. Daddy worked in town on the railroad after he came home from Vietnam."

Enos moved away from the window and returned to the present. He listened to the stillness of the house for a moment. What had he heard? A sound had started somewhere, from deep within the house itself, it seemed. But that couldn't be. Nothing inside could make such a sound, like dull drums in a barrel. It must come from outside.

Enos ran to the front door and jerked it open. Indeed, the sound came from off in the distance. It filled the night with a steady percussion, with more sounds added by the moment. He waited. The guns were in the basement, but against this sound guns would be of little use.

He studied the night sky, the stars. What evil could be on the way? Slowly he knew — English machines that fly in the air, helicopters, and many of them. This could not be from wandering thieves. The *National Guard* Regina had spoken of must be out tonight. Did they look for evil, or were they evil themselves?

Regina had mentioned no ill in connection with the Guard, but he sensed evil in the air, coming across the fields. He watched as lights appeared. They flew low to the south. It didn't appear they would cross his farm. He could only hope they were headed some place far from here.

Should he awaken Regina? Would she want to know? Surely not, if these were only helicopters that flew in the sky. But then she knew things he didn't, so he should get her opinion. He ran upstairs and knocked on her door. She opened it, with a blanket wrapped over her shoulders. Her face was hidden in the darkness.

The words rushed out. "There are helicopters in the sky. Many of them." But he didn't need to say it. By now the percussion of their sound rocked the house.

"I'll get dressed and come down." She closed the door again.

Enos went downstairs to wait beside the kerosene lamp. The helicopters still thumped in the distance and didn't go away. Why was this? They should have been past by now. Was there some logical explanation?

"What do you think it is?" Regina came up behind him to touch his shoulder.

"I don't know." He walked to the kitchen window again. "But they are up to no good."

"Let's go see if they stop." She took his hand in the shadowy darkness and led him to the back of the house. They watched through the living room window as the sounds rumbled in the distance.

"I think they might be transporting troops in or out," she said. "That's what the *National Guard* does. The governor might be calling for more, which wouldn't surprise me with how things were going in town."

"I don't think so." His voice was troubled. "But I don't know why. Should we get the guns from the basement?"

"Against helicopters?" She laughed. "I don't think that would be wise. And these are government people. You don't want to be involved, believe me — both for practical and moral reasons. I don't think we ought to fight against lawful authority."

"My faith believes in violence against no one," he said. "I have already broken that law and killed a man. There is no higher law to break."

"Then your faith would be wrong." She stroked his arm. "There is killing to protect oneself, and there is murder. There is a difference."

"But you come from the *English* world," he told her. "You would say so."

"Aren't you of this world?" she asked.

"I am now." He pointed with his finger. "But look. There is fire."

They watched as flames lit the sky. They shot upwards as the sound of deep percussions reached them. The roar lingered and seemed to explode again before it faded away.

"They blew something up." Her voice caught. "Do you know what lies in that direction?"

"Homes, farms, a lot of our people." He hesitated. "Also the *English* people's house where Clare lives. But why would the helicopters blow up their place? They were only giving out medicine to those who needed it."

"That and giving you guns, right?" She looked up at his face in the low light. "What are you thinking?"

"That I want to get the guns and see if this is what I think it is."

She pulled on his arm. "We'll leave the guns, but let's go see what happened. I doubt if you'll sleep much until we find out."

"I will get the horse ready then." He moved towards the front door.

Her words followed him. "But we can drive my car — it's quicker."

He shook his head. "Not tonight. They won't know where we came from — if someone asks questions or stops us. It is best that I look like an Amish boy."

"So much for the *English* look." She followed him outside.

Enos used his flashlight to harness the horse, and gave Regina the bridle and the light to hold while he pushed out the buggy. "Shine it on the buggy shafts while I hitch the horse."

He swung the horse in and fastened the straps. "Now climb in."

When she did, he threw in the buggy lines and swung up himself. He left the lights off and allowed the horse to take his time.

Regina's voice came out of the darkness. "If I wasn't so tense at the moment, I'd be enjoying my first buggy ride."

He smiled, his gaze on the fiery blaze in the distance. It would take a little time to arrive, and he wasn't in any great hurry; better to approach cautiously than to barge in, he figured. Beside him her hand slipped through his elbow, and she drew close.

He pulled back on the buggy line as they broke out of the woods. Before them the flames from two burning houses and barns rose high into the air. The fire lit up the night sky and showed the astonishment on her face. She let go of his elbow and leaped out of the buggy.

"The helicopters are gone," she shouted. "It couldn't have been the National Guard. They wouldn't do something like this."

"Hush," he muttered, as he tied his horse to a fence post. "It couldn't have been good people who blew up this place."

Chapter Thirty-One

Enos moved closer to the flames as they shot from the burning house. Regina clutched his arm and sobbed quietly. A higher burst of fire drove a wave of heat towards them. Enos shielded Regina's face with his hand as he pulled her backwards with him. They waited and watched the fiery embers drift into the darkened sky.

"They are all dead." His voice was hushed. "I don't see how anybody could escape that."

"I can't believe this," Regina whispered. "Our own people did this. They really are blowing up buildings."

Enos stared at the flames. "These are strange things to me. I only know that I have killed, and may have to kill again."

Regina pulled on his arm. "There is no right in this."

Enos shrugged. "They have killed Joe and Clare. So of course this is wrong, but even so we are taught not to disobey the powers that be."

The words exploded out of her. "Well, confound your preachers and what you have been taught, Enos — this is not right. You don't blow up your own people in the middle of the night."

"Come." He took her hand. "Let's walk around and make sure nobody is alive. I don't see how there could be, but sometimes there are miracles."

Her voice shrieked. "Don't talk to me about miracles. Not in front of this destruction."

"There are always miracles, Regina." Enos squeezed her hand. "No matter how bad things get." A blackened object on the ground caught Enos's attention. "There." He pointed and broke into a run.

The shifting wind brought the heat in his direction and drove Enos back. He waited, his arm over his face, before he advanced again. As he drew closer, the light from the fire showed the charred remains of what had once been a human being.

"What is it?" Regina's voice was distant.

He didn't answer, but searched the ground. He seized a board that still sizzled at one end and beat out the coals. When the smoke no longer rose in the air, he slid the board under the body and dragged it with him as he retreated.

"You know what it is," he said in answer to her questioning gaze.

She gasped and held both hands over her mouth.

"I'm going to see if I can find something to cover it with." He ran towards the small wooden shack that sat between the house and the barn. Its roof smoldered with smoking debris, but nothing had ignited yet. Enos jerked open the door. A woman rushed out and clutched him by the throat while she screamed obscenities into the night air. He tumbled over backwards.

Enos tried to dislodge her from him. He pushed upwards while he turned his head to breathe, but she was heavy. He was held down with the sheer force of her weight. It would take drastic measures to get rid of her, he figured, measures best taken soon.

His fingers found her throat and he squeezed hard, which brought the noise to a low wheeze. With her grip weakened, he wiggled out from under her. She broke into screams again when his fingers broke loose from her throat. He saw Regina running towards them. She grabbed the woman from behind.

"You're crazy." Regina helped pin the woman to the ground. "Shut up, Nellie, it's me — the girl who brought you over in the car."

Enos stood back and stared at Nellie. "So what was she doing in there?"

"What do you think I was doing?" Nellie screamed. "Clare told me to run, and that was the first building I came to. Thank God I had enough sense not to hide in the barn. They blew that up."

"Where are Joe and Clare?" Enos asked her.

"They were shooting the last I knew." Nellie pointed towards the sky. "I told them to give me a gun, but they said to run instead. I guess they didn't trust me with a weapon, and now look what happened to them."

"I don't blame them one bit for not giving you a gun," Regina snapped.

Nellie snorted and got to her feet.

Enos ignored Nellie now to enter the small building. He soon came back out again. "I don't see any bag I could use to cover up the body."

"Do you have to?" Regina made a face. "Surely the fire department will be here soon, and the police."

Enos laughed. "You know they're not coming. Nor is anyone else. We are the only ones stupid enough to be out here. Unless my people come, but they have troubles of their own."

"So why are there horse and buggies pulling in the field where we parked?" Regina tugged on his arm.

Enos turned to look but said nothing. The sight caused pain to burn in his heart. Near him the fire sent bursts of light in all directions. Regina had spoken the truth; his people had come. Men climbed out of the buggies to tie their horses, and even women were there. They stood still and waited on the men.

A great lump rose in Enos's throat, and tears stung his eyes.

"At least someone cares," Regina whispered. "Thank God for that."

Enos watched the dark-clad forms as they approached. He mouthed the words. "These were once my people but I am no longer one of them."

Regina must still have heard him. "Don't say that. We will always be a little of what we were raised to be."

He groaned as Nellie screamed again. "The ninja turtles are coming. They flew in from the sky, blew us up, and now they're walking in."

"Shut up." Regina clamped her hand over Nellie's mouth. "I've had about enough out of you. Those are nice Amish people."

Nellie sputtered and Regina removed her hand.

"Are you going to be quiet now?" Regina demanded.

"I guess so." Nellie's eyes still darted about. "I just never saw Amish people walking up in the dark."

"I don't think you've seen a lot of things in life," Regina told her.

Enos turned to face the man who came forward first. His hat was pulled down over his forehead, and wild firelight played on his beard and exposed face. No wonder Nellie thought strange creatures had approached. Not that long ago Enos would have stepped forward with gladness in his heart to greet the man, but now he felt like a stranger and the man a stranger to him. The thought was as dark and wild as the night.

"Good evening," the man spoke first.

"Good evening, Lester," Enos replied. "I'm surprised you're out here after what happened."

"Do you know me?" Lester stared out from under his hat. "I don't remember seeing you before."

Of course I know you, Enos wanted to say. *I grew up around you and played with your children. You are my father's cousin.* But obviously he had changed too much for Lester to recognize him. A great sadness crept into his voice. "I'm Enos, Lester."

"You're Enos?" Lester stepped closer, pushing back his

hat. "*That* you are! But you're all soot covered and your hair. What happened? Bishop Mast said you had been thrown out, and now I see why."

"Ah. . . ." Regina cleared her throat near them. "I don't know about who's throwing out who but these people have just been blasted into eternity. I think that's what we need to be worried about."

"Who is this woman?" Enos stared at Regina now.

"She stays with me at the house," Enos said. It was none of Lester's business, but he wouldn't be satisfied until he knew where Regina belonged.

"Is this the woman you've been sleeping with?" Lester pulled back a step.

Regina gasped, "You people are something, you know."

Enos held up his hand. "No it is not, Lester. I'm not sleeping with anyone."

Lester snorted. "In your fallen state you'd say anything Enos. And it is the state of your soul that lays heavy on my mind. But let's not quarrel, I say."

"The truth is still the truth," Enos muttered, but it was useless to protest, he knew.

"Aren't the *English* coming to take care of their own?" Lester changed the subject.

"I doubt anyone's coming," Enos replied.

"Then I will tell the others what has happened here." Lester moved away to hold a whispered conference with the ones who had come with him.

Behind Enos, Regina spoke in his ear, "Were you sleeping with the woman who was *kind of your sister?*"

Enos shook his head. "I was not, but I was sorely tempted."

Regina let out a long breath. "You are something, aren't you?"

"That's what she said."

"I can see why."

Silence fell between them as he hung his head. Regina

seemed to have forgotten him as she spoke into the night sky. "What is wrong with the world, God? Is there anything left to believe in? The government is killing its own citizens with bombs and helicopters, and it's killing them in converted prisons…." Her shoulders quivered. "It's all gone. My church, my boyfriend — well, my *sort of fiancé* — and the government is evil and corrupt."

"I'm sorry." Enos came closer to place his hand on her shoulder.

Should he say the words or not? Enos wondered. They seemed wilder than the flames that shot heavenward, crazier than the blown-up buildings around him, and yet the thought was brighter than the stars that peeked through the smoky haze. Enos cleared his throat before he spoke, "We must not allow hate to take everything from us. We must still believe in love."

"I've heard that before." Regina forced a laugh. "But never from a more unlikely source. You surprise me, Enos."

He searched for words. "I don't know … perhaps it's seeing you. Being with you."

"You know I'm no angel." She turned towards him as the shadows fell over her face.

"I'm sorry," he muttered. "For everything. I really am." He met her gaze and sighed.

Chapter Thirty-Two

The cruiser lights came up the road towards the burning buildings and grew stronger until the piercing strobes penetrated the smoky haze. The vehicle stopped by the road. Regina stood beside Enos with the small group of Amish people a short distance away. Nellie looked ready to scream again but cowered when Regina sternly shook her head.

An officer stepped out of the car and waited a few moments for another to get out the other side. Together they walked across the lawn. They gave perfunctory nods to the Amish group and came straight towards Enos and Regina.

"Good evening," Enos greeted them.

The officers nodded. "What happened here?"

Regina cleared her throat, but Enos answered first. "I live down the road a ways, and we heard helicopters going over. There was an explosion, and this is what we found when we arrived. Nellie over there was in the house at the time. She took shelter in the storage shed and survived."

"Did you find any other survivors?" the officer asked.

"No sir," Regina spoke up, and the officer looked at her for a moment.

"What about you?" he asked Enos.

"Only the charred body over there." Enos motioned with his chin. "We've been here for some time, and no one has come over from the site across the street. We had planned to look but got distracted."

"Okay then." The officer took charge. "I'd suggest you get back to your place. We'll take it from here."

"Why weren't you here sooner?" Regina didn't move.

The officer looked taken aback, his eyes cold. "Well, ma'am, as you can imagine, things are very busy right now. They aren't quite normal, you could say. I don't think I have to explain that to you. So the two of you just leave now."

"Ah, we'd like Nellie to come with us," Regina said. "We have plenty of space at the house."

"I'm afraid that's not possible," the officer said. "We have to take her in for questioning. She might be able to give us information on what happened."

"You know good and well what happened here," Regina snapped. "The government took out this place."

The officer came a step closer with a menacing look on his face. "You are accusing us of doing this? Do you have any evidence to back up this crazy claim of yours?"

Regina didn't flinch. "I don't, officer, but I stand by my words. No one else would do something like this."

The officer laughed. "I guess the good citizenry cannot be blamed for wild conspiracy theories. I can't say I wouldn't come up with a few myself with what's been going on. Why don't you folks go on home and get some sleep."

"We're going." Enos pulled on her arm. Regina resisted, but gave in when he pulled harder.

"They'll take you in if you don't stop," he whispered as they walked away.

"Good night, Nellie," Regina said as they went past. The woman had a big smile on her face. She appeared happier than she had all night.

"At least someone likes the government showing up," Enos said when they were out of earshot.

"Talk about changing your mind in a time of crisis," Regina added. "She hated the government a few days ago. I hope the poor woman lives to see the morning."

"That depends on what she saw if you ask me."

"You know what? I believe you and it's frightening me."

Enos shook his head. "I could have told you that a long time ago."

They approached the group of Amish people, and Lester stepped forward to meet them. "What did the officers want? Are they going to bury the bodies?"

"I think so." Enos glanced over his shoulder. "But they want us off the place. I guess they want to hide their dirty work before anyone sees more of it."

"You shouldn't be accusing God's lawful government of wrongdoing," Lester said, "although it doesn't surprise me. Man's power only corrupts the man who holds it."

"Well, don't start preaching now," Enos told him. "We need to talk about what we're going to do."

"Going to do?" Lester stared at him. "What do you mean, what we are going to do? We are having nothing to do with you. Of all people, you should know that, Enos. There is no fellowship between the people of God and the unfruitful works of darkness."

"Forget about that, Lester, okay?" Enos lowered his voice. "You don't have to sit down to eat with me, but if you don't do something, there won't be many people of God left in this area. Believe me, before long gangs of thieves will be searching the countryside for food."

"What has that to do with us?" Lester glared. "We are not thieves."

Enos ignored the barb. "Can you imagine where these thieves will be going? They will go straight to any Amish home they see. The wise thing would be for you to make some agreement with your *English* neighbors. You could make your places look like the *English*. You could share some of your food and get their help."

Lester gasped. "And make an agreement with the world? I say Bishop Mast has already made enough of an agreement with the world. Sure it has saved many of us, including my family, but at what cost? I ask myself that often, Enos, lying at home in my bed. Who will pay for what we have done?"

Enos faced the man. "So you would have been like my father?"

Lester glanced away. "Many are now saying they wish they had taken that road. Your father lost much, but he has now recovered, and his testimony is strong. He has made peace with Bishop Mast. His story of how he was visited with help from the heavens is giving us all strength."

Enos choked back the words he wanted to throw at Lester. But the truth of what had happened wouldn't do any good. It would be his word against his father's, and he would not be believed. Even if he were believed it would only give Edith, and his two surviving brothers, a black mark. They would have been saved by disobedience.

"You do not know what you are speaking of," Enos finally managed. "Rosemary and her parents died for nothing. I do not see why you have to do the same."

"None of us die for nothing." Lester's voice rose. "Not when we die in the *will of the Lord*. If our people do anything, we will gather and pray. That will be good enough, and I am sure Bishop Mast will agree."

"Okay," Enos sighed. "Don't say I haven't warned you."

"You had better heed our warning concerning your soul," Lester said. "There is still time for repentance while there is life. Think about that."

"I will." Enos turned to leave. "But I must do what I have to."

Regina cleared her throat. "Perhaps you should listen to him, Lester. I don't know you of course, so I'm sorry for intruding, but Enos is a strong man. He does what he believes is right. You shouldn't disregard that."

"You must believe what you wish." Lester didn't meet her gaze. "We will have to look to our own ways. But one thing I do know is that we will not need the help of one who has been shut out of the Kingdom of God."

"I won't argue with you," Regina said, "other than to say I think you're wrong. Enos is a strong and good man."

"He used to be." Lester glanced towards Enos. "As to what he is now, only time will tell. We will be praying for him that he finds repentance."

Regina continued, "You do know that he speaks the truth about the danger your people are in?"

"I do." Lester glanced towards the officers who stood by the burning buildings. "I think we should all be going. We have been lingering here much too long."

"May God help all of us," Regina muttered.

Lester smiled for the first time. "To that I agree. May *The Lord* have mercy on you, too."

He turned to go, and Enos waited until they were all in their buggies before he led Regina to theirs. Somehow it seemed better that way—that his people go first, the holy before the unholy. He knew he was unholy; the darkness in his soul screamed the words at him. He waited for Regina to get in the buggy and threw her the lines before he climbed in.

"We will have to help them," Regina said as they drove back towards the house.

"How?" Enos slapped the reins. "You can see for yourself that they don't want any help."

Regina searched for words. "Sometimes ... maybe people hide what they want deep inside of them. I think you do."

Enos laughed. "That's easy for you to say. So what do you want?"

Regina didn't hesitate. "I want nothing but to help people. I've never wanted anything else as far back as I can remember."

Enos glanced at her in the darkness. "You're helping me. Be happy with that at least. My people on the other hand — only God can help them."

"I don't know." Regina sat up straight in the buggy. "Maybe you are right, and I'm here to help—maybe more people than you. And to learn as well. You call me back to what I've left behind and thought I'd never return to. Do you think that's wrong?"

"That's a little deep for me." Enos shifted on the buggy seat. "I'm not exactly following the ways of my father either."

Silence settled between them.

"Do you think any of this will ever make sense?" she finally asked.

"I'm not the one to say," he muttered. "I only wish I hadn't killed. Though I hated what they did to Rosemary. They tore her body apart. But you saw my people tonight. They believe in forgiveness. They lay down their own lives for their enemies. Why do you think I was not able to do that?"

"You poor thing." She stroked his arm. "I wish I could help you."

"Maybe you already have."

She said nothing as he turned into the driveway. Enos pulled to a stop by the barn and climbed down to unhitch from the buggy. She waited while he led his horse into the stall. When he returned, Regina helped him push the buggy inside. They walked together into the house and parted at the base of the stairs.

"Good night," he said.

"Good night." She gave him a tender smile. "*The Lord* will yet help you. I know He will."

Chapter Thirty-Three

Long moments later Regina stood at the top of the stairs. The dim glow of the light beneath the door below wavered. It seemed to come closer before it went out. Enos must be on the couch by now, she figured, ready for bed. She shook her head. Her own troubles rushed in upon her. Her world spun out of control, with the familiar comfort of home gone. Perhaps that was what unsettled her tonight. Both Travis and the future were over. How would she ever obtain another position in a church with that on her record? A resignation, perhaps, but she had been fired. Explanations would have to be given, phone calls made, but it was useless, really. She was done. No black church would ever take her on, and certainly no white church would either.

And the professor was gone—in jail. Regina saw his face in the restaurant, lined with concern. But he only wanted to enlist her in the cause, whatever that was — a cause that had ended in handcuffs on his wrists and a fiery death for his accomplices. No, the professor was worse than Travis when it came to establishing anything of lasting value into her life.

Somehow she must find a way to serve again. God would open the doors; he always had before. He wouldn't change just because of this. And yet everything had changed. The world would never be the same again even if all the madness should end. And Enos had awakened something inside of her she wanted. But what was it?

Enos was tormented, but he kept control over his emotions. He said he had killed a man but he had done no wrong — if the rest of his story was true. And why should she doubt him? She must help him see that he had done no wrong. The man made no pretense of virtue. In fact, Enos felt he had lost all virtue when he killed, and yet he remained good in some inexplicable way. She wanted that. She wanted it desperately.

Perhaps it was the fire, the destruction tonight, or all the destruction in the days before tonight, that revealed the truth in her heart. Or was it just the way she grew up, the innocence of childhood carried into adult life? Regina jerked open the bedroom window. She looked out across the night sky, where in the distance the fires still burned with a red glow on the horizon. This was so like her life, she thought. It too burned down slowly but surely.

Regina took the kerosene lamp and moved down the stairs. She listened to the sharp squeaks of the steps, louder than she could have imagined in the silence of the night. Enos would hear her come, but why did she care? She wanted to speak with him. Regina's hands shook, and the flame from the kerosene lamp flickered on the walls of the stairwell. She pushed open the door and stepped into the living room. Enos was asleep on the couch.

She glanced at him before she felt her way over to the kitchen table. She lowered her head into her hands, stifling her cries. He must not hear, and yet he must. If he would only come, somehow this would all be made right again.

Regina listened. Enos had heard. His soft step, the mere whisper of stocking feet on wood, pulled her head up to peer into the darkness. Above her the flame of the lamp played shadows on his face; questions flickered in his eyes. His chest was bare. She lifted her arms and reached for him. He came closer to receive her embrace.

"Sit, please," she whispered.

He complied and took the kitchen chair. "It's been a hard night. Shouldn't you be in bed?"

She met his gaze. "I couldn't sleep."

He smiled. "I was dreaming of you."

She laughed. "Of me? That couldn't have been much of a dream."

"Oh it was." He reached for her hand. "It was a very nice dream. A dream of angels."

"You keep saying that. But I'm not an angel."

"Come." He stood to his feet. "We can talk better over here."

Enos carried the lamp and they entered the living room. He helped her sit on the couch before he placed the lamp on the floor and sat down himself. He glanced at her. "Shall I tell you a story of our people?"

She nodded.

He thought for a moment. "It's an old story from our faith, but it will show you why I appreciate you." He cleared his throat. "There was once an Amish family who lived on the frontier a long time ago, when this country was still young. The Indians came one night, doing what the Indians sometimes did in those days, surrounding the cabin, calling to the family to come out. They refused and stayed inside. The two oldest boys wanted to shoot at the enemy, as their neighbors would have done, but their father refused to allow any shooting. So the Indians soon set the log cabin on fire, and the family retreated to the basement. There the boys and father kept the fire at bay, pulling apple cider from the root cellar to splash on the flames. When they were almost overcome with smoke and thought the Indians had left, they climbed out. One Indian had stayed behind to eat apples from their orchard and announced his startling discovery, calling the others back.

"They killed the mother and the daughters. The two sons and father they took captive. Later one of the sons escaped to tell his story, which now lives as a legend of our faith, a testimony to how a man who follows God will live. He will not kill."

"That's a nice story." She exhaled slowly. "But they might have died anyway, even if they had tried to shoot their way out. Many did in those days. Guns were not always enough."

"You don't sound like my people." He smiled. "They teach us the lesson the family left behind. It is better to die, they say, than to kill another human being."

She studied his face. "You said this story had something to do with us."

"It does," he said. "Now you see how great my sin was, and how precious your understanding is to me."

"I'm glad of that." She paused. "And I hope you find help—through whomever." She forced a smile. "But I have my problems, too. That's what I came down to talk about."

He leaned back on the couch. "I'm listening, but I doubt I can be of much help. I don't fill the void like you do, since I lost my people."

She looked away. "You should stop saying things like that. I'm not as wonderful as you think. I have plenty of troubles of my own. My work, my old boyfriend, my whole world. I think it's all gone."

"I suppose so." He ducked his head. "Yet *The Lord* has brought us together. We should be thankful for that. Because I know that it will not be long for us. Our time together is short. But I will always remember your goodness."

She laughed. "You're quite a surprise, Enos. You know that, don't you? And you are making me feel better."

"I'm glad for that." His face saddened.

"Was she beautiful?" She reached out to touch his hand.

He hesitated. "*Yes,* she was very beautiful. But we had best not speak of Rosemary."

"I know." She got to her feet. "Perhaps we should go to bed?"

He nodded and pointed at the lamp. "That's yours."

"Good night," she whispered. "Thanks for helping me." He still sat there with his head down when she closed the stair door.

Chapter Thirty-Four

Enos was fixing breakfast the next morning when Regina stepped out of the upstairs doorway. He had the kitchen half filled with smoke and the window open as he waved his arms around.

Regina laughed as he turned to look at her, his face full of alarm. "Don't tell me you've never fixed breakfast before?"

"Of course I have," he snapped. "It's this crazy bacon. It's not acting like normal bacon."

"So exactly how many times have you fixed breakfast?" She came up to stand beside him. "Here, let me take over the bacon pan."

She looked at him. His cut hair stuck out every which way and his face glowed from the heat. Her laugh filled the kitchen.

"I'm not that funny," he muttered. "But you're right. The bacon is fried to a crisp."

"Nearly." She stabbed with the fork to pick bacon pieces out of the hot pan. "I know you have never done this before."

"I did this a few times," he protested. "But obviously I didn't learn much. Some things in life take a woman's hand."

"Then why don't you set the table instead?"

"Bossy, bossy." But he got the plates out of the cupboard.

"Don't you like bossy women?" She glanced over her shoulder. Had she dreamed it last night, or had he told her a story on the couch? Whatever had happened she felt much better.

"I love bossy women," he teased. "They make wonderful wives."

She laughed again. "I think you're lying."

He sat at the table. "Come, let's eat."

"Bossy, bossy," she repeated, and his grin broadened.

They ate in silence with brief glances at each other.

"What?" she finally asked.

"Nothing. You're more like an angel in the morning light than you were last night."

She made a face. "It usually works the other way, I thought."

He shrugged, but a smile played on his face. When they were finished, he got up to move his plate to the counter. He cleared his throat. "Ah, if you don't mind, would you come into the living room for a few minutes?"

"Another story?" she teased.

"Not really," he said, and vanished.

She moved her own dishes to the counter and walked into the living room to find him on the couch with a Bible open on his knees. She sat beside him.

"You preach, don't you?" He offered her the Bible. "I thought we could read a portion of scripture. It might do us good for what lies ahead."

She hesitated for a moment before she opened the book and began to read. "I waited patiently for the Lord and he inclined unto me and heard my cry. He brought me up also out of a horrible pit, out of the miry clay. . . ."

He appeared calmer when she finished.

"You have the same scriptures we do." She tried a tease again.

He smiled. "I suppose so. I had never thought of that before."

"Shall we pray," she suggested.

"Yes, but you lead out. I can't find the right words." He knelt beside the couch.

She knelt beside him and took his hand. "Our great and blessed Father in whom is neither darkness nor shadow of turning, shine now on our hearts, give us the light of your day;

bring peace to our troubled souls, that we may find strength for the journey that lies ahead. Thank you, Father, for Enos. Thank you that he has been so kind to me and given me a place to stay. Thank you for protecting us last night from dangers that we did not even know we were facing. Keep the souls who died in the fire safely in your hand and grant them mercy and grace. We know that you will do all things by the counsel of your own will. Thank you Father. Amen."

"That was a nice prayer." He stayed on his knees. "Thank you."

"You're welcome."

"Can you ask *The Lord* for my forgiveness?"

"For what, Enos? I told you there was nothing wrong with self defense."

He ignored her comment. "Then ask for my many sins."

"You can ask God yourself."

"I would rather you would."

She shrugged and bowed her head. "Please, Father, forgive Enos's sins, whatever he has done, and mine also. We ask this by your mercy and grace. Amen."

"Amen," he said, then added. "I'm sorry for what I've done Lord. If you can help me, I would really appreciate it."

"Amen." She tacked on at the end.

He glanced at her. "I will always remember this moment."

She forced a smile. "You're sweet, you know. But maybe we should start planning the day?"

He nodded. "I want to visit my father's place. That might not be pleasant, but I need to."

"Okay," she agreed. "I'll go with you, but first I should listen to the news — on the radio — and see what's going on."

Enos stood to his feet and disappeared out the washroom door a moment later. She watched him go across the front lawn until he closed the barn door behind him. Regina turned back to set the radio on the kitchen table and fiddled with the dial. There was the usual hissing static. Her first choice, the voice from New Zealand, was silent. He apparently only broadcast in the evening hours, on U.S. time, or perhaps he had quit. Languages like biblical tongues rose from the speakers, the excitement the only understandable part. They were everywhere, but few in English. There must be some uproar of some kind.

An English voice came on then faded away again, so she adjusted the dial.

" … taken overnight," the voice said. "I repeat again, in an unprecedented measure, taken overnight, the president of the United States has declared a sweeping emergency, nationalizing all of the states' National Guards, many of which were already out on the streets maintaining order. In the capital, federal troops have been ordered into positions on all the main streets. I repeat, the marines and smaller units of air force paratroopers are out in force, surrounding all government buildings and the White House.

"Traditional communication networks are now under the full control of the U.S. government – one would assume for their own uses, as heavy-handed as that sounds. If the National Guard is unable to keep order, the president has promised to use military troops, suspending all necessary laws to make this possible.

"These are unprecedented times that call for unprecedented measures the president says. In related news, the stock market has crashed to below four thousand on the Dow Jones, and the US dollar is currently trading on world markets at near junk bond status. The president has ordered a freeze on all food prices and essential commodities at their current levels. Where this will all end, no one knows. Congress is threatening to enact articles of impeachment against the president, but no one knows at this time when this will occur or if it will have any effect in alleviating the current crisis.

"We will be repeating this bulletin at regular intervals throughout today." The voice faded into silence.

Regina turned the dial to search for confirmation. She caught voices in English now and then. All of them said much the same thing. "Martial law has been declared … the president has taken on emergency powers … mobs are roaming the cities, burning and looting … Chicago and San Francisco have shut down all the main roads in and out … Miami is under a twenty-four hour curfew … food is running out in the food chains … semitrailers filled with goods are being pulled over on the interstate and vandalized …."

She shut off the radio as Enos walked back into the house.

"It's finally happening." Worry was written deep on her face. "The worst has come, and we have to warn your people."

He stared at the radio. "What is it?"

"It's not good. The president is taking over the country."

He drew in a sharp breath. "Come, we must go then. It may not do any good, but we can try."

"I'll wash the dishes first," she said.

Enos nodded and stepped up to help dry them. He seemed in no hurry, his face a mask.

"There will be much killing." His gaze lingered out the window. "It will destroy so many things."

"I suppose killing always does," she said. "But it can't be helped. Is that how you plan to protect your people?"

"I might as well be useful, since I have already killed."

"You don't think their praying actually makes a difference? Maybe God will protect them?"

"Like he did Rosemary and her parents? She died in that bedroom over there, Regina. She loved me, as I loved her. We were never allowed to say the wedding vows together. We were not given time. I only know the angels took her before the worst. They had to. She was not guilty of anything."

"I'm sorry." She touched his arm. "But don't your people teach you must forgive — even that? Like *The Lord* forgave you this morning. I'm not saying I could, but don't they say to?"

"They do." He hung his head. "But I don't know if I'm forgiven yet."

"Please, Enos, don't say that." She stroked his arm. "We are allowed to seek justice, but not revenge."

"It is all hatred in my heart, Regina. That is all I know."

She hesitated as the sorrow grew deeper on his face. "I'm sorry, Enos, really I am. Simple answers don't seem right at the moment."

He tried to smile. "Have you spoken with your father lately, with your family? Do they know where you are?"

She shook her head. "I haven't since I was asked to leave the church. I guess I was ashamed. Dad said they were all fine the last time I spoke with him. Anyway, the phone lines are down right now. Nobody can call around. The radio said so."

Enos looked deeply concerned. "What is happening with the government? You didn't really say."

She sighed. "The President declared an emergency, and perhaps martial law. Do you know what that is?"

He shook his head. "You don't have to explain. I know it's bad. Anything with the government is usually bad."

She laughed and wiped the last of the dishes. "Talk about two different worlds. Where I come from the government is the best thing since apple pie."

"But you know better now? So perhaps our worlds are coming together?"

She smiled as tears sprang to her eyes. "I wish they were, Enos. But we're still very far apart."

"I know," he said. "Isn't it strange?"

"Not stranger than everything else." She turned back to wipe down the table. Where was the professor this morning, she wondered. Was he still alive? These latest events certainly meant he and his people had been right all along — a lot of good that did them.

"Hello." Enos interrupted her thoughts. "We're all done here … so shall we go now?"

"Yes." She rushed about. "Let me grab some cash. You never know when it might come in handy."

"We'd better take the buggy and the guns," he said. "I usually carry them under the seat."

"Why not my car? That would be faster."

"We need the car to stay here. It makes the place look *English,* remember? We don't need our food stolen or worse."

"It might happen anyway." She followed him out the door.

"Then we had better pray like my people do." His voice carried little conviction.

But at least Enos didn't tease, Regina thought. The whole country was in trouble—had been for some time. She just hadn't realized it.

Chapter Thirty-Five

Regina clung to his arm as Enos drove the buggy towards his father's place. What was his father like? Regina wondered. Enos hadn't said much other than the obvious about being expelled. But what strict religious order wouldn't throw out its members for the things Enos had done? Though she supposed the killing would be reason enough for the Amish, if more reasons were needed one needed only to look at herself. Enos lived in the same house with an "English" girl with no one around to verify the propriety of their relationship.

If their exchange at the fire the previous night was any indication, these people seemed to have some form of communication that baffled her. They rejected technology. Of course, she didn't have a cell phone either, but that was from a quirk of her own. Otherwise, she used the phones like normal people did.

"I wonder how your father's doing," Enos said, interrupting her thoughts. He glanced at her with concern on his face.

"So do I," she replied. "I would have you drive into town so I could call, but they said the phone lines are down."

"Perhaps you should try anyway." Enos's voice was kind. "They could be wrong."

"That's nice of you to suggest, but how could I do that? I should have called before I left the parsonage, but I guess I was too upset."

"There is an *English* neighbor on the next road who lets us use their phone for emergencies. This would be an emergency, I would think."

"That's sweet of you to offer," Regina told him. "I don't think the call will go through, but we can try."

"Okay." He turned the buggy south at the next stop sign.

They pulled into the driveway of the one-story ranch house with its obvious power lines running overhead. Enos stopped near the front door and Regina climbed down. A woman answered, middle-aged, her face lined with concern. "Is there something I can do for you, ma'am?"

Regina pointed back towards the buggy. "Enos said you sometimes allow your phone to be used for emergency calls by the Amish?"

"I'd be glad to," the woman said. "But everything's down. Haven't the Amish heard what's going on in the world?"

"We have," Regina replied. "Although I'm only staying with Enos for a short while."

"Oh, I didn't think you were Amish," the woman said. "But I can't say I blame you for moving around. My husband and I are thinking about going somewhere, but God only knows where that would be. No place sounds any safer than sitting tight right now. We should have gotten out of the country years ago, but Chip would never listen to me. Now look at the mess we're in. We'll do good not to starve to death before this is all over with. Gas was ten dollars a gallon in Farmstead yesterday. Wal-Mart had almost nothing left on the shelves. Can you believe that?"

"No I can't," Regina said. "And I'm sorry to have bothered you. I wanted to call my folks in Georgia."

"I'm sorry too," the woman told her.

Regina nodded. "Is the power still on? I'm just curious."

"So far," the woman shrugged. "We'll have to count the small blessings, I suppose. How we'll pay the bill in a few weeks is beyond me. The government sure isn't going to be able to help."

"Thank you." Regina retreated down the front steps, and turned to wave from the buggy. The woman still stood there, watching her leave. Her face was even more distressed than before.

"The phones are down," Regina told Enos as he drove out of the driveway. "Gas is over ten dollars in Farmstead. I think I'd better leave the car parked in your driveway until this is over."

"If it's over soon — I have a bad feeling about that." Enos slapped the reins.

"I wonder what martial law would look like out in the country?" Regina leaned out of the buggy door to look around. "I don't see the National Guard anywhere."

"They probably stay around the cities."

"I don't think that's good for some reason."

Enos didn't answer her fears but motioned with his chin as he pulled into a driveway. "This is my home."

He stopped by the barn. Regina climbed down and took her time to look around. It appeared much the same as where Enos lived now. The barn was set back from the house a ways, and the driveway ran in between. The house was a white two-story with wrap-around porches on the front. Not that different from what she had grown up with, only larger. Of course there had been no barn, only a shed, and no horses.

"You never told me about your mother." Regina waited as he tied the horse. "Will I be meeting her today?"

"Mom's gone." Enos didn't look at her. "Also two of my sisters and my brother after me. There's only Dad, two brothers, and Edith left now."

"I see, and I'm sorry."

His face was dark as he led her towards the house. Enos didn't knock but walked in the front door. She followed to stand beside him when he stopped in the middle of the living room floor. All was silent. No one seemed to be around.

"Hello?" Enos hollered, making Regina jump.

The swift patter of feet came down the stairs, and the door burst open. A slight girl, her white *kapp* askew, raced out and flung herself into Enos's arms. He caught her and hugged the girl tight to his chest while she sobbed.

"Now, now." Enos stroked her back. "What has happened, Edith? Tell me quickly."

She let go of him and threw herself on the couch to cover her face in her hands. Regina pushed past Enos and put her arm around the distraught girl. Enos shook his head and bent down on one knee in front of them. "What's wrong, Edith?"

Regina whispered, "I'm Regina. Can you tell us what's happened?"

"Father and the boys have gone to the schoolhouse," Edith said. "Bishop Mast called a meeting for the men. There are terrible things happening in the community and they want to talk about it."

"What has happened?" Enos stood to his feet.

Edith lifted her tear-stained face. "I'm not sure. I couldn't hear everything, but Emory Yoder's were robbed last night. They live the closest to Farmstead. Lester came to tell us. There were a bunch of pickup trucks and men. They pulled up to the basement door and took everything out, all the canned goods, the bags of potatoes. They even took the wheat in the barn. Emory and his family have nothing left."

"God help us." Enos turned his face away.

"That's not the worst," Edith continued. "They were also at Jonas Troyer's place and now he's dead."

"Dead!" Enos shouted. "How did this happen?"

Edith burst into tears again as Regina hugged her tighter. Long moments passed before Edith found her voice. "You know how hot-headed Jonas is. He stood in front of the cellar door and wouldn't move. They shot him, Lester said, then dragged his body out in the yard. They still took everything. I guess Bishop Mast will go over to bury him at the graveyard this afternoon."

"And Father left you alone?" Enos exclaimed. "With men like that about? I can't believe this."

"He said *The Lord* would take care of me." Edith broke into sobs again.

"I'm taking you home with me until this is over," Enos said. "I've had enough of this. What if someone attacks you again?"

"I can't leave, Enos." She wiped her tears. "You know that. Father won't allow it."

"Come." Regina took Edith by the hand. "Let's go talk about it somewhere. Shall we?"

Regina left Enos to pace the floor, while the girl motioned towards the kitchen table.

"You'd be welcome to come and stay with us," Regina said once they were seated, her hand on the girl's shoulder. "I'll even talk with your father, because Enos is right, you shouldn't be alone in the house with what's going on. A lot of very bad men are roaming around."

"I know," she nodded. "Enos killed one of them. Did he tell you?"

"Yes, but I'm sure Enos wasn't to blame," Regina said. "He was defending a girl. Shall I ask your father whether you can stay with us?"

Edith studied Regina's face for a long moment before she whispered, "You're staying with Enos then? You're the woman?"

Regina smiled, "No, dear, it's not like that at all. But I do stay with Enos. Believe me, it's all above board."

Edith didn't appear convinced. "I don't know what all that means, but Enos killed a man, so I don't know if Father will allow it."

"Okay," Regina told her. "Shall I stay with you awhile until your father comes back?"

"You don't have to. I'm okay upstairs. I won't come out of my room if someone else arrives."

"Are you sure?" Regina wiped a stray tear that ran down the girl's face.

"I'm okay." Edith put on a brave face. "Father will be praying for me."

"Well, that's sweet of him." Regina took the girl's hand and returned with her to the living room.

"I'm staying," Edith told Enos, her voice firm. "It's better that way."

"I suppose so," Enos agreed. "I wouldn't want to make trouble for you."

"Are you going with the angels when you die?" Edith looked up at Enos's face.

"No one's dying," Regina stated as she drew Edith towards her for another hug.

"We could all die soon." Edith's eyes were large. "Enos needs to be ready to go."

"I prayed this morning. Perhaps that will help." Enos tried to smile and patted Edith on the head. "We're going over to the schoolhouse to see if I can talk some sense into our people."

Edith disappeared up the stairs before they went out the front door. Regina noticed that the girl straightened her *kapp* as she went.

"The poor thing," Regina told Enos on the walk out to the buggy. "She's got to be scared to death, but she's still so brave."

"I should have insisted she come with us." Enos untied the horse. "It will be my fault if something happens to her."

"You really take too much on yourself," Regina told him as Enos climbed in and sat on the buggy seat beside her. She took a deep breath. They were all in a lot of danger come to think of it.

"I think you should preach that sermon to yourself." Enos glanced sideways at her with a slight smile on his face. "That's what my people would say."

"That's mean, you know," she told him. "But that was nice of you, the way you took care of your sister. You have nothing to be ashamed of in protecting her."

His face was grim as he looked straight out the front of the buggy. Moments later he said, "There's the schoolhouse," as he pointed with his chin.

"They have gathered to pray." She took in the long sweep of buggies and horses.

"They pray to a God who gives and who takes away."

She glanced at his face. "It's still nice that He gives."

"I don't know. Sometimes I wish He wouldn't bother."

"That heart of yours needs some healing, I see." She put her arm around his shoulder and pulled him tight.

"I'm not a baby that needs to be mothered," he muttered as he pulled into a field where lines of buggies were tied to the fence row.

"But you need to be loved," she told him. "We all need that."

Chapter Thirty-Six

Regina pulled on Enos's arm as they walked across the schoolyard. Even longer lines of horses and buggies were tied behind the building. Men and boys in dark homespun suits stood outside the double doors, black hats on their heads, their faces grim.

"I don't think I should be coming in here," Regina whispered. "I don't see any women."

"That's because this is a men's gathering."

"Then I'm not going another step." Regina let go of his arm.

Enos stopped and turned around to face her. "It doesn't matter. We're *English* now, see . . . ." He ran his fingers through his hair. "And no hat."

She wasn't sure how much that changed things.

"I'm not one of them," Enos continued. "Come. It looks strange standing out here arguing.

Regina wanted to laugh. And Enos thought it was not strange to walk into a group of Amish males in black hats and dark suits who stared at you?

"We won't go inside," Enos said as they approached. "They don't want me in there anyway. Someone will come out to speak with us shortly I'm sure."

Apparently this was some compromise on his part. As they stood apart from the scattered group it didn't seem like much of a compromise. At least some of the young boys smiled, Regina told herself. A man came out the door moments later. He looked around before he walked over to them. Regina waited as the two eyed each other.

"I'm surprised you'd come here, Enos. You know this is hard on all of us."

"I know, Father," Enos told him. "But I had to. There is a great danger out there. Surely you are ready to do something about it?"

"You never give up," Enos's father said. A sad smile played on his face. "We will pray for you tonight when we gather with the women folk. The sorrow in your heart has driven you to do things that no man should do, yet I hope *The Lord* will be merciful with you, as He is with us."

Enos hung his head, and Regina walked over to take his arm. Enos's father nodded to her, his face sad. "I see you have an *English* woman with you now. I cannot give my blessing to any of this, even if I understand some of it. *The Lord* will have to judge you at the *Last Day*. And I hope He will remember your mother's dying words."

Enos said nothing.

"It's not how it may appear between us. Enos is an honorable man," Regina spoke up for him. "We were hoping there was something we could do to help. I know the police won't be of much help with everything else going on, but maybe you could gather at one place — like this schoolhouse — and protect each other in some manner?"

The old man shook his head, and his beard parted in the wind. "Perhaps you do not understand, but we do not ask man to help us in our hour of need. It is better to suffer death than to forsake the ways of *The Lord*."

Regina nodded, "I understand. Enos told me a story last night about your faith."

"Oh?" The man's face lighted up for a moment. "Enos told you about us?"

"Yes," Regina said. "You should be proud of your son. He is trying to do what is right."

"Proud!" He jerked his head back and swept his hand through the air. "No one should give in to pride. It is the sin that pulled Satan from the heavens."

"Ah, what about happy then?" Regina tried again. "Is that better? Enos should give you joy in your heart."

He leaned forward to study her face. "You can never know the sorrow that lies upon my heart at the loss of my son. My heart was broken to where it will never recover again. Killing is the first sin man committed after being thrown out of the garden. Enos has killed his brother."

"I know. That's what he said, but couldn't there have been reasons perhaps?" Regina asked. "He was defending one of your girls."

"There are always reasons," the old man said. "But we are the ones who make the choices. That is what counts in the end."

"Come." Enos pulled on her arm. "I'm sorry, Father, for what I have done. And I know the way back is closed to me, even if I wanted to come — which I don't."

"We will pray for you." His father stood still with a bowed head.

"Come," Enos said again, and Regina followed him back to the buggy. She looked over her shoulder to see the old man still there with tears running down his face.

"You should see if you can fix this problem, Enos, and mend the rift between you and your father."

"He killed my mother, Regina. He wouldn't let us take the medicine Clare and Joe offered us. He killed my sisters, and would have killed us all including himself if I had listened to him. He has me to thank that he's even breathing."

"You hadn't told me that," Regina responded. "But I must say he looks like a man of conviction."

Enos laughed. "He's stubborn, that's all — blaming God for his own faults."

"Are you sure you aren't doing the same thing?" She looked up at his face.

"I don't know. How would I know? People can't see their own faults."

"Take me to see your mother's grave, Enos. Would you?"

"Mom's grave?" He nearly stopped the horse as he jerked back on the reins.

"Yes. Take me there. I want to see it."

"But it's in the field behind Father's house. There's nothing to see."

"Just take me, Enos. I also want to see where Rosemary is buried."

"The woman has gone crazy," he muttered.

She grimaced. "The whole world is crazy, so we might as well join in."

He shrugged and urged the horse on faster. Apparently he wanted to get this unpleasant request over with. At least he would humor her. And she had her reasons. She wanted to see where his pain came from.

Regina and Enos drove back the way they had come. They pulled into his father's driveway and parked out by the barn. This time his sister Edith ran out before Enos had the horse tied.

"What are you back for?" Edith asked, as she came to a stop inches from him.

"We've come back to show Regina Mother's grave. Maybe you should go back in the house and wait until we're done?"

Edith shook her head. "I want to go with you. I was never back there since that horrible night we buried her."

"Okay." Enos gave in. "But I still think you shouldn't come."

"I think it's a good idea." Regina took the girl's hand. "Everyone wants to visit their mother's grave."

Enos shrugged and led the way across the field. They soon reached the fence row with its mounds of fresh dirt heaped high. Wooden stakes marked the heads with names scrawled in white chalk.

"Paul, Mary, Esther, and Fannie," Regina read in a quiet voice. "Which one was your mother?"

"Fannie," Edith whispered. "She was a good mother. I wish she was back with us, because I miss her so much."

"Did your bishop help bury them?" Regina asked.

Enos shook his head as tears ran down his face. "We brought her out in the spring wagon, in the early evening, her body destroyed by the disease. Father was on the outs with the bishop so there was no one to say the prayers except Father himself, but it wasn't the same. Nothing is the same when you're on the outs with your faith."

The tears kept on as his voice continued. "She told us before she left that she heard the angels singing, that *Mommy* and *Dawdy* had come for her. She asked that I be sure to keep my heart pure so I could follow her. Then we buried her here. We threw the dirt on her body. And I have not heeded her warning."

Regina wanted to run up and hug him, hold him in her arms like a little boy, but he was a man now — a strong man who wept like a child. Instead she opened her arms to Edith, holding the young girl tight while she sobbed. They stood there for long moments, heads bowed, as the sun went behind the clouds and came out again. A wood thrush flew through the fence row. It made a racket in the branches of the small trees, but Enos didn't move. Finally he turned and without a word led the way back to the buggy.

At the house he took Edith in his arms, and the two wept again. "I have to go now," he said as he wiped his eyes. "Can you go back in the house and wait? Father should be home soon."

"Oh, Enos," Edith sobbed. "Can't you come back home again somehow? We need you. I need you. It's not the same with both you and Paul gone. Can't you please?"

"I'm sorry, Edith." He touched her face with his fingers. "But it can't be done. I know you don't understand, but a lot of us don't understand things right now. Maybe God will explain everything some day."

"Do you still pray, Enos?" Edith wiped her eyes to look up at him.

He nodded. "I do a little, but you must not worry about me, Edith."

"You are my brother," she whispered. "Of course I worry about you."

"I know." A ghost of a smile played on his face. "I'll always be your brother."

Edith returned the smile, her face lighting up. She turned to run back towards the house. She held up her dress to the knees as she bounded up the front steps.

Enos untied the horse but said nothing as he climbed into the seat beside Regina.

"Do you still want to see Rosemary's grave?"

He guided the horse out to the main road while she took a moment to answer. "I do. And I think you should see it too. Have you been down there since it happened?"

He shook his head.

"And yet it's close to here, isn't it?"

"It is, but it's not something I want to see."

Regina left him to his thoughts but held his arm on the ride to the graveyard. She took his hand after he tied the horse. Together they walked across the fields to the other side, where they came up on a small knoll. Fresh dirt was everywhere, with three Amish boys, their hats on the ground, busy at work on a fresh grave. Enos led the way to a line of three mounds that rose against the sky, the sides washed out by the recent rains.

Regina looked up at his face and waited. She squeezed his hand and stroked his arm, but still there were no tears. Enos stood frozen, unable to move.

"Why are there no markers?" she asked. She remembered the wooden chalked ones at the other field.

He cleared his throat. "I guess they were expecting me to put some up, but I never did."

"Did you bury them yourself?"

"No, they helped me. The women washed the bodies, and Bishop Mast said the prayers. That's what they do if you are not on the outs with the church."

"Tell me about Rosemary." She squeezed his hand again.

He waited for a long moment in silence. "The grave on the right belongs to John, the middle one to his wife Esther, and the last one to Rosemary. She was my love since we were young. We made eyes at each other sitting in our school desks. Mostly it was me growing red, I think, and she laughing at me, but I made it through those days. Rosemary was the most beautiful girl of all the Amish. She could laugh with a sound like water in a brook running over stones. When she smiled the whole world changed around her. I thought I would die sometimes sitting beside her in the buggy.

"She was too wonderful to die like this — torn apart by an evil man's hands. I saw her before they buried her. The devil must be evil in ways we can never understand to so use a body only God could have fashioned with His own hands. That man must have been full of the devil."

"You loved her, didn't you?" Regina felt his fingers move in her hand.

"She taught me how to love, and how to hate. It is something I cannot change."

"I'm sorry, Enos. I really am. You are a brave man to go on living. Don't forget that."

"But I cannot go on hating for long." His voice was cold. "It is eating me up inside. Even your love cannot long stay alive in such a heart, but I don't know what to do."

"I know." She held his hand as the sun went behind the clouds again and sent a chill through the afternoon air.

Chapter Thirty-Seven

Regina cleared the last of the supper dishes from the table. She paused to lean into the kitchen doorway. Enos sat on the couch, his face lit by the glow of the gas lantern that swung from the nail in the ceiling. He had needed a good supper, she thought, which was why she had made him one. An instinct from her Georgia upbringing, she supposed, from watching her mother take such good care of her father.

There were few things like a good meal to reach a man's heart. At least that's what her mom always said. In her father's case it seemed to have worked well. Enos was another matter, but then her father hadn't lost his mother to illness and his promised one and her parents to a violent attack. Still, overseas duty in Vietnam wasn't a cakewalk, and even though her father never talked about such things, he surely had seen his share of pain.

Perhaps Enos needed some time alone to think through things. He was far from healed on the inside. Thankfully he still talked with God, the great physician. Regina turned to wash the dishes and listened to the soft tinkling of the china edges as they met under water. With a clean towel she wiped them dry and placed them back where she had found them.

This world was far removed from what she was used to. It was hard to reconcile the two. Travis, the parsonage, the professor — it all seemed a dream, like her life was caught in a time warp. Regina smiled. Perhaps she was in one. The lives these people lived were very real. Different from hers, and in many ways better, she decided. Even if she could never be like them.

The leftover food she put in the gas-powered refrigerator. It had no light inside, so she brought over the lamp and set it on the counter. The salad bowl teetered sideways since all the shelves were full. There was no lack of food in the house, she noticed. That was something to be very thankful for.

"Dear God," she prayed, "help Enos, or help me to help him however I can, because I really don't know how."

Regina leaned around the kitchen door for another check on Enos. He still stared out into the fast-falling dusk. She lifted the shortwave radio off the floor and set it on the table. With a sigh, she began to turn the dial. She sat down and listened to the urgency of the English voices, wherever she managed to find them. They were on the same subject.

"Enos." She got up to call from the kitchen opening. "Come listen to this."

He rose to his feet, his face lined with the deep pain of his sorrow. "Is something wrong?"

"Yes, come listen to this."

He came in and sat at the kitchen table. She fiddled with the dial and the voice improved considerably. "... streets of Washington DC are patrolled by the Marine Corps, under the control of General Worland. The president is currently confined to the White House. Congressional committees are holding hearings even now as we speak, looking into charges that the president has been directly involved in many of the atrocities committed by government officials throughout the states.

"When these hearings began early this morning, spurred on no doubt by the president's declaration of martial law some hours before, the president ordered the members of Congress arrested who were involved in any investigation into these conspiracy theories, as he called them.

"General Worland refused, ordering the troops under him to disregard the order. Marines now encircle the Capitol Building where Congress is in session, lining the streets throughout the city. The Speaker of the House has called for

General Worland to bring in reinforcements if he needs them, and we have been told that he may have decided to do so, as there are reports of troop movements towards Washington from Fort Bragg.

"Our source at the Capitol could not tell us what the charges are that the congressional committees are looking into but he assured us they are *impeachable offenses.* Which is apparently what motivated the president into his unprecedented actions earlier, ordering the arrest of another branch of government.

"We do not know when a vote for impeachment could come to the floor of the house, but hopefully this drama will be resolved soon for the good of all. Never have troops been used during peacetime to protect the workings of Congress, but that goes without saying. Perhaps this is war, just in a way we have not seen it before. Let it be said with certainty that we really are experiencing the making of history right before our eyes."

Regina turned down the volume.

"So what does all that mean?" Enos clasped his hands.

"It means we could all be in a whole lot of trouble." Regina got up. "I think I'm going down to pray with your people at the schoolhouse."

"Really," Enos said. "Well, I'm not going with you. But tell me more about what is happening. Is the president doing things he shouldn't be doing?"

Regina laughed, "That's putting it mildly. But of course nothing is proven yet. Though I'd be very surprised if the president wasn't involved in what has been going on."

"No one's perfect." The look of sorrow returned to his face.

"This goes well beyond some little mistakes, Enos. I was hoping the martial law declaration was a thing of necessity, but it could well not have been. It might have been a cover-up for what was going on."

"You always see the best in people, don't you?"

"Of course." She reached over to ruffle his short hair. "It's the best way to live, although I'm beginning to doubt that."

"Thanks." He attempted a smile. "And don't stop being that way. It feels good."

"I don't have to think the best of you. You're already a good man."

"I wish," he said. "But be that as it may, I'm not going with you to the schoolhouse. I've had all of my people I need at the moment."

"I'm taking the car, since I'm certainly not driving your buggy."

"That's okay." He shrugged.

"There goes your protection."

"I have my gun, and I'll use it," he said.

"Now please, Enos." She ran her hand through his hair again. "There are rules, you know. Different rules than you grew up with, but still rules. You don't go shooting people for no reason, okay? They have to be threatening your life. So shoot in the air, things like that, but don't kill anybody if you don't have to."

He nodded. "There always seem to be rules. I'll be careful."

"I'll see you then." She took her purse and jingled the car keys in her hand. Enos went to the door and kept watch until she reached the car. She knew, because she turned around to look. He stood in the doorway, a silent dark figure framed by the low light. She waved, and he lifted his hand to wave back, then closed the door as she started the car.

Regina drove back over the route they had gone earlier in the day, past Enos's father's place, the farmhouse and dark barn. They must all still be at the prayer meeting, she thought — Edith, James, Andy, and his father. While in prayer they would find respite from the sorrows this world had heaped upon them.

A warm glow flowed through her body, radiating outward

from deep inside of her. How wonderful these people were, in spite of the way they used Enos. There was something endearing about their stubbornness, which seemed almost like devotion. Or was it the other way around? They lived close to the earth and held dear the simple things of life.

Enos was blinded by the sorrow he had suffered. She needed to help him see that he should make peace with his past. He had too great a thing here for him to throw it away for vengeance. Of course, if Enos made his peace, he was lost to her. But that couldn't be helped. Their worlds would never blend in that way.

Regina wiped away the sudden tears. She must place what was right above all else, as they did. Enos was a wonderful man, and he deserved to live in peace, un-tormented by the travails of the *English*. She would never meet anyone better than Enos. Not in ten years, not in twenty years, not ever. What better thing could she do than help him make peace with his past and return to where he would be truly happy? There couldn't be any better choice of action, even if her heart objected to the thought.

Ahead of her the schoolhouse came into the reach of the headlights. Even more buggies than this morning were parked all along the fence row and into the back yard. She parked a distance away in a small pull-off by the lane.

She would have to walk a short distance, but this was the way it should be. Her car belonged down here, apart from them. She was not one of them, and yet they would not turn her away. The women would be there tonight, all of their hearts open in prayer.

Several small boys stood outside when she approached the double doors. They looked at her and pushed their small black wool hats back on their heads.

"Hi," she smiled. "Is it okay if I come in?"

The tallest one smiled. He nodded but said nothing. They moved aside as one to allow a way in and up the steps into the main auditorium. Only a few hand-drawn pictures from the schoolchildren adorned the off-white walls.

Regina paused at the top to gather her wits. The men prayed on one side, and the women on the other. Everyone knelt at the plain wooden benches with their faces hidden in their hands. The school children's metal four-legged desks were stacked high on both sides of the large open room.

A man's voice from the front lead out in *German,* with words she couldn't understand. Regina slipped into the back bench on the woman's side and turned to kneel as they did. It felt strange, this humbleness of the spirit that seemed to go along with the bent body. But perhaps it was simply the spirit of the place, the deep tones that rose in prayer. Behind her, the man's voice ceased and another rose to take his place.

They must be ministers who prayed, she thought at first, but after an hour realized there couldn't be that many ministers in the room. The men must take turns by some system she couldn't understand. But perhaps they were simply leading out as they had opportunity.

Words from the past began to take focus in her mind, German spoken by one of her teachers in college — only it wasn't quite the same. They seemed to be using some dialect, with normal German words slightly mispronounced scattered about.

Gott she understood, and *Liebe, Gnade, Heiligen Geist, Helfen Uns,* and *Vergebung* — words drawn from the distant past, somehow transported into the twenty-first century in all their power and potency. Yet was not the cry of the heart in any language the greatest voice this world could hear? She mouthed the words in her own tongue — *Love, Grace, Holy Spirit, Help Us,* and *Forgiveness.*

That last word pulled at her heart as she pressed her head into her hands. How many things in the world needed forgiveness? How many sins had been committed today, every day, by all of the fallen members of the human race? If hatred was the standard for human relations, then none of them could last long.

But could she forgive what had been done already? The woman in the car who drove her own child to its destruction and took herself with him. The man at the hospital driven to such extremes. People abandoned in their greatest time of need by the government they trusted. And if the charges being debated before Congress were true, there were a whole lot of things that would need forgiveness.

The shuffling of feet around her aroused Regina from her thoughts, and she stood to her feet along with them. The women seemed surprised to see her, yet offered to shake her hand. No one asked what she did here. Perhaps they thought she was one of the *English* neighbors who lived close by, and had been driven to prayer by the extremities the nation was in. She left while the somber voices still talked in the schoolhouse. Apparently the Amish would visit for some time yet. No doubt they drew strength from each other as they had just drawn strength from God.

The tall boy at the double doors smiled at her as his hands held open the door. She smiled back. He would make a good husband for someone some day if he survived this horrible time. He would find some young demur little girl perhaps who sat among the women even now, who would hold his hand in marriage.

"Good night," she told him, but he only smiled.

At the car she turned to look back and gasped at the sight above the schoolhouse. She put her hand over her mouth to still any sound as she leaned against her car. What looked like mists moved above the roof line and drifted skyward. But they were not mists; they were angels that took form for a few minutes then faded away again. Others seemed to come to take their place, holding steady for a moment before their wings wafted them away in the night air.

"Oh God," Regina whispered. "I can't believe this."

As she stared with eyes wide open, the vision faded, leaving only ordinary clouds that drifted in from some river or pond in the fields behind the schoolhouse.

Regina shook her head and climbed back into the car. She drove past Enos's father's place, the house still draped in darkness, back to where she had started. She climbed out of the car and walked into the house. She might as well not tell any of this to Enos. He wouldn't believe her anyway. He would think she was trying to move him to reconcile with his people. Indeed she wanted to do that, but she was not about to use this vision. Right now it seemed too sacred a thing to subject to anyone's skepticism. Perhaps in the morning she would tell him.

"Hi," he said when she walked inside. "I think we need to go patrol the community. Those men could be back again."

"I don't think that's necessary," she told him.

He looked at her. "Are you like my father now, believing in prayer?"

"I think I do," she said. "And I'm going upstairs to get some sleep."

A look of pain crossed his face, but he dropped his eyes. "Okay. Maybe I'm wrong. I wouldn't argue that point. But I'm going out on my own."

"Good night, Enos." She closed the stair door behind her.

Chapter Thirty-Eight

The three pickup trucks rode the back roads. They slowed briefly for the stop signs before roaring on through. Two trucks held three men each and the other held two, their guns on the racks behind them or propped up between their knees. A low light in the house window ahead caught the attention of the lead truck, which pulled abruptly into the driveway.

"I like this place," the driver said. "Anyone with a light on at this late hour has got to have his basement well stocked."

"You sure it's an Amish place, dumbbell?" his companion said as they bounced to a halt beside the barn. The other two trucks stopped behind them. "We don't want to be storming some house where they go calling the police on us."

The driver laughed. "Like the cops care about us. They're too busy fighting each other and Congress is fighting the president. I say we get ourselves what we can while it lasts."

"I guess that light looks like a gas lantern. Some poor soul must still be up praying for his sins."

They laughed loudly and poured out of the trucks, then broke down the front door with well-aimed kicks. No one tried to turn the knob. The old man who sat at the kitchen table stood to his feet, his face lined with worry.

"Can I help you?" he asked. "It seems you could've knocked. The door was unlocked."

They fired into his chest, and the sound exploded in the small quarters.

"Ha, now that's the way to take care of opposition," the driver said.

"We're going to stop killing them soon," another said. "We have to. We need them to work so we can keep ourselves going."

"Not with the prices we're getting for this stuff," the driver said. "We can retire in a few weeks."

They laughed. "Well, how about starting to load the stuff then. I suggest you pull up to the basement door as usual."

"You boys get started," the driver said. "I'm checking the upstairs. I don't like surprises."

"Tie them up for me," someone said. "And we'll check in later."

To more laughter, they found the basement door while some went to bring up the trucks. The driver barged up the stairs with his flashlight and flung open the first door he came to. He found nothing but an empty bed, a quilt flung out into the floor, its occupants having fled.

He pushed open the closet door and smiled at the long line of plain dresses that hung there. He worked his way out into the hallway and pushed open the bedroom door on the other side with his gun barrel. The hinges screeched in the still night air.

"Ha." His flashlight beam caught the face of a young girl huddled in the middle of a large bed. Two young boys stood in front of her. "I see where she's gone."

The boys said nothing, but they launched themselves at him without a sound. Their hands reached out like willowy phantoms, throwing wild shadows on the wall. He hollered before they struck him, then staggered back under the force of their bodies. He dropped his weapon to throw them off him. On all fours he scrambled across the floor. The flashlight clattered against the wall and revealed their forms crouched for another leap. Apparently these youngsters would not submit without a fight.

Both of the boys looked at the gun that lay near their feet. He figured they would seize it, turn the weapon on him, and fire away at will. Cold sweat broke out on his chest; his heart pounded from fear. What had seemed only harmless fun moments before had fast turned into the grim reaper himself.

He measured the distance with his eyes, but there was no way he could reach the weapon before the boys did. They looked like hardy farm fellows, their young arms rippling with muscles in the light of the flashlight. He waited. What else could he do? They looked at each other, then at the gun, then back at each other.

He watched as they shook their heads and launched themselves over the gun at him again. With a wild cry, he dove between them and slid across the floor. His arms reached for the gun. He found the steel under his fingers and spun around, firing at anything that moved.

His hands shook when he stopped. There was no longer any movement and he reached for the flashlight. They were dead, no question about it, their heads twisted at strange angles. Blood dripped onto the hardwood floor. He kicked them with his foot and fired again, but still his heart pounded. He moved the flashlight beam and found the body of the girl sprawled across the bed. Her hands hung down almost to the floor.

"That wasn't necessary," he muttered.

Feet sounded on the stairs and he hollered, "I'm in here. Don't shoot."

They came in with their own lights to probe the dark corners of the room.

"You are one sorry son of a gun," one of them laughed, the sound eerie in the silent room.

"Let's get out of here," the driver said. "Have you loaded everything yet?"

"Next time we'll keep you with us if you can't stop shooting," the other said as they stomped out of the room. They paused long enough to shine their flashlights around one last time.

Downstairs they loaded the last of the canned goods, the bags of potatoes, the onions, and the wheat onto the trucks. With two vehicles filled to the sideboards, they parked the third beside the barn to nab the goodies there. They found bags on a stanchion wall and scooped them full of oats, then threw them into the truck bed.

When the truck could hold no more, they pulled out of the driveway and headed to town. They avoided a roadblock on 460 by a side road. In the dark a cruiser passed them, turned around, and turned on its lights. They pulled over in front of a large two-story house just west of Farmstead. No one offered any resistance while the officer called in backup. Surrounded, they were arrested and taken into Farmstead to be questioned further.

Chapter Thirty-Nine

Enos stood at the kitchen window after breakfast and watched the early morning fog lift off the road to the south. Regina was a better cook than he had thought at first. She prepared food that matched anything he had grown up with as a child. She must wish to smooth things over after what had happened last night.

He had gone to patrol the community by himself for an hour, driving through the main roads of the community with his buggy. Everything had been quiet enough. He had watched the families arrive home from their prayer meeting at the schoolhouse and waited until the lights winked off in the houses. It had all seemed so useless, such a waste of energy, he told himself. The world had gone crazy and there seemed little he could do about it. Perhaps prayer was the answer after all?

As they ate together this morning, Regina had told him the story of the angels she saw over the rooftops of the schoolhouse. He had smiled at first, but believed her. At least that she had seen them. Regina was sure they had been a sign of divine protection over the gathered Amish community.

Now she listened to the radio again as the voice of the man spoke excitedly: "… for the first time in the history of the United States, the charge of treason has been leveled against the president, with articles of impeachment to be debated on the floor of the house. The congressional committee claims the president is guilty of the highest crime in the land, committed against the Constitution of the United States which the president has sworn on oath to protect.

"Debate is scheduled to begin within the hour on charges of gross abuse of powers and of complicity by the president himself in high crimes and misdemeanors against the citizenry of this country. Security around the Capitol has increased overnight with soldiers flown into Reagan International from Fort Bragg in North Carolina. Others are en route by convoy, our sources tell us, but have not arrived yet."

Enos turned his head away when he saw movement on the road. He looked closer as a horse and open buggy took shape. The driver pushed his horse so hard he was near a gallop. Without a word to Regina, Enos burst out the front door to meet his cousin Henry as he pulled into the front yard.

"Come at once," Henry shouted in German. He moved over on the seat of the buggy. "They're all dead. We found them this morning."

"Who is dead?" Enos asked. His body refused to move.

"Your father and the rest of them," Henry told him. "We've sent for Bishop Mast, and I came for you."

"But ... ?" The question died in his mouth as Enos leaped on the buggy. Henry turned the buggy around and nearly overturned in the barnyard. Enos looked back to see Regina standing on the front porch with the now silent radio.

"My family is dead," Enos screamed back at her. The sound roared from his chest like a mighty earthquake. Her hands flew to her mouth and the radio crashed to the porch floor. There was no room for her in the open buggy, Enos thought, so she would simply have to stay behind. This was his sorrow, and these were his people. She didn't belong among them.

Henry drove his horse hard, while Enos hung on to the sides of the rail until his fingers turned numb. There had to be some mistake, his mind told him, but Henry wouldn't have gotten things mixed up. It simply wasn't possible.

"Was Edith disgraced?" he asked between clenched teeth.

"No." Henry's face was white as the wind drove the mist across his face.

"How do you know?"

"Because I found her myself upstairs in the bedroom with James and Andy. She was shot in the head and chest, but all her clothes were still on her. They were not torn. I would have known."

Enos nodded, his whole body numb.

Henry cleared his throat. "You must never tell anyone, but James and Andy were attacking the man. The signs were very clear. That's why he shot them, and that's why he never got to Edith. She must have fled to the boys' room for protection."

Enos groaned.

"Do you think their souls went with the angels?" Henry's voice trembled.

"How do I know such things?" Enos said. "I only know I hate the people who have done this thing to my family. I hate them with everything that's in me."

"You must not say such things," Henry gasped. "It can only place your own soul in awful danger."

"I've already been thrown out from our people," Enos said. "How can it be worse than that?"

"You must still not say it," Henry said. "It is a high and grave sin."

"Yes, the worst," Enos said. "And I have done it all."

Behind them the sound of a car approached. Henry turned his head, but Enos didn't look.

"It's that woman who stays with you," Henry said. "She's not passing."

Enos turned around and shouted over the buggy seat, "Go away, this has nothing to do with you."

Whether Regina heard or not, she shook her head as Enos pointed back towards the farm. Her car didn't fall out or turn around and was still with them when they pulled into the barnyard. Their horse gasped for air.

"I'll take care of him," Henry said as he leaped to the ground. "You go on to the house."

Two buggies were parked in the yard, their horses not tied up, the reins hanging to the ground. Enos walked past them with small steps. He wished he wouldn't need to arrive anywhere ever again. How wonderful it would be to just walk to the edge of the world and step off into nothing. There he would hold out his arms and feel his body drift away, falling down, down, down until he reached the bottom. His bones would shatter, his flesh would tear on the rocks, or if there was no bottom he would continue forever and ever.

"I'm so, so horribly sorry." Regina came up behind him to take his arm. He said nothing but allowed her to stay. What else could he do?

They entered the house arm in arm and walked to the living room, where the bodies were laid out. Women wept as the men guided them to the forms covered with white sheets. Enos pulled back the covers one by one in the order they had laid them.

His brother James, the strong one, the one who always spoke up first; Andy, the tender one, the scholar, the one who understood people's feelings; his father, the one who gave him life, the one whose hand brought him up to work the fields.

He pulled back the sheet on the face of his sister Edith and wept. Regina touched his shoulder, and he felt her like a distant movement on a body he no longer owned. Edith was gone. She would never see the light of the sun again. She would never see love rise in the eyes of her beloved. She would never say the sacred vows. Edith was dead. They were all dead.

Chapter Forty

The yard had filled with more buggies when Regina stepped outside on the porch. She searched their faces. Perhaps she would recognize someone from the night before. They at least would know who she was and why she was here. Someone needed to report this crime, but no one seemed to take any steps in that direction.

Should she leave and find a police officer since the phones might still be down? But that might not be wise. She should at least tell one of the Amish people what she planned to do. Enos was in no shape to be asked. Thankfully Lester, the man from the night of the fire, stood beside the barn where he spoke with another bearded man.

Regina nodded to the Amish people she passed on the lawn and they nodded back. Lester and the man beside him fell silent when she approached.

Regina cleared her throat. "I followed Enos over from the house and I have a question."

"Yes." Lester's face was sober. "I am sorry that you have to see this great tragedy *The Lord* has allowed to be visited upon us."

"I want to help," Regina replied, "which brings up my question. Shouldn't someone report this crime to the police? That's normally how things are done."

"I understand," Lester said. "But these are not normal times. I think the *English* people seem to be having enough problems of their own."

"We don't report such things," the Amish man beside him said.

"I know the bodies are already moved," Regina told them. "But the police need to be told. They'll understand."

The two men looked at each other for a moment.

"And you would do this?" Lester looked back towards her.

"I'll do it right now." Regina turned to leave. If they hollered after her, she'd have to stop. But they said nothing as she got in the car and drove out the driveway.

Another buggy came down the road, the elderly man bearded and sober-faced. He sat beside his wife, her bonnet pulled far forward on her head. Regina pulled aside to allow them to pass. Enos would have plenty of comfort for his loss, there was no question about that, but perhaps not the kind of comfort he desired. These people had thrown him out of their company and yet they gathered when he suffered.

A cell phone would come in handy now, but those might not work either with the phones down. The closest police would be at a roadblock. They had to be around, she thought, and headed towards 460. The little town of Puckett came up in minutes, along with the roadblock. Two officers stood outside their cruiser and motioned her to a halt.

Regina handed them her driver's license and vaccination card before they even asked. The officer at the window glanced at them, nodded, and waved her through.

"Excuse me," Regina said, "but I need to report an attack on an Amish family last night. I just came from there and need to go back."

"Did you discover this yourself?" the officer asked.

"No," Regina said. "I'm staying at their son's place. One of his relatives came to report the crime to us. We went there first. The Amish are reluctant to report these kinds of things, but they agreed that I could."

"And what would the address be?" the officer asked. He scribbled it down when Regina told him. He made no objection when she pulled forward to a driveway, turned around, and drove back through their station. The officer she hadn't spoken to was on the radio in his car.

Before she reached the first turn in the road the officers had pulled up their roadblock. With their lights on they soon passed her. When she arrived back at Enos's father's place the cruiser was already parked in the yard. An alien sight, she thought. The multiple-colored lights bounced off the sides of the horses and black buggies.

Enos still sat in the living room with his face in his hands when she walked in. The old man and his wife from the buggy sat on either side of him, their arms around his shoulders. One of the officers stood near the bodies, the other nowhere to be seen. The stair door was open and voices drifted down. Apparently the missing officer had gone upstairs to investigate. Moments later the officer came down the stairs followed by a young Amish boy, the one who earlier had driven Enos in his buggy.

"Everyone needs to clear the living room and the upstairs," the officer said. "We have another squad car coming and need to do the investigation."

The old man seated beside Enos stood to his feet as tears streamed down his face. His voice choked, "I am the bishop. If I could speak for my people, may I say something?"

The officer nodded, "Of course."

The bishop cleared his throat. "It would be our wish that you not punish any man who has done this. *The Lord God* will seek his own vengeance in His own time, and it is possible that those who have done this may yet come to repentance through the pricking of their own conscience."

"You want us to walk away from this?" The officer stared.

"I do not know what you call such things," the bishop said. "But we do not wish to see anyone held in judgment for this."

"I'm sorry, but we can't walk away from this. And I can assure you it's not your fault. That's how we do things."

Regina spoke up. "These people have been having trouble with vandalism the last couple of nights, I think. They've had another murder, and they've lost quite a few items. Someone is clearing out their basements of food items."

"You go check the basement," one of the officers said to the other, who left through the kitchen doorway, pulling his radio off his belt clip as he went. "And now the rest of you please move out. We have our duty to do. It's the way things have to be done."

The bishop stood to lead Enos by the elbow towards the kitchen. Regina followed and no one objected, but perhaps they wouldn't even if they didn't want her around. She glanced at the women's faces in the kitchen. No one seemed to pay her any mind. The bishop and Enos took chairs at the table, and she slid onto the bench against the wall to seat herself across from them.

The bishop spoke in German to Enos, who seemed to notice Regina for the first time. His eyes were stricken with a deep sorrow, his face streaked with tears.

"This is Bishop Mast," Enos whispered to her.

Bishop Mast regarded Regina with steady eyes. He seemed to measure her very soul with his intense gaze. Regina wanted to look away, to flee the room or hide under the table. Yet she couldn't move. She sat as if riveted to the spot on the hard bench.

Apparently once he had arrived at some conclusion about her, the bishop spoke. "Enos tells me you are a minister."

"Yes," Regina said, because it was true. Even though it seemed like another world, far distant from this world of bearded men and black buggies.

"Do you believe in forgiveness of your fellowman?" Bishop Mast asked, still regarding her. He seemed to ask the question out of deeper motive than mere curiosity. They could hear the sirens of another police car arrive, but neither of them looked towards the kitchen window. Behind them a few of the women left through the washroom door, the click of the latch loud in the silence of the room.

"I do," Regina said. "It is the doctrine Christ taught."

Bishop Mast's eyes didn't leave her face for a long moment, then he nodded. He turned back to Enos and laid his hand on his shoulder. Enos didn't move, his eyes fixed on the tabletop, the tears still on his face.

"*The Lord* has chosen to give you a cup of great suffering," Bishop Mast said. "It is a cup that few of our people have been asked to drink. Our hearts go out to you, Enos, and it is my belief that I should use this moment to welcome you back into the goodwill of the people. If you will forgive, Enos, then God will also forgive you — even what you have done in killing a man."

Enos didn't move, his hands still on the tabletop.

"Can you do this?" Bishop Mast asked, his eyes on Enos's face.

Enos still said nothing. His breath came shallow, and his chest didn't move.

"This may be the only chance you get," Bishop Mast told him. "If you do not forgive while your heart is freshly torn, then it will only get harder and the task more difficult in the future. Can you, Enos? Can you let go?"

"Forgive all this?" Enos screamed. He towered over Bishop Mast and pointed towards the living room. The officer stuck his head in the opening, then withdrew it again as Enos collapsed into his chair. "This is too much to ask of any man."

"God has carried the load of this sin upon his own shoulders," Bishop Mast said. "You should not carry it upon your own, Enos. No man is strong enough for such a thing."

Enos groaned, his face in his hands. "They killed Rosemary. Men like these did it, and now they have killed the rest of my family."

Bishop Mast's eyes sought Regina's face, as if pleading for help. She drew in her breath. The bishop apparently wanted her to address Enos, but she was not from his people, so why did he ask? What if she didn't side with the bishop? Wasn't this a big chance for the man to take?

She could easily doom his efforts to draw back one of his flock. Yet it was true that hatred froze the heart and haunted the soul, and that wasn't what she wanted for Enos. Why shouldn't she help? She didn't want him to roam the countryside with his guns, seeking revenge. He might as easily be killed in this tense environment as find the revenge he looked for. She sighed and nodded to Bishop Mast.

"Enos." Regina reached across the table to touch his arm. He didn't look up, but he listened. "I think you should listen to what Bishop Mast is saying. It is not good to hate. You know what your mother said before she died. It's best that you listen to what your people are telling you."

Enos lifted his head, his eyes bloodshot. "You want me to forgive what they did to Rosemary?"

Regina stroked his arm and ignored the astonished look on Bishop Mast's face. If he wanted her help, then she needed to give it the only way she knew how. "It is better to love, Enos. It is always better. Remember? You believe that. Let God take care of the details. Please, Enos? Okay?"

His eyes said it first, as the light blazed in them. For long seconds he sat frozen before he dropped his head into his hands again.

"He'll do it," Regina whispered to Bishop Mast, who looked back towards Enos.

"Will you, son?" the bishop asked a few minutes later.

Enos nodded but didn't take his head out of his hands.

"Will you forgive the death of Rosemary and her parents?" Bishop Mast intoned. "Will you forgive the death of your father, of Andy, of James, of Edith?"

"I will." Enos still didn't look up.

"And will you forgive your father for whatever you hold against him?" Bishop Mast continued.

Enos leaped up from his chair and cried out, his face contorted. "It was his fault that Mom died — and Rosie, and Mary, and Paul."

Regina glanced towards the opening of the living room. No officer's head appeared, so they must have gotten used to what was going on in the kitchen. Bishop Mast stood to his feet and put his arm around Enos' shoulders. "Yes, Enos, you must forgive your father. He did what he thought was right."

Enos lifted his face towards the ceiling and screamed like a man whose very soul was in torment. "He would have killed us all."

"But you must forgive him, even as God forgives you," Bishop Mast insisted. Regina stood and reached across the table to draw Enos back into his seat.

"Let go, Enos," she whispered. "It's better that way."

Long moments passed as they waited. Slowly his breathing returned to normal, and his hands ceased to shake. Regina still held them until he lifted his head to meet her eyes and nod. His face was grim. Bishop Mast patted his shoulder, a pleased look on his face.

"Welcome back home, Enos," he said. "You are now one of us again, and *The Lord God* will wash your heart of your sin."

Regina let go of his hands and walked around the table to stand beside him. He might be lost to her now, returned to his own people, but she would still stand with him until this day was over. She would not leave until the task was complete, a task she apparently had been sent to this place to perform. How strange that a liberal minister would find herself in Amish country, and that she would help a man like Enos find peace again.

Chapter Forty-One

The late afternoon light hung in the air, the sun near the horizon, ready to drop behind the low bank of clouds that rose in the west. Bishop Mast stood at the head of the newly dug graves, his prayer book in his hand. The men who had dug the graves stood with their shovels ready. Regina clung to Enos's arm, her head bent towards his shoulder.

More than a few women had given Regina strange looks as the afternoon progressed. Apparently they wondered why she was still there. The look in their eyes said it clearly — they had forgiven Enos his past transgressions, but if she didn't clear out soon there would be new ones marked to his account. But she would stay until this was done. She would follow Enos home in her car and tomorrow be gone, never to bother him again.

The tears stung her eyes. She had a right to cry, she told herself. She deeply felt Enos's sorrow, both for his loss and for his struggle this morning to forgive. Hadn't she been there for both of them? She glanced up at his face, still drawn from the pain he had been through. It must not be an easy matter to lose and to forgive those who had taken so much from you.

"And now let us pray," Bishop Mast said, and they all bowed their heads. "Oh God, our great and gracious Heavenly Father, we serve and worship you alone. We love you and seek to keep Your word. We follow after your mercy and your compassionate heart. We confess our sins today. We seek your forgiveness as we also give others forgiveness."

Regina felt Enos' arm move and glanced up at this face.

The first trace of a smile played on his features. The sorrow was still there, but from somewhere he had found at least a touch of peace.

A great swell of emotion rose up inside of her. Not only was he strong on the outside, he really did have that inner strength she always thought he had.

Regina lay her head against his shoulder and whispered her own prayer: "Dear God, please give me the strength to go on."

Enos turned his face towards Bishop Mast as the prayer continued. "Yes, Lord, we are all your children, and lead us now as you led your people, the children of Israel, with a strong hand out of the bondage of Egypt. Your great name was glorified, so now also glorify yourself with the works of your hands among us, your unworthy and broken servants."

These indeed were a great people, Regina thought, steeped in Old Testament theology. They lived out their lives under the belief that God was in everything they did. What would it be like to be one of them? Was such a thing even possible? Could she leave behind her world to join that of Enos and his people? A life of silence? A life lived close to the land? A life of humility before the Will of God in the most intimate details of life? What would that be like?

Regina sighed. Even if possible, that would ask a lot of her. It was likely more than she could give. When she left, she would put her life back together with the same grace that enabled Enos to put his own back together. She would return to Georgia, to family who understood her as Enos's family understood him.

Bishop Mast concluded his prayer, his voice nearly a whisper. The shovels began to move and the dirt fall. Regina allowed the sobs to rack her body — cries for herself, for Enos, for those still here to face this world, most of all for the loss in her own heart. But had it not all been worth it? She comforted herself.

The question found an answer in Enos's face. As he watched the dirt fall on the last of his immediate family, he had a sudden look of joy and lifted his hands towards the heavens. They stopped work as one man to look towards him.

"Go on," he told them. "I just saw the angels leaving. They were flying away towards the sun."

Regina turned to look but saw only the fiery blaze of the sun, the bank of clouds that reached up to swallow the last of its brightness. Perhaps Enos had seen angels, just as she had seen them above the roof of the schoolhouse. God moved in ways He chose, and He could well choose in these times of great pain to reveal Himself in special ways.

"To God be the praise," Bishop Mast said. At least he apparently approved of what Enos had seen. Then they began to shovel again.

When they were done, Regina stayed with Enos on the walk back to the farmhouse. He moved with his head down until they arrived in the barnyard.

"You had better go back to the house," he whispered. "I'll come later after everyone leaves. Someone brought my buggy over, I think, and if not I can catch a ride."

"Do you want me to make supper?" she asked. They had not eaten all day, and hunger gnawed at her.

He nodded and squeezed her hand. She left him to walk back to her car, the only English automobile still at the farm, the officers gone hours ago. They had assured her that patrols would drive through the Amish community for the foreseeable future. They had said that an arrest of several men with pickups loaded with canned goods and bagged grain had been made that morning west of Farmstead. Again, it looked as if her purpose here was complete.

Regina glanced back over her shoulder and saw that Enos had gone inside. She wiped away the tears, started her car, and drove out of the driveway. The fuel gauge, she noticed, was on the three-quarter mark. She wouldn't need fuel anytime soon.

Not until she returned to town. What was life like there by now? Everything had to have changed. Were the phone lines up so that she could call her father? She would have to try at the first chance.

She arrived back at Enos's place and parked the car by the barn. She approached the house but paused on the porch to glance around. The likelihood that anyone had vandalized the place was slim, but still fear bubbled up inside of her. She pushed it away to enter the house and then descended the stairs to check the basement. Everything was as she had remembered. Upstairs, a quick check of the bedrooms and closets revealed no intruders.

She would prepare mashed potatoes and gravy tonight, Regina decided. It might not be made how Enos was used to, but hopefully close. She set the radio on the table and found a station that carried a fairly clear voice, then she put the bowl of water on the counter. The potatoes were in the root cellar, the flour and other ingredients in the pantry. While downstairs Regina grabbed a can of corn.

When she returned she found the radio in the middle of an announcement that the vote on the impeachment of the president was about to take place. Regina waited, but soon continued her work when no fresh news came. Then with a tremor in his voice the announcer proclaimed that the vote on the floor of the house had begun. Regina paused to listen as the moments ticked past.

"The president's party doesn't hold the majority of the seats in the house," the announcer said. "So once again an impeachment of the president is likely. They should reach the required votes without any problems."

Regina continued her work, only half listening to the announcer's voice. She was in the middle of peeling potatoes when the excited announcement came.

"By a vote of 314 to 121, the Congress of the United States has once again passed articles of impeachment against its president. And we have another surprise in the midst of a day of great surprises. A large number of the president's own party have joined in voting *yea*. These articles will be taken over to the Senate tonight, our sources have told us. Because of the extraordinary times, the Senate is to begin the trial stage of this drama tomorrow morning at ten o'clock, an unusually early hour for that chamber."

It would take more than an impeachment of a president to heal the nation, Regina thought, if even half of all she had heard was true. Many state and local officials must have been involved. It would not surprise her if Travis and the town council of Farmstead had known to some degree about the atrocities that had occurred under their watch.

Yet that was hard to take in. Travis was in many ways a nice man. Sure he had shown his dark side that one night, and then he had gotten rid of her at the first sign she didn't support the party line. But perhaps there were reasons for his behavior. A guilty conscience could no doubt do much to unsettle a man.

How great it would be to stay here, hide out from the world at an Amish farm, marry an Amish man, and never see the rugged, raw side of modern life again. Yet modern life had found Enos and no doubt left him scarred. These people would survive though. Enos would survive. She would survive.

They would not seek revenge or harbor bitterness for long, as she also must not. How strange that the very thing her own world would consider the worst response to such a tragedy—that of peace and forgiveness—would in fact ensure that these people not only lived beyond the event but thrived.

It was a lesson her own world could use. Perhaps she had been brought here for that reason? Maybe God wanted her to carry back the message so seldom spoken. That in forgiveness of others — even for their worst sins — our own hearts are cleansed.

Men had fought their wars for thousands of years now, and seemingly each generation had to fight them all over again. Was their loss of life any less than what these people had suffered? She wondered as she prepared supper and watched the road for Enos coming home with his buggy. How strange everything was here, and likely nothing would ever be quite normal again in life. Especially not after the things she had seen.

With supper prepared she waited, listening to the radio and its ongoing commentary on what could happen tomorrow. The president was still confined to the White House. If the Senate failed to convict, there could be consequences beyond what anyone could imagine. The people responsible for the impeachment vote would surely be punished, as would the military leaders who had defied the president's orders.

Enos came home after dusk had fallen. His low buggy lights flickered on the road before they came to a stop out by the barn. Regina ran out to meet him but restrained herself from a hug when he climbed down from the buggy. The time approached when she would have to leave, so she must begin her withdrawal from him now.

"Are you hungry?" she asked.

He nodded as he unhitched the horse. Had Bishop Mast spoken with him again and ordered her out of the house — perhaps tonight already? Was he allowed to even eat with her? She held the buggy shafts for him as he led the horse forward.

"Please take the guns out from under the seat of the buggy," he said. "Maybe you can take them into town tomorrow and get rid of them."

"Okay." She removed the guns while he was in the barn. Hopefully the Amish person who had taken Enos's buggy over hadn't seen them. But if he had, he likely would have considered it a sin in Enos's past. And it was his past now; she had to remind herself of that.

Regina followed Enos towards the house, and halfway there he took her hand. It felt warm and cozy, his shoulder strong.

"Sorry about your folks, Enos, and all that you've lost."

"It's okay," he said. "*The Lord* will make it right. He always does when He gives and takes away."

"I'm glad I got to know you, Enos," she told him. "But I guess you know I have to leave tomorrow. I don't want to mess up your renewed relationship with your people."

"I know." He squeezed her hand. "But I'm glad you're here tonight."

"You are?"

"I'll never forget you." A smile played on his sorrow-stained face. "You have helped show me the way back to God. I never would have found it on my own."

She leaned against his shoulder and wiped away the tears.

Chapter Forty-Two

Regina had breakfast prepared for Enos as the first streaks of dawn blazed across the sky. This would be much harder than she had thought, but it must be done.

She watched him walk across the front yard from the barn, his hands in his pockets, his hat pulled low over his face. She wondered what it would be like to be born Amish. To look forward to this kind of life, to rise before the dawn and prepare food for a man who came in hungry from his chores. It was a privilege of birth, and one she was locked out from. Even her humble beginnings in Georgia had not prepared her for this. Enos knew that, she knew that, and the time had come to leave.

"Good morning," Enos said as he came in the mud room door. He ran his fingers through his hair.

"Good morning," Regina returned the greeting. "Breakfast is ready."

He sat down and waited until she was seated before he bowed his head to pray. Tears had filled her eyes by the time he lifted his head. He reached across the table to touch her hand, so he must have noticed. "Don't you think something could be done — about you and me?" he asked. "*The Lord* has already done so much to heal the sorrow."

"Do you think God could — bring our lives together? You know how far apart they are."

"I don't know." He met her gaze. "It would be wonderful if He could."

"You know I can't come and live in your world."

He nodded. "And how could I live in yours? It's so far away."

She smiled. "You make it sound like India or China. It's only in Farmstead, but I know what you mean."

"It's like the picture we used to have in school of the Grand Canyon. The other side is far away, even though it's close enough to see."

She pressed her lips together as she passed him the bacon and eggs. "You say it very well, Enos, and so it is. But I am glad I got to know you. My life will always be richer for it."

"My life will never be the same after knowing you. I know that," he said as he moved several eggs onto his plate.

"You'll find yourself a wonderful Amish girl — after this is all over with and the world has settled down. She'll be the vision of your dreams." Unlike me, Regina wanted to say, but choked back the words. She shouldn't become melodramatic about things, like some teenager who reached for what couldn't be. Reality was reality and had to be faced.

"Will you be going back to the parsonage in town?" he asked.

"For the time being, as long as no one is living there. They had told me I could stay there until they found another pastor. I can't imagine they've found one in this chaos. It'll be a miracle finding one when everything gets back to normal."

"*The Lord* can do miracles," he said. "His angels are very close to us right now. I think God does that in troubled times."

They sat in silence and then she asked, "Do you want more eggs?" He shook his head. In fact, he seemed unable to eat more than a few bites. She stood to wash the dishes.

"You'll be gone then when I come in from the fields." He got up from the table.

"I suppose so. I packed my suitcase last night."

"Thanks for everything." He opened his arms wide.

She stifled a sob and accepted his embrace. They clung to each other for a long moment, until he let go.

"May the Lord go with you wherever you go." He touched her cheek with his hand. "You are wonderful."

"Don't say things like that." She laughed and looked away.

He nodded and left by the washroom door. Regina listened to the soft noises he made as he pulled on his boots and closed the outside door behind him. She peeked out the kitchen window to watch him walk across the lawn again as the rising sun blasted rays across his face. He didn't lower his head or turn around to look back. The barn door opened and closed, and he disappeared.

How selfish of me, she thought, on this, their last morning together, to not comfort him over the death of his family. That was her duty, her gift, and yet he had seemed to be the one who comforted her. How was that possible? Never had a man reached her with compassion before she reached him. Perhaps her father had, but that had been a very long time ago.

She finished the dishes and put them away, sliding each plate and utensil in place. She lingered long at the task; she wished to savor her last few minutes in this place. But how could such sweetness rise out of the very house where death had come so violently? Was Enos correct? Did God come closer with his ministering spirits in times of great trouble? Did He go out of his way to bring love into the world wherever evil left its hideous mark? She was a minister. She ought to know.

Then why could God not do a miracle between Enos and herself? Was this kind of love only to be for someone else? But how selfish had she become to even ask the question? She had always cared about others first; now she wanted something for herself, something that could never be. Was that to be the agony of her soul, her punishment for reasons unknown?

With a sob, Regina took her suitcase and radio and walked across the front yard. Enos had been here only moments ago, his steps firm. There were no men like that out in her world; Travis was weak compared to Enos. Yet she deserved nothing like Enos. She deserved her own world. And she needed to stop reaching across the fence for what didn't belong to her.

When Regina arrived at the car, she placed her suitcase in the backseat and waited with her hand on the latch. She could see Enos in her mind's eye burst out of the barn door and race across the yard to shout that he wanted her to stay, wanted her to be his wife, and wanted things to be like this forever. She would open her arms and welcome him with laughter, with hope that welled up inside of her, with a proclamation that she had always known things would turn out okay.

Instead, Regina steeled her face and climbed in the car. She turned the key and left.

Out on the blacktop Regina looked back over her shoulder, but the door of the farmhouse was closed, the side of the barn empty. She really had left and she really wouldn't come back. She held in the tears and took deep breaths as she approached the first roadblock.

They were National Guard Units from their insignias, their faces strange to her.

"Excuse me," she said, once the officer in charge waved her through. "Have things been quiet in the area overnight?"

"As far as I know," the officer said.

"No more trouble with the Amish people?"

"Not with them," he said. "They don't make trouble that I know of."

"I mean with people bothering them. Stealing and murdering."

The officer shook his head. "I would have heard if there had been. We've got orders to seal this part of the country down pretty good. Does that satisfy you, miss?"

"Thank you," she said, as he waved her on again.

The officer was shaking his head and talking with the others when she glanced in the rearview mirror. Surely her questions hadn't aroused suspicions. They likely were talking about the awful things that had already happened in the area.

Regina shuddered and drove towards 460. How closely love and hate walked together. Yet in the end they led to such different places, one to joy and laughter, the other to death and destruction.

If she never saw Enos again, she still would know how deeply he could love. These hadn't been times for much laughter, but laughter would someday come for Enos. He would laugh on the morning after his wedding vows, at the birth of his first child, on the evenings he sat on the porch swing with his loved one. Life would be filled with laughter, with joy as well as sorrow, with bubbling emotions too deep for expression except through smiles and tears.

Regina saw another roadblock coming up and quickly took the side road. The guns were in her trunk, and sooner or later her car would be searched. She stopped and waited by the side of the road. Would the officers follow her? Would they assume she had avoided them?

When no one came she eased into a lane sheltered by trees and moved deeper into the forest. There she stopped, opened the trunk, and threw the guns behind a log, hiding them with leaves. That's all that mattered anyway — that they were out of sight until she was gone.

She had only one box of ammunition. The others must still be in Enos's basement, but he could deal with that. She tossed the box into the leaves as well, then backed out to the road and headed for the roadblock again. The officers said nothing as they checked her license. They didn't even ask for the vaccination card. So the epidemic must be on the wane, she figured.

On the edge of town another roadblock appeared with multiple officers to man it. They searched her car, behind the seat and in the trunk, then waved her on. As she approached the center of town she saw little wisps of smoke that still drifted upwards. They rose like signals from another time and place.

She hadn't been gone that long, but it seemed like an eternity. Was this really her town, her place in the world? Likely not. She would spend the night in the parsonage and head for Georgia in the morning. That is, if such a thing was possible. The last gas station had fuel for $12.59 a gallon. Apparently the order to freeze prices didn't amount to much.

She bypassed the smoky section of downtown and drove south to the Benchmark bank. The teller gave her the $300.00 she asked to withdraw and made no comment, though her face was tense. Back at Krogers the shelves were bare of everything except the basics. Regina selected a loaf a bread, a half gallon of milk, and a box of Wheaties.

"We hope to have more things in by tomorrow night," the checkout clerk said.

Regina smiled and nodded. She should have thought to bring food from Enos's place. He wouldn't have minded. The bill climbed higher and higher in front of her eyes, ending at $27.73. Nobody's money would last long with these prices, she decided.

"Thank you." Regina left with her meager bag.

Back on Main Street she approached the parsonage. Would it still be there, or was it too gone with further riots or attacks? The sight of the low two-story white house beside the towering red church brought tears to her eyes. Beyond the church the streets were still strewn with bricks and concrete, the sidewalks blocked off with yellow sawhorses and orange tape. The National Guard manned the posts, their vehicles parked in the still-standing Bethesda Plaza.

The Baptist church had a huge tarp draped over the back side where the explosion had left a gaping hole. Otherwise there were no visible signs of clean up, or any attempts at restoration. Things must still be too unstable for anyone to think of such things.

Regina drove behind the parsonage, parked, and got out to try the back door. It still opened to her key, and no one answered when she hollered. She paused as tears stung her eyes again. Here she also had loved and lost. Her work, her passion had come to an end here. Was that to be the legacy of her life?

But it couldn't be. A new world would have to grow out of the one that had been destroyed. Because things had to start anew again, didn't they? God wouldn't be God if they didn't. With a sigh she went and retrieved her bag of groceries and the radio. She left the suitcase for last.

Chapter Forty-Three

Regina tried the phone again, for the third time, and still had no dial tone. The evening light grew dimmer outside the parsonage. How was she supposed to travel to Georgia tomorrow if she didn't know the status of her parents? What if something had happened to them in this time? But then, that was only more reason to go. Perhaps she ought to set out tonight already?

She pondered the thought as she replaced the phone. It would be a long journey — she shouldn't try it in the night. There were safety issues to consider and the cost of fuel. She ran the numbers in her head and came up with $300.00 as an estimate.

That was if fuel prices didn't jump again, and that cost didn't include food. Perhaps a better idea would be to simply sit tight here until things settled down. If Travis hadn't found anyone to take over the parsonage by now, he likely wouldn't anytime soon.

With little else in the house to eat, Regina poured herself a bowl of cereal. It felt weird to eat breakfast in the evening, but then the whole world was weird outside her window — the downtown gone, the Baptist church in ruins — so it might as well be weird inside the parsonage.

Enos would eat some of the meat loaf tonight she had left him. Tomorrow he would have to fend for himself, but tonight he had only to reheat what was already there. He would know how to do that. Would he think of her, remembering her presence in the house, or was he already into the newly restored life with his people?

Regina pushed the thoughts away. She really needed to think about her own life, which was far from restored. And what had happened with the trial in the Senate? All day she had not once thought of it, her mind occupied with more important things. Yet in the end it would affect them all, so she might as well know.

Regina plugged in the power cord and turned up the volume to fiddle with the dial. It wasn't hard to find news and commentary, but she kept on until she found an actual feed into the Senate proceedings. She listened as sworn witnesses made their charges. Most of them weren't a surprise, reports of unrest fomented by the government.

If the reports from the professor had been correct, that was the case when the Farmstead and Roanoke bombs were set. The same apparently had happened elsewhere along with the attempts to cover it up.

"The government wanted reasons to take over through martial law," the witness said, "and used internal attacks as the basis, blaming them on militia groups. Many of these groups — some of them belligerent, but many of them harmless — were destroyed in order to back up the government's claim."

"We will need further verification of that charge," a senator's voice came on. "Will this be forthcoming, Mr. Chairman?"

"Yes it will," the chairman said. "We have a governor and a general slated later in the evening. For now we will move on to the whole area of the government's handling of the epidemic."

Regina turned off the radio. She already knew what they would say and didn't want to hear it. The pain of what had happened in the streets of Farmstead was bad enough. But to have the cause be those who were supposed to help was even worse. The president ought to have jail time ahead of him instead of only a possible impeachment.

She stood to pace the floor and felt bitterness rise up inside of her. Why did people betray each other and speak the right words only to have them proven worse than lies? Darkness seemed close tonight. It lurked in the shadows of this town and hovered over the whole country. Could they ever come back from this awful abyss? Could they ever find firm ground again?

Perhaps the Amish would, with their simple ways and hearts given to forgiveness and mercy. But would anyone else? How easy it would be for the country to slide into hatred, pursue grudges, seek revenge, and demand it all in the name of justice.

Without question the road ahead would be hard. Maybe this was another benefit of her foray into Amish country. The world could learn much from these people, and she had a pulpit — or did — to speak the message. Somehow she would find a way to gain another position. Travis and the board might do their best to prevent her with a negative reference, but everything could be overcome. That was what her father would say.

Her thoughts were interrupted by the sound of a car pulling in from South Main. It stopped by the front door. Regina stood and tried to catch a glimpse of who was coming. It was none other than Travis, now waving at her through the front window. She unlocked the door and felt a chill run through her. There was a smile on his face, but his eyes were cold. He embraced her and she didn't resist. But it would go no further, she told herself. Or there would be a mighty struggle.

"What is going on?" She pushed away with both hands.

"Now, now." He forced a laugh. "Don't be acting like you aren't glad to see me. I sure am glad to see you. I've been looking for you everywhere the last few days. Where in the world did you disappear to?"

"I don't know that it's any of your business where I've been," she told him. "I'm only stopping in here for the night, since you said I could stay here until you found someone else. Tomorrow I'm heading for home and Georgia."

"Have you contacted your folks? Are they okay?"

Travis tried to appear concerned, she thought. "No, the phone lines are still down."

"Good. I thought you had received bad news or something."

"You know it's over between us, Travis. So perhaps you'd better go. Unless that's a problem, and then I can leave." Where she would go she had no idea. But a night in her car was better than what Travis might have in mind for her.

He grinned, the effort intense. "Now don't get testy with me, Regina. There is good news. I have decided to reject your resignation and ask you to reconsider. And this could really look good on your resume someday, Regina — turning down a position at one of the oldest black churches in Farmstead because of personal convictions, only to have the board ask you to stay on."

Regina held up her hand as she gathered her wits around her. This she had not expected. "You'll have to back up and give me more details."

"There aren't any to give, Regina. And don't be making this harder than it already is. You know how humiliating it is for me to lose face like this? I'm backing down, in front of everyone. Isn't that a reason for you to be thankful? And now we can be in this together. Isn't that wonderful, Regina? Everything can go on as before."

"Nothing is going on as before, Travis, especially between you and me. Let me make that abundantly clear."

"Wow, what has gotten into you?" Travis stood to his feet. "I'd like to see a little thankfulness from you for what I'm doing."

"You are not *The Lord* who can give and take away." She wiped a tear from her eye as she heard another voice from what seemed years ago say the words with great sorrow in his voice. Enos knew what they meant. He knew like she would never know.

"Well, of course I'm not," Travis laughed. "But I am making the offer again. That counts for something."

He must have finally noticed her tears and took her hand. "I'm sorry, Regina. I know it must have hurt you much more than I can imagine, but we can put that all behind us now and go on again. The church needs you. I need you, Regina."

She pulled her hand away. "How involved were you in all that was going on in this town, Travis? In the bad things?"

"Hey, I didn't know." He threw his hands in the air. "I had no idea. Sure there were little things that seemed amiss, but I trusted like all of us did. I'm telling you the truth, Regina."

"You didn't know about the faulty vaccine people were being forced to take? Well, certain people. Or the prisons being used like concentration camps? I told you about what I saw, Travis, and you *shushed* me. Why did you, if you didn't know anything?"

"I'm not blind, Regina." He was on his feet now. "Of course I could put two and two together, but none of it was my idea. I simply figured others knew better than I did."

"And you think that will be enough of an excuse? Maybe to some people, but what about me? What about God?"

"Okay, I'm sorry, Regina." He threw his hands up again. "I should have spoken up, but how much good would it have done? None at all. Perhaps I made things better by staying quiet like I did. Look at yourself. You would have lost your job, and it wouldn't have come back if this had happened any earlier. Do you think you gained that much?"

"I gained plenty, Travis, but I think you're lying. The board is offering me nothing back. Now are they? You think you can convince them, but I'm not interested."

"Come on, Regina. Why are you playing hard to get? Remember what we used to have together. I love you baby." The hunger shone in his eyes again.

She stepped back. "I have been taught many valuable lessons in the last week."

"That's what I like about you, Regina." He grinned. "It's what I've always liked about you. We'll make a fantastic team again, even though you're a little sore right now. Time will heal. I promise you. Now, if you don't mind, I need to go. As you can imagine there are more things than possible to do around this town, and there are people at the hospital to visit. Mrs. Good and Mr. Lewis, the last I checked. They will be looking forward to seeing you again, I'm sure ... as I will be in the days ahead."

She kept her voice steady. "I'm not staying, Travis. I'll make the visits to the hospital while I'm here, because I like the people, but that's it."

"I know you will, Regina." He smiled his best smile. "I'll be back, and you'll let me take this to the board, won't you? I need this Regina."

When she shook her head, he left. He waved through the window and roared his car out of the driveway. That much hadn't changed — Travis at his flamboyant best. Yet the colors had faded. The old world would never be the same. And his eyes had been cold the whole time. Travis was lying about the position at the church. He wanted nothing more than to save his own skin by using her. How, she wasn't quite certain, but she wouldn't fall for his tricks anymore.

She and Travis would never be. He might not believe it now, and he might not believe it for a long time. When it did sink in there would be fury and anger, but she would be long gone by then, well on the way home to Georgia.

Moments later, in the glow of the streetlights, which by some miracle still shone, Regina walked up the street to the church steps. The officers at the barricade looked ready to approach her until they noticed where she was headed. She entered the building, turned on the lights in the sanctuary, and walked to the front.

She shouldn't come here; it would only torment her soul. But she needed the goodbye at least. Somewhere she would find a voice again and bring the message that already stirred in her, one she had learned anew in the last few days — that mercy and forgiveness pave the way for love to grow in the heart of mankind. That hatred and revenge drive us from God and from each other.

She would have stories to tell of death, of destruction, of unimaginable pain, and stories of how in the midst of all that she had seen people believe that God was greater than what they suffered, greater than their agony. He was God, and they honored His attributes. They believed we must honor ourselves and pull our own natures out of the pit.

Now if only Enos were here. If he sat in the pew, how wonderful everything would be. How perfect the world, even though it was fallen apart on the outside. Regina wiped away a tear and approached the pulpit to turn and look out over the empty seats.

Enos wouldn't be here because Enos was from another world. One she had been allowed to glimpse for a brief moment. For that she ought to be thankful and lift her heart in praise to God.

"Thank you, Jesus." She lifted her hands towards the ceiling and wept.

Her heart would go on, she thought; she would pick up the pieces. But a part of her would always remember what it was like to be held for a brief moment by the strongest man she had ever known. Travis with his burly attitude was a child compared to Enos. He could never touch the power of Enos's soul.

Regina smiled and allowed the tears to flow. She would live a better life than before. By the power of God, she would. In the stillness of the long moments, she walked up the aisle through the double doors and started back to the parsonage.

She turned on the sidewalk and whispered, "goodbye."

Chapter Forty-Four

THE CABLE NEWS BEGAN TO CARRY the Senate trial on the third day. As if by some secret formula the news honchos had divined the outcome, Regina figured, and decided to cast their fortunes on the right side. On her part from day one she had already concluded the vote would be to impeach.

The weight of the evidence was simply too much. If she had known what went on, then others among the citizenry also knew. That tidal wave would rise. It would sweep its opinion towards Washington. Senators would listen, if for no other reason than to save their own political hides.

By now, though, the testimony needed no further proof.

The cable news girl had said this morning in astonishment, "People of course are not calling their Congressmen or Senators, since the phone lines are down, but even mail is down to a trickle. There are no polls being done as the country sits transfixed by what has been happening in our government."

Regina drove to the hospital to fulfill her promise. A walk was out of the question, with the wide detour she would have to make. It would take years for someone to get downtown rebuilt and High Street open again for traffic.

The roadblocks were still up as the officers checked for security, but the request for vaccination cards was no longer given. Whatever the outcome of the trial in Washington, the country was still a long ways from getting back on its feet, even as the flu epidemic faded.

Thankfully Travis hadn't been by again. Apparently he

thought to wear her down. He figured the loneliness of her personal life would grow stronger. He figured eventually she would give in and accept his offer to tie their lives together.

After she parked at the hospital lot, Regina got out of the car and blinked in the bright glare of the afternoon sun. A dirty piece of paper blew across the pavement, driven by the wind. None of the horrors from those nights long ago remained. Someone must have changed the orders within the health care system, whether out of fear or compassion no one would ever know. Perhaps there were simply not as many sick people to deal with.

The worst atrocities would not be repeated soon, though. Not after what had been revealed at the Senate trial. Other men, hopefully better men, would soon be placed in charge. But no one had said anything yet about how to deal with the financial mess that had wrecked the country.

Regina shook her head as she walked towards the hospital. It really was time for her to quit worrying about things she couldn't change. There was plenty she could do within her own sphere. For starters, she had to make this hospital visit. It helped to narrow things down like that and reduce them to small chunks of manageable time.

"Mrs. Good and Mr. Lewis still in?" she asked the girl at the front desk.

"They're about ready to be discharged," the girl smiled. "Mrs. Good's in 211, and Mr. Lewis in 256."

"Thank you," Regina told the girl, and took the elevator up to the second floor. She saw no one. When she got off a nurse passed and gave her a weak smile. Someone's family came out of another doorway as they spoke their cheerful goodbyes to loved ones. Regina smiled and nodded to them.

"Good evening," Regina greeted Mrs. Good as she entered. "How are you doing?"

"Much better, I'd say. I'm glad to see you're back again."

"Well, I'm back in town for a little bit."

Mrs. Good smiled. "I mean back as in the church. That Travis is a load, that's all I can say. I hope you give him a hard time for what he tried to pull off — throwing you out because you spoke up against that mob attack. Why, there's not one of us who would have supported such a thing."

"I'm glad to hear that," Regina said. "But I'm afraid I'm not coming back."

"Oh, I'm sorry to hear that," Mrs. Good said.

She looked it, Regina thought, which was nice.

"Thank you," Regina told her.

"Who were the people promoting the fuss that burned down all those buildings? Out in the country we don't find out much about what goes on."

Regina shook her head. "Let's say they're probably sorry for what they did by now."

"You always were the sweetest person. Come here and let me give you a kiss."

Regina sat down beside Mrs. Good. She bent her check towards her, then gave the elderly lady a kiss on her own cheek. "There, so are you getting ready to leave soon?"

"Tomorrow morning, Lord willing. I can't wait for Charles to pick me up. The service in this hospital has gone right out the door. They don't hardly do anything for you anymore. I think they must have one nurse for this floor, and a doctor or two. What's the world coming to, Regina?"

"I don't know, but we'll make it through." Regina took the woman's hands in hers. "At least we still have each other to be thankful for."

"You can say that for sure," Mrs. Good beamed, "and the Lord too, of course. I think He's helping me get better fast, even with the hospital care the way it is."

"I'm sure he is." Regina squeezed the woman's hands. "How many grandchildren do you have now?"

"Eight, and everyone survived the flu. Praise God. Even all the mommies and daddies made it through. Can you believe how good *The Lord* has been? I thought I might be the one to go, but here I am, ready to go home tomorrow."

"*The Lord* has been good to all of us." Regina got to her feet. "Let me go check on Mr. Lewis, then I'll be on my way."

"Thanks for stopping by," Mrs. Good said as Regina left.

She walked up the hall to find room 256 empty. A check at the floor desk confirmed that Mr. Lewis had been released earlier that morning. The service at the hospital had obviously gone downhill. They didn't even know who was in and who wasn't.

"Thank you," Regina told the girl as she left to walk down the hall.

Regina took the hospital elevator down, then waved to the girl at the front desk. There was no sense in trying to correct the mistaken information on Mr. Lewis. Life held more important things at the moment.

She drove around to the south side of town. What a temptation it would be to drive down 460 and pull up in front of Enos's house in the morning. He would welcome her, wouldn't he? He had feelings for her, as she did for him. Or was it all her imagination, a mirage raised by the stress they had been under?

She had better leave well enough alone, Regina thought, as she took the turns back out to South Main Street. Their worlds were simply too far apart, and she had no right to even wish that the beauty and peace of his world be disturbed to satisfy her own desires. Enos was too wonderful for this town, for the violence it had expressed, for the people who became snared in the twisted politics that nearly burned it down.

She parked behind the parsonage and went inside to turn on the television. The breathless girl was on again. She monitored a live feed on the vote in the Senate. Already the number was over the two-thirds needed for impeachment, and the vote was not yet completed. Regina sat at the table to watch the conclusion. Moments later the last vote was cast, which came to seventy-two for impeachment and twenty-eight *nays*. The result was not even close.

"A very first in our country ... " the girl gushed.

Regina turned away from the screen. It would take more than the impeachment of a president to right the country's wrongs, but perhaps this was a start. The girl's voice caught her attention again. "We also have a report that the vice president has resigned, effective immediately. There is no word yet on what the Speaker of the House's response will be, but our best guess is, since he is from the other party, that he will accept the Presidency."

Regina heard a knock on the front door and turned off the television. She had heard no one walk up, and Travis wouldn't have arrived so quietly. With a puzzled look on her face, she opened the door to find the somber unshaven face of Professor Blanton.

How long her mouth was open she never knew.

"May I come in?" A slight smile played on his face.

"Of course, why of course," she sputtered. "But you were in jail."

His smile widened. "So you noticed. I've been waiting across the street for the last hour until I saw you drive up. It took me a little while to gather up my courage."

"To see me? Like I believe that." She stared at him.

"Of course I came to see you. Don't all jailbirds stop by to see their beautiful women?"

Regina sobered. "I feared you were dead."

"Well, I'm not," he said. "Aren't you a little glad to see me?"

She took a deep breath and gave him a quick hug. "Is that enough of an answer?"

"It's all I need." He laughed. "That is if you could allow me to stay around for a bit."

"So you've graduated from following me around to moving in?"

"I can sleep in the spare bedroom," he said. "I won't violate your moral principles. I promise."

"So the professor is asking me for something again? And where will this one lead?"

"Wasn't the last trip interesting?" He grinned.

"You don't have the law after you, do you?"

He shook his head. "They let me go. I imagine they hope I will disappear quietly. I think the rats are running for the sewers."

Behind them the phone rang and Regina went to answer.

"Hello," she said.

"Yes, Dad, I'm okay. And you and Mom?"

"It's Dad," Regina mouthed towards the professor. "They're all okay."

"Good," he whispered.

"Yes, Dad," Regina said into the receiver. "There's someone with me right now, and I really am okay. We're coming to visit as soon as we can get down there."

The professor raised his eyebrows.

Regina shrugged and smiled.

"Yes, Dad .... Of course we will be careful .... I have a friend along who will take care of me .... I'll introduce him when we get there .... Goodbye ... and you take care too."

"I can stay then," he said, when she had hung up.

"You don't have to look so smug."

"That's what comes from following beautiful women around." He settled into a kitchen chair with a sigh. "When do we embark upon this trip of yours?"

"As soon as we can get out of here," she said. "Georgia and Daddy here we come."

"The enthusiasm of some people," he muttered. "It never grows dim."

7424563R00170

Made in the USA
San Bernardino, CA
04 January 2014